HIGH STICKING THE HEART

MARIE M.

To those who give more than they take and carry all the emotional weight on their shoulders while trying not to let anyone see them falter. It's okay to let someone come and lighten that load so you can fly.

NOTE FROM THE AUTHOR

Having Mexican representation in my book was very important to me. That being said, even in the Mexican community, we are not a monolith. This story is written through the lens of a *no-sabo* kid raised to love her culture by her immigrant mother. A woman who had the balls to break through the *machismo* stigmas placed upon so many Latina daughters.

You may not relate to some of the situations in this book, and that's okay. I hope you have a good time anyway.

This story is pretty light, but it does involve a toxic parental relationship, parental manipulation, and attempts at social isolation by a parent.

Betty

ONE

ARIELLA

I'M A STRONG, INDEPENDENT WOMAN WHO DOESN'T NEED ANYTHING FROM A MAN— EXCEPT FOR HIM NOT TO TALK TO ME

I'D NEVER REALIZED swamp-ass was a *literal* thing and not just a figure of speech.

"Why didn't you tell me you lived in the bowels of hell, Graciella?" I yelled into the open doorway, wildly throwing my head around in an attempt to redirect another droplet of sweat threatening to run into my eye.

It had been two weeks since I'd breathed freely, living in air-conditioned air so cold I was left with a choice between switching to thicker sports bras or heading out to endure hell's atmosphere.

"There is a *river* running between *mis nalgas* at the moment. This is not *a little* humidity. This is the end of times or something."

Sure, I knew logically that moving out of California meant leaving California weather, but I hadn't fully grasped what that would look like.

My new reality?

Every time I stepped outside I resembled a drowned

rat with my hair plastered to my head thanks to perspiration, all while I sucked down breaths, hoping I'd finally inhale something other than hot, thick air.

I looked at my cousin's blunt bob, contemplating chopping mine, but since my wardrobe consisted solely of black leggings or shorts, my long hair and colored sports bras were the only fun, girly accessories I had.

Fine. I'd learn to endure the torture.

Gracie's voice cut through the inner bitching. "Foul, Ariella. That was foul. And don't let a Texan hear you speak poorly on their state."

I rolled my eyes at the warning. They had to know their weather sucked, right? Who was happy in these conditions?

"Well, you know what would have been nice to know before I decided to move out here with you? That there was enough humidity in the air to drown you," I said, carrying in the last of the boxes I'd shipped to my new residence.

In typical cousin fashion, Gracie only shrugged, ignoring my suffering. "You're the one who decided to move here at the end of August." She tugged at my shirt and wrinkled her nose. "Yeah, that shade of gray? Never wear it again. At least not in summer."

My groan echoed off the brick walls.

"I wish I could say you get used to it, but you don't," she added unhelpfully, reclaiming her spot on the worn green velvet couch so she could watch me play live-action Tetris with my boxes of shit.

There were only three of them, but Gracie's place—now *our* place—was the size of a rich housewife's walk-in closet. Not tiny, but we had to take turns walking in certain areas.

Nearly every corner had bits of her style—yellows and greens with dainty details. But now there were also bits of my bright oranges and hot pinks, as well.

Our personalities were as different as our favorite colors, yet somehow, we worked. Like the sun and the moon, we complemented each other.

She was sunshine and fun, always seeing the best in the day. I was fiery and fierce, and my mood was liable to shift on a dime.

"Thanks for helping me carry that, by the way," I bit out with faux irritation, shooting her a glare over my shoulder when the final box was precariously placed on top of the others.

She shrugged, unfazed by the attitude. "¡Órale! What was I supposed to do with these?" She gave a pitiful attempt at flexing her bicep. "You're the one who has a job showing men how to pick up heavy things. Mine requires me to keep up with what's trending."

"Strength and conditioning, Graciella," I explained for the hundredth time. "I'm a strength and conditioning coach. You should know this—you work in sports too."

She waved a manicured hand in the air dismissively. The stupid smirk on her face told me she hadn't forgotten what it was called.

"Correction, I work in sports *marketing*. It's not the same. I have to make sure my clients' brands look good and capture content for sports shit. *You* yell at men in the gym." She smirked. "It's honestly perfect for you. Anyway, the point is, you're the strong one. We both know if I need something carried, I'd delegate it to a man. You should try it sometime," she said, pointing at me over her screen.

I clucked my tongue at her awful idea.

"I'm a strong, independent woman who doesn't need anything from a man...except for him not to talk to me," I said, pulling off my sweat-soaked shirt, grimacing at the wet plopping noise of it hitting the concrete flooring.

She rolled her eyes. "Are you done yet? I'm ready to do something fun," she complained, tucking a stray hair behind her ear and setting her phone on the table, giving me her full attention now that she was bored.

Gracie's outlook on a fun night was very different from my own. To me, a *fun night* consisted of some cafecitos, no bra, and a murder show. Maybe throw in an overpriced FoodRun delivery.

Hers usually involved a margarita and a man.

I walked to the kitchen, taking my time to finish the heavenly cool water I'd poured myself so I could weigh my options on how to respond.

I'd put her off since getting to Dallas, and if I didn't agree to go out with her soon, I was afraid she'd hire someone to kidnap me and force me out of the house.

Probably one of the guys she matched with on an app because, apparently, that was how my cousin got everything she needed done.

Leaky sink? Get a Tinder match.

Need new tires? Get a Tinder match.

I wasn't sure if she was setting female empowerment back or shooting us forward...

Sighing at the thought, I finally asked, "When you say *fun*, what exactly are you talking about, Graciella

Xochitl Barrera?" She opened her mouth to answer, but I cut her off, concerned by the twinkle in her eyes. "I do mean, *exactly* what are you talking about? Because I do not want you to tell me we are going to some kickback at your friend's with only a few people, and then I find myself crammed into the random room of a frat house off of 11th and San Antonio St. where a random dude is playing his DJ set while a bottle of UV Blue is being passed around. It's shocking we are even alive," I scolded, my hands on my hips to keep from flailing them around.

A habit that was hard to break, truthfully. I was pretty sure it was a trait ingrained in our cultural DNA to talk with our hands and add emphasis with sound effects.

As if to prove my point, Gracie made a clucking noise with her tongue, waving away the accusation. "Well, the first problem in that scenario is we aren't in San Jose, so there's no chance of that. Plus, how pathetic would it be if two twenty-five-year-old women showed up to frat parties to get drunk? I'm not *that* desperate for a man. You, on the other hand..."

She fell into a fit of laughter when I chucked my sandal at her, grazing the top of her head while I called her every insult I could think of.

"Okay, okay." She held her hands up in surrender, attempting to control herself. "No men. It will be a *primas* night. One of my clients knows of a sports bar's soft launch happening tonight. The guest list is all athletes, agents, and marketing people." She sat up on her knees, looking like an excited puppy. "It will be fun," she promised, wagging her eyebrows, trying to entice me.

There was definitely no way I was getting out of going somewhere with her tonight.

"So let me get this straight. You want to have a *primas*-only night at a bar crawling with hot athletes?" I asked, the cold stainless-steel biting into the exposed skin of my torso as I leaned against the countertop.

Her smile was so sickly sweet I was shocked she still had all her teeth. "*Nothing* says girls' night like free margaritas and staring at athletes' asses," she said.

"Oh, now the margaritas are free, too?"

"They are if you wear that black halter top that makes it look like your boobs are in your chin."

I shook my head at her logic. She wasn't wrong, but I wouldn't tell her that. It would go to her head.

Pointing my finger at her, I tried my best to sound stern, "*Mira*, we will go—" An ear-piercing cheer cut me off.

She'd been hoping for that answer for days, but I'd avoided going out until now, using that time to try and adjust to the new time zone, weather, and the fact I didn't live in my childhood home anymore.

There was a reason I'd applied for the job in Dallas. I'd needed a reprieve from my family's expectations, and there was no way in hell they'd be okay with me moving out of state by myself. Explaining that concept to my white friends was always a humiliating experience. It led to some variation of the same questions.

"*What do you mean you can't make those decisions yourself?*"

"*But you're twenty-five...you're an adult.*"

Yeah, it wasn't that simple in my household. Cultural

expectations and generational normatives loved to cock-block a woman's independence. What made my situation particularly difficult was that I loved my family.

It would be far easier to be the family's disappointment if I didn't care what they thought. Sometimes I wished they were shittier to me so I could justify cutting them off completely and living my life on my terms.

Ironically, thousands of miles didn't stop my dad and brother's onslaught of questions or attempts at control. They wanted to know what I was doing, where I was going, or the million-dollar question—who would I see?

I sighed, rubbing at my chest. I hoped that with more time apart, they'd start to see I was living my own life and that the weird sense of guilt sitting on my sternum for wanting to do my own thing would subside.

Gracie hopped off the couch, rushing to the mini bar she'd set up on a wall shelf. "This calls for a shot."

The declaration caught my attention. Tequila and Graciella had trouble written all over it.

If I was being honest, tequila and *me* had trouble written all over it.

"No trying to set me up while we're there, Gracie." She rolled her eyes at the warning, passing me a shot glass. The clear liquid balancing precariously at the top of the rim threatened to run down the side of my hand. "I'm being serious. I'm out here for my career, to show everyone I can do this..." The last part was barely above a whisper.

Her eyes softened, the corner of her pink lips pulling into a sad smile. If anyone understood the cultural pressures coming from home, it was Gracie.

She'd managed to break the hold when she left for

college, but it came at a price. My *tío* still refused to speak to her. Despite the differences in opinions on how I should live my life, I had comfort in knowing my family would never cut me out the way my uncle had with her.

I shook my head, needing to clear the sour mood.

"*Vamos,*" I said, raising my glass and waiting for Gracie to join. "To new opportunities, breaking generational machismo—"

"And amazing cousins who let you move in with them," she added.

I smiled at her, all of my earlier worries suspended for now.

"*¡Salud!*"

TWO

DALTON

WELCOME TO HOCKEY SLANG

"YOU CALL THAT SKATING, boys? Pathetic. Looks like none of you want to keep your damn jobs. Again!" A chorus of groans echoed across the rink, swallowed by the sharp blast of Monroe's whistle.

Goddamn lines.

We'd done so many this off-season that I'd lost count, and my legs were toast. The promise of sweet, sweet release in the form of a massage was the light at the end of the hellish tunnel Monroe was putting us through.

The chill coming off the rink did nothing to stop sweat from trailing down my face, threatening my concentration.

"Winners always finish first, Dalton. And I don't associate with anyone other than winners."

Vincent Langley's harsh mantra played on a loop in my head, driving me to go faster, to edge out my teammates. I pushed harder. Dad didn't believe in soft encouragement—just brutal expectations.

At least with me.

Fire burned through my quads as I powered myself

forward, pumping my arms like my damn life depended on it, the blades of my skates cutting into the ice. Our defenseman, Jimenez, was right on my heels, giving me the final boost to push through the discomfort. I nearly collapsed when Monroe's whistle sounded, marking the end of today's torture session.

"Bring it in, boys," he called right as one of the rookies hurled, barely getting his helmet off in time.

"Welcome to the big leagues, Roberts," Jimenez snickered beside me. "Coach, why you got us ripping lines like that? Robby over there isn't just sucking wind. You got 'em blowing chunks."

I bit down on my mouthguard to smother a grin.

My best friend loved giving the guys shit, and the new winger, Roberts, would never live this moment down.

The kid was a good sport, though; he skated over, wiping his mouth with the sleeve of his practice jersey, a goofy smile plastered on his face. He reminded me of a puppy with his happy-go-lucky attitude and blonde mullet that peeped out of the bottom of his helmet when we played.

"Three... two... one..." I counted under my breath, bracing for it.

"Up-Chuck," Jimenez yelled out right on cue, pointer finger tapping on his bottom lip like he was deep in thought. "That's what you'll be called now, Roberts. Up-Chuck."

"Wow, Jimenez." I leaned against my stick, looking over my shoulder at him. "Real stroke of genius there."

The second the words were out, I regretted them. You couldn't say anything even remotely suggestive around the guy without it being turned into a sex joke. It was like he'd been hardwired to spit out that shit on instinct.

And I knew better than to say the word *stroke* within his earshot.

He broke out into a shit-eating grin. "That's what the ladies call me. Stroke of Genius." He mimed grabbing a woman's hips. "No wonder you can't get pussy, Up-Chuck. Your cardio is shit. Me, on the other hand, I can go all night long, baby," he said between thrusts.

The whole team broke out in laughter until we caught Coach's scowl.

Want to talk about someone having a hardwired reaction?

I wasn't sure Josh Monroe knew how to make any expression besides a scowl anymore, not since his nasty NHL career-ending injury a few years prior.

Well, that wasn't entirely true.

He looked at his daughter, Goldie, like she hung the moon, but that softness was reserved solely for her. We got the hardass coach who pushed until we broke and then built us back better.

At thirty-two, he was young for an NHL coach, but what had made him a great center made him an even better coach. Monroe could read the ice like no one else. Everything I knew, I'd learned thanks to him.

Grew up idolizing the guy, begging him to let me tag along to shit. Only reason he had was because our moms were best friends, and Aunt Cindy had practically forced him to put up with me.

"You should be too fucking tired from practice to even

think about pussy," he seethed. "At this rate, you can kiss your playoff dreams goodbye."

That shut everyone up real quick. I knew he wasn't completely serious. I'd grown up with the guy—hell, I'd looked up to him, too, since he was about seven years my senior—and while he communicated via grunts ninety-five percent of the time when he was fired up about something, he had *no* problem finding words to express it— passionately.

"You've got a month left, and we're gonna use it. Only two of you were explosive out there." His gaze cut toward me and Jimenez before sweeping over the others. "The rest of you? Looked like you've spent the summer sitting on your ass. We're going to be putting work into our strength and conditioning this month. Good seasons start during this downtime, boys."

He was right. The pressure that always lingered just below the surface surged forward.

We couldn't have a repeat of last season—I couldn't have a repeat. Not with me barely crawling out of the emotional hole I'd been in.

"Yes, Coach," I called out, glaring at the others until they followed suit.

For a split second, I thought I caught the ghost of a smile twitch at the corner of Monroe's mouth. But it was gone so fast, I couldn't tell if I'd imagined it.

"You dumbasses better be ready to work because I'm making some changes come Monday," he called over his shoulder, storming off toward the team office and leaving us to slink off to our locker room.

The distinct *eau de* locker room replaced the crisp air

from the rink. Bleach barely masked the lingering scent of sweat-saturated hockey gear—not even the best air filtration system money could buy eliminated the smell completely.

I smiled, thinking about my mom making me store my stuff in the outside shed because of the stench. Same reason I never put the top on Betty, except when it rained or snowed.

"Dalt, you're coming with us tonight, right?" Jimenez asked as I approached our neighboring lockers. He ran a tattooed hand through the top of his black hair, shaking loose droplets of sweat.

It was less of a question and more of a statement with a thinly veiled threat that I better not bail on them—again. I wracked my brain for a believable excuse for not going out with the guys, but those few seconds were like blood in the water to him. He whipped around when I didn't answer fast enough.

"Dalton, you're coming tonight." There was more bite in my best friend's tone that time around. If I pissed him off anymore, he'd start cursing me out in Spanish. "You're coming up on four months of living like a damn hermit, man. Start acting like you're twenty-five instead of fucking seventy-eight. You're a star athlete in the prime of your life."

"I'm not acting seventy-eight," I threw back, catching his eye roll as I pulled my jersey over my head, stripping out of my gear. He was right, but I didn't have to admit it to the fucker. "I just don't want to end up on the front page again."

I'd practically become a shut-in over the last few

months, but it was better that way—no tabloid run-ins or news articles could be written if you never stepped foot outside of your apartment.

Jimenez's heavy hand gripped my bare shoulder, forcing my attention. "Dude, who fucking cares if the paparazzi are there. I'm sure you're old news now. You know how short their attention span is."

The whole locker room chimed in with their agreements—nosy bunch of assholes.

Dread formed like a pit in my stomach. I was being pulled in two separate directions. On the one hand, disappointing my team hurt like being hit with a slapshot, but was that feeling enough to get me to go out?

"Sure, *normally* their attention spans are short, but not if you have an ex-girlfriend who happens to be *part of* the media," I mumbled the last part, grabbing my towel.

His expression flickered with sympathy, but it vanished as quickly as it came, replaced by his signature grin. His calloused hand was back on my shoulder, holding me in place.

"Ah, man, don't worry about that. We're going somewhere she probably wouldn't go. It won't be a problem. Besides, you can't keep letting other people run your life, Cap. You deserve to do what you want to, and I *know* you want to come out with your best friend and party before Monroe tries to kill us next week." I leveled my gaze at Jimenez's attempt at puppy dog eyes. "Please?" he begged pitifully, dragging the word out like it had twelve syllables.

The hockey world might have an image of him as a playboy who could hit a party as hard as he hit a player in his defensive zone, but he'd always had my back, and I wanted to repay him for it. Even if that meant pulling me out of the cave I'd shut myself in.

He was right. I'd let this go on too long. It was time to start living again.

"Alright, I'm in, but only if you're sure she won't show up."

Tonight I would enjoy myself and my team. It would be the start of a new chapter.

THREE

DALTON

BOOBS: THEY'RE WORTH MENTIONING TWICE

FOR BEING PACKED WITH PEOPLE, the bar felt comfortable. The murmur of conversations mixed with the sound of televisions playing various sports. I could see it becoming the new spot for the boys, especially since it was only down the road from the arena.

"I told you going out with us was the cure to all your troubles. Boobs, booze, and boobs," Jimenez slurred, his arm draped across my shoulders. I rolled my eyes at the goofy grin plastered on his face. He got it every time he drank.

"You said boobs twice."

"They're worth mentioning twice, *jefe*." He slapped my back before socializing with someone on his other side, giving me a chance to scan the place. No one had given me a moment to breathe since the locker room.

Jimenez had practically poured alcohol down my throat, figuring I'd be less likely to bolt if I was buzzed, and then he'd plastered himself to my side like my personal handler. They were all afraid I'd bail.

Fair assumption, really.

In true Christian Jimenez fashion, he'd failed to mention that his long-time buddy owned the bar we were going to, and that tonight was their soft opening. He'd apparently promised we'd make an appearance at Goaltender so they could take pictures of the team for marketing.

They'd offered us free drinks in exchange, but there was no way in hell I'd let them do that. Clearly, the owner had no idea how many beers a hockey team could put away in one sitting.

The place reminded me of the dive bar we'd gone to in college after our games—minus the dive part. Goaltender managed to straddle the line between a high-end restaurant and comfort bar with its polished concrete floors and elegant light fixtures accented with some of the most iconic sports jerseys and memorabilia.

This is like the adult version of our college escapades.

The thought soured when I remembered who else had been there to celebrate our wins. I sipped my beer, hiding my frown with the rim, the cold liquid quenching my drying throat.

"They did great with the place, huh?" Jimenez's attention was back on me, oblivious to my mood. "You should hire someone for your place once you're done wallowing," he said, waving at someone across the room.

I might've been the team captain, but Christian was essentially the team representative. People fucking loved the guy, and he loved the attention. We'd been friends long enough for me to know the signs of how badly he wanted to be out there schmoozing it up with the owner, Carlos.

The tapping fingers, his ass hanging halfway off the barstool, the way he practically pouted every time he looked over there. All of it was a clear indication that he *hated* the role of babysitter.

I nodded toward where a crowd milled around in the center. "Go."

"You sure, Cap? I don't mind being your wingman."

I snorted into my glass at his bullshit line. "I'd have to be trying to pick up women to need a wingman, Jimenez. I mean it. Get out of here. I'm fine to sit at the bar all by myself."

He held my gaze a beat longer, dark eyes searching for a reason to stay by my side. "Alright, but if you need me, wave me over," he said, already halfway out of his stool.

I shook my head at the loud cheer he got before going back to scanning the crowd. Most of the people in the new bar ran in the same circle as us—athletes, agents, and marketing people in the business.

I'd spent the first hour giving out head nods like candy while shooting daggers at the back of Jimenez's head since he'd promised me a "low-key and chill" night.

It made me slightly uneasy. This crowd was the same one Emma ran in. Thinking about our breakup and the following weeks left a bitter taste in my mouth.

Dating a sports reporter was all fun and games until they broke up with you. She'd loved the spotlight, and unfortunately for me, that meant that when she broke things off, my name was dragged into the press to keep hers relevant.

An infectious sound pulled me from my darkening thoughts. The woman to my right flung her head back, laughing, causing the corners of my mouth to tip upward involuntarily. Something about the laugh's carefree nature gave me the same warm feeling as when sunshine hit my face.

The happiness was quickly chased away, though, my bad mood crashing down like a rogue wave, reminding me of how trapped I'd felt lately. When had I last felt open and free anywhere besides the ice?

Hell, I wasn't even sure I felt it there anymore.

I had the oddest urge to walk over to her and ask what her secret was.

"That's enough alcohol," I muttered into the glass, downing the rest of my beer before signaling to the bartender.

"Did you want to close out, Mr. Langley?"

Internally, I cringed at the use of the name but didn't comment. "No thanks. You can leave it open for the guys. Would it be cool if I stopped by tomorrow to pick it up? And could I get some water, too?"

The guy nodded, running off to get my drink, and like a magnet, my attention returned to the woman.

My mother would whack me upside my head for staring at a woman the way I was, but I couldn't look away. Dark brown waves covered most of her back, hitting right where her waist tapered in slightly. Tanned skin peeked through the silky curtain whenever she moved her head.

Bet her skin is soft.

I jerked back at the thought. *Where the hell did that come from?*

That should have been my sign to leave, but I was too engrossed in observing how animated she was as she spoke to the person beside her. Muscled, arms waved out to the sides, and a chuckle slipped out when I noted how her friend rolled her eyes at one particularly animated movement that made it look like the mystery woman was lifting weights.

I was lost in the moment, but the smile I hadn't realized I had fell the moment I heard a familiar voice coming from the front door.

Emma.

Like a trigger response, my ass was out of the chair and moving before my brain fully processed what was happening. The need to get out of there before she spotted me was visceral. I cringed, realizing that was impossible, considering my whole team was there. And a six-three man darting through a crowd of people like his ass was on fire wasn't exactly inconspicuous.

A curse slipped out as someone stepped in my way, slowing me down while my pulse did the opposite. God, this was the same feeling as when we were a goal down with ten seconds left on the clock, but the other team had the puck.

Dread slid through me like a toxic sludge, contaminating any happiness I'd felt tonight. Looking over my shoulder toward the door, I checked where she was at.

The knot in my chest loosened a bit.

Emma still stood at the entrance, her lips pursed in a way that made her look irritated, blonde hair pulled back into a tight ponytail. Any relief I'd felt at the distance vanished because her head snapped my way, sending my heart slamming into my rib cage. I nearly gave myself whiplash to avoid eye contact.

Shit. She's for sure going to make her way over to me.

A mantra of "get out, get out" played on repeat in my mind until it was interrupted by the laughter from earlier.

Like a freaking moth to a flame, my body moved toward the woman, toward that laugh. She now sat alone, laughing with the bartender.

I had no clue what came over me, but one moment, I was practically sprinting out of the bar to avoid my ex, and in the next, I did one of the dumber things I'd done in my life—I slid next to the random woman.

I was never drinking again because what was I doing?

I should have been halfway out the door by now, avoiding Emma, not sitting on a barstool that was too small next to a woman with what? A nice laugh and back? I was seconds away from standing and apologizing before making my exit when she turned, stopping in my tracks.

Large brown eyes peered over at me through thick black lashes. My pulse jumped into my throat, a nervous excitement that set my blood on fire.

She was gorgeous.

Soft waves framed her face, giving a clear view of her high cheekbones and glossy lips, which were clearly moving. It took my brain a second to catch up with what she was saying.

"Can I help you?" she asked again with irritation, her dark brow quirking up in an arch.

"Um." I cleared my throat, trying to jumpstart my vocal cords into working.

Demon possession had to be real, because what I'd

meant to say was, *"No, so sorry for bothering you,"* but instead, what came out was, "Actually, yes. I realize this is extremely weird, and I am not trying to hit on yo—"

"Saying you're not hitting on me sounds *exactly* like trying to hit on me." She cocked her head to the side, eyes daring me to argue with her. But I was too distracted by her glossy lips wrapping around the straw, taking a sip.

Heat crawled up my neck at the inappropriate thoughts the sight invoked. "Point taken, ma'am, but this is worse than some pickup line," I admitted, smiling at the way she narrowed her eyes at me in suspicion.

God, I needed to touch some grass. This was not how I usually reacted to a woman.

"Okay, I am going to humor you because my cousin's in the bathroom, and at the very least, this will provide a great story to tell her." Her big brown eyes raked over me in a way that felt like she was assessing me for weaknesses.

It was fascinating that she didn't seem the least bit intimidated by me. Not that I wanted to intimidate her—quite the opposite—but with my stature, most *men*, let alone women, looked at me with caution.

Not her, though.

I leaned forward, resting my elbow on the polished bar top, moving into her personal space. There was no way I wanted anyone else to hear what I was about to ask. A warm and sensual scent hit me, and I had the strangest urge to run my nose along the column of her throat.

Instead of backing away, she only arched her brow higher. "Watch yourself, cowboy. I've got damn good aim when it comes to kicking someone in the balls."

Of course she did. That only made me like her more.

"Good to know, but I hope you haven't had to use that move too often." The idea of men bothering her had protectiveness stirring in my chest, which didn't make a lick of sense.

She shrugged a shoulder. "Most of the time, my glare is enough to scare them off. But that didn't seem to work with you..." A small smirk played at the corner of her mouth when I didn't respond. "So, Longest Ride, were you going to ask me your question or continue to stare at me? Oh, and by the way, if you're going to ask for my number, the answer is no."

I opened my mouth, but nothing came out. Probably because I'd been out of my damn mind to think it was a good idea to stop and talk to a random woman.

What was I supposed to say?

That her laugh reminded me of sunshine?

This was ridiculous.

I couldn't pull a stranger into my shit.

"You're right, that's what I was going to ask, so I'll just..." I moved to stand up, but a small, calloused hand gripped my wrist with surprising strength.

"If you're going to lie, at least *try* to sound convincing. Because, unfortunately, there is this sick trait in me that can't allow you to leave now without you asking me your real question. Otherwise, I will lay awake all night long wondering about what you were really going to ask."

"Would you pretend to be my date?" The words tumbled out before I could stop them, immediately horrified I'd voiced the idea.

Who the fuck asks a random person that?

She blinked a few times before throwing her head back and laughing.

It was even better from this angle. It didn't matter that she was laughing at me—I couldn't stop the stupid grin plastered on my face.

When she looked back, her face fell.

"Hold on, you're serious."

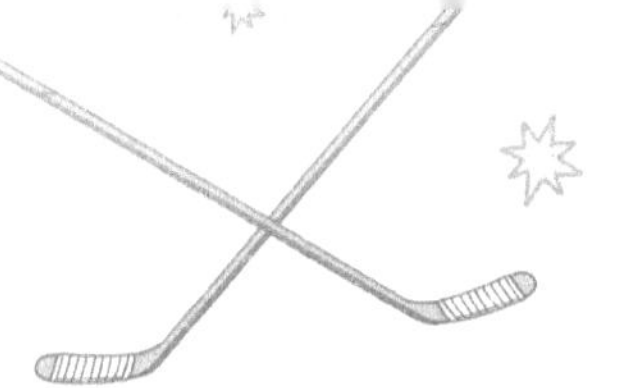

FOUR

ARIELLA

LOOKING PRETTY, FEELING PETTY

HE MIGHT BE DROP-DEAD GORGEOUS—*CLIMB him like a tree* hot—but he was also out of his damn mind if he thought I was about to pretend to be his date, especially with such little information. Had he never watched Dateline?

Ugh. To be a man and never have to think of those things must be nice. Also, where the hell was my cousin?

"Ma'am, I'm afraid I'm dead serious." His voice was smooth, with a slow southern drawl that curled around the edges.

He tipped his felt cowboy hat just enough to let those green eyes lock onto mine. With the moody lighting of the bar, the color reminded me of the forest. I'd seen a lot of hot men in those hats since moving to Dallas. They were on every street corner practically, or that's how it felt after coming from the decidedly cowboy-free Bay Area.

But none of them wore one like *him.*

His thick, corded arms and broad chest filled out every inch of his white T-shirt. I didn't want to look down at

what he was wearing below the bar top because if his thighs were as big as the rest of him, it would take an act of god to keep me from saying yes to whatever he asked.

"Ariella, dance on top of this bar." Yes, hot, mysterious cowboy man, sir.

I should have turned him away before I started drooling, but the desperation in his tone and face was like kibble to me. Curse the Contreras' trait that made me a *chismosa.*

He took my silence as a green light to keep pleading his case. "Look, it will only be for a minute. Then I'll be out of your hair. I promise. In fact, for your trouble, I'll cover your tab for tonight, too."

I'd been distracted by the slight stubble on his chiseled jaw, wondering if the hair under his black hat was the same honeyed brunette color. But the second he got to the paying-for-shit part of his pitch, I snapped right out of my hot-man-hypnosis.

"Why does every man think that they can throw money around to get women to do what they want?"

"I—that—" His eyes widened in surprise. "That wasn't what I was trying to imply, miss. I'm sure you don't need me to pay for anything. I was just trying...I apologize."

The ice over my heart thawed a bit at his genuine response.

Truthfully, it was adorable how flustered he was and how he sheepishly kept his gaze locked where his rough hands were splayed on the marble, like he needed the support. I'd clocked the callouses when he rubbed his face as he fumbled for a response. Hands like that had seen hard work before.

Against my better judgment, my attention traveled downward. I almost laughed when I reached his thick thighs. Of course they were covered in light-washed jeans. I'd bet every dollar to my name that stitched on his ass was that sexy Wrangler W.

This was god tempting me. I was sure of it.

Here I was, minding my own business, sticking to my vow of celibacy, and a hot man just happened to need me to be his date. Or...

I leaned closer to him, the alcohol skewing my depth perception enough that we were practically nose to nose. His nostrils flared slightly, but there was no indication that our proximity bothered him.

"Did Gracie put you up to this?" I asked, ignoring the fluttering feeling low in my stomach.

"Who?"

"Short, Mexican woman with a cute bob and bossy personality, but in a weirdly cheerful way. She probably got you to agree to this before even realizing it?" He looked more confused with every word.

"I have no clue what you're talking about," he answered, eyeing me like I'd lost my mind.

Huh.

That last tequila shot I'd taken was a mistake because, at this point, I should've told him to get lost. Instead, the opposite sentiment fell from my liquor-loosened lips.

"Who's this act for?"

"You'll do it?" Shock colored his tone.

"Didn't say that." I gripped my drink, resisting the urge to massage away the wrinkle forming between his brows at my words. "Amazing how men manage to survive with your atrocious listening skills. I asked *who* you need me to fake being your date in front of?"

"Well, uh, it's for my ex." He winced, dragging a hand over the back of his thick neck, the apples of his cheeks tinged with pink.

And just like that, all the positive thoughts I'd had about him vanished.

Of course. It's always an ex-girlfriend, a current girlfriend, or some kind of messy situationship. Here I was, giving him the benefit of the doubt, thinking maybe this act was for an agent or a boss. But nope. Odds were, he'd screwed her over, and now he wanted me to help him dodge the fallout.

"Sorry, Longest Ride," I said with a shrug. "Girl code. I can't help you hide from your ex."

He sighed, running a hand over the back of his head like the weight of the world sat on his shoulders. "You're right. I'm sorry for bothering you. I don't know what I was thinking." He shifted, ready to leave. "Have a good night, ma'am."

I opened my mouth to say something—what exactly? I had no clue—but a sharp voice cut me off.

"What a surprise seeing you here." The words dripped with condescension. I turned toward the source, finding a tall blonde sauntering toward us, her expression dripping with contempt. "Really? This is what you decided to wear the first time you crawl out from that condo you've been hiding in?" She plucked at his shirt with a manicured hand, dropping it and brushing her fingers together like she touched a dirty rag. "God, you can't function without me, can you? What's your father going to say about this outfit?"

He stood perfectly still, his chest barely rising, like he was holding his breath. His expression had gone blank, but there was something almost *too* controlled about it, as if every muscle in his body was locked in place to keep him from reacting.

Instantly, my red-flag radar went off.

There was no way I knew what this man was thinking —hell, I didn't even know his name—but somehow, deep in my gut, I knew he wished the polished concrete beneath his boots would crack open and swallow him whole.

Or her. Though honestly, maybe that was just me.

"And you wore *that* hat?" She sneered, ignoring how uncomfortable she was making him. His body language was practically screaming for her to leave him alone.

He hadn't said a word.

My eyes bounced between the stunning woman who grew uglier by the minute and the equally stunning, silent mountain of a man beside me. The glint in her eyes was icy—malicious—and made the hair on the back of my neck stand on end.

But what got under my skin most wasn't her words. It was how he seemed to fold in on himself with every insult like he wasn't shocked at how she spoke to him. Like she'd done this before.

Rage simmered below the surface of my skin, threatening to erupt. I curled my fingers into fists, nails digging into my palms until little crescent moons marked my skin.

I didn't need to know a person's name to want to stand up for them.

She liked this. I could see it in the way she stood—head high, shoulders back—landing verbal blows, knowing full well he wouldn't throw any back.

The guy lucked out, picking me for this little charade. Because two things were true about me, every single time:

One, I was ordering the iced coffee regardless of the weather.

And two, I loved to throw back.

Plus, it pissed me off that she hadn't even bothered to acknowledge my presence. All I'd gotten was a quick, dismissive glance. The kind people give when they think you're too irrelevant to register, like I was the dirt beneath her outrageously expensive heels.

"Sorry, did you lose a contact?" I asked, layering on the condescension tone thick enough to cut with a knife. As I spoke, I deliberately shifted my body into her line of sight, making it impossible for her to pretend I didn't exist.

For a second, surprise flickered across her face. She blinked, working to process what I'd said. But then the confusion twisted into a sneer. Or maybe that was just her resting face. Hard to tell if the look of superiority was a permanent feature or reserved for people she thought were beneath her.

"Excuse me?" she snapped.

"Emma, back off," the once-silent cowboy said. The emotionless face from a moment ago was gone, replaced by something close to protectiveness.

Emma. Great. Another name I can't use for my future children.

Not that I was planning on kids anytime soon, but with the rate things were going, I was running out of options. I should've probably been concerned about how long my list was, but instead I was too busy enjoying how color crawled up her neck. Her perfectly-powdered skin was breaking out in angry red splotches.

"Ugh, don't be so sensitive," she said, waving a dismissive hand like I wasn't worth the effort.

"Don't be so rude," he shot back, his voice sharper this time.

Warmth spread through my chest. It was cute that he wanted to defend me. But he didn't know me well enough to realize I didn't need protecting.

You didn't grow up in a family as big as mine and not know how to hold your own. No one could come for your throat quite like *familia.*

The difference was, they were lovable assholes. This woman was just an ass.

Emma was about to be sorely disappointed if she thought she could rattle me with a few cheap jabs.

"I asked if you lost a contact." I motioned to her eyes. "Like, do you have bad eyesight and didn't see me sitting here talking with him? Or are you just naturally that much of a bitch, and barge into conversations without acknowledging the person you interrupted?" I asked, finishing it off with the sweetest smile I could muster.

He choked on a laugh, trying—and failing—to hide it with a cough. I could feel the amusement radiating off him, but I kept my eyes locked on Emma, unwilling to break the stare-off. Her mouth opened and closed several times like a gaping fish.

Speechless.

People like her never knew how to handle someone who didn't shrink under their glares, bad attitudes, and cutting words. I was a good judge of character, and something told me he wasn't the shitty one in their relationship.

"Who the hell are you? I've never seen you before." She looked me up and down, taking me in for the first time. "And how *dare* you speak to me like that. Did you hear what she just said to me?" she asked, whipping toward him, expecting backup. "You're just going to let her tal—"

"Oh, he doesn't *let* me do anything," I interrupted. "And how ironic that *you* are suddenly concerned about manners when you haven't shown any since you walked over."

Her blue eyes narrowed to slits, lips twisting like she'd just sucked on a lime. "Listen here, you bi—"

"Emma," he cut her off, his voice low and laced with warning. "I'd be real careful about what you say next. Because I promise—finishing that word won't bode well for you."

Her face was comical. Wide-eyed and slack-jawed, she even threw in the scandalized gasp, loud enough to draw the attention of some of the other patrons. Her reaction to him shutting her down told me everything I needed to know. He was probably a stand-up guy, and she used that to her advantage, knowing he wouldn't push back. The guy probably spent most of their relationship absorbing her toxicity in silence.

It pissed me off.

People who maliciously took advantage of others were

everything that was wrong with the world, and while I couldn't fix every injustice, I could help him out. I just hoped he would catch on and not ruin the performance I was about to put on.

"Babe." I reached over and rested my hand on his thigh, causing his eyes to widen for a split second, but he didn't miss a beat.

"Yeah, Sunshine?" he asked, intertwining our fingers and lifting them to his mouth to kiss the back of my hand. Acting like it was the most natural thing in the world.

Butterflies erupted in my stomach.

He doesn't know you. This isn't meant to be sentimental. It's fake. You're doing a good deed.

This is just the tequila...

Why is he staring into my soul like that?

Strawberry lip gloss coated my tongue as I swiped across my bottom lip, suddenly aware of how dry my mouth was, and those mossy eyes tracked the movement like a predator stalking its prey. Never in my life had I experienced being turned on by something as small as that.

"What the hell is going on here? What do you mean, *babe*? There's no way you've moved on. I would know." Emma's voice had so much disdain that I had to physically stop myself from rolling my eyes—or decking her. I couldn't tell if her irritation was that he'd moved on, period, or moved on with someone who didn't look like her.

"Well, maybe you should stop stalking him," I said.

"Yeah, seriously," he muttered under his breath,

barely loud enough for me to catch. How long had she been bothering him?

Before I could change my mind, I slid off the stool and stepped between his powerful legs, pulling my hand free and looping both arms around the back of his neck. From this position we were at eye level, and my breath hitched at the intensity of his attention.

The fire in that gaze was as palpable as the heat radiating from his inner thighs. Every part of this interaction sent electric shocks coursing through me. I should have thought this through, but I hadn't predicted my body would react like this to a stranger.

It took Herculean strength to pull my eyes away and look at his ex, who stood not a foot away now. She looked mad enough to spit.

It was borderline comical.

"He's moved on, but maybe you haven't? I mean, I can't for the life of me figure out why you're still standing here bothering us."

Rough hands landed on my hips, his thumbs brushing the sliver of exposed skin between the waistband of my jeans and my top. Suddenly, I was no longer standing between his thighs but sitting on top of them. Caged in by a pair of strong arms.

"There's no way he's moved on from me," she spat, stomping her foot.

His chest rumbled against my side as he spoke. "Believe it or not, Emma, the world doesn't revolve around you. And neither does my life. I've left you alone, and I'd appreciate it if you did the same."

She scoffed, rolling her eyes. "Please, you were always so sensitive."

That was it. She'd done enough damage to this poor man for one night.

"Babe." I leaned in close like I was sharing a secret meant only for him, but my voice was loud enough for her to hear. "Let's get out of here. Go somewhere more... private."

I squirmed on his lap under the intensity of his gaze, gasping when his grip tightened as he held me still. "If you keep moving, we won't be going anywhere very soon," he said with a smirk. It took a second to catch on to what he was implying, but the firm bulge pressed to my hip clued me in pretty quickly. I bit my bottom lip, and he smirked.

What the hell did they put in these drinks?

This was so far outside my normal behavior.

"But yeah, darlin'," he said, his voice as smooth and warm as honey, the Texan gentlemen really coming out. "We can do whatever you want."

I had to focus to keep from melting into a puddle at his feet.

This is fake. This is fake. This is fake.

The mantra didn't do shit when he shot me a smile that was borderline boyish, like he meant what he was saying. That he wanted to do whatever I wanted. I stood, needing to cut the connection before I did something rash like kiss the stupidly handsome face of a man I didn't know.

"I hope you find your contacts and a better attitude," I said, hitting his ex's arm with my shoulder as I pushed past her, pulling him behind me.

FIVE

DALTON

GIRL CODE ONLY COUNTS IF YOU'RE NOT A CUNT

SHE LED us toward the main dining area, which was being used as a makeshift dancefloor tonight. For such a small woman, she carried herself with authority and had zero trouble dragging me around.

"What happened to Girl Code?" I whispered in her ear, needing to cut the distance between us. I'd itched to get close to her again since she slid off my lap—to smell her warm coconut scent wafting from her skin.

"There's a very clear clause that states you forfeit your right to Girl Code if you're a cunt. And your ex is a cunt. Shit." She turned so suddenly I nearly ran her over. I grabbed at her hips, using them to steady her while her hands found my forearms.

My fingertips once again found that smooth strip of skin. I choked back a groan, my mind creating inappropriate thoughts of how it would feel to grip her there while doing things that were not appropriate in public.

"Sorry," we said in unison, still holding on to one another.

"Sorry? What are you sorry for?" I asked.

"Well, calling someone's ex a cunt isn't exactly good manners." The smirk on her face said she wasn't too torn up about it.

"Ma'am, I'm the one who should be apologizing. Emma is..." I tried to think of something to say about my ex that didn't make me come off as an ass.

I mean, I probably already gave this mystery woman a shit impression.

First, I asked her to pretend to be my date, and then my ex treated her like shit. She handled herself fine, though. More than fine if I were being honest.

I thought back to the fiery look that blazed in her eyes when Emma cut in without a second glance. It wasn't jealousy over me that caused her reaction; it was my ex's lack of common decency. Same look the team got when someone hit our goalie in a game. When someone blatantly disregards the agreed-upon etiquette of life.

"A cunt." She lifted a brow in a challenge, amusement in her tone, then tugged me toward the dance floor before I could form a response. "Come on. No one is going to believe we're a couple with us standing a mile away. Let's see if you have any rhythm, *güerito*."

My mother's words echoed in my mind. *"Live a little, Dalt. You deserve to do things you like, too."* That subject was a sore spot between us for the last few years. I wasn't sure my mom meant *this* when she told me to live a little. On second thought, with that woman, this was probably *exactly* what she meant.

There was no stopping the smile on my face as my fake date dragged me onto the floor, pushing through the crowd with ease. She looped her arms around my neck, and I hesitated, not knowing where to place my own.

"Come on, Longest Ride, don't tell me you don't know how to hold a woman on the dance floor," she taunted, placing my hand on her back before pushing it lower. Low enough that the tip of my pinky grazed her ass, our bodies softly swaying to the music.

Was this a nightmare or a fantasy? Because my restraint was being tested within an inch of its capabilities.

I cleared my throat, running through every bad game I'd ever played, trying to keep my growing hard-on at bay. "Well, I appreciate the assist there..." my words trailed off, giving her an out if she didn't want to give me her name, but damn, did I want it.

I wanted to know what it felt like rolling off my tongue.

Her brown eyes twinkled under the lights, a look of mischievousness painted on her beautiful face as she chewed on her bottom lip. She had to tell me. I'd beg if I needed to.

What is wrong with you? You just met this woman.

Maybe Jimenez had a point when he told me that my lack of interaction with the female sex was going to cause me to lose my mind because I was seconds away from dropping to my knees.

"Ariella, but my friends call me Ari," she answered, cutting through my internal argument.

Ariella. It would roll off my tongue nicely if I moaned it. Fuck.

Like a man possessed, I leaned forward, my mouth so

close to her skin that my lips brushed her ear when I spoke.

"Tell me, Ariella, are we friends?"

Her soft gasp went straight to my dick. But, of course, she wouldn't let me have the upper hand. I'd known this woman all of ten minutes, and that was plenty of time to tell she was a ballbuster.

Without missing a beat, she whispered back, "Well, I don't know. Being friends usually means we both know each other's names, and you've yet to give me yours."

We pulled away, both grinning from ear to ear. I didn't know what it was about her, but somehow, she made me feel at ease. Like the carefully curated person I wore for the public wasn't needed.

"Dalton, but my friends call me Dalt."

"Tell me, Dalton—are we friends?" Her brow arched, a teasing smirk tugging at the corners of her lips, playful but daring, as if testing the boundaries between us.

"Yeah, Ari. We are." My voice was low and steady, nothing like the pounding beat inside my chest as I slid my left hand slowly up her side, tracing the curve of her shoulder. Her toned muscles were warm against my touch. When I reached her hand, I took it in mine and shifted our stance, pressing my thigh between hers to lock us into frame. Her smirk bloomed into a full, radiant smile.

Sunshine.

She tilted her head slightly, her dark eyes sparkling. "Do you know how to dance Bachata, Dalt?"

I chuckled, letting my thumb brush the back of her hand. "My best friend is Dominican. It was pretty much a requirement for me to learn so we could stay friends. You should have seen him teaching me how to dance it properly. I've never had another man's junk that close to mine," I said, unable to stop the thought from tumbling out.

She barked out a laugh, completely unfazed by the confession. "Alright then. Let's see what all that junk rubbing taught you."

"Never should have told you that," I said, guiding her backward, sliding into the first slow step, thankful that she'd worn heels. It helped even out the height difference between us.

"Oh, come on, I thought we were friends. Aren't we supposed to share secrets?"

Her body melted into mine effortlessly, her hips swaying to the beat. I let my hand settle at the curve of her waist, fingertips barely grazing her skin as I matched her movements, every shift in her weight a signal I responded to, drudging up the memories of how the dance went—*right, left, right, tap.*

The bar around us faded. We moved together—*push, pull, lean, sway.*

"Okay then, Ari. Tell me a secret."

She stumbled at the request. The easy smile she'd been wearing faltered and shifted into something more guarded. I clocked the way her throat bobbed as she swallowed. "Listen, this is not something I normally do."

"What's not something you normally do?"

"This." She gestured between us with the tilt of her chin. "Pretend to be some stranger's date. Let him hold me on the dance floor. Honestly, Keith Morrison would be so disappointed in me."

I laughed, her comment catching me off guard. "The guy from *Dateline*?"

She arched a brow, the corners of her lips pulling up into a bewitching grin. "What do you know about murder shows?"

"Enough to know that if I were a killer, I wouldn't be dancing with you in a room full of witnesses."

"Hmm." She narrowed her eyes playfully, and I used the moment to spin her out and reel her back into my arms. Her body fit against mine like she belonged there, and my heart kicked up in response.

"You've got a point," she admitted, voice breathier than a second ago. "But we need to go over some rules. No last names, no job titles, no phone numbers, no addresses. Got it?"

I frowned, leaning back slightly. "Why's that? Am I that bad of company?"

Her gaze softened. "No. You're too good of company." She exhaled a soft, bitter laugh. "I can't afford to be tempted by a handsome man with pretty eyes. If I don't know anything about you, I won't contact you later...when I'm feeling weak."

Her honesty hit me harder than I expected.

"That's...weirdly logical. I'm equal parts disappointed and impressed with your self-discipline," I responded, confused as to why my chest ached at the idea of not knowing these things about her when my head knew it was for the best. I'd decided I needed no distractions this season, and Ari would be the biggest kind of distraction.

The music shifted to something faster, but I wasn't ready to lose this moment—not yet.

"Well, if we're only going to have this one night..." I paused, rubbing at the back of my head. "How about we make it a real date?"

I'd meant what I said earlier. We'd do whatever she wanted, especially now that we had an expiration date.

But the moment the word "shit" escaped her lips and she yanked out her phone, my stomach dropped.

Idiot. I was a complete idiot. I didn't even know if she was single. Hell, I didn't know if she liked men.

The silence between us stretched, sharp, and unbearable. I forced myself to stay still, even though every instinct screamed at me to backtrack—crack a joke—anything to escape the awkward, sinking feeling building in my chest.

She tapped furiously on her phone, biting her lower lip. "I just need to check something real quick. Remember my cousin that I told you about?" She looked up briefly as if she were seeing if I was still following. "Well, in the excitement of telling off your ex, I forgot she's supposed to be here with me."

I exhaled, though it didn't make the knot in my gut untangle. Maybe this wasn't the part where she reminded me we were strangers and I needed to get lost.

"*Pendeja,*" she whispered, shaking her head. "Sorry about that."

"No problem." My voice cracked, but she didn't seem to notice. Or if she did, she let it slide.

Her lips curled into a sly smile as she furiously typed a message.

"You're in luck." The rock on my chest was a little lighter at those words. "Apparently, my original date for tonight is...horizontally occupied. She says not to bother waiting up for her." She shook her head, tucking her phone back in her pocket.

"Well," I said, my confidence returning, "Want me to grab us another round?"

She tilted her head, studying me with those sharp brown eyes. I got the distinct feeling she was weighing whether or not to let me in.

I saw the moment she made up her mind. Her eyes lit up, and those glossy lips of hers formed a mischievous smile. She made me both nervous and excited when she looked at me that way.

"All right," she finally said. "But you're not taking me anywhere. I'm taking *you* somewhere."

With my hand still in hers, she dragged me through the crowd, tossing out a half-hearted "excuse me" when needed while shoulder-checking professional athletes without a second thought. The whole scene had me smiling like a fool. She carried herself with effortless confidence, and I'd be a liar if I said that didn't make her hotter.

"Now who's the potential murderer? Where exactly are you taking me?" I asked, leaning over her to push the door open. I'd let her pull me around all night if that's what she wanted, but there was no way I was letting her open a door.

The look she shot me as she stepped outside told me she might not feel the same way.

"Ari, is this going to be our first friend fight?" I leaned in close, keeping my voice low to avoid being overheard. One downside to being an NHL player, privacy was a luxury I didn't always have. Lately, it seemed like everyone was looking for a way to worm into my life, whether I wanted them to or not. "Because when I'm around, you're not opening a door for yourself."

She huffed, the air blowing a piece of her dark hair into her face. "Women can open their own doors, you know."

"Oh, I know. I'm sure you can do a lot of things all by yourself, Ariella, but that doesn't mean you should have to," I said, my voice low, tucking the brunette lock back behind her ear.

Her lips twisted, and her sharp eyes narrowed like she was trying to decide exactly where to aim her next argument. There was no hiding my cocky smile when she rolled her eyes and relented, realizing she wasn't going to win this one.

"Fine." A black polished nail poked at my chest, and she winced a bit when she hit the muscle. "But you're not paying for my meal, okay? I can buy my own stuff, Longest Ride."

"Not a bull rider," I said with a laugh. "Besides, I thought there were no job titles allowed."

She let out a noncommittal hum, her eyes raking up and down, lingering a little longer than necessary on my legs.

"My eyes are up here, Ari."

"Thanks for the anatomy lesson," she sassed, though I could swear her cheeks were a shade darker than before. If I'd been Jimenez, I might've offered to give her a hands-on anatomy lesson—but that wasn't who I was.

Or how I was supposed to act.

"Do you have a car?" she asked, pulling out her phone. "Because if not, we'll have to RideOrder."

Mine was at the rink, and we could easily walk there, but she'd yet to show any signs of knowing who the hell I was, and part of me really liked that I got to be a nobody for once. It was the closest I'd felt to myself in a long time.

"Sorry, no car," I said, only half-lying. "Came with some buddies."

She nodded and opened the rideshare app. "Should be here in a few minutes. I'll let you pay for half the ride," she added with a sly grin. "I'm not *that* into my independence."

God, her bright smile and how her warm brown eyes seemed to twinkle from within had my head spinning. I wanted to chalk up my reactions to the months of celibacy and the fact that I hadn't talked to a new woman in years.

Emma was my college sweetheart. We'd met our freshman year after a hockey game, and the rest was history—or so I'd thought. The months apart had given me a new perspective on our relationship. Looking back, I wasn't sure I'd ever been in love with her.

And deep down, I knew she'd never been in love with me.

I'd been so determined to be a good partner, to show up and be everything someone needed, it never even crossed my mind that she might walk away.

That I wouldn't be enough.

But then, around four months before, a nearly six-year relationship had ended with a note saying she needed a break.

A silver Corolla pulled up to the curb, but I was too lost in thought to reach for the door.

"Hah." Ari shot me a look of victory. "After you, sir."

She dipped into an exaggerated bow, giving me an eyeful of cleavage in the process.

Maybe not always being a gentleman had its perks. Very, very perky perks.

"Quit staring at my boobs and get in, Dalton."

I grinned and folded myself into the tiny car.

"If you'd let me open the door," I muttered as she slid in next to me, "we wouldn't have had that problem."

"No, but then you'd be staring at my ass," she quipped, slamming the door shut behind her.

She was so different from my ex, who'd preferred to be catered to, never wanting to pay for a single thing. Hell, I'd footed the bill for lunches I hadn't even been invited to. Emma had loved being taken care of—she'd never once held a door for me, asked what I needed, or offered to split the burden.

Ari, on the other hand, seemed allergic to the idea of letting me take that sort of initiative. She wouldn't even let me open a door without a fight.

And, for reasons I couldn't fully explain, I liked her even more because of it.

This couldn't be the only time.

My pulse kicked hard at the realization, and I let myself believe that maybe, just maybe, this wouldn't be the only night I'd get with Ari.

SIX

ARIELLA

WE WANT MEN VOCAL IN BED...AND QUIET EVERYWHERE ELSE

THIS GUY WAS full of surprises, and I couldn't quite get a read on him. He was polite and respectful—hell, I could still feel the heat of his hand on my lower back from when he'd moved me away from the edge of the sidewalk as we walked up to my favorite place. I was pretty sure he hadn't even thought about it...being a gentleman came naturally to him.

Now we were seated at a table at what had quickly become my favorite restaurant in Dallas, and Dalton leaned in, his elbows resting on the table. "So, what's the 'usual' that you're feeding me?" He looked at me with more trust than anyone I'd only known a few hours should.

"We're getting a night-out essential... chilaquiles," I announced with both hands raised. It earned me a chuckle from him, and for some reason, it made my heart feel lighter.

He leaned back in his chair, arms folded across his

chest, giving me his undivided attention. But not in a way that was suffocating, just...present.

Like I was the only thing that mattered in that moment.

God, it was unsettling how much I liked his attention. Of course I would find a man who didn't instantly piss me off at this critical time in my life and career.

I shook the thoughts away, focusing back on our conversation. One night—I was allowed one night to set my carefully curated plan aside and enjoy living before it was back to the grind of my goals.

"Most people think chilaquiles are a morning-after-drinking meal. But that's where they're wrong." I leaned closer, lowering my voice like I was sharing a secret. "You eat them the same night you drink, so they can soak up all the alcohol. Prevents the hangover—sometimes. Not that it matters...they're delicious either way." His deep laugh rolled through the space between us.

Right at that moment, the server came over, and Dalton's expression was downright comical, like a starved man who hadn't eaten in days.

"Based on how you're looking at that plate, I'm guessing you're happy with my choice," I teased, grinning as he stared down at the food. "Okay, so chilaquiles are fried tortilla strips—sometimes people use chips—smothered in salsa de tomatillo, then topped with onions, cilantro, cotija cheese, créma, and—this is the best part—two fried eggs, over easy." I grabbed my fork and sliced into one of the eggs, the yolk breaking and oozing across the plate. "If the yolk isn't runny, you're not doing it right,"

I added, my eyes flicking up to catch his reaction as he mimicked my move.

He took a bite, chewing slowly. Then his head tilted back slightly, and a deep, guttural, "Holy shit," slipped out around his mouthful.

I couldn't help it—I burst out laughing. "You always that loud, Dalt?" I teased, raising an eyebrow.

He froze for a second and I could see the mischief brewing behind those green eyes of his. He leaned in, lowering his voice to a deep rumble that had my pulse jumping.

"Sometimes, you gotta let a woman know what a great job she did."

I choked on my bite, coughing as I tried to refill my lungs with air. He gave me that cocky, lopsided grin, clearly enjoying himself.

"Not great at swallowing, Ari?"

I knew that under the polite cowboy's outer shell laid something...else.

Now all I could picture was his...nope, not going there.

Clearly not waiting for an answer, Dalton tore through his chilaquiles. "Okay, no last names, no job titles, no phone numbers, no addresses. What *can* I know about you?" he asked, shoveling in another bite of his food.

"Oh, come on, there are plenty of other things to share besides those four." I rolled my eyes. "Like all the random little shit you don't tell anyone else. Here, I'll start. I love Topo Chico, specifically the lime ones, but those things are so expensive now I never get them."

"Uh, what's Topo Chico?"

My mouth dropped open at the comment, a scoff falling out at the same time. There was no way I could, in good conscience, let us end the night without him trying one, even if it was going to cost me four damn dollars, or whatever the going rate was for them. Without another word, I slipped from the table.

"Topo Chico." I took a giant gulp before sitting back down and sliding it across the table, waiting for his reaction. He took a drink without hesitation.

Holy shit, I need sleep.

I'd never given a second thought to sharing a drink with someone, ever. Coming from a family as large as mine, food and eating was a communal experience—we all shared everything. But there was something about watching his lips wrap around the same bottle mine had just been on that had me shifting in my seat. Suddenly, I wanted my drink back to see if it tasted like him...

You don't need sleep. Jesús Cristo, that's what you need.

He coughed, a giant hand covering his mouth, before giving me a weak smile. "So...spicy water?"

"You hate it," I laughed, pulling it back to my side.

"I don't *hate* it, but I'd never willingly choose that to drink."

He was so much sweeter than my brother or cousins would ever have been. The crisp bubbles ticked my nose as I watched the way Dalton watched me. At the sports bar, he'd been tense, shoulders practically in his ears, back rigid. But here, where it was just the two of us, he was relaxed. His strong legs were spread out over on my side.

The heat radiating off them was a constant temptation to bump against them with my own.

"Your turn," I rushed out, taking another bite, in desperate need of something else to focus on.

"Hmm," he mused, finishing off the last of his food. He probably would have licked the plate if I wasn't sitting across from him. The mental picture had a smile stretching across my face.

"My favorite candy is those chewy orange and yellow rings covered in sugar, but they have to be the off-brand from the gas station. They taste better." His smile was so different from the one he'd given earlier, and I couldn't help but think I was receiving information he rarely gave out.

"The only candy I like I don't think you'd classify as candy, because they're all spicy."

He balked before quickly covering up the reaction. "Spicy candy? How is that even candy, then?"

God, he was adorable.

"Wait 'til I tell you I put hot sauce on my popcorn and lime on my fruit," I said, leaning forward and lowering my voice like I was letting him in on a secret. Really, I just wanted to be closer to him since our impromptu one-time date was coming to an end.

Our time was slipping away, and the thought of the night ending felt like a knot in my chest.

This must have been what Cinderella felt as the clock approached twelve—as if reality loomed at the edges of the fantasy, threatening to steal her from the bubble of temporary freedom. Maybe that's why I let the next sentence tumble out. I wanted to experience the freedom of that moment.

"I start a new job next week, and I'm so nervous."

I hadn't admitted that to anyone. Not even my family...especially not my family. Maybe it was easier with Dalton because I wouldn't see him again, or maybe it was because I sensed that he wouldn't judge or make me feel small. "It's not that I don't know what I'm doing, I'm confident I can do my job, it's just that..."

"Just what?" he asked, our foreheads nearly touching, his green eyes steady on mine as he pulled my hand from where I subconsciously picked at my callouses. "You're going to make them bleed," he said gently, brushing his thumb over the rough skin. "Go on, tell me what you're worried about so I can help alleviate those worries."

Heat pooled low in my stomach.

Indecision churned inside me. Each thought colliding with the next.

Letting anyone in on my insecurities felt like a cardinal sin, like admitting defeat. I'd always handled things on my own. Had to. Seeking help usually carried the same shame as failure. It meant I wasn't strong enough. That I couldn't carry the weight I was meant to shoulder. But for one night, with someone I'd never see again...maybe I could let the wall fall.

It didn't mean I couldn't handle life on my own.

"Pinky promise you're not gonna tell anyone?" I asked, holding out my smallest finger. My heart lurched when he wrapped his around mine, the sensation far more intimate than it should have been.

"Pinky," he said, low and sincere.

I took a breath, heart hammering as I unloaded some of my worries. "It's in a field that's not known for having women, and there are going to be a lot of men. I don't want them to think I don't know what I'm doing. I have to keep this job. I worked too hard for too long to get out of my ho—to get here."

Dalton's whole body went still, but he didn't interrupt or try to offer a quick fix—he just let me talk.

"And my family..." I trailed off, chewing on the thought. "They already don't think this is a good career path. They keep waiting for me to realize it won't work out." My throat tightened. Saying it out loud made it feel so much heavier. They wanted me to settle down and start a family, to find a good Catholic Latino who would take care of me and the babies I gave him, like my mom and all my *tías*.

But the thought of giving up on everything I wanted felt like drowning on dry land.

Dalton brushed his thumb across my callouses. The caress was like a pressure release valve, allowing the weight on my chest to lessen. "I get that. But I think it's a sign you'll do a kick-ass job."

He gave me a lopsided grin, but I saw the flicker of something darker in his eyes—something heavy. "I still get nervous in my profession. Constantly going over everything I did right or wrong and where I can improve. Hell, I get the added bonus of working for my dad, which..." He glanced away, his jaw tightening for just a moment. "Let's just say it takes a lot to make him proud."

Dalton let out a humorless laugh, staring down at our joined hands with an intensity that told me he was mentally somewhere else. "I'm not entirely sure I ever have..." he said, so quietly I would have missed it if I weren't so wrapped up in him.

The comment made me frown.

My parents didn't get what I did for work, but I'd never thought of them as not being proud of me. It was more like they were proud I was trying, but waiting for me to realize it wasn't going to work out the way I'd always thought. And outside of that, there were plenty of things my parents had been proud of me for. Surely he couldn't mean his father had *never* been proud of him.

I didn't get to ask because Dalton lifted his head, throwing on one of the curated smiles he'd had on at the sports bar, and that told me all I needed to know. We were moving on from the subject.

"Those nerves mean this matters, Ari. You're gonna prove to them—and yourself—that you belong. Give 'em hell."

Dalton stood, tossing a few bills on the table despite my protests. "Don't argue," he said, that soft, confident grin slipping back into place. "It's already done."

I rolled my eyes. *Already done my ass.*

From my purse, I grabbed enough cash to cover my plate and overpriced spicy water, adding it to the pile. The rest could be the tip, a thank you for dealing with us at this hour. Dalton shook his head but didn't look surprised— smart man didn't argue either.

We walked out beside each other in comfortable silence, the muggy night air hugging my skin. For a moment, we stood on the curb under a flickering streetlight, both knowing what was coming but neither willing to address it.

"This one's yours," he said softly, nodding toward the RideOrder that had pulled up.

Neither of us moved.

My chest tightened. It was supposed to be easy—a clean break—one night to step out of my comfort zone, no strings attached. But the thought of not seeing him again scraped against something raw inside me, and I wasn't ready for how much it stung.

"I had a really good night, Dalton," I whispered, more to myself than him.

His smile softened, the sheepish grin back. "Me too, Ari." His voice was quiet, but there was something in the way he said it that made my heart stumble. "A lot better than I expected, if I'm being honest."

Maybe I should just hop in the car and run away, lessen the blow of goodbye...

Ariella. When did you become a whiny bitch? Take what you want, and enjoy your one night.

It's not like I'll see him again.

He tilted his head, eyes glinting under the streetlight. "What's that look for?"

"I was just thinking of something that would make the night perfect instead of just good," I answered, the electric tension humming between us.

I wasn't sure who moved first, but Dalton's hand slid along my jaw, his fingers brushing just below my ear. It was like I forgot how to breathe for a second. His touch was warm and steady.

The regret I halfway expected to feel was noticeably absent. I *wanted* this.

He closed the distance. The kiss started soft, like he was testing if this was okay. His lips were warm and smooth, with a hint of hesitation as he waited for my reaction. Waited for my lead.

That realization made the kiss better.

There was no rush, no demand—just patience.

I pressed in a little deeper. The scratch of stubble against my skin had me sighing in pleasure. His lips curved into a smile against mine at my reaction.

God, that stupid smile.

His hand shifted, thumb brushing my cheekbone in a way that sent a maelstrom of shocks down my spine. The kiss was unhurried, as if we were both savoring something we knew might never happen again. When we finally pulled back, I swallowed, keenly aware of the tension crackling between us and the temptation to dive back in.

"That," I said, my voice a little breathless, "wasn't bad."

He chuckled, the low sound curling around me. "Not bad, huh? That's all I get? Because if I remember correctly, you practically purred."

"Don't get cocky."

"Too late," he whispered, brushing one last kiss to the corner of my mouth, light and teasing.

My heart did this weird little flip, and I had to bite my lip to avoid smiling too much. Even without the kiss, tonight would linger in my thoughts.

Maybe not everything needed to be so rigid in my life. Maybe there was room for spontaneity.

I slid into the backseat of the RideOrder, my heart doing another weird flip I wasn't used to as I looked up at Dalton.

"I'll see you around, Ari," he said, though we both knew it was a lie.

"Yeah," I whispered, unable to bring myself to correct him.

The soft click of the door sounded too loud in my ears. Too final. The driver pulled away, and I used every ounce of discipline not to look back one final time.

SEVEN

ARIELLA

GRACIE'S SERIAL KILLER TRAIT IS SITTING IN THE DARK UNTIL SHE CAN INTERROGATE YOU…

MY MOVEMENTS WERE on autopilot as I slipped my key into the door, busy committing everything about Dalton to memory. I wanted it all. The way he looked, the way he moved, every detail accurate for when I dreamt of us rolling around in the sheets. It seemed like my recurring dream with Maluma was getting a fresh lead—a tall, sandy brunette with green eyes and an ass you could bounce a quarter off of.

I may or may not have peeked back at Goaltender.

"Ariella María Elena Contreras, where the hell have you been?" Gracie's voice caused me to yell out into the darkened apartment, dropping my keys and phone as my cousin ranted on. "Really? What if I was an intruder waiting for you at the apartment? That's what you would do? Yell out and drop shit? Where have you been, *prima*? I thought for sure you'd be asleep in bed."

The apartment's lights suddenly flicked on, revealing Gracie sitting on the couch—aka my pseudo-bed—

tucking her dark chin-length hair behind her ears like it might let her hear the *chisme* better. Because that's what she was after if her shit-eating grin was anything to go by.

I rolled my eyes, toeing off my shoes while trying to figure out how much to tell her about my night. We told each other almost everything, but if I wasn't careful, she wouldn't let me sleep, too busy demanding to go over every moment in detail for hours so she could dissect what everything meant.

Which would be fine if I was seeing Dalton again. Hell, I'd probably want that boy-crazy mind of hers to tell me what everything I was feeling meant.

But since tonight was a one-time thing, I decided to shift topics.

"Why are you sitting in the dark like a freak?" I asked, plopping down next to her. "Weren't you supposed to be out getting your back blown out?"

Dark brows knitted together, her full lips forming an irritated pout. "That would require him to last longer than a few minutes. Honestly, I should have done it in the bathroom at the bar and then gone back out with you. Then I could have classified it as a hot quickie and not a waste of my time." The look of disappointment morphed into a smirk as she playfully smacked my leg. "But then you wouldn't have gone slinking off with a man," she said in a sing-song tone.

"How do you know it was a man?" I challenged, tamping down the stupid smile that threatened to form.

Her toffee-colored eyes nearly got stuck in the back of her head with how hard she rolled them. "Please, you only get all defensive and evasive like this when there's a man involved."

She had a point there. I should have known she'd pick up on it right away. We were only a few months apart and more like sisters than cousins. Our moms often told us we were just like them growing up—except my *tía* and mom were actual sisters.

"So," she drawled out, practically vibrating with excitement, "what's his name?"

There was no getting out of this conversation.

"Dalton." Even I could hear the smile in my tone.

There was a moment of silence before she piped up again. "Dalton? That's all you have for me? What's his last name? Date of birth? Star sign? Credit score? Hell, condom size?"

I shot her an unamused look, brow practically in my hairline. As close as we were, Gracie and I were worlds apart in some things. Part of me envied her ability to be so open and fearless. Unafraid to dive into connections without worry.

"I don't know any of that. We agreed to no personal info."

She shot out of her seat, her hands landing on my shoulders to shake me. "*¡Dios mío!* Did you have your first one-night stand? I'm so proud," she squealed, pulling me in for a hug.

"No..." My cheeks heated. "I, uh, took him to get chilaquiles after the bar...and maybe pretended to be his date to help him avoid his ex." I rushed out the last part, bracing for the shit I'd receive.

She pushed away, throwing herself onto the couch

with enough dramatic flair to make a telenovela star jealous. "*Perdóname*, did I just hear you say you pretended to be his date so *he* could avoid his ex? What happened to Girl Code, Ari? Was he really that hot?" Her usually raspy voice had jumped a few octaves in shock.

"No. Well, yes, he is that hot, but that wasn't the reason I did it." I let out a frustrated sigh. "I told him no, but then she came over and was mean to him."

"Mean to him?" Gracie asked, placing the back of her hand on my forehead. "Are you okay? When has a woman being mean to a man bothered you? Correct me if I'm wrong, but normally, *you're* the one being mean to men."

I swatted her away. "If you give me a second, then I could get to the part where she completely ignored me, as if I was nothing more than dirt under her expensive shoes, and you know how I feel about that." I pointed at her for emphasis. "And I am not *only* mean to men. I'm mean to anyone who deserves it; it just so happens that most of those people are men. Another aspect of life the patriarchy has successfully infiltrated."

She snorted and her hair broke free from behind her ear as she nodded. "First of all, I gave you plenty of time to tell me all of that. You were staring off into space, drooling, but this makes way more sense. Girl Code doesn't count if you're—"

"A cunt," we said in unison.

Gracie stood, moving toward her bed tucked in one corner of the studio while I prepped the couch for sleep. The narrow cushions, lumpy and threadbare from years of use, seemed to mock me as I tucked my hot pink checkered sheets around them, a stark reminder of why things with Dalton couldn't go anywhere.

I had goals, and sleeping on a couch at twenty-five was not one of them. Neither was moving back into my parents' house, where I'd get stuck fending off all the suitors my family threw my way. They'd probably take it as a sign that the dreams I'd worked so hard for, the ones they disapproved of, had failed.

This new job was it—my all-or-nothing. There was no room for the emotions or distractions that came along with a man.

"So," Gracie's voice pulled me from my thoughts. She was curled up on her side, having settled into her own bed, watching me with a smirk. "When are you seeing him again?"

"I'm not." My voice held more bite than I'd meant it to. "I told you we didn't get phone numbers or anything, and I have to focus on work." I tossed my blanket over the sheets. "And on making enough so you can have your space back."

Even in the dim lighting from her twinkle lights, which hung as a makeshift headboard, I could make out my cousin's frown. "You know you can stay here as long as you'd like. And meeting people is a good thing, not a distraction. What are you planning on doing? Working *all* the time and never having fun? Or getting laid? A *novio?* Life's about more than work, Ariella."

I dropped onto my makeshift bed. The well-worn cotton sheets were like a warm hug, the checkered fabric cool against my skin. I lay there, cocooned in that familiar fabric, feeling a gnawing restlessness I hadn't anticipated.

Tonight shouldn't have affected me this way. Yet there I was, wondering if Gracie had a point.

Fucking mescal.

After a while, my cousin's even breathing told me it was safe to whisper out my insecurity. The one I kept buried deep inside.

"I don't know how to do both. And I don't want to get stuck like our moms."

My lids fluttered shut, the buildup of emotions draining me and pulling me under. But right before drifting off, a *cha-ching* sounded from my phone, and my eyes flew open.

EIGHT

ARIELLA

SEEEE? IF HE WANTED TO, HE WOULD

AT FIRST, I was confused about who'd be sending me money, until I remembered Dalton had scanned my CashPay in the car ride over to the restaurant.

> CASHPAY:
>
> $15 from Dalton55
>
> CASHPAY:
>
> $1 from Dalton55
>
> The first one was for the ride. This one is because I apparently have to send you money to message you, and I had a feeling you'd skewer my balls if I sent you more than a dollar. Thanks for the best date I've had in my life. Good night, darlin'.

Butterflies went wild low in my stomach as I read the message over and over. Damn it, why did he have to be so charming? I gnawed on my lip until the point of pain, fingers typing and deleting messages for a solid five minutes until I tucked my phone under my pillow.

As I drifted off into a restless sleep, images of a chiseled jaw peppered with stubble popped into my mind.

This was the only place where I could have Dalton—in my dreams.

NINE

DALTON

LISTEN, I KNOW BOYS ARE DUMB, AND
VIOLENCE IS BAD, BUT GOD DO I LOVE IT
WHEN THEY GET ALL AGGRESSIVE OVER THE
GIRL...

THERE WAS something seriously wrong with me.

All weekend, I'd sent Ari messages via CashPay, hoping for some kind of response. The fact that she hadn't sent back the six dollars was a good sign...right?

"You alright, Cap?" Jimenez asked as I scrubbed my palms over my face, trying to shake off the mental hoops I was putting myself through.

I'd considered asking his advice, since he was the team's self-proclaimed expert on women. But I didn't know if his advice was the kind I was looking for. Plus, what would he say when he found out I was messaging her through a payment app because I didn't have her number? And worse, that she hadn't even responded.

What was the line for moving into stalking territory?

"He's probably tired from the action he got Friday night," Roberts shouted from across the locker room. "Did you see her, Jimenez? Damn, she was fine."

"The fuck are you talking about, Up-Chuck? Cap

here didn't get any pussy Friday night." My best friend turned to me, lowering his voice. "Did you?" he asked, almost hopeful.

I yanked on the ties of my sneakers a little harder than necessary. "No, I didn't sleep with anyone Friday." Just another disappointing reminder that I hadn't asked Ariella to come home with me. I'd replayed it a hundred times, all the things I could've said. But if I was being honest with myself, I didn't want her as a one-night stand.

I wanted more of her, period.

I let out a ragged sigh. Maybe she was right to keep it to just one night. She wasn't the only one who had life circumstances that demanded attention. All of my attention needed to be on making it to playoffs, winning the Stanley Cup this year, and keeping out of Emma's warpath. In retrospect, making her think that I had a date may not have been the best move.

Damn, Ari had more discipline than I had—and that was saying something.

The drafted message in CashPay burned a hole in my shorts pocket. I needed to move on.

She already had.

"Oh, come on, Cap, don't hold out on us. Look how cozy you two look. You had to hit that after looking at each other like *that*." Roberts said, shoving his phone at me.

On the screen was a tabloid picture of Ari and me with the headline: "Star Hockey Player Dalton Langley Steps Out with Mystery Woman." And in a block of smaller text below it: "Was She the Cause of Surprise Split with Longtime Girlfriend Emma Faulk?"

"Sources say Langley was seen cozying up to a

mystery woman after snubbing his ex. The two even shared an intimate kiss before leaving together in a cab," Jimenez read over my shoulder, smacking me on the arm when he got to the kissing part. "Damn it, man, why didn't you tell me you finally kissed someone other than that *bruja*?"

"Because I didn't kiss her. Not then, at least," I muttered, irritated, looking closer at the photo of me and Ari. The angle from where the picture was taken told me everything I needed to know about who'd snapped it.

I should have anticipated Emma doing something like this.

I studied the grainy photo. Roberts wasn't wrong. We looked at each other like we couldn't wait to get home. She'd captured the moment I tucked a strand of Ari's silky hair behind her ear. All weekend, I dreamt of that hair sprawled across my pillows or gripped in my hand as I pulled it.

Roberts's voice shattered the fantasy. "So, she's free game then? Because let me tell you, I—"

Without thinking, I shot out of my seat, shoving the rookie back with more force than needed. Jimenez caught him before he fell on his ass, arching a brow at me. I ignored the silent question, too fired up to think rationally.

"She's not free game, rookie." The locker room fell silent, all eyes on us.

Roberts held both hands up in the air, a sly smirk on his baby face. "You got it, Cap. She's your girl."

She wasn't my girl, but I couldn't seem to get those words out.

Luckily Monroe walked in, saving my ass from

explaining to Jimenez why I went off on a teammate over a woman I barely knew. "Hey, assholes, let's go. You've got about thirty minutes before meeting your new strength and conditioning coach this morning. Let's not start off with all of you being late." Grunts of agreement mixed with the slamming of locker doors as everyone geared up.

We worked in the weight room all season, but concentrated on it most during the off-season and pre-season. The guy we'd had last year had left about a month before for health reasons, leaving Monroe in a rush to find a replacement.

"Dalt, your dad wants to see you in his office," he added, giving me a nod. "Make it quick."

The protein shake from that morning turned into a rock at the bottom of my stomach. "Got it. I'll head over there now," I said, making my way out of the locker room and toward my dad's office near the entrance of the practice rink.

A giant photo of the man in question hung on the wall right outside the double doors. Vincent Langley, former star NHL player, owner of the Dallas Desperados, self-made millionaire, and my father. His intense stare in the image almost captured how imposing the man was in real life. I knocked once, waiting for the go-ahead. Dad had a rule about players entering his space uninvited. Called it a show of disrespect if they did.

No one on the team was called to meet with him as much as I was, though.

"Dalton, you're not just a player. You're a brand. You represent my legacy, and I won't have you tarnishing my image."

"Come in," a deep voice snapped.

I walked in, closing the door behind me. "You wanted to see me, Dad?"

The office was an extension of the man who owned it, exuding strength and elegance with its charcoal walls and masculine furniture. Jimenez once asked me if my dad's desk size was a reflection of his dick size, which, of course, left me with a mental image I'd *never* wanted.

Without looking up, he gestured toward the club chairs, engrossed in whatever paperwork lay in front of him. "Sit, Dalton." That's how it was with him. He gave a command, and I followed it. Whenever it rubbed me the wrong way, I reminded myself that this whole father-son thing was new—at least for me, it was.

"Let's talk about this season and what I expect," he finally said, folding his large hands in front of him on the cognac leather blotter.

Seeing the same mossy color I saw staring back at me in the mirror every day reflected in his gaze was always unnerving. And our eyes weren't the only similarities between us.

My build clearly came from my father, same with the sharp jaw, and before his head of hair turned salt and pepper, we'd shared the same sandy brown hair color, too. Still, I always felt I saw more of my mom in myself. Maybe that had more to do with growing up with only her around —I hadn't known another parental figure to try and find bits of myself in.

"Sure, Dad. What exactly are you wanting to go over?"

His lips thinned. "Vincent. Or Mr. Langley, Dalton. 'Dad' suggests unprofessionalism."

He'd hammered that concept into me more times than I could count. You'd think breaking that habit would've been easy since I wasn't used to calling anyone 'dad' until my senior year of college.

"I expect the team to make it to playoffs this year, and to win them. There *won't* be a repeat of last year, understand me?" I nodded, knowing that's all he wanted—a silent show that I heard him loud and clear.

He stood, coming to lean against the front of his mahogany desk. "Dalton, you're going to have a lot of eyes on you. People are already interested because it will be our comeback season, but you've added scrutiny due to the last name on the back of your jersey. A name I don't want tarnished. And with all the attention since your public breakup a few months ago...well, let's say you're not off to a good start in showing me you can handle the pressure."

I winced.

Yes, because it's easy to bounce back from being broken up with via a note on our shared apartment door after losing the playoff game in overtime.

I wondered if he'd seen the tabloid from this weekend and that was what sparked this conversation. Probably not, or he'd have brought it up specifically. The man didn't mince his words.

It wasn't that I had a reputation. I didn't share Jimenez's playboy status, or have a gravitas like Monroe, who was known to essentially only give grunts for answers.

But my dad was right, the last name on my jersey meant I drew attention, and since the split with Emma, I'd continued to be a topic of conversation, mainly by her doing. Far enough removed from the relationship I could see that I was just a way to keep her name relevant.

Hopefully, Ari worked in an industry far removed from the sports world, and she'd never even know she'd been dragged into my mess by the tabloids.

"It won't be a problem."

He arched a brow. "So far, all you've shown me is how well you can hide away."

God, the difference in how my mom and dad delivered pep talks was like night and day.

The heavily cologned air of his office filled my nostrils as I took a deep breath, trying to ground myself and swallow down my irritation.

I stood, wiping my clammy hands off on my shorts. "Don't worry, I'll make sure I represent you and this team properly, but I've got to get to the weight room for practice. Being late for the new coach wouldn't be a good look." His jaw ticked at the hint of an attitude in my tone, but he didn't object as I walked toward the door to leave.

"See that you do," he called after me. "And don't forget, the Media Day event is coming up. You're the primary face of this franchise. I expect you to set the tone for the season, Dalton. No slip-ups."

I gripped the door handle, saying nothing as the weight of his expectations settled heavily on my shoulders.

"This team needs a leader. If you can't handle the attention or maintain focus under pressure, let me know now, and I'll find someone who can."

My jaw tightened, muscles tensing at the insinuation that I wasn't capable of living up to his expectations. That I wasn't enough.

He seemed to sense my irritation and pulled me back in line with five words that always hit their mark.

"Go make me proud, son."

He looked at me with an expression that was as close to a smile as I got from him. Every time I saw it, I was sucked right back to being a kid, watching other dads look lovingly at their sons. Wishing I had the same moment to share with mine.

Now I did. My dad was in my life now, in a major way.

I should be grateful. He'd given me this opportunity—stepped back into my life. I owed him, right? I couldn't fuck it all up.

I gave a firm nod, reminding myself of my priorities.

No tabloids. No distractions.

No thoughts of Ari.

"Of course, Dad."

TEN

ARIELLA

I SHOULD HAVE BROUGHT a bag suitable for throwing up into.

Or maybe I should've kept my ass in San Jose and been fine living with my parents until a man came around to save me.

That thought only made my nausea worse, but it was exactly the push I needed to move through the front doors of my new place of work.

Langley Ice Rink, home of the Dallas Desperados.

The crisp air cooled my flushed skin. The temperature inside was a stark contrast to the weather outside and another not-so-subtle reminder of what I'd managed to get myself into. My lids fluttered close, blocking out the white wall with the team logo plastered across.

I needed a minute to shove down the nerves.

It wasn't like I was some clueless hockey newbie. I'd spent years working with hockey players, starting as an intern with San Jose State's hockey team in college.

After graduation, they offered me a job as their strength and conditioning coach, and I stuck with them until I got the call from Dallas. I was damn proud of the work I did there. Several of the guys had hired me outside of the season to prepare them for pursuing their NHL dreams.

I could have applied for the San Jose Stars, but part of me knew I needed an excuse to leave home, to start fresh somewhere that didn't hold all my family's expectations.

But that meant I only had one option—Texas.

My older brother Ricky would have lost his mind if I told him I was moving to a new city with no family around. I loved him, but god, was he nosy.

The thing was, in our culture, being the older brother basically made you a second father to your siblings. Asking him to stay out of my shit was practically a foreign concept and two weeks into my move I was expectantly waiting for him to randomly show up.

"Hello, ma'am. Can I help you?"

The receptionist's sweet voice reminded me I was standing in the middle of a lobby on my first day of work— not the time or place to space out and mull over my life choices.

"Yes, sorry. I'm supposed to be meeting with...Josh Monroe," I said, checking the email on my phone. "I'm the new hire on the coaching staff."

Her eyes widened.

I wanted to chuckle, her face giving away exactly what she was thinking.

"This five-foot-three woman in spandex shorts,

scrunchy white socks, and Converse is on the coaching staff?"

Sure, my outfit wasn't traditionally the picture of professionalism, but squatting in a three-piece suit wasn't practical. I had worn the Dallas Desperados tee shirt they'd sent me. She recovered quickly, flipping through her papers with a polite smile.

"Welcome! I'm Jasmine. You're the new strength and conditioning coach?"

"That's correct. Ariella Contreras."

"You're early," a gruff voice said from behind me, and I turned.

A large man in athletic shorts and a sweatshirt with the team logo walked toward me from a hallway I'd missed. *Walked* wasn't quite the right description—it was more intense than that. Everything about him seemed serious, from the subtle scowl to the neatly styled hair and sharp jawline covered in a five o'clock shadow.

"Is the company culture here to be late? If that's the case, these guys are in for a rude awakening when they walk into my weight room," I said, keeping my attitude in check. Professional Ariella was in the house, but that didn't mean I'd let people walk all over me.

Professionalism and respect were a balancing act.

I'd learned early on that respect needed to be demanded from day one. Otherwise, you'd be fighting an uphill battle. I'd spent enough time around players to know that some people—men and women alike—assumed that boobs somehow meant "unqualified."

I was here to show them I knew exactly what I was doing.

The man stopped in front of me, and I swore there was a ghost of a smile on his lips. "Not a problem at all. I'm pleasantly surprised at the initiative. Last guy who had the job sucked." He held out his hand out for a shake. "Josh Monroe, head coach. I'm the one who hired you, so you'll report directly to me. Understood?"

It felt like a coded instruction, but I shook his hand firmly. "Understood. You're my boss."

He watched me for a few seconds, then gave a curt nod before turning to the receptionist. "Jasmine, you have that new hire packet ready? I'll take it and make sure Ms. Contreras gets it to you by the end of the week. Right now, she's got a workout to lead."

Excitement snaked up my spine.

"You ready for that?" he asked, turning back to me.

I schooled my smile, wanting him to see I was all business. "Absolutely. I know what I'm doing."

"Good. I wouldn't have hired you if I thought otherwise. San Jose won three NCAA Championships while you worked for them," he said, leading us down the hallway he'd come from.

"They did, but it wasn't because of me." I gave a modest shrug, not used to compliments. "I wasn't coaching the game itself."

Monroe glanced over, a hint of respect in his gaze. "Right, but the improvements were hard to miss. Under your training, the players' explosiveness, speed, and agility saw a serious boost, and the team experienced fewer injuries overall. Your former employers all said the same thing—your priority was always the players' health."

I chuckled, remembering what I used to tell Randy.

"Yeah, I'd tell them my job wasn't to win games, that was theirs. Mine was making sure the players' bodies were ready."

"Which is exactly what we need," he replied with a firm nod.

I followed behind, looking at the wall of player photos hanging on the wall as silence stretched between us. I should have left it that way. Instead, I *had* to open my big mouth.

Gracie was rubbing off on me.

"No offense, Coach, but you seem kind of young for a head coach."

He glanced over his shoulder at me, slowing just enough so we were side by side. "And you seem kind of... female for a strength and conditioning coach."

I winced at the quip. "Touché. I should have known better."

The ghost of a smile appeared again, or maybe it was a grimace.

"Figured you'd understand," he said, pushing open a large metal door, revealing the most beautiful sight I'd ever seen.

"I think I've died and gone to heaven," I murmured, stepping past Josh.

I looked around in awe, unsure of where to focus first. I was so enthralled I didn't even care that I'd made the grumpy head coach laugh—or laugh-ish.

"Heaven to you is a room that smells like sweat and is full of gym equipment?"

The space was massive. There was a literal wall of squat racks, Olympic lifting platforms, bumper plates, turf, weighted sleds, boxes, and kettlebells—it was a playground of equipment.

"It's full of *Rogue* gym equipment," I corrected. "There are like six full squat racks in here." I turned to him and pointed to a machine I had only dreamed about owning. "You have a belt squat machine."

Honestly, they didn't even need to pay me. If they just let me live in this gym, I'd be happy. Hell, I'd pay *them* to use it.

Monroe smirked. "Looks like you don't need me to walk you through any of this. The far wall rolls up for access to tires and other gear outside. And over there," he pointed to a door tucked in the corner, "is your office. I'll go get the guys."

"Wait." My nerves spiked as he mentioned bringing in the players. I'd gone over my plans and routines for hours, but this was my first day—my trial period. First impressions would matter, and if I didn't prove myself, my ass was back on a plane headed to California and my pale pink childhood bedroom.

Monroe paused in the doorway, a foot already in the hallway. He raised a brow as if to say, *"What else could you possibly need?"*

"I'd like to meet and discuss specifics of what you're looking for with the players," I said, keeping my tone professional. "That way, I can tailor my programming to their needs. Sure, we'll focus on power and explosiveness, but I like to incorporate a focus on core strength." I fought the urge to bite my lip, instead standing tall. "Sometimes by using means players aren't used to."

"I knew you were the right choice. Do whatever you

want, Ariella, you don't need my permission for how you run your domain." Then he disappeared down the hall.

I blinked. *Okay, that went better than I'd thought.*

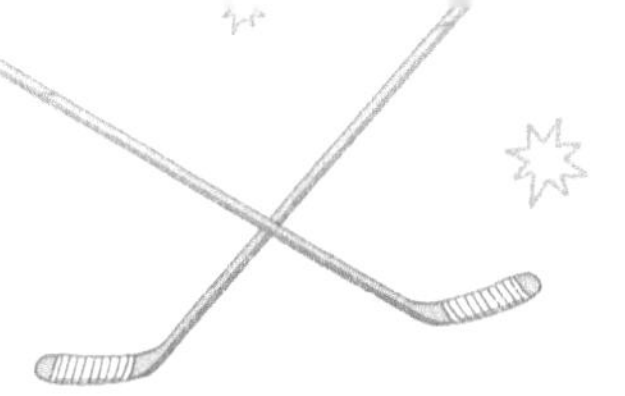

ELEVEN

ARIELLA

HOOCHIE DADDY SHORTS

I SET my stuff down by the giant whiteboard hanging next to my office door, picking up one of the markers to write down what I'd run the team through. I hadn't been sure if I'd be training the players right away or spending the first week doing all the boring onboarding. Thankfully, I'd come up with an introductory workout just in case.

The faint scents of bleach and Pine-Sol tickled my nose, covering me like a blanket of comfort. That bubble of familiarity and peace soon popped when shouts and loud conversation filtered in from the hallway, spiking adrenaline through my veins. I caught a few mentions of "new coach," and, "Monroe will kick our ass if we're late." As the voices grew louder, I ran a hand over my shorts—the slick fabric catching on my callouses as I attempted to wipe off the layer of perspiration.

"You've got this, Ari. You know what you're doing, and you can probably out-deadlift some of these guys," I muttered, bracing as the players finally spilled into the gym.

Several pairs of eyes landed on me, pausing for a minute before scanning the gym.

I clocked the exact moment they realized there wasn't anyone else here because they went silent. It was as if the whole room held its breath, waiting to see who would react first.

Put on your big girl chonies.

"Hello, team, I'm Ariella Contreras." I gave them a calm, collected smile as I scanned their faces. There were looks of shock, disinterest, and skepticism—nothing new.

I was about to say more when a deep, all-too-familiar voice cut through the room, freezing me in place.

"Ari?" An all too familiar green gaze locked on me, Dalton's expression a mixture of confusion and shock that I knew was mirrored on my own. "What are you doing here?"

What was *I* doing there? What the hell was *he* doing there?

This man was supposed to stay in my memory, maybe make the occasional cameo in my dreams. He was definitely not supposed to turn up at my new job, pinning me with that intense gaze that made my stomach flip. I forced myself to break eye contact, but if I thought looking at his stupidly handsome face was difficult, staring at his muscular thighs was way worse. My brain felt like static, and I had to bite my lip to keep from groaning—or barking.

Who did I need to talk to about getting him issued nine-inch inseam shorts instead of the five-inch ones he was currently wearing? Or sweatpants. A burlap sack would be even better.

"I—"

"Hey, you're Cap's new girl. I'm Roberts," a kid barely out of his teens shouted, breaking the tension as he shoved his way to the front and threw an arm around Dalton, extending his other hand to me. "You're even prettier in person," he said, earning him an elbow to the ribs. Dalton's look of confusion was replaced with irritation.

But the comment got my brain back online and functioning. "No, I'm your new strength and conditioning coach," I said firmly, working to rein in all of the emotions coursing through me in that moment.

"Now we know how she got the job," someone else snickered, barely loud enough for me to hear.

I didn't appreciate the insinuation, especially since I didn't know what the hell was going on.

Dalton didn't either. He untangled himself from Roberts, pushing through the other players and making his way toward the bearded guy who'd made the remark. "Watch it, Stephens. I hear you talk to her like that again, and you'll be missing a few more teeth." His tone was harsh and his hands fisted by his side.

A twinge of warmth stirred low in my stomach at seeing Dalton stand up for me, but I had to make it clear that I was here for my skills and nothing else. These were *my* players now, and if I didn't demand their respect from the get-go, I'd never get it.

I placed a hand on Dalton's chest, stopping him. "I can handle this."

He scanned my face in a way that made my heart beat faster before dipping his head. "Yes, Coach," he said with a slight smirk, stepping back and glaring at Stephens.

Was I ovulating this week? Was that what this was?

Because I'd been called Coach many times over the last few years, primarily by men, but none of those other times had made my stomach do a full lurch in excitement.

Stephens scoffed, rolling his eyes as he crossed his arms over his chest. The guy was massive and looked like his nose had been broken a time or two. I wondered if one of those times was from catching a woman's fist to the face.

"Did you have something you wanted to say, Stephens?" I asked, voice sharp and commanding as I closed the distance between us. He recoiled slightly, his eyes darting to the side as he shifted uncomfortably, looking for support from his teammates, but none came.

I crossed my arms, meeting his gaze without blinking. "I'd think carefully before you speak, because whether you like it or not, I'm your coach."

His mouth snapped shut, but the defiant fire in his eyes remained.

I stepped back, grabbing my whistle and glancing toward the trashcan near the gym doors. "Alright, looks like we're doing this the hard way. When you're hanging your head over that trashcan, Stephens, remember you brought this on yourself. We could've eased in, done a nice introduction workout while I got to know you guys. But now..."

Groans and muttered curses rippled through the group, and I hid my smirk before addressing them all. "Listen up. I was hired because I'm damn good at my job. You get one workout to get over whatever issues you have with me. After that, if you've got a problem, take it up with Monroe." I paused, letting the silence settle before giving them my biggest smile. "If you can still talk, that is. Gentlemen, welcome to your new hell."

"Y'ALL ARE ACTING like a bunch of babies," I called out, my voice competing with all the labored breathing. There was a slight possibility I'd gone a little too hard on the guys. But at least one of them didn't seem fazed. I was far too aware of how distracting it was to see Dalton dripping with sweat, hands on his hips as he paced the turf, catching his breath.

He'd come in first. Every. Single. Time.

Jimenez, as I'd come to learn his name was, had been right on his tail for the first few sprints but eventually fell away. Not Dalton, though. He was like a machine.

"Coach," Roberts groaned, struggling to get onto his elbows like sitting up was the hardest thing he'd ever done. "We're on skates all game. We're not cut out for this sprinting and dragging a sled shit."

I had to fight my smile at the whine in his voice. He sounded like my little cousins when we didn't allow them into the living room with the adults.

"Oh, I'm sorry," I replied deadpan. "I didn't realize you don't use your legs in hockey." Just then, the door opened behind me.

Josh walked in then stopped, blinking a few times. "Why are all my players lying on the floor?"

A flicker of worry snaked up my spine. Josh was hard to read. He'd seemed confident in his decision to hire me, but that was before he walked into all his players looking like broken toy soldiers.

I cleared my throat, keeping my tone steady. "Some of them had doubts about my qualifications, so I thought I'd introduce them to my methods firsthand."

Dalton's voice cut in. "Turns out we suck at weighted sled sprints and not being judgmental dicks." He glared at Stephens, who was busy studying his feet. At least the guy had the decency to look embarrassed.

Josh's gaze cut toward Dalton, the two exchanging some silent communication I couldn't quite read, ending in the corner of Josh's mouth pulling up slightly. "Well, assholes, it looks like y'all earned yourselves lines on the ice to finish up. Get your skates on. You have five minutes. I add a line for every minute you're late. Stephens, you have an extra five for being an ass."

Ignoring the groans, Josh turned toward me, holding a fist I tentatively bumped. "Knew I picked the right person. Now you're needed over in HR. I'm guessing they're wanting you to sign this shit," he said, handing me the new hire packet.

"Thanks for having my back."

A heavy hand landed on my shoulder. "Trust yourself, Ariella. You've got the résumé to back it up."

"Not at the NHL level," I said, unsure why I was arguing about this.

He held my gaze. "Yeah, well, I didn't either before getting this gig. But I believed in myself enough to know I could do it." Monroe paused, arching a brow in what felt like a challenge. "And I thought you would too."

His words were the kick in the ass I needed. Monroe

was right, I'd earned this. I could do this. Straightening my shoulders, I gave him a curt nod. "You're right. I'm the right choice for this job." The statement was as much for me as it was for him.

"Of course she is," Dalton cut in, startling me. I hadn't realized he was still standing there. His expression was unreadable, but I appreciated the respectable distance he kept between us.

I'd pushed our situation out of my mind the entire practice, but we'd have to address this at some point.

Josh looked at him with surprise. "Dalt, what the hell are you still doing in here? You're never late to the ice."

He shrugged, holding my gaze with a gleam of mischief. "Just wanted to talk to the new coach. Introduce myself properly since we'll be seeing a lot of each other." He winked before heading out the gym door behind Josh.

The hidden message in those words left me sweating. It was coded, sure, but I knew exactly what he meant by it.

TWELVE

DALTON

I FEEL LIKE A SHOWER HANDY WOULD MAKE FOR EASY CLEAN-UP…

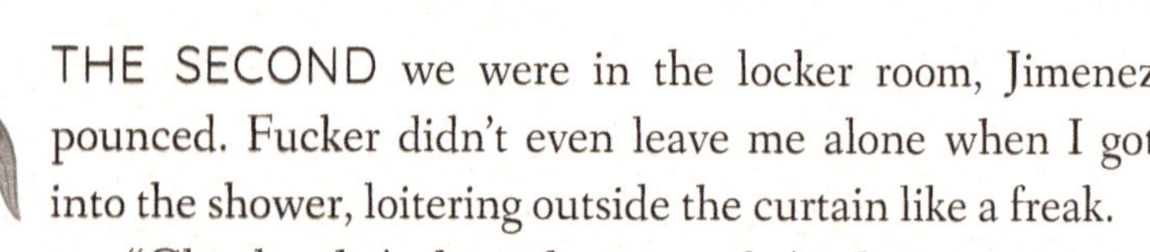

THE SECOND we were in the locker room, Jimenez pounced. Fucker didn't even leave me alone when I got into the shower, loitering outside the curtain like a freak.

"Clearly she's here because she's the new coach, Christian," I said, answering what felt like the hundredth question in the span of fifteen minutes.

"No shit, Dalton. You know I mean did *you* know she was coming today? That she was going to be on staff?" There was a rustling outside the stall like he was contemplating opening the white liner so he could see my facial expressions.

"Don't you open that curtain," I called out, the final word cut off a bit by the stream of water turning on, giving me a few minutes to collect myself.

"Fine. But I want some fucking details here, Cap."

No, I didn't know the beautiful woman who'd given me one of the best nights of my life in years was going to show up Monday as my new fucking coach.

I wracked my brain for a single clue I'd missed, but

she'd been so insistent on not sharing personal information that there'd been nothing about her work, other than her mentioning she'd been worried about her new job in a male-dominated field.

I smiled, dipping my head under the water to wet my hair. She'd killed it today. Hell, she'd practically killed us, but those assholes had deserved it.

"Did you drown, or what? I'm still waiting here."

Persistent asshole, I thought with a smile.

"Couldn't you tell by my reaction I didn't know shit?" I shook my head remembering my shock when I'd walked in and seen her, reaching for the bar of soap. "We didn't talk about that kind of stuff the other night. We just..." The words dropped off as I soaped over my chest, trying to think of how to verbalize what that night felt like.

"You just enjoyed being together," he said, voice suspiciously sincere. Not even an ounce of his normally suggestive humor laced in his tone.

"Yeah," I breathed out, not sure he could even hear me over the noise of the locker room.

"So, what are you going to do now? Are you two even allowed to date?"

I let out a heavy sigh, dropping my head to the cold tiles. "I don't know man. She's a coach, and there's probably some rule against it." I didn't voice the fact that she may not want to do anything—or *be anything*—with me.

That idea stung more than it should have about a woman I'd just met, but damn did I want to be something with her.

Jimenez's voice cut through the internal wallowing.

"Look, I'm sure it'll work out fine. I mean, your dad owns the team. That's got to get you some special privileges."

I tried to ignore the absence of his usual confidence.

"Yeah, I'm sure it will all work out," I said, letting all the unspoken words hang in the air as I returned to the task of washing off the hockey sweat from my body.

"Exactly." I heard him move away, going along with my bullshit response. Neither of us could be sure it would work out.

My mind wandered now that I was alone.

This morning, I'd been convinced that I needed to move on, not turn into some stalker freak and start showing up at the restaurant she'd taken me to every day until I saw her. Which I'd considered doing.

Fuck, and now...

Now, I would see her everyday. And hear that damn laugh. And stare at that smile that lit up a room...and see her in those damn small spandex shorts that hugged her ass, highlighting her muscled legs.

My cock stirred at the mental image seared into my mind.

Then there was that little issue of how fucking attracted I was to her. Without thought, my hand wrapped around my cock, giving it a slow pull. My mind drifted to the sensation of my lips on hers...

Was I really about to fuck my hand in the team locker room while thinking about my new coach sprawled out naked on a weight bench?

Yeah. I was.

This has to be a fucking HR violation.

THIRTEEN

ARIELLA

KICKING MY FUCKING FEET!

I'D BARELY REGISTERED the walk down to HR's office, passing the white walls in a daze. The guy I was never supposed to see again because he was too distracting was now one of my players? Of course this would happen to me.

"Ms. Contreras." The nasally voice snapped me out of my spiraling thoughts. "Please, come in and have a seat."

"Mr. Monroe said you wanted to see me," I said, reaching into my bag for the packet he'd sent me with. "I haven't filled this out yet. Want me to finish it here?"

"There's actually no need for that, Ms. Contreras." Her flat tone and the way she avoided eye contact sent a chill up my spine.

Confused, I stilled, watching the middle-aged woman adjust her wire-rimmed glasses, her eyes darting down to the paperwork.

"I don't understand. Am I supposed to fill it out online or...?"

She cleared her throat. "What, exactly, is your relationship with Mr. Langley?"

Mr. Langley?

I forced a polite smile, trying to keep things professional. "I'm sorry. I'm not sure what you mean. Mr. Langley's my boss, but I haven't actually met—"

She cut me off with an exasperated sigh, as if she'd heard enough. "No, no. Not that Mr. Langley, his son." She lifted her gaze, finally meeting my eyes, her expression sharp and assessing.

I'd been on the receiving end of plenty of judgmental looks—the kind where a person looked at me like I was clueless—but this time, I actually was. I leaned forward in the scratchy office chair, trying to sweeten my tone. "Look, Ms..." I peeked down at her name placard, "Adams, it's my first day. The only people I've met so far are the receptionist, Jasmine, and Josh—"

"Let me stop you there. I'm not interested in games." Her voice dripped with impatience as she slapped a photo onto the desk. "Now, I'll ask you again. What is your relationship with Dalton Langley?"

My breath stalled as I looked down at the photo. A perfect snapshot from that night. Dalton tucking a loose strand of hair behind my ear, his eyes on me like we were the only two people in the room.

It was intimate, sure, but not scandalous.

"Aha. So you do know Mr. Langley," she said, her tone as smug as it was infuriating.

I forced my expression to stay neutral as I pushed the photo back toward Ms. Adams, my brain whirring with this new information. "I wasn't aware that my private life would be subject to scrutiny," I said, keeping my voice even. "I wasn't lying to you, I don't commonly think of Dalton as Mr. Langley."

Because I had no clue that was his last name until two seconds ago...

"Nevertheless, our policy is clear, Ms. Contreras. We do not hire individuals with former romantic ties to active players. Mr. Langley, Dalton's father, has a strict mandate against any risk of entanglement that could jeopardize his team's reputation."

She said it as if my fate had already been decided.

A rush of frustration tightened my chest. This was completely unfair. "Ms. Adams, I was hired based on my skills and experience. Whatever assumptions this photo suggests don't change my ability to do my job."

Her gaze remained unyielding. "It's not personal, Ms. Contreras. I simply enforce the rules. And given your...previous connection, I'm afraid your employment here can't continue." She slid a severance packet across the desk. "Please sign this NDA regarding the nature of your termination. Afterward, you'll receive severance and be escorted from the premises."

I sat there, feeling my dreams slipping through my fingers. I'd worked too damn hard for this job, this opportunity, to make my own way, to have a photo derail my future.

If there was one thing my parents had taught me, it was when shit got hard, you worked harder. I'd experienced firsthand how my parents had fought and scraped to carve out their own place in this country, never giving up even when those more privileged told them their efforts were a lost cause.

I wouldn't either. That lethal combination of desperation and determination kicked in, and I spat out first thing that came to mind.

"Is there a policy against employees dating?"

Ms. Adams looked surprised by the question. "No..." she dragged out the word, shifting her gaze to her computer, typing away. "Hmm. There doesn't seem to be a policy prohibiting current employees from dating if no conflict of interest exists..."

Her response sparked something reckless in me, and I took a steadying breath, forcing myself to sound calm—like it wasn't my last hope.

"Then let's clarify something," I said, meeting her gaze. "Dalton and I aren't ex-anything. We're currently dating."

Her eyes narrowed as she processed my words. "Excuse me?"

I leaned in, slipping the severance packet back across the desk. "You said the policy allows for employees currently dating, and we are. So there's no violation here."

This move wasn't winning me any brownie points in her book. She looked conflicted, like she wanted to push back but knew it wasn't her place to do so. I only hoped this lie didn't blow up in my face before I could come up with a more permanent solution.

"Fine, Ms. Contreras. I'll inform Mr. Langley of this... development. But know this, any improper conduct and you'll be out the door without question."

"Understood."

Leaving her office, my heart raced, equal parts relief and anxiety swirling inside me, because *what the fuck did I just do?*

"Note to self. Always ask a man's last name and occupation," I muttered, storming down the hall, pushing open a metal door with bold black letters.

When I barged into the locker room, a chorus of shouts followed, but I ignored them all. I was a woman on a mission, and no one was stopping me from reaching my destination.

"Where's Dalton?" I barked at Roberts. The look of shock on his baby face would have been hilarious if I wasn't so pissed. The walk over here had only added fuel to my fire.

I was ready to fight a full-grown man.

"Now, Roberts."

"Uh—he's over there." He pointed. "Cap uses the one on the left."

He'd barely gotten the second part out, and I was already halfway across the room, yanking open the curtain. Steam billowed out of the tiled stall, hot water sprinkling my face.

"What the hell, Jime—Ari?" Dalton scrubbed a hand down his face, looking at me as if I'd grown a second head.

"You are going to fix this, do you understand?" I seethed, jabbing a finger into his chest. "I worked too damn hard to get this job and finally move out of my parents' home to have it all fall apart on the first day. Do you know what it's like to be twenty-five and have to sleep in a twin-sized bed at your parents' house? Of course you don't because you're apparently the son of the man who owns this whole damn thing." My voice rose another octave higher as I waved my arms around. "And yeah, currently, my bed is about the same size, but at least when I want to leave the house, I don't face an interrogation. I mean, I love my family, but damn, now that I know freedom...I'm not going back, Dalton. Do you hear me?"

I was out of breath by the end of my rant-turned-information dump.

It happened sometimes when I was overly worked up.

I was honestly surprised I hadn't switched to Spanish midway—or maybe I had.

He blinked a few times, his lips twitching in a way that told me he was trying not to laugh. Which only pissed me off more. "Darlin'...I'm going to be honest. I have no clue what you're talking about."

I rolled my eyes. "Don't you, *darlin'* me."

Of course, he didn't. HR *would* only speak to the woman involved. Because why on earth would they talk to the man in this situation? Pinching the bridge of my nose, I unleashed a string of Spanish curses under my breath.

"Ariella, babe?" came Jimenez's voice from beside me. "There a reason you're in the men's locker room? I don't know how HR would—"

"Oh, are you worried I'll get fired, Jimenez?" I snapped, turning to unleash my fury on him. "Because that's exactly what they tried to do."

Professionalism had left the building. Hell, it wasn't even in Texas anymore.

Silence fell over the room.

"What? What do you mean they tried to fire you?" Dalt growled, reaching for the knobs on the wall. And like blinders being lifted, I was suddenly aware of the droplets rolling down his chiseled chest, making their way to—.

"Oh my god, you're naked." I slammed my eyes closed, covering them with my hand for good measure. I needed to go to confession because, honestly, I wanted to peek through my fingers and see a bit more.

Jimenez burst out into a fit of laughter at my expense. "*Mami*, what did you think you would see when you ripped open the shower curtain? Cap in a pair of swim shorts?"

My stomach swooped at the thought of what I'd almost seen, and a tinge of disappointment that I hadn't looked lower.

Dalton cleared his throat. "You can look now." A white towel hung low on his hips, and I had to fold my arms over my chest to hide the effect it had on my nipples. "Jimenez, go tell the guys to get some damn clothes on."

"Sure, Cap. I'll let them all know you'll beat their ass if they flash your girl," he teased, yelping when I grabbed an extra towel off the hook and snapped it at him. "Fuck, you got my nipple." For good measure, I did it again. "Ow, shit. How are you so good at that?" he asked, covering both with his hands like a makeshift chest plate.

"I've got an annoying brother and *primos* who are a lot like you. Perfected this shit years ago."

He backed away, shaking his head. "She's all yours, Cap. But I'd be careful, bet she's deadly with a *chancla*, too," he said, leaving a half-naked—and wet—Dalton and me alone.

"Okay, Ari," Dalton said, gingerly gripping my chin

between his thumb and forefinger, directing my attention back to him. "Start from the beginning so I can fix this."

But all that move did was make my head fuzzy and my heart beat faster.

I took a steadying breath, trying to focus on his words instead of the warmth of his hand or the fact that we were standing inches apart, him still dripping and wrapped in a towel.

Professionalism, Ari. Stay focused.

"I don't need you to fix anything, Dalton." I released a frustrated breath. "I already did. But to get around your father's ridiculous policy, I had to lie."

His brows furrowed, concern flickering in his gaze as he slowly dropped his hand. "I'm not following..."

"The Desperados don't employ any 'ex-romantic interests.' Too much risk for bad press, according to your father," I said, irritation lacing my tone. "Apparently, that includes fake dates to avoid your real ex. HR called me in, slid a picture of us together across the desk, and handed me a severance packet. The real kicker was they wanted me to sign an NDA that wouldn't allow me to discuss the reasons for my release."

A spark of anger crossed Dalton's face, his jaw clenching. "They tried to fire you over a single photo? They couldn't even talk to me?"

"Exactly." I felt the frustration building all over again. "And when I tried to stand my ground, she dismissed me."

His gaze softened, a flash of something protective in his eyes. "So, what'd you do? You said they *tried* to fire you. Are they changing the policy?"

I took another breath, steadying myself. "I improvised.

I asked if there were any rules against employees dating, and when she said there weren't..." the rest of the words seemed to get caught in my throat, but I took a breath and steeled myself. "I told her you and I were currently dating. That I'm not an 'ex' anything." My heart was racing, and I fought back the urge to fidget, waiting for him to freak out.

Dalton's eyes widened in surprise, but then his lips quirked into a half-smile. "You told HR we're together?"

"I didn't exactly have a lot of options," I said defensively, crossing my arms. "It was either that or hop on the next plane back to California and try to explain to my family why this opportunity fell apart on day one. So yes, I told HR we're dating. Now, you're going to play along until I can figure out a better solution. Please." I winced at how harshly I bit out the please, but I felt like a live wire.

"Hey, hey." He pulled me into his arms, and I tried to ignore how it felt to be pressed against his skin. "You're not going to have to move back, okay? And you're not losing your job."

I pulled back far enough to look up at him. "Promise?" For the first time since this disaster happened, I felt some of my worry leech into my voice, needing to release some of the building pressure.

"Pinky," he said, with confidence, wrapping his finger around mine. "I'm sorry, Ari. This mess is on me, and I'll do whatever it takes to make it right. I'm with you on this —whatever you need."

I felt a wave of relief mixed with something I didn't want to investigate. "Thanks, Dalton," I said, my voice quieter than intended. "I know this wasn't part of the plan for either of us, but...I appreciate it."

He gave a small, reassuring smile, releasing me as I stepped back out of his embrace. "Anything to help, Coach. I'll be the best fake boyfriend you've ever had."

I forced myself to look away, trying to ignore the towel still slung dangerously low on his hips.

God, I needed to get out of there.

"Okay, I'm leaving now," I said, clearing my throat and stepping back. "The last thing I need is HR finding another reason to fire me before I've even fixed this one."

Dalton laughed softly. "Wouldn't want that."

With one last nod, I spun on my heel and left the locker room, my heart pounding as I slipped out the door.

What the hell did I get myself into?

FOURTEEN

DALTON

YOU KNOW YOU LIKE A SLUTTY LITTLE SHORT CHAPTER...

I WALKED out to my car, trying and failing to hold back a grin. I knew I *should* be upset about the injustice of Ari's situation.

And I was, on principle. But it would be a bold-faced lie if I didn't admit that Ari needing me to be her fake boyfriend was the best news I'd gotten in a while.

If she'd burst into my post-workout shower two seconds later, she'd have caught me trying to relieve the hard-on I'd had since stepping into the gym. Seeing her standing there with those damn spandex shorts and a shirt with my team name across her chest, yelling out instructions—I was done for.

"Come on, Dalton, that all you've got?"

"Give me more."

"Harder. Drive. Drive. Drive..."

How the *fuck* was I supposed to work under those conditions? Were there *any* cues that wouldn't have me fighting for my life not to pop a boner during a workout? I'd have to wear five pairs of spandex shorts from now on.

Or think about the face my father made when I disappointed him.

The smile fell from my face, and I shook my head, attempting to brush off the negative thoughts as I plopped into the driver's seat. This situation was complicated.

But damn, was it worth it to get to see her again.

Worth being her boyfriend...even if it was fake.

FIFTEEN

ARIELLA

"DID HE JUST SEND YOU TWO GRAND? HE'S
LIKE A SUGAR DADDY! FORGET WORKING,
LET HIM PAY FOR SHIT."

"*MAMÁ, esta bien.* Ugh, I have to go, Ariella just got home," Gracie said, standing in the kitchen with her phone pulled away from her ear and a finger gun to her temple. Even from the door, I could hear my aunt rattling on, and it wasn't on speaker. Gracie returned the phone to her ear, hurrying out a final, "*adiós, Mamá. Te quiero.*"

"What did my aunt want?" I asked, tossing my gym bag by the couch and hopping up on one of the two counter stools in our little kitchen.

"*Ay.* She's pissed at me because I'm not adding water to my dish soap." Gracie huffed. "*Me dijo que soy* wasteful. It's not even like she's the one buying the soap."

Her irritation made me laugh. There were some things a Mexican mother would argue about 'til her grave. Diluting your soap, shampoo, and conditioner with water was one of those things.

"Wait 'til she finds out that you put your tortillas in the microwave sometimes."

Graciella spun so fast that her jaw-length hair managed to slap her in the face. "That was *one* time, and it was because I was drunk and didn't want to burn down the fucking building." I shrugged a shoulder, popping a grape into my mouth with a sly smile while she continued her rant. "Anyway, enough about me, how was your first day? Are they hot? Can I come watch them all sweaty? Do they wear slutty shorts?" Her eyes widened. "Do any of them have thigh tattoos?"

Damn it. I knew her interrogation was coming, but somehow I still wasn't prepared for it. She'd managed to ask all those questions in a single breath. If she wasn't in marketing, she could pursue a career as an auctioneer.

"You know how I went out with that guy the other night?" I peeked through my lashes at my cousin, who was practically crawling across the top of the counter to get closer to the *chisme.*

"The mystery man you refused to get any more details on."

"Yup," I said, popping the *p*. "Turns out, he's the captain of the Dallas Desperad–"

A loud squeal that probably broke the sound barrier cut me off. "Shut the *fuck* up, Ari. Hottie is from the team you're coaching?"

"Oh, it gets worse. They tried to fire me because there's apparently a tabloid photo of us, and they didn't want the owner's *son* working with an ex."

She slapped a hand over her mouth, eyes widening to a comical size. "Wait, what do you mean *tried* to fire you?"

My cheeks heated, embarrassment crawling up my

neck. "I may or may not have told HR that we're currently dating, since there was no policy against that. Which," I winced, "ended with me storming into the men's locker room and telling Dalton he better go along with it until I find a better solution."

Gracie let out another shriek, dancing around in a circle chanting *holy shit.* "This is totally like a romance movie."

Regret about telling her was already setting in. She always was the romantic—even if, weirdly enough, she was adamantly against relationships. We'd tried getting into the details of that once, but it hadn't gone well.

"What are you talking about? It's nothing like a romance movie. He's just helping me keep my job. Or did you miss the part about me nearly getting fired because of some asinine rule made by *his father?*" I added some extra emphasis on that part to really drive it home for her, but it didn't dim the hearts in her eyes. "A man who's also my boss, and who I'll have to pretend not to be pissed at when we finally meet...shit. I hadn't thought about how that's gonna go."

Gracie finally had an appropriate reaction and grimaced. "Maybe he's always wanted a Mexican daughter-in-law."

Her face wasn't all that convincing.

I shrugged, fiddling with the pop holder on my phone, trying to avoid thinking too hard about what I'd gotten myself into. Spiraling wouldn't help, but the uncertainty was already knotting in my stomach.

Cha-ching.

"What was that?" Gracie asked.

I flipped my phone over, ignoring her question as the noise sounded a second time. I knew exactly what that noise was for, but that didn't prepare me for the numbers flashing on my screen.

CASHPAY:

$1000 from Dalton55

Ari, no one is going to believe this if I don't at least have your number...

CASHPAY:

$1000 from Dalton55

If you don't text me back I'm going to start sending higher dollar amounts. Which, weirdly enough, would only entice others not to respond...but I have a feeling you'd be pissed. (214)601-3330

"*Dios mío*," Gracie said from beside me.

My cousin was loud ninety-nine percent of the time, but the other one percent she went into CIA mode and would pop up where you least expected. Like over my shoulder, trying to sneak a peek. I pulled my phone away, but it was too late.

"Did he just send you two grand? He's like a sugar daddy! Forget working, let him pay for shit."

"Graciella." I shot her a look, but she just smirked and started listing off all the things I should let Dalton buy me. Most of them being food.

"Wait." She stopped mid-kitchen pace. "Why is he messaging you over a payment app?"

She had CIA-level observational skills, too, apparently.

"Because I didn't give him my phone number," I mumbled, picking at the callouses on my palm to avoid eye contact. There was a slight pause before Gracie busted up in laughter.

She dropped onto the couch, her legs kicking up as she gasped for air. *"¡A la verga!* Ariella." Sitting up, she pointed a perfectly manicured finger at me. "That's the definition of *if he wanted to, he would.* How many times has he sent you messages on there?"

I could feel the beads of sweat above my upper lip; they appeared when I was nervous or embarrassed. "I don't know, like six or seven...or more."

"Have you answered him?"

"No. I told you it was supposed to be a one-night thing, Gracie. I don't have time for boys."

A second later, a blur of pale pink smacked me in the side of the head. "Did you just throw a pillow at me?" I yelled, tossing it back.

She signed and pinched the bridge of her nose. *"Porque eres una idiota,* Ariella. Text that man back before you do lose your job. How long do you think he will be nice to you if you ignore him?"

I groaned, staring down at my phone. Dammit, she was right.

Before I could chicken out, I opened my texts and typed a quick message.

ME:

Let's meet up and go over our story and, you know, set some ground rules for this whole…situation.

He responded almost immediately.

DALTON:

Please tell me this is you Ari.

ME:

And if it wasn't?

DALTON:

Then I'd keep sending you a thousand dollars until you responded.

ME:

You're insane 😊 and I am sending back your money

DALTON:

Don't bother sending it back. I'll reject it

DALTON:

How about I pick you up for work tomorrow?

"You're smiling at your screen," Gracie said, sounding far too smug, so I made a point to frown. It was going to be my next facial expression anyway because I did *not* like his answers.

ME:

First of all, absolutely not. I am not keeping TWO THOUSAND DOLLARS. And isn't picking me up a bit much? I mean I don't need a chauffeur and I can handle getting there on my own.

A few seconds later, his reply popped up.

DALTON:

I'm not doubting your capabilities. But the team's already seen me with a girlfriend before and trust me they know what to expect. If we're going to sell this we can't give them a reason to think something's off.

ME:

Fine. But we are quickly letting them know that I can get myself to work and it doesn't mean anything suspicious.

DALTON:

Noted. Just an honest boyfriend letting his independent girlfriend do what she pleases. Nothing to see here.

A smile crept onto my face despite myself, and I quickly typed back a simple, *"See you tomorrow,"* before locking my phone.

Gracie was practically hanging over my shoulder, her eyes glinting with excitement. "*Ay*, that man is totally into you, *y no te hagas*—you like it," she teased, giving me a playful nudge.

I clucked my tongue, making a noise of disapproval. "Please. This is just for work. He's only *acting* interested, so we can make this look real."

"*Mmhmm*, sure. And what about the other night, Ari? Those feelings fake too? *Tú sabes que te gusta*," she called out over her shoulder, headed for the bathroom.

Her words lingered.

"It's just a crush—infatuation really. It'll go away after

I spend time with him," I said even though she'd shut the door, pushing away from the counter. "Then he'll feel like every other guy I've met—a distraction from my goals, something that'll just get in the way."

Why did that feel like a lie?

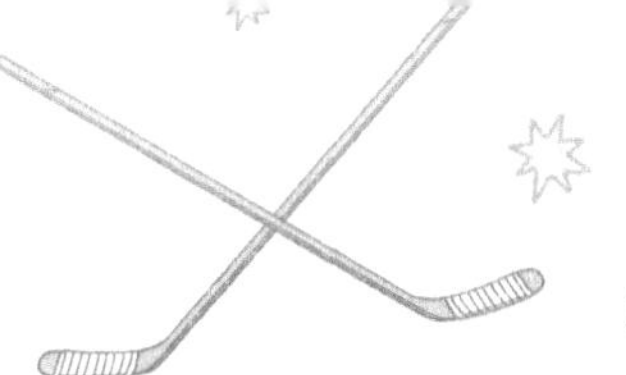

SIXTEEN

DALTON

IS SENDING MONEY TO THE GIRL WHO GOT AWAY BUT TURNED OUT TO WORK FOR YOUR DAD'S HOCKEY TEAM A TAX WRITE-OFF?

A WEIRD FEELING looped through me, growing the closer I got to Ari's place. A mix of nerves and excitement. Maybe a dash of fear for the fiery strength coach.

Ari's bite was already growing to be one of my favorite parts about her. And boy, did she try to bite my head off when I told her I was picking her up this morning.

Something about her telling me off turned me on. My competitive nature roared to life whenever she did.

I loved a challenge, and she was a challenge.

The passenger door swung open, and a thoroughly annoyed Ari dropped into the leather seat, tucking her gym back between her bare, well-muscled legs.

Faking attraction to her was not going to be a problem.

"Good morning." The look she shot me had me smiling from ear to ear. "Was that supposed to be intimidating? Because it's quite the opposite. I think you're adorable when you're pissed."

I couldn't seem to resist poking the bear.

She huffed, reaching for the seat belt. "Yeah, well, we'll see how you feel when I make you do lunges all workout."

"Here, I didn't know if you liked iced or hot coffee, so I got both." I held out my peace offerings, trying to hold back my laugh at her shocked expression. "Sorry if you don't drink either of those. I thought about ordering one of everything from the menu, but you don't seem like the type of woman who'd appreciate that type of excess. Plus, I don't have enough cupholders."

I paused my nervous ramble, trying to give her time to choose, but I couldn't take the silence. "I also got you every type of milk or creamer they had. Did you know there were that many sweetener options? I thought sugar was the only one, but I was wrong."

Her fingers reached out almost cautiously, like she was trying to figure me out. "That was really thoughtful," she said, looking at me strangely.

Maybe she didn't like coffee but didn't want to tell me? I should have called her. I'd just worried she wouldn't answer.

"Thank you. Iced coffee, always. Hot coffee in the summer is wild."

Her praise had me puffing my chest.

God, was I pathetic.

"Eh, it was nothing." I had to look away when she wrapped her lips around the straw. It felt too intimate to lock eyes when she did that with her mouth.

"How do you even fit in this tiny car?" she asked, eyeing the interior with a hint of disbelief. "I'd have guessed you'd drive a truck or something." Her gaze drifted over me, lingering just a moment too long. "Especially in those jeans."

Her words about the car hit a sore spot, though there was no way for her to know that. I swallowed down the hint of bitterness and kept my tone light. "What are you talking about? I'm wearing sweats." I managed a smile, pulling out of the guest parking spot in the apartment building's garage.

"I don't mean right now. When we met, you were wearing Wranglers that were—"

She went silent, lips pressed closed.

"They were what, Ari?" Something told me she was going to give a compliment before she cut herself off, and I desperately wanted to know what she'd thought when we first met. Because I knew what I'd thought about her. Yeah, she was gorgeous, but there was something about *her* that had grabbed my attention. She had an energy that pulled me in.

Her confidence, her laughter. Sunshine.

She was sunshine.

But there was no way I'd tell her that. It was a surefire way to freak her out. Freaked me out a little bit.

I cleared my throat, hoping to shift my focus to anything else. "Spill it or I'll carry you into the rink bridal style. Really make a grand entrance."

My eyes were on the road, but I could feel her irritated stare, and all it did was make me smile. Riling her up was quickly becoming a favorite pastime. I swore I saw her stick her tongue out at me.

"Fine," she huffed. "Your Wranglers looked like they

were practically painted onto your ass and thighs. Happy?"

She had no idea.

My cheeks hurt with how hard I was grinning.

"Ariella, were you objectifying me?" I asked in mock offense. "It's a good thing you're my girlfriend, or I'd have to report you to HR." The word *girlfriend* felt at home on my tongue. I liked how it sounded a little too much.

"*Pendejo*," she said, whacking my shoulder.

I snuck a quick glance, catching the flash of a smile she tried to hide. Her hair was pulled back into a high ponytail that swung mid-back, and the thought of wrapping my hand around it sent my pulse racing. This arrangement was supposed to be fake, but the way my heart pounded every time I looked at her felt anything but.

"Ready to talk about our new relationship?" I asked, shifting my attention back to the road, trying to sound casual.

"*Fake* relationship," she corrected. "This is only temporary, just until I can figure out another loophole or... maybe I'll get HR to like me enough to break the rules." Her voice trailed off as she stared out the window, watching as we passed the stark city buildings.

"Not likely. She's a stickler," I said truthfully, pulling Ari's hand into my lap and linking our fingers. I did it without thinking.

By nature, I had this drive to take care of people. It had been that way since I was a kid, but it really kicked in when I hit high school, and understood how many things fell on my mom's shoulders with my dad not around. There was this urge to comfort and support that lived inside me and, apparently, that instinct extended to Ari.

"Oh, great." She sat there looking dejected, but she hadn't pulled away like I thought she might.

I gave her hand a gentle squeeze. "Hey, you're not alone in this. We'll both work on finding a solution. I might be able to get my dad to change the policy..."

"Really?" She perked up, surprise and hope evident in her tone. "That would be perfect. I mean, it's a stupid rule anyway, and how does it make sense to have a policy about ex-relationships but not one about fraternization?"

Shit. I might have put my foot in my mouth. Convincing my dad to do anything that wasn't his idea was...difficult.

I forced a half-smile, my chest tightening. "It's possible," I said carefully. "But he's pretty set in his ways. We'll need to prove you're too valuable an asset to let go, even if we weren't together."

She nodded thoughtfully. There was this fire in her, this absolute drive to prove herself, and I admired it.

"That shouldn't be hard. I'm a damn good strength coach."

"Exactly. If he sees how much you bring to the team, he'll have a harder time enforcing that stupid dating policy. Or ex-dating policy, whatever."

I parked in my assigned spot, next to Monroe's truck and Christian's SUV, and felt the familiar pang of regret hit me in my chest. Ariella was right. I didn't like folding my body into this car.

Sure, it was nice—expensive—but it wasn't what I'd have chosen for myself.

It had been a signing gift from my dad, who insisted my other ride wasn't a good look.

I don't want you driving around in that thing, Dalton. Gives people the idea that I don't pay my players well.

A prime example of how Vincent Langley was a difficult man to get to change his mind.

Ari's voice pulled me from my thoughts. "Okay, next order of business to handle before we walk into our place of work as a sham couple," she turned in her seat, facing me fully now that we were parked. "Let's talk ground rules."

SEVENTEEN

ARIELLA

FERALLY CHEWS ON BOOK

HE JUST HAD to pick me up bearing gifts in the form of iced coffee and gray sweatpants, making it nearly impossible for me to concentrate on what I needed to talk to him about.

Gracie and I had stayed up all night going over my... situation. True to her nature, she'd broken out one of her fifty thousand notebooks and a pile of colorful pens so we could make a pro-con list and a code of conduct. She'd only agreed to help with the second part *after* I gave another play-by-play of every interaction between Dalton and me—again.

"*What does he smell like?*" she asked excitedly. Her legs crossed, chin in her hands.

"*Like...*" I paused, trying to figure out how to put his scent into words. "*Well, I don't fucking know how to describe it. What do I look like, an aromachologist? He just doesn't smell like sweat, and I kinda wanna rub my nose on his chest.*"

We'd reviewed the list this morning before Dalton picked me up.

Some of Gracie's pros felt more like cons to me.

*Will pay for shit
*You can be his date to events
* He has a car, so you don't have to RideOrder

Now that I was enveloped in soft leather and air conditioning instead of humidity, I had to admit that the last point was, in fact, a pro. Even if I felt the coupe didn't fit Dalton at all—either physically or personality-wise.

Or maybe it does. We barely know each other.

"Earth to Ari, you still with me?" Dalton asked, breaking the spell I seemed to be under.

I blinked up at his handsome face. The dim lighting of the parking garage cast a glow that made his jawline appear even sharper. His hair was perfectly imperfect, and I had to fight against the urge to reach over and touch it to see if it was as soft as it looked.

"Yeah, sorry." I pulled the colorful paper out from my bag, reading off the first bullet point. "First rule: when we break up, I'm breaking up with you," I said. Somehow, I needed to keep my dignity in this situation. Fake or not, hearing Dalton say, *"It's not you, it's me,"* might kill me.

His eyes lit up, mossy green and intense in the dim light of the parking garage. He looked at me like I was his favorite snack, and warmth crept up my chest and neck.

"Of course. No one would believe I'd let you go," he

answered, tone teasing, but the something in his words felt more like a confession. My stomach flipped, and a shiver of heat rushed between my legs. Maybe I'd survive this whole fake-dating thing if he'd put a bag over his head so his face wasn't so damned distracting.

"Okay, next rule," I rushed out, using the flimsy paper as a barrier, but he beat me to it.

"You're wearing my jersey when you come to the games."

"Absolutely not," I scoffed.

"Why not?" He sounded genuinely distraught.

I rolled my eyes, ignoring his pout. "Because, hot shot, I am on the coaching staff, not your personal cheerleader."

Instead of looking put out, he smiled. "Fine, we'll find another way."

"What's that supposed to mean?" I asked, suspicion growing. He took the shutdown way too easily.

"Don't worry about it." He winked, which did nothing to ease my concern. "Okay, my turn for a rule."

"You just made a rule."

"Yeah, and you shut it down. So I get a do-over." He turned in his seat to face me. "You let me buy you things *without* complaining."

I crossed my arms over my chest. "No way. That rule sucks more than your first rule."

He sighed. "I don't understand. Why not take my money? It's not like you'll owe me." His words raked over my skin like hot coals, despite seeming to be asking in earnest.

"Because, Dalton, some women are indebted to a man." I turned my head, the eye contact too much for this topic. "Some women give up everything in their lives because of a promise they'll be taken care of, only to have that security held over their heads later." My voice grew more clipped, each word tighter than the last. "I am not a charity case, Dalton. I can pay for my own things," I bit out, thinking of some of the women I knew stuck in awful marriages. Even if they were willing to break through the cultural stigmas of leaving their husbands...financially, they couldn't.

And I'd vowed a long time ago that would never be my reality.

I'd never be a part of a loveless marriage where I was just a commodity.

"Hey, hey. Look at me," he said, guiding my face toward him with a finger under my chin. The touch was gentle and tender, and the look on his face matched.

I was suddenly hyper-aware of how close we were. How alone we were.

"I never once thought you were a charity case, and I'd never hold money over your head. If you want to pay, pay. Hell, you can buy *me* dinner," he joked, pulling a laugh from me that loosened the knot in my chest. "But until the thing ends, you're *mine*, Ariella, and I'm going to make sure you're treated like a princess."

Something thumped low in my stomach at the territorial growl he let loose with that one terrifying word—*mine*. My brain screamed a warning to guard myself, to keep my walls up, but all I could feel was the pull between us.

How the hell was I supposed to respond to that?

My libido was like a devil on my shoulder, suggesting I climb over the center console and show him how badly I wanted to be *his*. But that felt like a *really* bad idea, so I went with something safe. Something that was supposed to throw up another layer of self-preservation. Because at this rate, he'd have me stripped bare before the week was over.

Both emotionally and physically.

"I'm not a princess." The argument was pathetic even to my ears, but he didn't bother pointing out my deflection.

He smirked. "Muscle mommy, then."

I burst out laughing, the final ties of the knot loosening. "Fine, I'll let you buy me shit if you promise *never* to call me either of those again."

"Deal." His hand slipped away from my face, leaving a trace of warmth I was already missing. As he shifted back, I caught him muttering under his breath, "I have a different nickname for you anyway."

But he kept talking before I got a chance to question him on it.

Dalton's voice turned serious. "Okay, now the most important rule. I need permission to touch you in public the way I would if you were *really* my girlfriend."

His intense gaze burned into me, making me want to look away. It was the same look of determination I'd seen on him in the gym—this was important to him. All the moisture in my mouth dried up and went south.

Great. Now, I was turned on *and* nervous.

"What do you mean?" I asked, my voice sounding breathier than intended.

The car seemed to shrink as he leaned in, resting his elbow on the center console. Our faces were only inches apart, and the heady scent of his cologne messed with my ability to think clearly. I wanted to shove him back in this seat because there was no way I could make good decisions with him so close.

"Ari, I was with Emma for years."

The mention of his ex left a sour taste on my tongue, which made no sense. Of course a star hockey player had a past with someone who wasn't me. And, realistically, this was just an arrangement. I didn't have any real claim to him.

But my head—or maybe my sex drive—didn't get the memo.

He continued, oblivious to my internal turmoil. "And I'm the captain of my team. I told you, pretty much all those guys were around when we were dating."

"And we're bringing that up because..." I asked, my voice sharper than intended.

The distance between us shrank even more. "Because," his eyes dipped to my mouth, "they are going to know this is fake right away if I don't have permission to *touch* you in public."

¡Híjole!

I cleared my throat, attempting to clear the lusty fog. "Okay, I'll agree to light PDA in public, but not during training. I don't want it looking like I got this job because we're together."

He nodded his head so hard I thought he'd give himself a concussion. "Light touching when we're not working, got it. What else?"

This giant of a man was adorably sweet, looking at me with eager eyes. *I was so over my head with this one.* An unexpected insecurity reared its ugly head. I pulled my bottom lip between my teeth, readying myself to rip off the Band-Aid.

"No seeing anyone else while we're together."

I might've overstepped with that request, but just *hearing* about his ex made the little green monster come alive. There was no way I could handle him being with someone else in private while we were pretending to be together in public. It didn't even make sense why this was important to me...but every time I pictured him with someone else, I wanted to hit his car door with a hockey stick.

His hand slipped down to my thigh, and I swallowed hard as he squeezed it gently. "I would never. I told you, you're *mine* until the season is over."

"Even if we aren't having sex?" I blurted out, horrified that I'd voiced *that* insecurity too.

His dimples made an appearance, voice thick with amusement. "I've got a hand, Ari."

My body forgot how to function. Thankfully, Dalton saved me the trouble of remembering how to speak and continued, oblivious that he'd broken my brain.

Or maybe he did it because he knew he'd broken it.

"So light touching, monogamy, anything else you wanna add?"

I cleared my throat, still trying to recover from his earlier comment. "When we are in the gym, I'm in charge," I said, holding out my hand.

He slipped his much larger hand around mine, swallowing it.

"Yes, Coach."

DALTON

INSTANT PUDDLE

"ARE YOU *WHISTLING*?" Jimenez asked, pulling a collared shirt I swore had glitter on it over his head.

Shit, was I?

I'd been walking on clouds since Ari and I had gotten out of my car. She'd run off to turn in her new hire packet with HR before she had to coach us through a workout.

"I suggest you don't eat anything," she'd called over her shoulder, looking straight up gleeful as she tossed out the warning. I grimaced at the memory. We were all about to get our asses handed to us.

"What, I can't whistle before practice?" I asked with a shrug, pulling on a shirt that was admittedly a size too small and cropped. And I might have worn some of my shortest shorts after noticing how Ari had stared at my quads last practice.

"Great, and now you're dressing like a hoe for training?" Jimenez shook his head. "Hoe behavior is reserved for me. You can't walk out there trying to outshine me," he complained, unwrapping a protein bar. He may go out

and party on a weekday during the off-season, but Jimenez didn't mess around when it came to his fitness.

I ignored his previous comment.

He wasn't wrong, I was exhibiting signs of his behavior. But I wasn't about to admit it aloud.

"Eh, I wouldn't eat that," I said, swatting the bar away from his mouth.

He growled, bending over to pick it up while counting to five under his breath. "And why the hell not?"

"First of all, the five-second rule does *not* count in a locker room. That is foul, Jimenez. And second, Coach suggested we shouldn't eat anything before this practice," I told him, pulling off my sweatpants and stuffing them into my locker.

"When the hell did he say that? We aren't even on the ice 'til later." His voice trailed off, eyes growing wide as it dawned on him who I was referring to. "Holy shit. He didn't tell us, but *she* told *you*." He hit my shoulder playfully before dropping his volume. "Shut the fuck up, Cap. Is she really your girl?"

I hated my personal life being the topic of conversation, but he was practically a brother. We'd come up together in juniors, got recruited to the same college, and when my dad had showed up to sign me, that was one of my negotiation requirements—Jimenez would get signed too.

Monroe coming on as coach was the other.

A pang of guilt shot through me for not telling either of them about my arrangement with Ari. I'd need to ask her about that, but until then, I'd have to get creative with the truth. "Yeah, we're a...thing. It's new and complicated because of her working here and all."

There. Not a lie, not really, anyway.

He beamed at me, slapping a hand on my shoulder and making me feel guiltier. "My fucking man. Now I understand the hoe aesthetic, but bold move going for the hoochie shorts because a boner will not be contained by those." He pointed to the honestly pathetic amount of fabric, then switched gears. "I'm so proud of you for getting back out there. I wasn't going to say anything, but the way you two were looking at each other in that picture —damn. It was hot. Thought you were going to pull her into the bathroom, and you know." He thrust his hips forward, folding his hands behind his head and biting his lip.

I laughed, shaking my head at his antics. Whatever woman he ended up with would have her hands full.

"Hey, assholes," Monroe popped his head into the locker room, "let's go. You're supposed to be in the gym in about two minutes. You already embarrassed yourselves yesterday. We're not doing that again. Got it?"

The locker room broke out in a chorus of "*Yes, Coach,*" as everyone started making their way out the door he held open. But he stopped me as I tried to exit.

"I need to speak with you for a minute. The rest of you get your asses over there."

"Sure thing," I replied, trying to keep my tone neutral. He always sounded pissed off, but something in his tone had rock settling in my stomach.

Monroe folded his arms across his chest. "What's this

I hear about you and Coach Contreras dating?" he asked when everyone had left the locker room.

My fists clenched at my sides. The last thing she needed was for Monroe to be on her case, too. "Yes, *Coach.* That a problem?" I challenged.

The distance between us disappeared, and he drove a finger into my chest. "Quit acting like a dick, Dalton. We both know your mom didn't raise you to like that. Don't you cost that girl her job." *If only you knew.* "She's worked fucking hard to get here. I saw her résumé, and it's impressive."

I swatted his hand away. "Fuck you, Josh, if you think I'd risk her career. You should know me better than that. You've been around me my whole life. How could you think I'd use her?"

Instead of anger, Monroe did something I'd never seen him do in a locker room—he smiled. "Yeah. I do know you're better than that. I'm just making sure you're still the same man you were before your dad walked back into your life three years ago."

He turned and walked away before I could question what the hell he'd meant.

"LANGLEY, want to explain why you're late?" Ariella asked, hands on her shapely hips, looking like my personal wet dream in her black shorts and Desperado's T-shirt. But it was the scolding tone that had my dick stirring.

Roberts piped up before I could answer. The kid was the youngest on the team, and it was evident in his behavior, but he was good people. "Coach?" She turned toward where he was stretching on the black mats with the rest of the team, who were all locked into their own conversations as they warmed up. "Um, no one calls him Langley. It's either Dalt or Cap."

"She can call me whatever she wants," I cut in, walking up to her, smiling at the way she arched a single brow my way. Of course, she was unwavering even as I practically stalked her down. I stopped when we were only inches apart. The only tell that our proximity was getting to her was the jumping pulse in her neck.

"Sorry, Coach. Monroe wanted to have a word. Is there a punishment for being late?" I brushed a strand of her hair off her shoulder, savoring her soft skin beneath my fingers.

"That what you want?" she asked, her voice too low for the others to hear, managing to stay the picture of professionalism, except for that damn tongue of hers. I would've been able to recover from the lust threatening to take over if it hadn't darted out and swiped across her bottom lip, making it appear wet and glossy under the gym lights. So fucking kissable.

Fuck. Should've gone for baggier shorts.

She moved back, regaining space between us, but not before shooting me a heated look. And not the '*I want to take your clothes off*' heated, but the '*I'll put you in your place*' heated.

Ironically, both turned me on just the same.

"Watch yourself, Dalton. Remember my last rule."

"Yes, Coach," I said, working hard to reign myself

back in from whatever demon possession had taken over my body. I ran a hand over the back of my neck, feeling really out of my depths. *Why was I suddenly so damn... affectionate?*

I'd lied to her in the car.

PDA wasn't my thing, or it hadn't been until her.

With Emma, I'd never felt this way. She'd hated the "touchy-feely crap," as she'd called it, and only leaned into public displays when cameras were nearby. Even then, it felt staged. Off-camera? We were borderline frigid, and every conversation ended in an argument about how I wasn't doing "enough" for her. By the end, I'd felt more like an accessory than a partner.

But Ari? She was fire and independence, someone who didn't look at me as a checkbook or a ladder to climb. Maybe that's why I couldn't shake this pull toward her.

"Why don't you go by Langley?"

Her voice broke my thoughts, and I tensed when the question registered, turning over in my mind how to answer in a way that didn't feel like a trauma dump of my childhood.

"Um."

A hand landed on my shoulder, and her deep brown eyes held a look of understanding. "You know what? Don't worry, it's none of my business. Cap or Dalt it is." Her smile was genuine, and it only made me want to tell her more, but I didn't get a chance.

"Or asshole."

The way she jumped nearly a foot away from me was impressive, and I would have laughed if she hadn't looked like a deer in headlights as she stared down Monroe.

"Hey, what are you doing here?" she asked, flustered. She probably hadn't seen him since the incident. I fought whether I should continue to stand there or move to the mats with the others. We'd never clarified when or how we'd tell everyone we were dating. Maybe she wouldn't say anything at all and just let them assume. I was about to move when she straightened her back, lifting her chin.

"I'm glad you're here, actually. Alright, let's address the elephant in the room." Her voice boomed through the gym, demanding the team's attention. "I'm sure you've all seen the photo of Dalton and me by now. To answer your question, yes, we are dating." She moved closer, gripping my hand as if we were shaking hands.

That's not going to work, Sunshine.

I tugged her closer, tucking her under my arm and dropping a kiss on the top of her head. She froze, and I chuckled at how she felt like a stiff board against my side. My little bubble of amusement popped when Stephens let out a scoff, making my jaw tick.

"How come you didn't admit it last time?"

The winger was asking to get his ass kicked. I opened my mouth to say as much but Ari beat me to it.

"Because, Stephens, I didn't want to, and you're not entitled to information about my personal life." The look she gave him was so fierce it could make a grown man cry. "I can share as much or as little as I'd like. At the time, we were working out details with HR, and that's all you need to know. Understand?" She looked around, making it clear she was speaking to everyone.

From where he stood against the door frame, Monroe gave a slight nod of approval and disappeared.

Ari's shoulders dropped away from her ears where they'd been glued since he'd walked in, like she'd been braced for backlash. "For any of you concerned about how this might affect my professionalism, the answer is, it won't. In here, I'm Dalton's coach, not his girlfriend." She shot me a menacing look. "He might regret dating me when he's in the gym with me."

"I'd never regret that," I said so only she could hear before addressing the others. "Any of you have a problem with it, you can come talk to me. Now go take a lap around the building."

Her elbow rammed into my rib while the guys filed outside, causing a grunt to slip from my mouth.

"Don't ever tell my players what to do while in *my* gym. It undercuts my authority," she practically growled.

Shit. "Sorry, you're right. Force of habit."

She crossed her arms, and I bit back a groan at the sight of her cleavage threatening to spill over the tip of her tank top, thankful that there was no one in here but us.

"You're killing me, Sunshine," I said, my voice low, wiping a hand over my face. Could I make it a rule that she could only wear turtle necks from now on? Baggy ones. Probably not. If I told her she wasn't *allowed* to wear shirts like this anymore, or to do anything she wanted to do, she'd beat my ass.

"Are you even listening to me?" That kicked me out of my inner musing. She rolled her eyes, repeating what I'd missed while fantasizing about her. "I said, you don't need to go all knight in shining armor either. I don't need you taking care of me, Dalton."

No, she definitely didn't.

I leaned down so my lips were close to her ear. *God, she even smelled like sunshine.* An intoxicating mix of coconut and something floral, maybe? Whatever it was, it was warm—tempting.

"Didn't we go over this? You may not *need* me to take care of you, but that doesn't mean I won't do it." My breath fluttered across her cheek, and I smiled at her sharp inhale. "And I need my guys to know that if they even fucking look at you the wrong way, they'll have to deal with me too." Her skin pebbled up on the column of her neck.

"I can keep them in line, myself, you know?" she bit back after a few seconds, her eyes burning with a fire that set my heart racing and dick twitching. Space, I needed some space between us before I did something caveman-esque, like throwing her over my shoulder and carrying her to her office.

"You can keep me in line, so I have no doubt you can do the same for them." I shot her a wink before escaping to run after the rest of the team.

God, running with a hard-on was going to be a bitch.

NINETEEN

ARIELLA

GRACIELLA'S DADDY ISSUES ARE SHOWING…

MY BREATH CAUGHT in my throat as I stood beneath a cascade of icy water. Droplets trickled down my body, tracing a path down to my feet, chilling my heated skin. It wasn't the humidity alone that had me feeling so flushed.

A certain athlete with the body of a Greek god was also to thank for that.

I stood there, embracing the chill, surrendering myself to the relentless stream, hoping it would chase away the images of his thighs. I thought riding in the car with him this morning was torture?

It had *nothing* on seeing him in the gym.

Fuck, every time he was in the rack squatting, I had to pull my eyes away from the way his shorts tightened around his legs at the bottom of the movement.

I want to identify as those shorts.

My groan echoed off the white subway tiles of the tiny shower, remembering when that man had done the unthinkable. The image was seared into my brain for all

eternity and was sure to be the material I used for self-care for years to come.

Him in his hoochie daddy shorts, reaching back and pulling his sweat-soaked shirt off with *one hand*. I'd seen plenty of male athletes' bare chests, and never in my career had I wanted to lick the sweat droplets off of their abs and trace that cut V with my tongue.

And the abs weren't even what had finally sent me into a mental tailspin. No, my downfall occurred when he took a drink of his water and then spit it onto the turf. Some sick part of my brain desperately wanted it to be my mouth he'd spat into.

My hand trailed down my body, and I imagined it was Dalton's palm caressing my torso, making its way toward my pussy. If I didn't release some of this tension, I was going to end up fucking my fake boyfriend, and that was the last thing I needed.

Or exactly what you need...

"Why do you have to be so goddamn hot?" I muttered to myself as the stream of water hit my face.

"Eh. It's genetic," a random masculine voice responded.

A scream ripped from my throat, my hands dropping to cover myself despite the shower curtain being closed. The bathroom door burst open, and a panicked Graciella yelled out, asking what was wrong, right as I opened the curtain enough to see who was in the bathroom with me.

"Who the hell are you?" I yelled, clutching the floral fabric to my chest.

A stranger wearing my cousin's fluffy pink robe stood by

the vanity, wagging his pierced brows at me. He looked like he was auditioning for the role of loser boyfriend in a band that practiced in his parents' garage, with his mop of messy box-dyed hair that hung into coal-rimmed brown eyes.

It wasn't that he was ugly, but he had *bad idea* written all over his tattooed-covered skin.

"Who the *fuck* are you?" I yelled at him again. He didn't even bat an eye at my outburst. Like being yelled at by women cowering behind a shower curtain was an everyday occurrence for him.

Maybe it was.

"Viper, I told you my cousin was taking a shower, and you'd have to wait."

My eyes shot to Gracie so quickly I thought they might literally fly out of my head. *Viper?* I mouthed to her, but all she gave me was a shrug. I cleared my throat. Maybe my next question would knock some sense into her. "You let a man named after a snake into our home?"

Her lips thinned, and I knew right away that it was the wrong thing to say. Gracie didn't take criticism of her romantic interests in her life well. To a degree, I understood it. In our family, the women were always under heavy scrutiny from our fathers and brothers; hell, any male in our life seemed to get a say on what we should or shouldn't do.

It was one of the few aspects of my culture I resented —the *machismo*.

I suspected her choice of men was a rebellion in the same way that my *lack* of a choice in men was. Both were a pushback on the cultural normative we'd been raised with, and normally I didn't give a shit who she chose to be with.

But none of the others had barged in on me when I was naked.

"*My* house, Ariella," she bit back with enough venom that she should have had the name Viper.

I lowered my eyes in a show of apology. "You're right, I'm sorry." My gaze snagged on the guy still casually standing in the bathroom. "But I'm sure you can see how I'd be a little bit creeped out that there's a grown-ass man in the bathroom with me while I'm *naked.*"

"He was supposed to wait until you were done," she said, frowning.

"Hadda piss, baby."

God, gag me.

There was no way this guy held doors open for Gracie. He probably made her pay for his meal.

I wanted to vomit at the thought of him peeing while I was less than two feet away. Ew. And he wore her robe while doing that, too.

"Okay, well, now that you're done, do you mind? I need to get dressed," I asked, desperately wanting to be wearing some clothes.

"Naw." He leaned back against the little blue cabinet, spreading his legs apart wide enough for me to see that he wasn't wearing pants—or shorts.

I hoped to god he wore boxers at least.

"I meant leaving, *pendejo.* Do you mind *leaving?*" I hoped the look I gave my cousin sufficiently communicated how much of a piece of shit her current hook-up was. The pink coloring on the tops of her cheeks left me hopeful that it had.

"Come on, Viper." She pulled him out of the bathroom by the upper arm, not looking back.

WHEN I WALKED out into the main portion of the apartment, Graciella was lounging on her bed—alone.

"Where's bargain store Andy Biersack?" I asked, opening up the fridge to grab a water. She flipped me off, not bothering to look up from her phone.

"He had to get to rehearsal."

I snorted at how right I'd been with my original assessment of him, which earned me her full attention.

"I'm sorry we can't all be dating a hot star hockey player. A hot, loaded hockey player at that." She smirked at me, and any worries I had about her still being pissed went out the window.

I plopped onto her apple-green striped duvet, laying on my side, head propped up on my hand. "Fake dating," I corrected.

"For now, but watch, you two are going to fall madly in love."

"*Ay.*" I sucked my teeth at her ridiculous claim, but she didn't take the hint.

"No, you mark my words. In fact, I'm putting it in my diary." From under her pale pink silk pillow, she pulled out a well-worn notebook. She wrote everything down in that damn thing. "What's today's date? Never mind. Ariella and Dalton will fall in love for real, and this will be their meet cute," she said, writing furiously while I rolled my eyes.

"Oh, right, because that will go over well with my family." I flopped onto my back, staring at the ceiling with its exposed ductwork and pipes.

"Sure, my uncle and *primo* will be a little bit pissed at first, but they'll come around."

I looked over at her, narrowing my eyes. "Did he pay you to be supportive or something? You don't even know Dalton."

"No," she drew out the word. "But I know *you*, and the fact that you even gave this guy the time tells me all I need to know. Think about it, Ari. You never go on dates with anyone, yet you took him when he was a complete stranger." I pursed my lips. She had a point, but I wasn't ready to relent. "And you trusted him with this whole charade, too."

"Yeah, but that's because I had no choice," I argued, but there wasn't a lot of conviction to my statement.

Gracie scoffed. "Please, no one can tell you what to do. That's why Ricky had such a hard time keeping you in line when we were in college. You don't fall in line. You stand up for yourself."

Her words simultaneously were like a warm hug and a kick to the gut.

On one hand, I was proud of paving my own path, but it was also a reminder that some of my choices went directly against what my family expected of me.

"Have you talked to them?" she asked, her voice soft.

I took a deep breath. I had, but every time they called,

I came up with an excuse to cut the conversation short. It wouldn't be long before they caught on, and then I'd have to explain why I was dodging them.

"Yeah, I've talked to them, but not since—" I shot up, pointing at Gracie, who was watching me with wide eyes. "*No digas nada*. Okay? Not a damn thing about me dating Dalton."

She pursed her lips and flipped me off. "Right, because that was my first instinct to tell them about your love life."

"I'm not in love."

"Not yet," she threw back, face sobering. "But seriously, what are you planning on telling them about you dating him?"

I flopped back on the bed, staring at the exposed ceiling pipes. "Nothing. I'm going to find a solution, break up with Dalton, and then resume life here as originally planned...they never have to know."

Gracie laughed so hard I thought she'd need an inhaler to breathe again.

"Ari, as the queen of ignoring my problems and living in delusion, even *I* know that's a dumb as shit plan. He's literally the NHL's golden boy. His dad *owns* a team. Like, you two are about to be all over the news."

She wasn't saying anything I hadn't already thought of. And she was right, I'd been pretending these realities didn't exist. "My dad re-watches the same soccer matches from years ago," I argued—with her or with myself, I wasn't really sure. "The man is *not* going to be watching the hockey game."

"And Ricky?" She gave me a pointed look. "You really

think your twenty-seven-year-old brother, who watches you like a hawk, isn't going to watch the team he knows you are coaching? Or look up your name to see if there's anything new about you online?"

I groaned, throwing my arm over my face.

She'd said the quiet part out loud—the only hiccup in this arrangement I'd been dreading besides meeting Dalton's father. Then, because the universe apparently hated me, my brother's name popped up on my phone screen.

Gracie and I stared at the vibrating device before locking eyes, both of us wide-eyed with panic. It felt like the time we both said we were spending the night at each other's house, only to sneak out to a party. Ricky called ten minutes to us being there, demanding to know where the fuck we were.

"Not. A. Word," I whispered to my cousin as I answered, pasting on my best innocent tone. "Ricky, so nice of you to call. I was just talking about you." *Oh, god, he's going to know something is up.*

"*¿Qué chingados estás haciendo?*"

I froze. "What...what do you mean? I'm not doing anything. Gracie and I are sitting in our apartment, doing nothing...not a thing."

She mouthed at me, "*What the hell?*" before cutting in to save me from my ramble. "Hey, *primo*. How's California?" she asked, pulling the phone away and putting it on speaker.

Ricky made me more nervous than my dad. It was like he could sense when I was about to do something he would disapprove of.

"Don't try to change the subject, Gracie," he replied, his tone softer with her but still firm. "I know my sister. Her voice gets high-pitched when she's hiding something."

"It does not," I protested, hearing the higher octave I was denying. "You're imagining things."

"Sure I am," he replied dryly.

"Whatever. What do you want, Ricky? I have things to do."

"I thought you said you two weren't doing anything..." *Pendejo.* "Listen, Ari, I didn't call to argue, just checking in. I know you've got your own plans out there, but I just want to be sure you're...you're thinking this through."

My shoulders tensed as I met Gracie's sympathetic gaze. Ricky loved me, no doubt, but he also felt like he had to step into the role of both older brother and father whenever he thought I was straying off course—his course. It was suffocating.

"Ricky, a little late to ask about that," I said, trying to keep the irritation out of my voice so it wouldn't cause a fight. "I'm already thousands of miles away."

Gracie snorted before chiming in with her own two cents. "Ari's doing great. She's settling right in."

"Right. And settling in involves what? Partying? Hooking up? Would Dad approve?"

That hit too close to home. I stiffened, feeling the surge of defensiveness rise. *So much for trying to avoid a fight.* "Ricky, I'm not a teenager anymore. You don't need to check up on every decision I make."

"Well, when you don't call for weeks and then pick up sounding like you're hiding a body..." His tone softened. "I worry about you."

My stomach twisted, torn between frustration and a flicker of guilt. He didn't understand why I'd moved out here or why I was chasing something that didn't line up with the life our family expected. Mainly because his decisions were never questioned, and he didn't have the same restrictions I had.

"Look," I finally said, forcing calm into my voice. "I love you, but I'm tired of being treated like a child. Maybe it's not what you'd pick for me, or what Dad would, but it's my life. And I'm figuring it out."

There was a pause, one that stretched long enough for me to feel the tension in the silence.

Gracie, sensing the strain, chimed in. "*Primo*, you gotta trust her. She's doing great out here."

Ricky's sigh came through, softer this time. "Okay, okay. Just...be smart. That's all I'm asking. Can you check in more often too? And if you need anything..."

"I know, I can call you," I replied, a small smile tugging at my lips despite the tension. "Thanks, Ricky."

The call ended, but a strange weight settled over me. I sighed, tilting my head back to stare at the ceiling, wondering if there would always be this tug-of-war between the life I wanted and the one my family imagined for me.

"It's your life, Ari," Gracie said gently, as if sensing my guilt. "You have a right to live it the way *you* want."

"Maybe. But sometimes it feels like I'll always be under the weight of their expectations," I replied softly. "Like being happy and making *them* happy can't exist at the same time."

"Ow," I yelped as Gracie whacked my arm—hard.

"Stop it." Her voice was firm, her eyes blazing. "Your family loves you—they may not understand you, but they love you. You keep pursuing your life, Ariella, and they will fall in line. This is all new to them; you're breaking cultural norms, and that means dealing with some fallout," her eyes turned sad as she stood and walked toward our bathroom. I knew she was thinking about my *tío*.

I also knew she was right.

"Oh, and Ari?" She paused, looking at me from over her shoulder. "Letting someone in while you pursue your dreams isn't a form of failure." Before I could respond, she disappeared into the bathroom, and the sound of the shower filled the silence.

What the hell was I supposed to do with that?

TWENTY

DALTON

WHEN YOU'RE STILL HOPING FOR WORDS OF AFFIRMATION FROM A TOXIC PARENT...

I WASN'T ENTIRELY sure what I'd expected when we'd agreed to this charade, but I'd thought I'd see more of Ari during the week.

Turned out, that wasn't the case. Tuesday was the only day we rode together to work, and I didn't even get to drive her back home.

I'd been hoping to learn more about her.

Honestly, I just wanted to be around her more.

But she'd disappeared after the workout before I was even off the ice every day over the last week and a half. I had a creeping suspicion that she was avoiding me.

Even Stephens had come up, brow arched, asking what I'd done to piss her off. To my surprise, there'd been a thread of protectiveness in his tone that I wasn't used to hearing.

"You and Ariella doing anything this weekend?"

I winced at the sound of Jimenez's voice. I needed to ask about telling him because keeping him in the dark was starting to eat at me. There was *no* way I could keep it up

for long. "Um, not sure yet," I answered, closing my locker and trying to play it cool. "I mean, it's only Thursday, we've got another day before the weekend."

"Well, what did you do last weekend?" he asked, shaking his head when I stared dumbly at him. "Y'all are new. You need to start thinking about these things ahead of time. Take her out. Wine and dine her. Women love that."

I couldn't help but laugh at that. "Not Ari," I said, a grin spreading over my face. "She's...more independent than that." I thought about how she'd chewed me out for not letting her give back the money I'd sent her before she gave me her number.

Not that I'd done much with it since. Just a quick text to get her address. After that, she'd insisted on finding her own way to work.

Honestly? I hadn't texted her because part of me was too chicken shit that she'd turn me down flat. Better to just avoid texting her altogether...right?

Jimenez snickered, breaking me out of my thoughts, and irritation coiled in my gut at his reaction.

"What's that supposed to mean?" I said, more defensively than intended. "There's nothing wrong with a woman knowing she can provide for herself. Maybe she doesn't want to come off as needy. Hell, maybe she doesn't want to give someone power over her."

Her words from that day in the car had stuck with me.

I'd grown up with a single mother, and she hadn't had anyone to help her. There were nights I'd lay awake waiting to hear her come home from her second shift of the day, wishing she had someone to help her pay her bills.

But now—now I wondered if my mom *chose* to make all her own money instead of letting someone else pay for our way of life.

My gut clenched.

Being a six-three white male came with a lot of privileges, most of which I often took for granted. But Ari's fear was actually one I could sympathize with.

Christian closed his locker and looked at me, blinking a few times before breaking out into a smile. "Damn. You really do like this girl. Never heard you get that defensive about your ex. And I talked a lot of shit about Emma."

I frowned. "Not to me."

"No, I definitely gave her backhanded compliments in front of you." He shrugged, picking up his gym bag and looping it over his shoulder. "Hoped it would convince you to run away from the bitch's icy clutches."

"Jimenez."

He held up both his hands. "I know, you don't like when I call women that word. But there's literally no other word for her."

"Your ex is a cunt."

"Cunt."

My best friend nearly choked on his own spit when I said that. I thought I might have to perform mouth-to-mouth.

"Excuse me?" he asked, clutching his chest like he was thoroughly scandalized.

I smirked, knowing he'd love this next part. "Ari said my ex is a cunt."

Just as I'd guessed, he broke into laughter, holding onto his sides as he slumped against our lockers. He caused quite a scene, and some of the other guys came over to see what had him losing his shit. He wiped up the tears forming at the corners of his eyes.

"Keep that fucking girl forever."

Why did that sound so appealing?

"DALTON."

Hearing my father call my name was the last thing I wanted to deal with. I was ready to go home and plop down on my couch.

No, you want to see your fake girlfriend.

I pushed all thoughts of her from my mind. "Hey, Dad, what's up?" I asked, turning to face him.

He sucked in air through his teeth, his hands curled into fists at his side. "My office," he said, making an abrupt turn on his Italian loafers and storming away. There was no need to check to see if I'd follow. He knew I would.

I let out a sigh, rolling out my neck in an attempt to loosen some of the stress he always seemed to cause in my upper shoulders. The man was cold and calculated, his image well-crafted. Which was what he wanted of me. But I seemed to have a hard time learning that particular lesson—along with not calling him dad when we were in the building.

Oh, is that the only time he doesn't want you to call him that?

Pushing away the negative inner voice, I moved into his office, closing the door before sitting in my usual chair.

He'd ditched his suit jacket and was at the bar cart pouring two glasses of scotch.

I hated scotch.

"Dalton, what is this I hear that you are dating someone on staff?" He handed me the low ball.

There was one sure thing about Vincent Langley: you weren't going to know what he was thinking or feeling until he wanted you to. And at that moment, he didn't want me knowing jack shit.

I took a sip of the amber liquid, letting the sting of the alcohol clear my mind before answering. The only reason this conversation hadn't happened earlier was that he'd been in New York. I kept my face schooled, attempting to play his own game.

"Yes, I'm seeing our new coach," I replied casually. "Figured it would be an advantage. Get some extra gym time from it. You know, improve my game a little more."

My stomach soured. Even lying about using Ari made me sick, but I knew how my father worked. If he assumed I was using this relationship to gain an advantage on the ice, he'd be more likely to change the policy to keep her. At least, that was my hope.

"Hmm." He took a swig of his drink, peering at me from over the rim. "So this thing with the girl isn't serious?"

Ice crawled up my veins, but I kept the panic out of my face. "It's only a few weeks old. And you know how long I was with Emma. I'm not sure I'm ready to get *that* involved with a woman again. This is all just fun, and like I said, I can get some extra conditioning time in."

My lower back was soaked with sweat. Lying was not my forte.

It felt like eons before he finally gave a curt nod and moved from in front of me to sit in his office chair.

"Well then, that sounds like a smart move." From how his mouth pulled up at the corner and the glint in his eyes, I knew I wouldn't like what he was about to say. "I'm sure this goes without saying, but make sure you wear a condom if you are sleeping with this girl, and *never* use one that you didn't bring yourself. You know how women like that can be." The smirk on his face, as if we were bonding, had irritation itching under my skin like hot needles.

The comment felt an awful lot like a dig at my mom, and I was thankful he'd sat in his office chair so he wouldn't see my fisted hands.

"I'm not sure I do." The green of his eyes seemed to turn icy at my words. "Women like what?" I asked, hiding my mouth with the rim of the glass.

He huffed, throwing back the rest of his drink. The thud of the glass hitting his desk filled the silence. "Dalton, men with power and wealth like us are a meal ticket for women like her. All I'm saying, *son*, is to be careful and not let this girl too close. We pay well, but still. You're in a different tax bracket. You have a bright future ahead of you." He let out a condescending chuckle. "I'm not even sure if she's good at her job. I let Monroe hire a new coach. Didn't expect he'd pick a woman."

I battled to keep my anger under control.

If it were a player who spoke about Ari like this, he'd have been on his way to the hospital. But it wasn't a player, it was my father. Honestly, that wasn't really enough to hold me back from clocking him. What had me hesitating was the fact that he wrote Ari's checks, and she was trusting me to help convince him she was an asset to the team.

"Actually, she's damn good at what she does," I said, trying to keep my tone cool.

"I look forward to meeting her then at Media Day," he said smoothly, leaning back in his chair. "If she's as good as you say, maybe she'll prove to be useful as more than just our inclusive hire. But even if we have to bring in someone better at the job, having her on staff will make us look good."

Rage boiled in my gut, threatening to spill over, but I fought to keep a lid on my reaction, not wanting to cause Ari more problems.

"She's the right person for the job." The bite in my voice didn't go unnoticed, likely because I almost never spoke back to him.

His dark brow quirked upward, a look of interest on his normally blank face.

"I can't wait to get to know this woman who has you so...invested. See if she's as good as you seem to think," he said condescendingly, like he didn't trust my judgment.

I gave a curt nod, ready to finish this meeting, and stood, swallowing back the frustration boiling under the surface. I could almost see it. Him meeting Ari, evaluating her with that intense gaze of his, and either finding her valuable or dismissing her without a second thought.

But if he just saw her work—saw her dedication and talent—he'd have to acknowledge she was an asset.

I turned to leave, not wanting to drag out the conversation any longer. "See you later," I said, letting the door click behind me without waiting for his response. Ari had worked hard to get here, and I had to believe he'd see her potential.

I took a deep breath, my frustration giving way to a sense of resolve.

I'd find a way to get him on board. To change the policy so her job wasn't in jeopardy.

Though part of me hoped not before I got to spend more time with her.

I'd just gotten into my car when my phone went off. My heart nearly stopped when I saw her name at the top of the screen, but the excitement died the second I noticed it was a group message with the rest of the team.

ARI, CHRISTIAN JIMENEZ, & OTHERS:

Meet me at this address tomorrow, boys.
I suggest you get a good night's sleep
and maybe book a massage for after...
3121 N Fitzhugh Ave, Dallas, TX 75204

Well, that's not ominous.

Then another message popped up, this one just from her.

ARI:

Sooo, does your offer of being my ride
still stand?

ARI:

If you can't, I can get a ride from another
member of the team it's no biggie

In what world did she think I would be okay with that? Just the thought of one of my teammates driving her around had me fisting my hands at my sides. She was about to hate what I wrote back. But you know how it is, all things are easier to say over text...

ME:

There is no way in hell that I would ever let another member of this team drive you anywhere. You're my girlfriend, so you'll be in my car.

Those three dots played with my heart, appearing and disappearing for several seconds. What I would give to be next to her in that moment. To watch the wave of emotions on her face and body language. She should never enter a poker tournament because her feelings were broadcast for all to see. Unfortunately for me, just because I got a glimpse of her feelings didn't mean I knew what she was thinking—or what she'd do.

Like right now. The text message she was typing out could tell me to go fuck myself, or she'd come back with something that could be borderline flirting...on second thought, they were both flirting to me.

The chime drew my attention back to the lit screen.

ARI:

You don't tell me what to do, Dalton.
Jimenez is picking me up now.

So defiant.

I smiled as I slid into the front seat. The fuck he was.

ME:

What time do you want me at your place?

Another round of the three dots appearing and disappearing played out, before her response came through. I could almost picture her debating how stubborn she wanted to be.

ARI:

8...

ME:

Good girl.

As I slipped my phone into my pocket, I couldn't shake the grin on my face. She'd make me pay for that tomorrow, and for some reason, I couldn't wait.

TWENTY-ONE

ARIELLA

ALL VALID QUESTIONS

I SAT on my cousin's bed and stared at the text from him for *far* longer than appropriate.

Good girl.

Why am I breathing heavy?

Why are my *chonies* wet?

Where the hell is my vibrator?

Why could I hear that in my head with his voice...

And the most important question of all...

Why the fuck did I want him to call me that again?

TWENTY-TWO

ARIELLA

I LOVE WATCHING MEN GET HUMBLED.

DALTON'S CAR rolled up right on time, his familiar, easy grin greeting me as I opened the passenger door and slid in, feeling the same jolt of nerves I tried to ignore whenever I was around him.

"Morning, Sunshine." His voice was warm and casual as he pulled away from the curb.

"No coffee today?"

I tossed my bag into the back seat, trying to avoid eye contact, afraid that he'd take one look at me and somehow figure out I'd spent half the night dreaming about him—dreams I couldn't forget even if I tried. My saving grace was that today I was making them do something I could almost guarantee none of them had before.

I'd probably be so busy laughing my ass off that I wouldn't have time to think about how his shorts always bunched at the crotch, giving me way too clear of a picture of what he was working with.

"Earth to Ariella." I yelped at the sound of Dalton's

voice, my cheeks heating at being caught thinking about his junk. "Distracted much? Look in the cupholder."

"Really?" I asked, trying to grasp onto the new subject before he could ask what I was busy thinking about. Sure enough, there was an iced coffee in the holder, and it was the perfect color, too. "You're a godsend."

"I know." I swore he puffed out his chest at the compliment. "Always iced coffee, even if we're in a blizzard. But you're from California. You have *no* clue what cold weather is like. I bet you rethink that whole *no hot coffee, even in winter* thing."

"I bet you I don't." I held up the cup, examining it. "Where did you get this? It's the best coffee I've had since getting to Dallas. They made it perfectly..." My voice trailed off as I searched for the name on the cup and found none.

He looked over at me warily. "Uh, it didn't come from a coffee shop. I made it this morning.

"You...you made it?" I asked, trying to wrap my head around the fact that my favorite coffee didn't come from a shop, but from him, and that he'd taken the time to make me one before picking me up.

He rubbed the back of his neck. "Technically, my mom made your coffee."

That comment made me choke. Great, even white boys have their moms do everything for them? *Oh god, did he say who the coffee was for?*

Dalton was utterly unaware that I was spiraling and kept on talking. "She needed help getting down some containers, and apparently that project couldn't wait 'til I saw her on Sunday, so that didn't leave me enough time to run and get you a coffee. I tried to do it, but she told me I was ruining her fancy machine." The tips of his ears were tinged pink. "I did add the two coconut sugars and half-and-half 'til it was...well, whatever shade of brown that is," he said sheepishly.

So, he didn't ask his mom to do everything for him.

I blinked, caught off guard by the confession. It was strangely endearing, picturing him in the kitchen trying to work what was, given how good it tasted, probably a very nice espresso machine to make me a coffee. "How did you even know this was how I liked it?"

"I notice things, Ari," he said with a shrug. "You mixed your last drink like you were a mad scientist. Hard to miss."

No. Those things *were* hard to miss. Gracie still asked what I wanted even though my order hadn't changed in years. He saw me prep my coffee *one* time and then managed to get it perfect. My cheeks warmed, and unwanted butterflies exploded in my chest. *Why did he care to pay attention to that?* The question was on the tip of my tongue, but I chickened out.

"You didn't tell your mom this was for me, did you?"

"Of course I did," he said, like it was no big deal.

Meanwhile, my heart literally stalled in my chest, a million questions swirling in my mind.

What did she say?

What did she do with her hands when you told her?

What did her face do when she heard about me?

"She knows I don't drink coffee, so there was no way it

was for me. Oh, by the way, she told me to tell you that she hopes you kick all of our asses." He relayed his mother's words with a shake of his head.

I wanted to smile, but I was too busy fighting off a panic attack that he'd told his *mom* about me.

"Did you tell her about us?" I blurted out.

His gaze cut over to me, something like guilt flashing in his eyes. "No. I didn't tell her we were dating, just that you're the new coach...and that...I like you."

Of course, that was the exact moment we pulled up to the studio, so I didn't get a chance to grill him on what exactly he'd meant by that last part.

The guys were already outside, shooting wary glances at the door like they'd been led into a trap. Jimenez eyed the studio sign with open horror. It wasn't like I'd kept where we were going this morning a secret. One quick Google search would have shown them where the address led. Honestly, how were men still alive and making it through natural selection?

A woman probably helped.

Dalton let out a bark of laughter as he cut the engine. "Oh, they are going to *love* this."

The nerves induced by our conversation melted away, and a smile pulled at the corners of my mouth. "They're going to hate it, but I'm going to love witnessing the suffering," I said with a smirk, moving to open the door, but the lock engaged as soon as my hand touched the handle.

"Don't you dare," Dalton warned, already halfway out of his side.

"What the hell? Locking me in won't get you out of

this practice," I yelled after him when he slammed his door shut, pointing at me through the windshield as he rounded the front of the car. My irritation faded when I realized what he was doing.

He yanked my door open, a boyish grin plastered on his face. "Darlin', before you tell me...yes, I know you can do this yourself. But I'll be damned if I pull up in front of all my teammates and let them see you open your own door." His warm hand wrapped around mine and practically pulled me into his chest. The scent of clean laundry and cologne enveloped me, making me feel even more unsteady than I already did. "My momma raised me to be a gentleman, Ariella. 'Fraid you're going to have to get used to it."

First the coffee, now the door opening.

Strawberry gloss coated my tongue as I gnawed on my bottom lip, trying to tamp down my feelings. If I was being honest, I liked it when he did things for me. Which was a bit of a mindfuck since I prided myself on my independence—but maybe both things could exist at the same time.

"You going to carry my bag too?" I sassed, trying to regain some semblance of control, even though I let him continue to hold my hand against his chest, his thumb absently stroking my skin.

"Naw, Sunshine. I like watching you lift heavy shit." His gaze raked over my body like a physical caress. "It's fucking hot."

"Hey, lovebirds. Let's go," Jimenez yelled, reminding me I was supposed to be working.

Shit. Focus.

Dalton chuckled as I scrambled to get around him, practically running so I could put some space between us. Though part of me asked why I was trying to get away. Wasn't the point supposed to be that they all believed we were dating? I was going to have to find a balance between girlfriend and professional.

Fake. Fake girlfriend.

Before I could mentally dissect why I kept forgetting that little key detail, Jimenez distracted me. "What are we doing here?" He looked from me to Dalton like this had to be a prank.

"Pilates," I said simply, pointing to the giant sign. His face was priceless. I patted his shoulder, fighting off a smirk. "This is what your core conditioning is missing. It's great for stability, strength, and balance. It'll help you on the ice."

Stephens gave an exaggerated groan, but otherwise didn't say much. He'd seemed to come around over the last week, no more judgmental remarks about how I might have gotten the job. He'd even asked me to help improve his squat form.

Jimenez shot Dalton a horrified look. "Pilates? Like the shit rich housewives do?"

"Better than pushing weighted sleds, right?" he responded with a shrug. Dalton's body radiated heat from where he stood behind me, not too close, but it still felt... territorial.

We walked through the door, the little bell over the entrance announcing our arrival as if we needed it.

"If that's the case, it's practically a vacation. It was

hard to sit down to shit for days after that practice," Roberts called out, causing the instructor to nearly choke on her water.

"Boys, let's behave in a way that wouldn't have your mothers smacking you upside your heads." I glared at Roberts, who looked at his feet, bright spots of pink staining his cheeks. I turned toward the woman, who looked at us like a deer in headlights. "Sorry, they sometimes forget they need to use manners and not their locker room talk."

She smiled, tucking her blonde hair behind her ear nervously. "Oh, that's okay. Welcome everyone. I'm Lisa. Glad to have you in today." She waved her arm to the side, directing everyone's attention to the main portion of the studio. "Go ahead and choose a reformer. Your coach has already gotten grippy socks for you all, and each station has been prepped with your props."

They all stood there awkwardly, eyeing the straps, springs, and pulleys like they were torture devices—which might prove to be true for some of them.

"Hey." I clapped my hands to get their attention when they still hadn't moved. "This is still a workout, not an optional activity, so get your asses in gear and act like you're professional athletes and not a bunch of babies."

Like a switch had been flipped, they all scrambled to get to a reformer. Lisa smiled shyly, nodding her thanks.

"Be mean to them. They like it," I said, leaning over so only she could hear.

Her smile widened, and confidence started to take hold. She straightened her back, standing taller as she addressed the group. "Okay, gentlemen, have any of you done Pilates before?"

I rolled my eyes at the cocky snorts, positioning myself at the front of the room so I could assist with form. Of course, Jimenez answered for the group, turning on the charm. "We haven't, but I'm sure we can handle it, *mami*," he said with a wink.

"Well, in that case," Lisa said, utterly unfazed by his overt flirting,"you should know this class will challenge every muscle you know you have and a shit ton you weren't aware of." She walked over toward the front of the room, a pep in her step.

Dalton settled onto his reformer with ease, looking at me with a challenging glint in his eyes, while Jimenez and Roberts snickered to one another as they put their socks on.

"This is gonna be easy," Jimenez called out, slinging his arm across his chest in an exaggerated stretch.

These poor, ignorant souls. They had no idea the pain they were in for...

WE WERE BARELY thirty minutes into the class, and every one of my players had a different expression of regret plastered across their faces.

"Keep your core tight. Drop it lower, boys. That front knee should be at ninety," I called out, watching them struggle. "Roberts, those weights are supposed to be out in front of you."

Lisa giggled as I reached for his arm, guiding them up toward where they should be. He let out a groan that sounded like he was dying.

"Oh my god, this is...impossible. When did three pounds get so fucking heavy?" he gasped, his face red with exertion.

Beside him, Jimenez said every expletive he knew in English and Spanish. "Coach, this is some medieval torture. Why are my legs shaking like this?" He pulled the carriage back so he could come out of the lung and looked down at his limbs in horror. "The sides of my ass cheeks hurt."

"Get back into it, Jimenez," Lisa called out from where she was demonstrating the move, looking like she was out for a walk in the park while the guys were at death's door. The shy girl from earlier was nowhere to be seen. She was running this class like a drill instructor, and I loved every second of it.

"Come on, we're going to pulse it," she shouted. A laugh burst from my lips at the protests from everyone on the team. "For ten, nine, eight—"

"Bro, there is no way," Roberts called out, face twisted in pain while she continued to count down.

Dalton moved through the exercises with steady concentration, but I could see the strain tightening his jaw. The sweat beading up along his brow.

"Up two inches, down two inches," I said, pressing my fingers to the crease behind his knee, ignoring the flutters at how close I was to his half-naked body. He'd ditched his shirt at some point, and I'd been actively ignoring him, because every time I looked at his body, all I could picture was him using those broad shoulders to hold my legs open and using that ton—

"You this mean to all your boyfriends?" The deep rumble of Dalton's voice cut off my fantasy, and I squirmed under his attention. *God, did he know what I was thinking about?* His eyes sparkled with amusement, making my stomach flip and heat shoot straight to my core.

Why the hell was my mouth so dry? I swallowed, trying to get my voice to work and willing it not to come out sounding breathy and turned on. Because I was. Something about watching all of his muscles ripple under his skin as he moved was tantalizing. And for some fucking reason, that desire to lick the sweat off his body was back...

"Oh, this is nothing," I replied, fighting with my libido. "Wait 'til next week."

At the other end of the studio, Stephens let out a frustrated groan, attempting to hold his balance. "Who taught you to count? This has been way more than ten seconds."

"Okay, boys, on your backs," Lisa called out, ignoring the jab. Probably because she had kept them down in that pulse longer than ten seconds, and if her smile was anything to go by, she did it on purpose.

"Oh, thank god," Jimenez said, collapsing to the carriage.

"Feet in straps, Pilates V. You're going to draw your legs in and then zip them back up." She called out, showing off the move. "Low back stays glued to the carriage the whole time."

"Cap, what the fuck did you do to piss your girlfriend

off?" Stephens yelled. "Fix it...fast. Because I am positive she's trying to kill us."

"Why do you assume this is my fault?" Dalton's response came out strained as he struggled to get the loop around his foot.

I laughed, deciding to help him out so they knew this wasn't some form of group punishment.

Well, not entirely. I did enjoy watching men suffer a bit.

"You're doing this because I want you to perform at your best. Pilates will make you faster and more stable on the ice. Plus, stronger obliques mean better puck control." I looked around the room. "Trust me, you'll thank me when you see the results."

The class wound down with a series of stretches, and I stifled a laugh, watching them stumble off the machines. They were going to feel this tomorrow...or tonight, to be honest.

"It was so nice meeting you all," Lisa said as they started to filter out. "Can't wait to see you next week."

The chorus of curse words had me dying.

"So," Dalton began, leaning against the wall and watching me. "Turns out Pilates is...intense." He gave a small chuckle, brushing a hand through his hair.

I rolled my eyes, collecting a few stray towels. "What, you thought it would be a walk in the park?"

"Maybe. I see women doing it all the time with ease. And, like an ass, I figured it was because the workout was easy, not that they might be strong."

That was one of my favorite traits about Dalton. He wasn't too prideful to admit when he was wrong or sexist, and he didn't get angry about a woman being better than him at something. It made him that much more attractive.

"Next time, I'll join in and show you how it's done."

He pushed off the wall, stepping into my space. "How about a private lesson?"

"Do you know how much those cost?" I teased.

"I've got money. Charge me for it, Coach."

We both fell silent, the air between us buzzing as his eyes dipped to where I pulled my bottom lip between my teeth. "Who do you think paid for this class?"

His brows furrowed for a moment before he barked out a laugh. "Did you seriously pay for this with the money I sent you?"

"I told you I didn't want your money."

All he did was hum and reach out to stroke my cheek. For a moment, it was just the two of us, surrounded by the quiet hum of the studio. "Come on a date with me this weekend."

My breath caught in my throat at the request, and I froze. What would it mean if I went out with him? This was all supposed to be a show for work, but going with him somewhere...was that for show, too?

"I..." I struggled to figure out what I was feeling—what I wanted. "Gracie and I are super busy this weekend. Lots of plans," I rushed out, stepping back.

His expression changed, blinking as if coming out of a fog. "Right, of course," he started, dropping his hand away, tone shifting. The heat from a moment before evaporated, and my stomach dropped. It was as if I could feel the way a chasm was now placed between us. I should have felt relief, but instead it felt like my heart was placed in a vice grip.

"Um, I talked to my father yesterday—"

I cut him off without meaning to. "What did he say? You think that will work?" My adrenaline spiked, half from nerves, half from hope.

He hesitated, jaw ticking as he looked off to the side. "I honestly don't know. He's...stubborn. But if he sees you're an asset, maybe we'll have a shot. It's all about showing him he doesn't want to lose you, no matter our relationship." His green eyes caught mine, sincerity in their mossy depths.

I nodded, mulling over his words. "Right, so we stick with the plan of acting like we're dating until I show him I'm valuable."

"About that." Dalton sighed, shifting his weight, clearly uneasy. "I was thinking of telling Jimenez the truth about us. Just him. He'd cover for us if anything slipped. Keeping him in the dark doesn't feel right. He's been my best friend since middle school. We're practically brothers. But I'd need your okay first."

Something warmed in my chest, both at his loyalty to Jimenez and his consideration of my feelings. "Yeah, of course. If you trust him, then so do I. Besides, Gracie knows, so it's only fair you have someone too."

He nodded, a smile blooming as his shoulders dropped slightly like the question had been weighing on him. "Awesome. Also, Media Day is coming up next week. We'll need to be ready. Our 'relationship' is bound to come up."

The reality of our situation sank in further.

"Hey," warmth radiated from where his hand gripped my shoulder, "it's going to be great. Now, let's get you home so you can get started on your weekend plans with Gracie."

There was no judgment in his voice, but they still hit right to the chest. Because I didn't have plans. I just didn't know how to handle the feelings swirling around in my head for him.

TWENTY-THREE

ARIELLA

PSH. THERE WENT MY CHONIES TOO, GURL...

SWAPPING SPIT with a man while your cousin lay only feet away was wild behavior. But also very on-brand for Gracie.

My noise-canceling headphones were fighting for their lives, trying to keep out the sound of them going at it. Tingles ran up my left arm, which had gone numb about five minutes earlier. To make matters worse, I desperately needed to pee, but I was too afraid of what I might see if I crawled out from the sheet I'd hidden under.

What a way to spend a Sunday night.

Honestly, this situation was one wrong move away from someone committing a crime—either indecent exposure or attempted murder, depending on who broke first.

"I do look good in orange," I mumbled to myself, turning up the volume on my phone.

I couldn't really blame Gracie. I was the one crashing on her couch, not the other way around. And she'd held off on bringing anyone around all weekend.

Until tonight, that was.

A notification popped up at the top of the screen, the name sending my heart into overdrive. I hadn't spoken to him since after the Pilates class on Friday. The amount of texts I'd started but never sent to tell him that I wished I'd taken him up on his date offer was criminal.

I was bad at *regular* relationships but apparently even worse at fake ones.

It would be so much easier if I didn't have a damn crush on the guy because how the fuck did this all work into my plans?

The screen lit up again, reminding me of the unread text and firing up the butterflies that now permanently resided in my stomach.

DALTON:

Hey. What are you doing?

I rolled my eyes, but my lips pulled up at the corners.

ME:

Is that the best you can do?

Those three dots toyed with me, and I found myself gnawing on my bottom lip, wondering if he would respond. My fingertips hovered above the keyboard, debating whether or not I should send another message.

I couldn't take the suspense and shot off something.

ME:

I'm actually being held hostage on the couch by my cousin and a random man making out...

DALTON:

Wait, what?

DALTON:

I'm aware being a hostage usually means
you are unwilling, but my brain can't
manage to figure out how you got into
this situation. Can't you like…move
rooms?

A picture of how his brows were probably furrowed in confusion popped into my mind, causing me to grin like an idiot.

ME:

Studio apartment. Nowhere to go unless
I hide in the bathroom, but I already
experienced another of her hook-ups
walking in on me while I was in the
shower.

Why was I sharing all of this with him?

DALTON:

Get dressed. I'm coming to pick you up.

DALTON:

Don't bother arguing. I'm already on
my way.

My bottom lip was back between my teeth, a maelstrom of giddiness overtaking my body. Normally, he'd be right, and I would argue, but I really wanted him to come to get me—and not only to escape the weird sexcapade happening on my cousin's bed.

But I needed to at least pretend to play hard to get.

ME:

> You don't even know which apartment I
> live in...

His response showed up almost instantly, as if he'd already prepared it and was ready for when I pushed back.

DALTON:

> Don't try me, Ariella. I will knock on every
> damn door in that building until I find you
> and carry you out over my shoulder.

Never in my life had I experienced the urge to squeal and kick my feet until that moment.

Knock on every door? Carry me out over his shoulder?

I popped up from under the floral flat sheet, shielding my eyes and scrambling to find a matching pair of tennis shoes.

Shit. My hair.

Gracie called out after me, but I was too busy running to the bathroom to throw on mascara and deodorant. I had to put that shit on everywhere with the heat in Dallas.

"Where the hell are you off to?" she asked, standing in the doorway. I smirked at her bob, which had obviously had a hand running through it—and not her own. "You know you don't have to leave."

Through the vanity mirror, I could see that while her words said one thing, her face said another.

"It's no problem. You have your sexy time or whatever you two are doing." Our eyes met in the reflection. "Dalton's picking me up."

Gracie lit up with excitement, and she literally jumped up and down for joy at the news.

"Ahh! It's happening." She clapped her hands, ignoring whatever his name was as he called out, asking what was going on. "I'm telling you, you two are going to fall in love."

I rolled my eyes, focusing on taming my hair.

"This whole thing is fake, Graciella. Remember?"

She let out a hum, turning to leave. "Until it's not, Ariella. Until it's not..."

DALTON:

Ariella, you better come get in the car. Or your neighbors are about to be pissed that I'm banging on their doors.

DALTON:

And I'll tell them it's your fault for not following directions.

DID he speed here or what? And why did my stomach do a weird flip when he mentioned me following his directions?

It felt like he'd just told me he was coming to pick me up, and now he was rushing me to get out the door and into his posh leather seats. I'd be lying if I didn't admit that part of me wanted to stay where I was to see if he really would knock on every door to find me, but the sounds coming from Gracie's bed made that decision for me.

"Bye, kids. Make sure you use protection," I called out,

running and trying not to look too closely at what was happening in the blanket they were hiding under.

God. I really needed to move into a place where I'd have my own bedroom—with a door.

The door was the key element.

I practically skipped down the stairs to the guest parking spots in the garage, my stomach performing acrobatic feats the closer I got. When I rounded the corner, I stopped in my tracks. Instead of waiting inside the way I'd expected, he leaned back, booted feet crossed at the ankles.

My mouth went dry the farther up his jean-clad legs I dragged my gaze. They fluttered shut when I hit his thighs and that sinful spot where his jeans bunched up at the crotch, giving just enough of an impression of what was behind the zipper.

He had *plenty* going on there. I already knew from his shorts.

Híjole, I needed to find a confession booth for these mental images.

"Are you praying?" My eyes popped open at the sound of his deep rumble. The crooked grin, slight five-o'clock shadow, sharp jawline, mossy eyes...it was all too much. "Plan on sinning tonight, darlin'?"

And there went my panties.

Had I been out of the game that long, I'd forgotten the mouths on men? Or was the particular skill of incinerating my *chonies* a specialty only Dalton had?

My guess was the latter, but I didn't want to dwell on that reality too long.

He chuckled at how he'd left me stunned, unable to

come up with anything remotely appropriate to say. Dalton never failed to surprise me with his mouth.

Wholesome hockey captain to the public, but this man had something else lurking under that polished surface, and I liked what he showed me.

Finally, I managed to get my mouth working.

"Depends, Dalton." I moved in close enough that we were nearly touching, trying to act as casually as possible while my heart raced like a workhorse.

I relished the way his Adam's apple bobbed in his corded neck, how his eyes nearly glowed as he dragged them over my body, stopping when he reached the sliver of tanned skin below my white cropped tank and above the waistband of the cut-off jeans shorts I'd thrown on.

He cleared his throat, uncrossing his legs to stand with them splayed out. I smirked, guessing what might require adjustment.

"On?"

"If you use that line on all the girls you threaten to throw over your shoulder?"

His expression grew serious, and he closed the gap between our bodies, so close I had to tilt my chin to keep our eyes locked. "Let's get one thing straight. I've *never* told another woman I'd knock on every door in a building to find her. And it wasn't a threat, Ari. It was a promise."

Damn.

His words lingered between us, thick and charged, and I had to force myself to breathe, my pulse pounding in my ears. He leaned closer, his gaze dark and intent, and for a moment all I could think about was the heat rolling off his body and how much I wanted to close the gap entirely.

"Dalton," I murmured, finding my voice, "I—" my eyes caught on something I hadn't noticed when I first walked out, too distracted by his dickprint in those jeans. "Please don't tell me you went and bought a new car because of that comment I made about you not fitting in yours." I pushed him aside to get a better look at the pale blue restored Bronco. "I mean, it's gorgeous, but that's insane to buy a new vehicle because of me."

A smirk flickered across his lips, and he raised his hand, brushing a stray hair from my face, not bothering to take his attention off me. "I didn't get a new one. I just have an *old* one I thought you might like to see."

TWENTY-FOUR

DALTON

"I'LL GIVE YOU MY PROTEIN STYLE." —THAT'S WHAT HE SAID.

JUST LIKE THAT, she'd managed to crack open something in me without even trying, and she didn't seem to have any idea that she made me feel...I didn't exactly know what it was I felt.

I studied her as if there would be a test. Like I'd need to answer questions on how her button nose wrinkled in confusion or how she squinted her chocolate eyes like what she was looking at might not be real, or maybe I'd be asked to describe the exact way the thin line of her mouth blossomed into a smile wide enough the corners of her mouth had hurt.

She whipped her head around, her hair flying wildly behind her, "Is this really yours?" The excitement in her voice mended hurts I hadn't realized I had.

I nodded. "Yeah, Betty's mine. '67 Ford Bronco." The words came out more gruff than intended, my throat thick with emotion at seeing her reaction.

Emma had hated my Bronco.

She thought it rode too rough and complained it didn't

scream *"I'm wealthy"* when she was in it. That was exactly why I liked it. That and the fact that Betty was the first thing I'd ever bought for myself. Worked coaching youth hockey and private lessons for two whole summers so I could buy her.

I didn't know why I'd given in when Emma demanded I start parking it at my mom's. Which was where it'd been until today, when I finally brought her back home with me after our weekly meal. As much as I told myself I'd done it because I wanted Betty back, a part of me wanted to show Ari—I just hadn't realized that opportunity would present itself so soon.

My chest warmed when Ari walked over, running her hands over the paint with reverence.

"So, how is it this thing's so nice if it's older than I am?" she asked.

"She didn't look like this when I bought her. Every penny I made working went into fixing her up. Rebuilt the engine, fixed a million and one things that were broken, but it was a labor of love." I smiled, reminiscing on my time under the hood. "My mom worked two jobs and put herself through school. I didn't want her to feel like she had to get me a car, too, and with hockey, I had a lot of places I needed to be, and I didn't want to burden her schedule with driving me everywhere. Enter Betty."

Ari's brows furrowed. "Where was your dad?"

There was a pang in my chest, the same one I got every time I spoke about it. "Um, he wasn't around until later." I flashed her a smile, attempting to keep my tone light.

He was her employer, after all, and eventually, she'd

meet him. I didn't want her to get the wrong impression about my dad. Vincent was a good guy...he just had a hard exterior shell.

Ari studied me for a beat before nodding, like she somehow knew the subject was delicate and chose not to dig deeper for my sake. "Why don't you drive this beauty every day? It's seriously gorgeous."

I should have known that question was coming, but I'd forgotten what it was like to have someone attempt to get to know you.

She didn't see my shrug, too busy making her way around the SUV. "Eh. The other one gets better gas mileage," I said lightly, digging out the single key hanging from the diamond-shaped keychain that read "Betty." My mom had given it to me when I got the car.

It wasn't a total lie, but it was definitely not the full truth. Telling her why I'd felt compelled to keep it parked, like some relic of my teenage dreams, was more than I was ready to share. What would she say if I told her I didn't drive the Bronco because my father hated it? That I drove the Audi, hoping he'd take note of how I listened to him and it would make us closer?

That I hoped it would help us come to have an actual father-son relationship...

Fuck. It was even more pathetic when I added that the entire time I'd rebuilt the Bronco, I'd been thinking about what it might be like to do it with my dad.

"I think we take her all the time now," she said, straightening her shoulders, chin held high like she was ready for a fight. "You've got enough money to cover gas. Hell, I'll help pay for gas." She hung onto the car like she was prepared to latch on and refused to move until I agreed. Her voice softened. "I just think it's a shame not to enjoy something you put so much of yourself into. Seems like she deserves better...like you deserve better."

My chest tightened at the sight of her pressed up against something that meant so much to me. Tanned legs, wild hair, and a smile I never wanted to see dim. And that final whispered comment about what I deserve hit me right in the heart.

"Yeah, Sunshine. We can take the Bronco."

The squeal she let out was music to my ears.

I'd agree to almost anything she asked of me, and she had no idea.

"WHO ORDERS protein-style with no animal fries?" she asked, hot pink toes wiggling up on the dash.

I'd nearly crashed when she'd kicked off her shoes, unfolding her golden legs to prop her feet up. When on earth did I start thinking ankles were sexy?

When you had a vision of hers slung over your shoulders...

"Dalton?"

"Huh?" I asked, coming back to earth from the fantasy land my mind kept kicking me into.

Her melodic laugh filled the car, carefree and warm, cutting through the sound of the wind rushing through the windows she insisted we lower. "I asked who orders protein-style and no fries, but then you stared at my feet like you've got some kind of fetish."

Swallowing, I plastered on a smile, hoping to hide how close to the truth she'd come. I didn't have a thing for all feet, but apparently I had a thing for hers.

I had a thing for all of her.

"Some of us," I began, giving her a sidelong look, "actually have to watch our figures because we skate around on thin blades and whack a small disc on the ice while other dudes try to beat us up with sticks."

She raised an eyebrow, crossing her arms as she leaned back into the seat, a small smile on her lips. "Poor baby. Must be tough being a big, strong hockey player."

"Ha ha, hilarious." I nudged her shoulder with mine, the bright lights from the In-N-Out sign casting a glow over her beautiful face. "Maybe we should trade places, then, huh?" I added, smirking. "Let's see how long you'd last on the ice, getting slammed into the boards."

She shot me a look, her eyes glinting. "You know, that's the hottest part of a hockey game," she said, taking a big bite of her burger.

A bit of sauce caught on her cheek, and my body moved before my mind could stop it, bringing my thumb up to wipe it away.

"Is it now?" I murmured, voice low. "You like the rough play?"

"Guess you'll have to see how I hold up in the rink someday." Ari's voice was breathy, her gaze pure fire, and I didn't know if we were still talking about hockey or something more.

I held the digit a fraction of an inch from her mouth,

pulse pounding in my chest. I was fully addicted to the challenge and mischief dancing in her brown eyes. My breath caught in my lungs, and I waited on pins and needles for what she'd do next.

Fucking hell.

Those sinful lips of hers wrapped around my thumb, licking it clean in one slow, deliberate movement without breaking eye contact. Then—because she truly did want to kill me—she moaned around my thumb, the sound imprinting onto my psyche. How pathetic that my obituary would have to list the cause of death as cardiac arrest from having her suck on my thumb.

The spark between us was instant—electric.

Blood pounded in my ears, at least the bit of it that hadn't made its way south. My cock was rock hard behind my zipper. She pulled back, leaving me tingling from the warmth of her lips and mental images of me shoving something else between them.

"Delicious."

It was downright erotic. Her gaze was unflinching, daring me to respond, bringing to life my competitive nature.

"Sunshine, I can give you all sorts of things to lick clean if that's what you want. I was also taught it's rude not to reciprocate." I wrapped my hand around hers, covering everything but her pointer finger. A tiny moan slipped from her lips as I used her finger to gather up some of the sauce, guiding the digit to my mouth and wrapping my tongue around it. Flavor burst in my mouth, but it wasn't what I wished I could be tasting.

Her pupils were so blown that only a thin ring of chocolate was still visible.

"Thanks for sharing," I said, biting the tip of her finger before kissing it.

It was like she was in a trance, unable to respond beyond a nod, and damn if that didn't make me feel all sorts of ways. Now that I'd gotten my hands on her, there was no way I could stop. Her silky strands slipped through my fingers, my hand finding the back of her head, holding her in place.

"You touch me a lot. You know that?" Her teeth pressed into her bottom lip.

"Not in all the ways I want, Sunshine."

I'd wanted to kiss her every day since the night I met her, to seal our mouths together and consume everything she gave me. To bite down on the plump flesh of her bottom lip like she was and taste the berry gloss on my tongue. Hell, I wanted to taste, bite, and lick every inch of her flesh. See what heady noises she'd make as I made my way down her body.

Thoroughly marking her as mine.

Need washed over me. I'd been unsure if she'd ever let me kiss her again, but right now felt like a good time to see. The center console dug into my stomach as I leaned across, holding her face in my hands.

She gulped, her eyes wide, not in surprise but in anticipation, our breaths mingling. I paused, giving her enough time to pull away if this wasn't what she wanted. Her shallow panting breaths led me to believe her mind was in the same fucking gutter as mine, but I needed to be sure.

Needed *her* to be sure.

"Ariella, can I ki—" my words were cut off by a blinding flash that shattered the moment.

We blinked, disoriented.

"What the fuck was that?" I asked, looking out the car window, keeping her shielded with my body. A small crowd of photographers gathered outside, cameras pressed against the glass, popping bright flashes. Voices rose above the clicking shutters, each question more insistent than the last.

"Dalton! Over here! Is this the woman from the bar?" one reporter shouted, his face illuminated by flashes bouncing off the windows.

More questions poured out, overlapping, each one louder than the last. "Who is she? Another fling, or the real deal?"

"What about Emma? Is this the reason you broke it off?" another called, his camera pressed against the glass like a vulture. The tint probably blocked any good shots.

The energy in the car shifted instantly. Ari stiffened beneath me, her fingers curling in her lap, jaw tense. "It's probably frowned upon to hit them with the car door, huh?"

"Assault is generally frowned upon, and there may be too much photo evidence to prove it was an accident, but if you decide to do it, I'll back you in court." I tried to lighten the mood, but the statement sounded rough and pissed off. Which was accurate to how I was feeling about being cock-blocked by paparazzi.

My stomach turned with regret at the all too real reminder that *I* was the real reason she was in this mess to begin with, because my name brought attention like this.

I'd dragged her into a lifestyle she hadn't asked for when I'd approached her in that bar.

"I'm sorry you have to deal with this shit because of me. Let's get out of here," I murmured, throwing the car into reverse and weaving out of the parking lot and away from the flashing lights.

"Hey, unless you're the one who called to tip them off, this isn't your fault." She reached over and intertwined our fingers. I glanced into the rearview mirror, watching the crowd shrink smaller the farther away we got. Logically, I knew she was right, but that didn't lessen the weight of the rock sitting on my chest.

"Yeah, but you wouldn't be in this if I—"

"Let's get one thing straight, Dalton. *I* make the decisions for my life, so stop speaking about this as if I'm trailing behind you helplessly."

"There was no way for you to know who I was that night," I argued. "That being around me would equal *that* kind of attention."

She sucked her teeth, pulling her hand away to throw it in the air. "*Ay.* I was at the private soft opening of a sports bar with athletes and agents on the guest list. You're six fucking three. Let's not insult my intelligence and think I didn't have an inkling that you were an athlete with your Greek god-like body." I smirked at her angry rant. Half of this stuff she never would have voiced if she weren't so fired up. "Sure, I thought you were a bull rider given your outfit and, you know, being in Texas, but still, I knew what I was potentially getting myself into when I said yes."

I nodded my head, the weight lightening.

"And another thing," she shifted in her seat to face me and I had to force myself to keep my eyes on the road. "I might have been desperate when I told HR we were a couple, but I still had choices. I always have choices, and I chose you."

Logically, I knew her words were meant to be platonic. They weren't intended to crack open the shield I'd placed around my heart since Emma—yet that was exactly what they did.

The truth hit like a high-stick to the heart.

I wanted Ari.

More than that, I wanted to convince her to choose me for more than this sham of a relationship. And I had no idea what to do about any of it.

TWENTY-FIVE

ARIELLA

"NO ONE'S THAT LOUD FROM A MAN."

SOMETHING HAD SHIFTED between us since the paparazzi run-in nearly a week before.

Maybe it was because I'd been two seconds away from climbing in his lap and dry-humping him in a parking lot. I was so painfully turned on by that moment, only to have paparazzi completely ruin me potentially getting laid in the back of a Bronco.

Instead what I'd gotten was a quiet drive back home and a lingering kiss on the forehead before I'd gotten out of the SUV.

Oh, and a deep regret of not getting my own place so I could have some *alone time.*

"I'm walking you up to your apartment this time," he said, drawing me out of my flashback, my cheeks heating at the fact that I'd nearly been caught thinking about humping one of my hockey players.

We'd had the same argument every day since that night, when he'd started driving me to and from work. He

wanted to walk me to my apartment, and I told him I was a strong, independent woman who didn't need assistance.

At this point, I think he only brought it up to irritate me.

"Dalton, I'm a big girl," I replied, unbuckling my seatbelt. "I've managed to walk myself to my apartment every day without you so far. What am I supposed to do this weekend when you're not here? Huh?"

He ignored me, cutting the engine and hopping out of the SUV to open my door. "Ari," He trailed a finger from my temple to my chin, tilting it until our eyes met. "Would you please allow me to walk you to your apartment?" His voice was soft, but there was a command hidden beneath the sweetness, his green eyes locking me in place until I forgot what we'd been arguing about.

The corners of his mouth pulled up into a sly smile. "Did I break you?"

I cleared my throat, rolling my eyes to cover the fact that, yes, he had broken me—just a little.

"Fine. You can walk me up. But not because I need you to." I gave his chest a playful jab.

His cheeky grin spread into a full-blown smile. "Obviously."

As we started walking toward my building, I tossed over my shoulder. "I'm only letting you for my neighbor's sake. And warning, she might kidnap you. She's *extra* nice to all the delivery men. I think she's on the hunt for a young white boy."

A bark of laughter filled the early evening air.

"I'll stop by her place on my way out then. I bet she makes some bomb food." His hand landed on my lower back, guiding me toward the entrance. "There's not a doorman, or a lock, or *anything*? Anyone can just walk in here?" he asked, pulling open the glass and metal door and eyeing it as if it had personally offended him. I'd always made him drop me off from the guest parking spots, so this was the first time he'd noticed the apparently subpar security.

Warm breath skimmed my ear when I only rolled my eyes in answer, and his voice dropped to a low murmur. "Ari, you're mine until this deal is over, remember? And I don't like the thought of just anyone being able to walk in here." He reached down, taking my hand firmly in his. "I know you're independent and strong, and you could prob-ably kick anyone's ass if they tried something. But for my peace of mind, would you please text me when you get back after practice or anything else?"

Surprisingly, his request didn't irritate me. He didn't make it sound like a command. There was room for me to say no, which made me want to say yes. Before I could answer, we were interrupted by some very vocal sounds emanating from my door.

I groaned. "Ugh. You have to be kidding me."

"Wow, they're really going at it." He scrubbed at the back of his neck, the tips of his ears turning pink when a particularly loud moan filtered through the apartment door.

There was no stopping my giggle. "She's faking it."

"How do you know?" he asked, horror on his face.

"No one is that loud from a man." I chuckled, but my mouth snapped shut when Dalton's gaze turned heated—any indication of embarrassment was long gone.

My back hit the wall as he stalked me down, caging me with his arms. I should have known better than to say that.

"I bet you'd be loud for me," he murmured, low and rough.

My whole body hummed with awareness, and I was distinctly aware of how close we were. His hand rested on my waist, anchoring me in place.

"Being cocky isn't cute," I whispered, trying to keep from closing the distance between our mouths.

I'd never understood what people meant when they said someone's eyes could darken—until now. The moss-green shifted to a deep forest shade, his nostrils flaring slightly as he held my gaze. My fingers flexed by my side, itching to grab the front of his white T-shirt to pull him closer and see if he'd make good on that promise in his eyes.

But before I could even process the thought, Gracie's voice cock blocked.

"Ow. Not *there*, *Dios mío*. I thought you were a doctor. You'd think you'd have a clue about female anatomy," she yelled.

Dalton looked at the door, like if he squinted hard enough he could see into the apartment. "Yeah, I'm going to say you're right, and she's faking it."

We both burst into laughter, the charged moment dissolving into comfortable silence.

"Well," I said, placing my hand on his chest, creating space between us, "you'd better get home, athletes like you need your sleep and all that."

"I will, as soon as you get into your apartment and lock

the door. Are you comfortable with that guy, or should I tell him to get lost?" he asked.

"Oh, I'm going to chill out here until they're done in there." I hiked my thumb over my shoulder. "Don't feel like watching a bad porno, you know?" Hopefully my phone had enough battery to last however much longer they'd be at it. I'd send her a text to wrap it up.

Dalton, however, didn't move to leave. "What do you mean you're staying out here? Don't you have your own room in there?"

"Studio, remember?"

I was back to being caged, but the heat in his eyes was different this time—protective. "Ariella, what's that supposed to mean? Where do you sleep?"

Shit. I knew he wasn't going to like my answer.

"On my cousin's couch," I said sheepishly.

One second I was standing by the door, and the next I found myself draped over Dalton's shoulder, eye-level with his toned, Wrangler-covered ass.

"Dalton. Put me down. Where the fuck are you taking me?" I pushed myself up, bracing myself on his lower back, looking around to see if anyone was coming to my rescue, but there wasn't a soul in the hallway.

"Home. I'm taking you home."

"This is my home." I wriggled around, trying to get free, but his grip was iron-clad.

"Not for tonight, it's not." My protest was silenced with a slap to my ass. "Stop moving, or you're getting more of those."

Thank god he couldn't see me bite my lip at the sensation of his rough hand rubbing away the pain.

He chuckled. "Or maybe that's exactly what you want."

Ignoring the fact that he was completely correct, I huffed. "You know this is a total overreaction, right?"

"Nope," he said easily, striding toward the elevator. "This is exactly the reaction you deserve for not telling me you've been living on a couch."

"DALT, I'm telling you, I don't need to stay here tonight. I'm just going to give her a little longer to get her freak on and go back." My argument died on my tongue when I stepped out into his darkened apartment.

Dallas City Center glittered beneath us through a wall of windows, each light a tiny spark against the night. The view was mesmerizing, like floating above the city. My feet carried me across the sleek plank floors, straight into his open, expansive living room, even though I'd sworn in the car I wouldn't step foot inside his place.

"Wow," I said, my voice no louder than a whisper.

"Wow is right."

I looked up, surprised at his proximity. But his attention wasn't on what lay beyond the glass. It was strictly on me. My stomach somersaulted at the intensity in his eyes as they locked onto where I ran my tongue along my bottom lip, pulling it between my teeth.

I tore my eyes away, taking in the apartment. Needing a reprieve before I did something stupid, like tackle him and make out with his stupidly gorgeous face, or see if stubble was a good inner thigh exfoliator.

It was beautiful—a designer's dream, with charcoal walls, metal accents, and an impressive display of sleek surfaces. But it looked too curated, like someone had staged the whole place without a single personal touch.

No photos, no plants, not even a cozy throw blanket.

I ran my hand over the back of the cognac leather sectional, making my way toward the kitchen.

"Did you just move in?" I asked, raising a brow. "Or did we break into a show apartment?" I turned to face him, walking backward and gasping dramatically. "Oh my god, you don't even live here, do you? Was this all to impress me? Because, if so, I'm already fake dating you. No need to catch a breaking and entering charge for me."

"The sarcasm isn't cute."

"Well, you must think I'm hideous because sarcasm is my main form of communication. With a dash of dark humor as a coping mechanism." I caught him shaking his head as I turned to press one of the flat wall plates, hoping it would turn on the lights and not do something weird like drop a disco ball from the ceiling, or whatever rich people had in their homes.

"Do you have a disco ball?" I asked, now curious.

He let out a surprised laugh. "Do I have what?"

"A disco ball? You know, those mirrored balls that hang from—"

"I know what they are, but why would I have one?"

I shrugged. "Because it would be cool. I mean, your living room is large enough to have a dance party."

The lights flickered on, illuminating the most stunning

kitchen I'd ever seen. Holy shit, it was impressive, with glossy white cabinets, stainless steel appliances, and a sink large enough for me to bathe in.

Dalton's eyes tracked me rounding the marble island from where he was leaning against the wall, hands stuffed into his front pockets, looking far too good for my health. His attention was like a physical caress on my skin. A shiver ran up my spine from the attention.

God, where was the parental supervision when you needed it?

"Holy shit. You have a drink fridge?" I asked, dropping into a crouch in front of the small refrigerator.

Small *empty* refrigerator.

Not having anything personal in his apartment was one thing, but not stocking a drink fridge? That was a crime.

"Why is it empty?"

Dalton moved to lean against the counter, looking slightly out of place in the swanky apartment, standing there barefoot in his white T-shirt and well-worn Wranglers, an easy smile on his gorgeous face.

"Maybe because I have a perfectly good fridge right behind you, and I don't have to drop into a squat for that one," he teased.

I rolled my eyes. He was missing the whole point. Luckily, I was there to enlighten him.

"A well-stocked drink fridge is the height of luxury." I pointed at it. "It's *the* symbol of wealth. That and those ice machines that make the little pellets of ice."

His shoulders shook with laughter as he unfolded his

arms and moved closer. "*Those* are the symbols of wealth?" he asked, offering me a hand.

I yelped when, instead of helping me stand, he lifted me and set me on the island. The chilled surface helped cool my heated flesh as he stepped between my thighs. There was no missing how perfectly aligned we were in that position.

"Well, Ari, I have both of those," he whispered, pulling back far enough to wink at me.

Everything about Dalton being that close was overwhelming. The clean scent, his sure touch, the heat radiating from his body—the way his voice washed over me, so deep and soothing.

I swallowed, desperate to fix my suddenly dry mouth.

His smile was so delicious I shivered. "Now, tell me, Sunshine." *There was that name again.* "What would you stock the fridge with?"

This was a good topic, yeah—something to think about besides the fact that if I were naked and scooched forward half an inch, this island would be ideal for fucking on.

"Ari?" he prodded, his rough hands landing on my bare thighs. Asshole was purposefully trying to fluster me if his smirk was anything to go by.

Two could play that game.

Against my better judgment, I hooked my legs around him, yanking him closer. It was intimate. Way too intimate. His jaw ticked, and I noted how he pulled his hips away just enough so we weren't touching—but there was no hiding the bulge tenting the front of his pants.

Oh, how I folded so quickly.

I was one move away from dry-humping my team's captain.

Oh god, it sounded so much worse when I thought of him that way. Also, so much hotter.

I cleared my throat, focusing on how to form words and unstick the syllables lodged in my esophagus.

"Well, I'd have Topo Chico. In the glass bottles, too." A laugh slipped out when Dalton wrinkled his nose.

"Spicy water. Got it. What else?"

"Sugar-free Red Bull," I said, my voice barely a whisper as his fingers crept higher, the edge of his thumb grazing just under the hem of my shorts, sending shock waves to my core. It was majorly distracting, and my lids fluttered closed, trying to regain some control.

"What size?"

"Um. I like the eight-ounce ones." *Why did I sound so breathy?*

"Anything else?" His voice was soft but a bit husky. The chill from the marble almost burned against my palms as I braced myself there, willing my hands not to touch him.

My lids opened again, only to find his green eyes glued to my chest. I was acutely aware that my nipples were now pebbled beneath my white tank top.

"Why are you asking?" My question sounded straight pornographic since it was more of a moan.

He dragged his eyes back to mine, a lazy smile on his lips as he dipped a finger under the frayed fabric. Somehow, I was both relaxed and completely worked up at the same time.

"I want to know everything about you." He leaned in,

pressing a kiss to my forehead. "The big, the small. I want to know all of it."

I froze, caught off guard by the sincerity of his words. It had been a long time since anyone had cared to know me. To ask me about my life and what I wanted. With that one sentence, he'd sent another battering ram to my carefully constructed fortress, and I scrambled to take cover.

Scrambled to get away.

"What would you stock the fridge with?" I asked, needing a distraction to give myself a second to process how he was looking at me—like I was the most important thing in the room.

He shrugged. "Doesn't matter. We're talking about you," he said, grunting when I hit his shoulder.

That was something else I'd noticed about him.

Yes, he was caring and considerate, but at times, I got the impression that it was at his expense. That he would downplay his own wants and needs for the benefit of someone else. And sure, there were times when that might be considered romantic or kind, but only if the people you extended that courtesy to reciprocate it.

Did Dalton have anyone putting his desires first?

Did he get a say in how things went in his life?

The thought left a hollow feeling in my chest and, maybe, a tinge of guilt. Dalton had been sweet, caring, and thoughtful since the start. Hell, I don't know that he'd ever acted like whatever this was between us was fake.

Maybe I didn't have to have all the answers as to what this meant for my future just yet. Maybe instead of worrying about the lines and boundaries, I could take a note out of Gracie's book and live in the moment.

"If you get to know about me, then I get to know about you," I said, my voice softer. "Your girlfriend should know the things you like."

He looked away, his jaw tightening for a second, but he couldn't hide the slight flash of surprise—or maybe relief. My heart clenched, wondering how long he'd been holding back his own wants.

"What's your favorite color?" I asked, hoping to keep the mood from turning sour.

His eyes snapped back to me, his tone confident—assured. "Yellow."

"Really?" I raised a brow in surprise. "Most guys say blue or green. Or black." I played with the collar of his shirt. "Yellow isn't common."

"It's a recent thing."

I laughed. "A new favorite color? At what? Twenty-five? Who picks a new color as an adult?"

His expression softened, and he leaned a little closer, the warmth of his breath tickling my skin. "Yellow reminds me of sunshine. That's why it's my favorite color now."

Sunshine.

Time seemed to halt. He'd said the nickname casually before, yet I'd never considered that it might have some meaning.

"Why Sunshine?" I asked, barely able to remember how to breathe.

He hesitated long enough that I thought he wouldn't answer. "Because the first time I heard you laugh, it reminded me of the warmth on my skin when the sun hits my face," he said softly, his voice a little rough around the edges, like he wasn't used to saying things like this.

Something inside me melted.

It felt terrifyingly real, more than anything I'd expected from this arrangement. On the one hand, I wanted more moments like this, more glimpses of the man behind that practiced public façade, but on the other, it went against everything I'd had planned.

His touch broke me from the inner turmoil. Without a word, he scooped me up like I weighed nothing, and I instinctively wrapped my arms around his neck as he carried me down a hall.

"Dalton, I can walk," I protested, but it didn't carry much bite.

"I know."

I didn't argue. Instead, I let myself settle into his arms, feeling the steady thrum of his heartbeat. He pushed open a door with his shoulder, revealing a guest bedroom as meticulously decorated as the rest of the place.

"Stay here," he said, setting me down on the navy duvet before disappearing.

I am playing with fire.

Silky fabric enveloped me as I flopped back, covering my face with my hands, hoping that all my questions and concerns would be answered when I pulled them away, but it didn't happen. The little voice in my head telling me to say "fuck it" and throw myself at him was getting louder and louder, though.

"Figured you'd want something comfortable," he said from the doorway, watching me with quiet intensity. I reached for the worn gray shirt he held out.

"Thank you."

I clutched the soft fabric in my hands, watching him take a small step forward. For a moment, I thought he might lean down and kiss me. My breath hitched, and I felt my pulse race as his fingers brushed my chin, tilting it up ever so slightly.

"Goodnight, Sunshine."

His lips pressed gently against my forehead again, thumb grazing my cheek one last time before he stepped back and left.

Like he hadn't just sent me further into a spiral.

What the hell?

Was this what it was like to have blue balls? I didn't even have a vibrator here to help relieve the tension he'd built up. A part of me wanted to yell after him. To demand he get his firm ass back here and give me something dirtier than a sweet forehead kiss. He had to know that every nerve in my body was buzzing with anticipation for something more.

But the other half was thankful he'd stepped away.

Why did he have to be such a good guy? Why did he have to make me *like* him and not just lust after him? Because just wanting to have sex, I could get behind. I could emotionally detach from a hookup arrangement. Get him to give me amazing orgasms and then bounce.

But liking him as a person? Fuck, that was different territory.

I tugged off my clothes, pulled on his soft, oversized shirt, and slipped beneath the covers, wrapped in his scent. My mind kept whirling, caught between wanting more, and fearing what that more might mean, as I drifted off to sleep.

DALTON
DOWN BAD & HORNY

MY FAKE GIRLFRIEND was sleeping in my guest bedroom.

What I'd give for her to be *not* sleeping in mine.

What I'd give for her to actually *be* mine...

Fuck.

Why did I only kiss her on the head?

DALTON

WHEN THE SCENE IS HOT, BUT IT ALSO MAKES YOU GO "AWW…"

SLEEP HAD EVADED me for hours after I'd shown Ari to the guest room—to her room. She didn't know it yet, but there was no way I was letting her go back to sleeping on a couch, or at least not for long. Not when I had an apartment that was far too large for just myself.

The only reason I lived in the Museum Building was because of my dad. He was in the other apartment on this floor. Not that I ever saw him. When he told me about the spot after my breakup, I thought it would be a good way for us to spend more time together, maybe do dinners like I did with Mom.

But I'd been here for months and had yet to even see him in the building.

I released a huff of breath, kicking off the sheets I'd managed to tangle up in my legs from all the tossing and turning I'd done. If I thought falling asleep to thoughts of Ari was hard, it was an entirely different ball game knowing she was across the hall, sleeping under the same roof.

I'd gotten up a dozen times tempted to ask her to join me in my bed.

The glow from my alarm clock was the only thing visible through the blackout curtains. The clock read seven in the morning, which was pretty late for me to just be waking up, even for a Saturday.

Groaning, I sat up in bed, my body protesting the shift, and quickly realized that walking around in just my briefs wasn't exactly an option with Ari here. Swearing under my breath, I grabbed a pair of sweatpants, half-scowling at the morning wood I'd have to deal with before I faced her. Resigned, I reached for my phone, unable to resist any longer, and typed out a quick text.

ME:

Morning, Sunshine. How'd you sleep?

I stared at the screen, feeling ridiculous, like a teenager with a crush.

The nerves ratcheted up higher, waiting for Ari's response. What if she'd already left?

ARI:

What the hell is this bed made out of?
Angel wings? I've never slept in anything
so soft.

ARI:

You should shave your legs just so you
can rub them back and forth on these
sheets. I'm telling you, it's like heaven.

I laughed, realizing I hadn't woken up like this in years —grinning, even if it was just at my phone. I was addicted to her sense of humor and that perfect mix of ball-busting and unhinged. For all the money in the world, I'd never be able to guess what she'd say next.

There were some things I'd like to hear her say, though.

ARI:

Want breakfast?

I smirked, knowing exactly how I was going to answer that question.

ME:

Yeah, I can think of something I'd like to eat this morning…

My dick twitched like a damn puppy that needed attention, as if I could forget that I still had that *little* problem to take care of.

The guest bedroom door flung open, and I heard the light patter of bare feet approaching my room. But then… silence.

"You gonna knock or stand there all morning, Ari?" I yelled, standing up and adjusting myself under the sweats.

"Well, what's the point of knocking now?" she called back.

"Because," I pulled the door open, looking down at her perfectly messy hair and the oversized shirt she wore—*my* shirt—falling over her bare thighs. "That's the polite thing roommates do," I practically growled at her, too distracted by the sight of her wearing that shirt. "Turn around, Ariella."

Her dainty nose scrunched in confusion at the command, oblivious to the fact that I wanted to wrap my arm around her waist and throw her on my bed.

"First of all, we're not roommates."

"We are."

"We're not. And why?" she argued, crossing her arms over her chest. The movement pressed my shirt closer to her body, and I realized she wasn't wearing a bra.

I braced an arm on the doorframe, leaning close enough to catch a faint whiff of her coconut scent. "Because you're wearing my shirt."

"Well, no shit, Sherlock. You knew this." She rolled her eyes, but I caught the darkening of the apples of her cheeks.

"Yeah, but I forgot I'd given you one of my college hockey shirts—one that has my last name on the back—and I want to see how you look with it." I twirled a finger, indicating I wanted to see her from behind.

And bent over.

She turned her head, trying to read over her shoulder the letters plastered there. "It doesn't say, Langley," she said as I physically moved her where I wanted as she tried to read the back of her shirt like a cat chasing its tail, but I stopped and bit down on my lip when I saw it.

Thatcher

Fuck. I got now why some of the guys on the team insisted their partners wear their jerseys.

"I didn't go by Langley in college," I said, still distracted.

God, she was beautiful in the morning, too. I doubted there was ever a time she wasn't gorgeous, if I was being honest.

"Is that why the guys never call you by your last name?" she asked.

"Yeah," I scratched at the back of my neck. "I played under Thatcher my whole life since it's my mom's maiden name, but uh, when my dad found me again, he insisted I play under the Langley name. Carry on the legacy." My stomach turned like it did every time I thought about this subject.

Her eyes narrowed, a look of irritation passing over her face, and my chest ached at the idea of disappointing her.

Not living up to the expectations of the people I cared about was my worst fear. One night, after too much whiskey, I'd told Christian I thought my dad left because I wasn't good enough. Fucker read me the riot act about how that wasn't true, but that seed of doubt took root years before, and I didn't think I'd ever rid the soil of those gangly threads.

Being a disappointment...it was my Achilles heel.

Now Ari had managed to make it onto my short list of people I cared for, and what she thought mattered.

"Did he ask you if that's what you wanted?" Her tone was laced with irritation.

"What?" The question caught me off guard. I opened my mouth, but no words came out. She stood there, hands firmly on her hips, radiating so much attitude and waiting like she would pry the answer out of me if she had to.

"Uh...no," I admitted, finally. "He just said—" I cut myself off, not wanting to recount my dad's exact words, knowing it wouldn't help his case. "Anyway, let's eat before we've got to go," I mumbled, deflecting.

Ari's lips pressed into a thin line, and for a second, I thought she'd push it further. My whole body tensed, bracing for whatever she'd say next. For years, I'd defended my dad against everything, keeping him off-limits in conversation with anyone, especially with my mom. Understandably, what he'd done to her was shitty, but my stomach soured every time I thought to say something bad about the man. The idea of hearing Ari criticize him... I wasn't sure how I'd react.

The proverbial blow I'd prepped for never came. Instead, Ari gave a curt nod, turned on her heel, and marched away toward the kitchen, yelling out over her shoulder.

"I hope your fridge is stocked better than your drink one is, Thatcher. I'm cooking you *huevos rancheros*."

I trailed after her, fighting a grin at her casual use of my name.

"So, does this mean you're accepting the roommate title?" I teased, watching her move through the kitchen like she belonged there.

She looked back at me with a smirk, rolling her eyes as she opened the fridge. "Let's not get ahead of ourselves. I'm just borrowing your kitchen—and maybe a few eggs. If I were your roommate, there'd be a dresser stuffed with leggings and sports bras, and you'd find ten different bottles of Tapatío in the pantry."

I chuckled, leaning against the counter, watching her with that stubborn, determined look on her face as she gathered ingredients.

She was joking now, but she had no idea how serious I was about making that threat a reality.

TWENTY-EIGHT

ARIELLA

THE CARDS SAY, YOU SHOULD FIGHT YOUR FATHER.

WHAT THE *FUCK* was I doing?

I'd been in my office for the last hour, attempting to finalize athlete profiles. Ice practices were already ramping up, and I liked to tailor my programs to emphasize athlete recovery while still building strength.

Hockey season was grueling on the body. Not only the game itself, but the schedule. Throw in potential injuries...all the planning on what I could do to prepare my players kept me busy. Problem was, work wasn't the only thing occupying my mind this Thursday evening.

Dalton and I had spent all day Saturday together, and then I'd avoided him like the plague on Sunday because I still had no damn clue how to sort out my feelings about him or whatever it was we were supposed to be.

Why face your emotions and work through things when you could ignore them and pretend there weren't Dalton-sized holes starting to form in the wall you'd built around your heart?

I could only patch them up so quickly.

Hot asshole? That I could walk away from easily.

But an attentive man who seemed to know me like the back of his hand? Fuck, that was harder to keep at bay.

Even after my radio silence, he'd still showed up Monday morning, leaning against Betty's pale blue body with a coffee and a smile. A smile that quickly turned into a frown when he saw that my breakfast was a protein bar.

Then Tuesday, and every day after, he was waiting with a breakfast burrito in hand, purchased from the spot I'd taken him to that first night.

It wasn't just him showing up, though. The man managed to touch me every chance he got when we were together, almost like he was making sure I was still there. A hand at my lower back, his arm brushing mine, even his fingers grazing any bare skin they could find.

I shook off the thoughts, trying to focus back on the notes. Lost in the quiet, I didn't even notice someone standing at my office door until a smooth voice cut through my concentration.

"Ms. Contreras, hard at work, I see."

I glanced up to find Vincent Langley leaning against the doorframe. I was struck by how different he was from his son. Sure, there were similarities, looks-wise, between him and Dalton, but the dead-eyed smile he gave me made them look worlds different. Thanks to Gracie's FBI-level deep-dive research on the man, I'd seen his photos online, but meeting him in person had me instinctively straightening in my seat, slipping into full professionalism mode.

"Mr. Langley," I replied, standing and extending a hand. "So nice to meet you. And yes, there's a lot to prepare before the preseason ramps up."

He strode in, glancing around my office with a gaze that felt too assessing, too sharp. I clocked the power move right away when he made me wait there with my arm extended, taking his time to accept the gesture. It took everything in me not to roll my eyes and to keep the polite smile plastered on my face when he wrapped his hand around mine, squeezing it as if we were doing a grip strength test.

I was a fan of a firm shake as much as the next person, but at some point you were overcompensating for something if you felt the need to squeeze the shit out of the other person's hand.

His jaw ticked when I didn't react or relent, but he let go, and I sat back down.

You're trying to keep your job, not lose it faster, Ari.

"I can see why Dalton's been talking so much about you. Very dedicated. Committed." The words were complimentary, but something about them felt like a hidden barb. "Not many people around here put in the same level of work ethic. It's refreshing to see."

I kept my expression neutral, but a prickle of unease crawled up my spine. Dalton never spoke poorly of his father, and the rest of the team didn't speak about Mr. Langley period, so I had no reason to have my guard up. Still, the unease was there, and I knew better than to ignore my intuition.

Something told me Vincent Langley didn't make casual visits to employees' offices. I'd been here three weeks, and he hadn't once bothered to meet me. For days, I'd expected to be called into his office after the HR incident, or at the very least after the news spread of Dalton and I dating, but *nada*. Yet here he was now?

"Thank you. My priority is that the team has the best support possible off the ice so they can perform on the ice as needed."

"Oh, absolutely," he agreed, leaning on the edge of my desk in a way that felt too close. "It's admirable, really. You remind me of myself, determined to get things done right." I nearly suffocated under the charisma he had dialed up as he peered down at me.

What the hell was going on?

"Thank you, sir. I'm honored to be a part of the Desperados organization and to showcase what I can bring to the team."

A faint smile tugged at the corner of his mouth, a cunning glint in his eyes. This was a man who wanted something, and now I was thoroughly on the defensive. "You know, I wasn't sure, but I think it could be a good thing Dalton's taken to you so well." He chuckled as if it were an inside joke. "He could benefit from someone reminding him what hard work and focus looks like."

I felt my spine straighten involuntarily at the backhanded compliment, trying to keep my face as impassive as possible. Was he testing me to see if I'd say anything about how he spoke about his son? Or was he just a dick?

Probably both.

"All due respect, Mr. Langley, but I don't think he needs any reminders from me. Dalton is one of the hardest-working people I've coached. He's a natural leader, and his dedication is inspiring. You should be proud."

There was a little more edge to the last part of my sentence than I'd meant, so I slapped on my sweetest smile, hoping he wouldn't notice. Because while his comment rubbed me the wrong way, this man still held my career's fate in his hands.

His eyes narrowed, the pleasant mask cracking briefly before it was back in place as if nothing happened. The chuckle he let out was so fake it was pathetic. "Of course. I only meant that Dalton has always been...well, susceptible to certain distractions, and I trust that you would want what's best for him and the team. You know how relationships can complicate things..." the words trailed off.

Maybe I'd been reading too many mafia books, because something about the way he spoke made me feel like I was being threatened.

"Don't worry, Mr. Langley. Our relationship won't get in the way of our careers."

He nodded but didn't look satisfied with my response. "That can be a difficult thing to balance. Emma managed to do a wonderful job. She was...quite the woman. You know all about Dalton and Emma, right?"

Heat crawled up my neck. Dalton's dad was definitely a dick.

My jaw worked overtime to keep my mouth shut so I didn't tell him what an asshole move it was to bring his son's ex up. Not that he needed to hear it—he knew what he was doing. The smug look on his face shown like a neon sign reading "guilty."

"Yes, we've met, actually. Gave her eyesight advice."

"She was perfect for him," he continued, like I hadn't spoken. "Emma understood the world of hockey, as a successful sports reporter. Was always there in the stands, proudly wearing his jersey. Knew exactly how to carry herself in front of the media, of course. Tall, beautiful girl. Made him look good."

He glanced at me, gauging my reaction. But if he was hoping to find tears in my eyes thanks to his cutting words, he had the wrong bitch.

"Wow, sounds like she must have really messed up to make your son not want to be with someone so *perfect*," I said, flipping him off from under the desk.

He cleared his throat, clearly caught off guard by the fact that I wasn't curled in on myself, feeling inadequate. Part of me wanted to know what he'd been planning to say if I'd melted into a puddle of self-consciousness. No wonder he liked Emma so much—they were two peas in a pod with how they treated people.

"Yes, well, I only bring this up because the media loves her. She's one of their own. Everyone loved seeing Emma and Dalton together, and they're bound to compare you two when they see you tomorrow."

Bullshit. He was bringing up my boyfriend's ex in some gracious act of *warning*? Unlikely.

"Thank you for the heads-up, Mr. Langley," I said, voice cool and unwavering. "But I'm confident I can handle any comparisons. As a woman in a male-dominated field, I've learned to grow a thick skin and be confident in what *I* can do, rather than worrying about what someone else is doing. And, quite frankly, the only person I care about preferring me is Dalton."

His smile froze for a beat before he nodded, the collected façade slipping. "G...good. I like to hear that. If you need resources or additional support, just let me know. We take care of our own here."

"Thank you, I'll keep that in mind," I replied smoothly, though his offer felt like it came with strings attached.

"I'll be around for Media Day, of course," he said, adjusting his suit jacket. "I look forward to seeing how you and Dalton handle yourselves. You're part of the Desperados family now, Ms. Contreras. I trust you'll represent us well."

Standing, I nodded to him, not chancing another of his handshakes. "Absolutely."

I held his gaze as he gave me a final assessing look before striding out.

Silence settled back into the office, and I let out a breath, feeling like I could finally think straight.

The audacity of that man to bring up Dalton's ex.

The entire interaction felt like he was testing for weaknesses to exploit. If he thought I'd crumble at the mention of a tall blonde who treated people like shit, he had no idea who he was dealing with.

Fuck, I need to lift some shit.

TWENTY-NINE

DALTON

HIP THRUST ME, DADDY

THE CLANG of metal plates reverberated through the gym as I stepped inside. The sharp tang of rubber mats and chalk hit me immediately, grounding me in the familiar space.

It didn't take long to find her.

Ari was at the squat rack, a barbell loaded with what looked like twice her body weight resting across her shoulders. Her form was perfect, her legs steady as she lowered herself into a deep squat, the muscles in her thighs and glutes flexing with the movement. My mouth went dry. She stood, her back to me, completely focused on her set.

She hadn't noticed me yet, which gave me a moment to take her in.

She wore those damn leggings again. The ones that should've been illegal for how well they fit her, paired with a sports bra that showed off the curve of her shoulders and the definition in her arms.

I had no right to be staring, but fuck if I could stop.

Watching her in her element, strong and unshakable, did things to me.

"You were supposed to meet me in the garage." My voice echoed in the mostly empty gym, making her freeze mid-rep.

She racked the barbell with a clang, then turned, wiping her forehead with the back of her hand. "I needed to blow off some steam," she said, her voice breathless but steady.

I raised a brow, crossing my arms as I leaned against the nearest machine. "So, you ditched me for squats?"

"I didn't ditch you. I just prioritized my mental health. Squats pair well with therapy."

There was a thread of something vulnerable beneath the teasing tone, and I wanted to know what it was that was bothering her. But that would require a careful approach.

"Fine," I said, pushing off the machine and moving closer. "But if you're going to make me wait, at least make it worth my while. Show me what you've got."

"Careful what you ask for." She gestured toward the bench and the loaded barbell nearby. "I was about to do hip thrusts."

Of course she was.

As if I hadn't already been struggling to keep my thoughts from going south.

"You're trying to kill me."

Her grin widened as she slid to the floor. "You're the one who wanted to watch. Don't blame me if you can't handle it."

I couldn't even respond. My brain short-circuited as

she rolled the bar toward her, positioning it across her hips. Her movements were precise and deliberate. Fuck, she was fully aware of how much power she held in every inch of her body. With her feet braced, she drove her hips upward, the barbell rising with her as her glutes contracted at the top.

My jaw clenched as I tried to tamp down how my body reacted to seeing her. Because as much as I enjoyed the view, I knew something was on her mind, and my cock tenting in my tiny shorts didn't help relay the message that I wanted to be there for her.

"You okay?" I asked, leaning against the rack as she set the bar down after another handful of reps.

"Yeah. Why wouldn't I be?" she asked, wiping her forehead with the back of her hand, avoiding my gaze.

"Bullshit." Her head snapped up, mouth parted in shock that I'd called her out. "When I'm blowing off steam this hard, something's usually up."

"Well, we're not the same person," she threw back, but there wasn't much heat on the words.

"Tell me I'm wrong."

She hesitated, her fingers tightening slightly on the bar. "Your dad stopped by earlier," she finally admitted. "To introduce himself."

My brows knit together. That wasn't totally unusual. He was the team owner, and they were bound to meet eventually, but there was something in her voice that I couldn't quite place. "How did it go?"

She broke eye contact, staring at her white Chuck Taylors. "Fine. He said he's looking forward to Media Day."

I was smart enough to know that 'fine' was not-so-secret code for not fucking good. "What else did he say?" I pressed, pushing off the rack to move closer.

She shrugged, but the movement was stiff. "Nothing too surprising. Mostly that he's excited to see how we handle ourselves for the cameras." She hesitated before adding, "He also told me how great Emma was. How well-loved you two were by the public eye."

Her words hit like a gut punch, and my jaw tightened. "He said that to you?"

"And I quote, 'She was perfect for him.'"

A bitter laugh escaped me. "Like he was even around enough to know," I muttered, the resentment bubbling to the surface. His praise of Emma was another reminder of how little he truly understood me.

Ari shifted, her gaze flicking to mine. "Sorry I'll never sit in the stands and wear your jersey. I'm sure that bothers you. I mean, you even tried to make it one of our rules—"

"Stop." I crouched in front of her, one hand bracing on the bench while the other tipped her chin to face me. Her eyes widened slightly, and I softened my tone.

"I'm sorry he did that to you. But listen to me." I cupped her face, needing to touch her. "Emma wasn't perfect for me. Not even close. She didn't support me. She supported the idea of what being with me gave her. The money, the attention, the title of being a WAG." I slid my thumb across her cheek, the roughness of the pad contrasting against her soft skin. "You don't give a shit about any of that. You're there for me in ways that actually matter. You push me to be better, you call me out when I need it, and…" Swallowing hard, I forced myself to say it. "I know you like me for me. Not the player, not the paycheck. Just me. He was right. You're nothing like her, and that's my favorite part. Understand?"

Her lips parted slightly, her expression faltering as she nodded her head.

"I've met Emma, and there's no way I feel the need to try and compete with her."

I smirked, recognizing her tactic to avoid talking about emotions, but deciding to let her have it—for now. "Good. Because if anyone should be trying to live up to someone, it's the other way around."

I stood, offering her a hand. She let me pull her to her feet.

"Thanks, Dalton," she said, her eyes saying more than her lips were. Now I was the one running from the emotions hanging in the air. I pulled my gaze away. "Alright, now it's my turn to work off some steam," I said, dropping to the floor and moving to where she'd just vacated. Because even though I was smiling at her, I was fucking pissed to hear my dad had cornered her in her office and decided to talk about how great my ex supposedly was.

"You going to just stand there or load more weight on the bar?" I taunted, drinking her in from where she stood above me.

God, she was mesmerizing. Sweat glistened on her well-muscled body. She'd put in years of discipline, and it showed, but the sexiest part wasn't how she looked. It was what she could do with that damn body. How strong and resilient she was, both mentally and physically.

She was as much of an athlete as I was.

"You want more, Dalt?" Her voice broke me from my drool session over her toned hamstrings.

As a response, I hip thrust a rep with my hands behind my head. "Give it to me, Sunshine."

My dick hardened at her tongue swiping along her full bottom lip.

That's going to feel great against the metal bar.

Instead of walking toward the rack of bumper plates, she moved in closer. I forgot how to breathe when she swung her leg over, positioning herself so she was straddling my body, ass sitting on the padded part of the bar—right above my cock.

Calloused hands landed on my shoulder, coconut invading my senses. She would manage to smell delicious even while working out.

"There's some more weight on the bar for you. Think you can hip thrust me?"

I reached up and turned my hat around because there was no way my mouth wouldn't find its way to her body. I'd been dreaming about it since that night in Betty, and then sleeping across the hall from her had been torture, but I hadn't wanted to push too far. I'd be damned if my hat was going to cock block me now that all the walls were coming down.

"How many thrusts do you want, Coach?" I asked already moving.

The top of the movement put her chest in perfect alignment with my mouth, and the sweat running in the valley of her breasts called to me like a siren's song. I was moving before I could think better of it. Saltiness coated my tongue as I licked up her chest, starting slightly below where her sports bra covered.

The gasp of surprise, followed by a breathy drop of my name, only fueled me. She was going to leave marks with how tightly she gripped my shoulders, but I didn't give a shit. Every rep I licked and kissed at a new section of her body, too far gone to put the breaks on the runaway train that was my libido.

Eight reps came and went too quickly, but I didn't care. I was ready to burn my fucking legs out just to keep tasting her.

"You've gotta stop, Dalton. You're going to injure yourself," she pleaded, sounding as disappointed as I felt.

I set her and the bar down, before pulling her into my lap.

"Look how wild you drive me, Sunshine," I breathed, pushing her down on the obvious bulge. Living for the moan she let out as her eyelids fluttered closed.

So much for not scaring her away, but I was too worked up not to show her the truth.

My hand slid to her waist, gripping her like she might disappear if I let go. Her long locks grazed my legs as she tipped her head back, letting out a soft "fuck." The sight of her pulse pounding in her throat made me lose my mind.

Every curve of her body fit against mine like she was made for me.

"Dalton," she whispered, her voice laced with want. "I—"

The sound of the gym door slamming open shattered the moment. We were being edged by the Universe.

"Hey, Cap," Jimenez's booming voice echoed through

the room, followed by the distinctive shuffle of feet on the rubber flooring. "You left your keys in—oh, shit."

Ari and I sprang apart, scrambling to stand. Her face turned crimson, her hand flying to smooth her hair, like that would erase the evidence of what had almost happened. I took a step back, trying to get my breathing under control while sending my best friend a death glare, promising a beat-down on the ice next practice.

Jimenez froze mid-step, keys dangling from his hand and his mouth agape as he looked between us.

"Whoa. Didn't mean to interrupt...whatever y'all were doing."

"Yeah, no shit," I growled. "What the hell? Don't you knock?"

"In a gym?" he shot back, clearly trying not to laugh. "Sorry, didn't realize this was a private session."

Ari groaned, covering her face with her hands. "Oh my god. I need to leave. Immediately."

"No one's leaving," I said firmly, pointing a finger at Jimenez. "Except him."

He held up his hands in mock surrender, his grin unapologetic. "Relax, man. I was just dropping off your keys. But hey, good for you, Coach. Didn't know you had it in you."

"Out," I barked.

He winked at Ari on his way out, earning him another murderous glare from me. "Later, lovebirds."

The door clicked shut behind him, leaving the two of us in awkward silence. I turned to Ari, who was now pacing in a small circle, her face still bright red. I desperately wanted to pick up from where we'd left off, but I could see by her panic that the moment had passed. Again.

"I can't believe that just happened," she said, her voice muffled by her hands. "I'm going to die. Right here. Please bury me under the squat rack."

"Darlin'," I said gently, stepping in front of her and prying her hands away from her face. "Hey, it's fine. Jimenez is an idiot, but he's harmless."

Her eyes met mine, still wide with embarrassment. "He's never going to let this go, is he?"

A smile tugged at the corner of my mouth. "Not a fucking chance. But I will kill him if he says anything to anyone."

That earned me a small laugh, and I felt some of the tension ease. "Can I help?"

"Of course." I tapped on her temple. "We're going to need all that murder show knowledge you've got up there."

She rolled her eyes, but the corners of her mouth were tipped up in a smile. "You're lucky you're cute. Otherwise, I'd be halfway out of here by now."

I chuckled, relieved to see her mood lifting. "You're not going anywhere but into the passenger seat of my car."

Picking up our bags, I led her out of the gym, my hand at the small of her back, as I tried like hell to ignore the worst fucking case of blue balls I'd ever experienced.

THIRTY

DALTON

PREACH, MAMI!

MEDIA DAY PREP was in full swing when we made our way through the side entrance of the arena. The rink was buzzing with activity. Photographers, marketing teams, and press were setting up, and I was about to head to where Jimenez and the rest of the team were gathering when a loud voice cut through the crowd behind us.

"Okay, where are all the hot men?" A woman with the blunt black bob came storming in, juggling a drink carrier loaded with coffees in one hand and an armful of chaos in the other. "So you're the fine ass white boy that has my cousin's *chonies* all wadded up in a knot," she said, dragging her eyes down my body in an assessing manner, stopping at my legs. "Do you have any thigh tattoos? Because if not, you really should reconsider it, she loves—"

Whatever else she was going to say was cut off when Ari stepped up and slapped a hand over the woman's mouth, looking mortified.

"*Ya cállate,*" she ground out, voice low, a warning in

her tone. But all the woman did was roll her eyes in false innocence.

Monroe stormed over, taking in the scene with a raised brow, clearly unimpressed.

"Everyone, this is my cousin Graciella," Ari said, her hand still pressed to her cousin's mouth.

"This isn't *Bring a Family Member to Work Day*, Contreras," Josh said in his usual gruff tone, crossing his arms over his chest and glaring.

Gracie peeled Ari's hand from her mouth. "Well, lucky for you, I'm here to do my job," she said with a smile, clearly unfazed by his grumpiness.

Monroe raised an eyebrow, nodding toward the coffee carrier and arm full of stuff. "What job's that? Crafts services?"

"No, actually," she said, not missing a beat. "I work in sports marketing, specializing in content." She flashed her pass in Monroe's face, coming within inches of hitting him. I tried not to laugh. "See, I was invited, thank you very much. Usually, it's my job to make people like *you* look better. Most of the time, I charge for this advice, but you look like you could use it, so here's a freebie. If you smiled more, they wouldn't think you're part bear."

The words were kind, hell even her tone was, but there was still something in her delivery that made it undeniable that she was telling him to go fuck himself.

Monroe's scowl deepened, but her grin only widened.

Ari shook her head. "Okay, gotta go," she said, pulling her cousin behind her.

I chuckled, watching Monroe's face twitch as Gracie winked at him over her shoulder.

She'd eat him alive. One sunny smile at a time.

I'D FORGOTTEN how loud the chatter in the press room was. The heat from the lights, the constant shutter clicks, and the conversations could all be overwhelming if you weren't used to it. We all shuffled behind the cloth table lined with mics. Jimenez and I settled into our seats next to Ari and Monroe, whose scowl only deepened when he caught sight of Gracie among the reporters, exaggeratedly miming for him to smile.

My attention kept drifting back to Ari, seated at my side.

She was gorgeous, seated in front of the Dallas Desperados logo, exuding confidence in her hot pink suit. Seeing her there did something to me. A swell of pride that was almost overwhelming. Hell, maybe I wanted *her* name plastered across my jersey. Or maybe a big foam finger I could wave that said "#1 Coach" just to show how damn proud I was.

I leaned over, my hand finding her knee under the table. "Ready for this?" I murmured, giving her a gentle squeeze. I caught her nod in my peripheral vision. "You're going to do great. I'm here to support you. Always. I want you to succeed."

In everything.

She looked composed and radiant, but I knew she was nervous. I started tracing small shapes on her thigh, hoping to ease the tension causing her shoulders to ride up near her ears.

Gracie flashed us a big thumbs up as the questions began.

Most focused on the team's plans for the season, our training schedule, and the roster, but then they made a shift toward the newest coaching member on staff, and I squeezed her knee.

One of the reporters in the front row leaned forward. "Dalton, how's the team handling the new training regimen under Ms. Contreras' leadership? Any noticeable changes yet?"

I straightened, giving a quick, confident smile. "Honestly? Yeah, we're already seeing a difference. She's bringing a new level of intensity and precision to our training. Her focus on injury prevention has us all feeling sharper and healthier. I think you'll see a team that's faster and stronger this season, all thanks to her."

A few reporters scribbled notes, clearly intrigued, and I could feel her eyes on me, a small, appreciative smile playing at her lips.

I wasn't kissing her ass, either. It was all true. Her focus on the functional training was resulting in real improvements on the ice. She didn't give a shit what we could bench. She wanted to see how well we could explode up out of a squat.

Another hand went up.

"Jimenez, what's been the toughest adjustment so far with the new program?"

He leaned to his mic, grinning. "Well, I'll tell you, she doesn't mess around. Brutal when it comes to running a tight ship." He glanced at her with a mischievous smile. "Honestly, I shouldn't have expected anything less from a Latina woman. Probably no one better equipped to handle a bunch of idiots like us." He shifted his attention back to the crowd of reporters, turning on the charm. "But the real challenge? The intensity. She has us pushing limits we didn't know we had. I had no idea three-pound weights could be so brutal! She's got us doing these front delt raises that make it hard for me to turn my steering wheel when I drive home."

The room broke out in laughter. Even the corner of Monroe's mouth twitched.

Gracie's smile was practically a spotlight in the crowd, beaming over the praise her cousin was getting. Hell, I was beaming. I could feel the ache in my cheeks from smiling so hard.

But the moment a familiar blonde woman stood up in the back row, my stomach dropped. *What the hell was she doing here?* Media Day was a closed event where only press from an approved list was invited, and I'd made it very clear *she* was not one of the approved.

Emma peered over the top of her notepad with that too-sweet smile plastered on her face as she adjusted her mic before speaking.

"So, Dalton. How are you feeling going into this season? Do you think the team is ready to support you in the way you deserve as a star player?"

I held back a wince at her voice.

Ariella's hand found mine under the table. Now she was the one giving me the encouraging squeeze. Or maybe she was so pissed she needed something to hold on to because her grip didn't let up.

"Oh, but the no ex-relationships rule doesn't apply to this?" she muttered under her breath. I coughed to cover up my laugh, shaking my head at the smirk on Ari's face, pleased that neither of us was giving Emma the reaction she was so clearly looking for.

I schooled my features before answering, the years of media training my father put me through kicking in. I was going to treat Emma like any other reporter and be professional.

"Every win and loss is earned as a team. We're there for each other, especially when someone's having an off game, including me." I meant it. My teammates meant everything to me, especially Jimenez, who'd always had my back. I might play well, but I wasn't anything without the rest of them.

"Sure," she said, her tone dripping with feigned innocence, "but last season, you didn't seem to have as many 'off nights' as your teammates. You're always on top of your game. It's impressive." She leaned forward a little, looking at me with a flirtatious smile, laying it on thick.

What the hell?

"Like I said, we're only as strong as we are together," I replied firmly. "That's the beauty of this team. We lift each other up. It's what gives us our edge."

"Of course." My stomach turned at the smile that spread across Emma's face as she shifted her attention to Ari. "This question is for Ms. Contreras. As the new strength and conditioning head coach, what do you think you bring to a team of this caliber? Are you truly qualified for this role? What if the team suffers because of your...in-adequacies?" Her lips twisted slightly as she pressed on, barely hiding her disdain.

My grip tightened around the mic, words ready to fire, and I could sense my teammates around me preparing to leap into this attack, too.

"Hey—"

Ari cut in over at least four male voices, her tone icy enough to freeze over the rink.

"I find it disappointing that a fellow woman would choose to tear another down rather than uplift." Her voice was calm, and the room went still. Emma's smug expression faltered slightly at the call out. "If I'm not mistaken, your question implies doubt in my qualifications because I'm not a man, which is an irrelevant qualification for this position. So, let me clarify what experience I have that *actually* matters. I graduated at the top of my class, summa cum laude, as a first-generation Mexican-American college graduate. I bring years of expertise in high-intensity training, strength conditioning, and injury prevention. I've dedicated my career thus far to building resilience in athletes, on and off the ice. And I know exactly what this team needs to reach peak performance because I know my players. Any other questions?" Pride burned in my chest.

Gracie stood, glaring at Emma in a way that scared even me before turning to her cousin. "Ms. Contreras, as a leader and role model in a traditionally male-dominated space, what's your message to women wanting to break into this field?" She paused, smile widening. "Besides not to be an asshole to fellow women."

Monroe made a noise that sounded oddly like a laugh but also like he might be choking to death.

Ari smirked before answering. "I'd say, push boundaries. Don't let stereotypes define you. Cultural, gender-based, or anything in between. Find allies who support your vision, and don't let fear keep you out of spaces you're more than capable of being in. That you belong in. Take up space because you deserve to."

Gracie broke into applause, smacking nearby reporters on the shoulder if they didn't join in quickly enough for her liking, and I could tell that Ari's cousin and I were going to get along just fine.

Meanwhile, Ari's cheeks matched her suit, and she shot daggers at Gracie for causing a scene.

I leaned over, my voice low in her ear. "You deserve every bit of this. You're amazing."

She glanced over, and our eyes locked, caught in a moment that felt like it was just for us despite the crowd watching. If we weren't in front of a room full of people, I'd have kissed her right then.

The lines between real and pretend weren't blurred—they'd disappeared completely. I wasn't sure they'd ever been there for me.

I was all in, and I wanted her for as long as she'd have me.

That last thought hit me like a punch in the gut. *How long would that be?* The question lingered, pulling at something raw and vulnerable inside me.

But before I could dwell on it too long, Emma stood again, barely contained smugness plastered on her face.

She held up her tablet, displaying a photo of Ari and me at In-N-Out.

"But isn't it convenient that she landed her position shortly after you began seeing each other?" Her tone was loaded, and she didn't even try to hide the implication. "Are you *really* saying her hiring had *nothing* to do with your relationship?"

What was her problem? We hadn't had any communication in months—not a text, a phone call, a fucking postcard—and now she was drowning me in compliments at the expense of my teammates and questioning Ariella's employment?

Ari's eyes narrowed, but this time, I did step in.

"Let me make this clear." I held Emma's gaze. "Ariella Contreras was hired by this organization solely because of her skills, experience, and the respect she's earned in this industry. She's one of the best at what she does, and every member of this team has already benefited from her approach and dedication." I worked hard to keep my anger in check, but I couldn't hide how I white-knuckled the mic. "My relationship with her has *zero* impact on her role here. And frankly, it's insulting to her to suggest otherwise. She didn't just 'land' her position. She earned it. So, to answer your question, no, our relationship had nothing to do with it."

Ari pried open the fist in my lap, intertwining her fingers with mine. Part of me had wondered if she'd be pissed that I spoke for her rather than letting her answer again, but when I turned, her eyes blazed with appreciation.

From the corner of my eye, I noticed Monroe leaning

forward in his seat, staring down my ex. "Just so we are clear, *I* hired Ms. Contreras well before she'd ever met Dalton. The next time you want to challenge someone's professional merit, I suggest you do it based on facts, not outdated or offensive assumptions. That's your whole damn job, right? The irony of you insinuating that she's unqualified, when you've come in here with baseless claims and personal vendettas."

Emma's face broke out in blotchy red patches. "I...well...she—"

"Sit down, Ms. Faulk. I think we've all heard enough from you," Monroe said, glaring until she complied before covering his mic and looking at me. "Why the fuck would they let your ex come to Media Day? Who do you think sent her?"

I wished I had an answer for him, but I didn't. Turning in time to see Emma slump back into her seat before glancing to the back of the room, I followed her line of sight, only to find my father leaning against the door-frame, watching the scene unfold with an expression I couldn't quite read.

That look in his eyes—it made my skin prickle.

Is she here because of him?

THIRTY-ONE

ARIELLA

THE MOUTH ON THIS MAN…

WE FILED OFFSTAGE, seeking refuge from the crowd in my office.

My body buzzed with the adrenaline of trying to keep my attitude in check that whole time. I'd be damned if I let someone who was clearly trying to rattle me succeed.

"What a cunt," Gracie exclaimed, storming in. "And that photo? Who the fuck cares about you two eating a burger? It wasn't like they caught him feeding you his protein-style meal."

Dalton choked, bending at the waist to try and catch his breath from the sudden burst of laughter. I should have warned him that her filter was nonexistent. In fact, that was her keeping it tame. Give her a few times of being around him, and she'd *vividly* walk through her horizontal tango escapades.

"*Ay*, Graciella." I pinched the bridge of my nose, fighting off my own laugh. It wasn't good to encourage her —it went straight to her head, and then suddenly, she thought she was a standup comedian.

She plopped down into a chair, making herself at home. "What? I'm just saying what we are all thinking."

A knock on the door killed our conversation.

"There you are, *son*." Vincent Langley said the word as if it were foreign to him. "Ah, and Ms. Contreras, you didn't do too bad up there." His smile widened, the edges sharp and predatorial. "Though I can't say I'm surprised that some questions rattled you. It's a different world when you're in the spotlight, isn't it?"

"I don't think she was rattled at all," Dalton folded his arms over his chest. "If anything, I'd say she did better than we could have expected given that Emma decided to show up."

Vincent's attention shifted Dalton, and the tension between them was palpable. "She's a reporter, Dalton. Is she just not supposed to do her job because you're dating Ms. Contreras?"

My eyes were pinging back and forth between the two men, and as much as I wanted to see Dalton tell his father he was a dick, I didn't want that to come as a result of him defending me. This was something the two of them needed to solve, and I didn't want to be the catalyst for a fight.

"Thank you for your support, Mr. Langley. I'm sure with more experience, I'll do even better," I said, cutting through the heavy silence that had settled over the room. I wasn't usually great at kissing ass, but I really put the effort in on that one.

Vincent's face morphed into a smug expression that told me he thought I was full of shit.

"Of course." He lingered a moment longer, his gaze

unwavering, as if waiting for me to slip up and call him out on the backhanded compliments.

When all I did was keep the fake smile that hurt the corners of my mouth, he gave a curt nod and strode out of my office.

The second he was out of earshot, Gracie let out a low whistle, shaking her head. "Your dad's got the charm of a rattlesnake." Dalton forced a smile, but the tension in his shoulders didn't ease. I shot her a glare, warning her from saying anything else. Her tone softened and she stood, placing a hand on his shoulder. "Don't worry, Dalty boy, if anyone can commiserate with having daddy issues, it's me," she said, patting him like he was a dog.

I gave her an appreciative smile, because I knew how much she hated talking about her relationship with her father.

"Anyway," she looped her bag around her shoulder, awkwardly walking towards the door. "I have work to do, and since Ariella won't let me date any of her players, there's really nothing else keeping me here, so *adiós*."

Dalton released a shaky breath when she left, closing the door behind her. His eyes were fixed on the floor, clouded with a mix of emotions I couldn't quite read. He seemed lost in thought, wrestling with something he couldn't, or maybe didn't want to, put into words. I rested a hand on his arm, hoping to offer some sort of comfort, but he just gave a sad, hollow laugh before plopping down in my chair. He cradled his head in his hands.

"You know, he's only been in my life a few years, and I just assumed that maybe he didn't know how to have a son after so many years apart. Ya know? That it would take time. That if I kept trying..."

The broken hope in his voice killed me.

I slipped into his lap, wrapping my arms around him. He tensed in surprise, as if he'd been so lost in thought he'd forgotten he wasn't alone, but then his strong arms encircled me. Latching on as if I were a lifeline, I swore he placed a kiss on the top of my head before resting his chin there. We sat there in a comfortable silence, nothing but the steady thump of his heart against my cheek.

I was bad at addressing my own emotions...I had no clue how to go about helping Dalton with his. But I wanted to try. I desperately wanted to be there for him, so I shoved away all of the panic that came with caring for him and what opening those doors would mean and was just...present.

"I think he's just worried about the season. I've just got to prove to him that I can date someone and still focus on the game." His voice was rough.

I tightened my grip when I heard how he tried to rationalize his father's treatment. He wasn't just trying to earn approval—he was trying to earn his father's love.

My heart hurt for him. While my family might not always understand or agree with my choices, their love was never conditional.

I'd never had to prove my worth to be a part of their lives.

"Dalton," I said softly, my voice catching, unsure how much I could even say. This wasn't my place. What right did I have to interfere with that relationship? We'd have to part ways eventually, and Vincent Langley would still be his father long after I was gone.

My gut clenched at that—everything about it felt sour and wrong. Tendrils of doubt about whether I truly needed to be alone to reach my dream seeped in, but Dalton's voice interrupted before I could fall down my own mental rabbit hole.

"Yeah, Sunshine?"

I shifted in his lap so I could look him in the eyes. "You're an incredible athlete. One of the best I've ever worked with. You're disciplined, talented, and this team? They're lucky to have you as their captain. You'll crush it this season, and your dad would be a fool not to see that."

His gaze softened, his fingers tracing a soothing line along my back, making their way to cup my face. "You are the most amazing woman I have ever met, and I would very much like to kiss you now."

I forgot how to breathe. How to function.

My heart threatened to jump out of my chest. It wasn't like we hadn't kissed before, but something about agreeing to *this* one felt different. Like I was opening up a door to something new, something not as fake as I was still pretending to believe. I couldn't get my words to work. All I could give him was a nod.

It was enough.

Dalton's sharp inhale was his only reaction before pulling me in and closing the distance between our mouths. It was like liquid fire flowed through my veins. I moaned against him, his tongue greeting mine with hunger, and I tilted my head back to give him more access, putty in his hands, clinging onto him as if he were my lifeline.

Nothing else mattered.

Everything slipped away the moment Dalton's lips moved against mine.

I felt his kiss everywhere, like it had a direct line between my thighs. His mouth was perfection, the softness of his lips contrasting with the roughness of his jaw. I wrapped my arms around his neck, digging my fingers into his hair.

"Sunshine," he moaned as I straddled him, his hands finding my ass while his teeth pulled on my bottom lip. I couldn't help myself and ground down onto him, moaning at the friction against my clit. He was so fucking hard that it short-circuited everything in my brain.

"Fuck," he gasped, head tipping backward as I circled my hips. "Having fun?"

I kissed down his jawline, nipping at the sensitive skin near his ear. I needed more of him, driven to show him he was wanted, and to wipe away the doubt and rejection.

"You have no idea, Thatcher," I whispered, pulling his lobe in my mouth and biting down, timing it with the apex of my thighs grinding down on his cock. His fingers dug into my flesh, breathing, picking up in pace. I wouldn't be surprised if ten fingertip-shaped bruises were left from his grip. And *fuck me* if that wasn't hot to witness a man falling apart from below you, sensing his need to touch you.

As if he read my thoughts, he slipped his hands under my shirt, trailing his fingertips from my back to just beneath my ribs, teasing the edge of my bra. Our tongues clashed as the kiss deepened. I couldn't stop moving on top of him, the need to feel more of him aggressively taking over my mind. My fingers found the edge of his shirt, bunching up the fabric as I pulled it over his head, needing to run my hands over the corded muscles of his arms, chest, and back.

He pulled back from the kiss, his eyes blazing with desire.

"Ari, can I touch you?" The low growl rumbled through his chest like he was barely holding himself together.

Holy shit.

"Yes."

The word escaped almost involuntarily from my kiss-swollen lips, sounding like a plea.

He didn't hesitate, hands moving under my shirt and bra to cover my breasts, his thumbs brushing over my hardened nipples, sending a thrill down my spine.

"Fuck, they're perfect," he murmured against my neck. "You're perfect."

Goosebumps erupted where his mouth traced down my throat, each graze making it harder to remember where we were or that anything else existed outside of this moment.

"Dalton, I need..." I didn't know what I needed or wanted. Hell, I didn't know what I was doing.

His lips found my temple. "Let me take care of you," he whispered, standing with me in his arms. My ass met the hard surface of my desk. "Let me make you feel good, Sunshine." Kisses peppered my clavicle before he dropped to his knees in front of me.

Those thick fingers were surprisingly agile, and he flicked the button of my pants open.

"Lift," he demanded, pulling at the pantlegs the second there was some space between the wooden desk and my body. Cool air hit my exposed skin, and his green eyes flicked up at me. "You always go around wearing no underwear?"

My cheeks heated under his stare. I'd been so caught up in the moment it didn't dawn on me 'til right then how he was staring at *all* of me.

I licked my lips. "I didn't want underwear lines to show up in pictures."

He blinked a few times, the wheels turning in his head. "I never see lines in your shorts either..."

A man was kneeling before my bare pussy, but what was making me embarrassed was the fact that he'd just caught on to the fact that I almost never wore underwear.

"Do you have a problem with that?" I challenged, lifting a brow.

"Yeah, I do. I don't like thinking about all the missed opportunities I had to slide my hand under your shorts and fuck you with my fingers."

There weren't a lot of things that left me speechless, but Dalton's mouth was one of them. I swallowed, trying to gather enough saliva to respond. "What makes you think I would have let you?"

All he did was smirk, like he knew full well what would have happened if he tried. He placed a kiss on the inner crook of my knee. "Tell me, Ari, does this pussy get wet when you see me working out?" Another kiss. "How does it feel to want to fuck your hockey player?"

I squealed when, without warning, he yanked me forward on the desk, stopping when my pussy was right at the edge. I must have manifested this moment because he shoved my legs apart with his broad shoulders, warm breath brushing against my core, and it was like he'd walked straight out of my nightly fantasies.

My eyelids fluttered close, anticipation building. The waiting alone was liable to cause me to come.

But nothing happened.

I look down to find him staring up at me, a cocky smirk on his gorgeous face.

"I thought you were in charge when we were in your gym, Coach."

"Huh?" I furrowed my brow, the lust making it hard to think straight.

"If you want me to eat your pussy, you have to ask for it." I froze, heat flushing my body at his words. He trailed the tip of his nose up my inner thigh, inhaling. "God, you smell so fucking good. You drive me crazy. Look at what you do to me." His fingertips dug into my chin, directing my attention to where his pants tented at the crotch.

Gone. Whatever reservations I had left were out the damn window. I only had so much willpower, and seeing him so turned on was my breaking point.

"Pull it out." My voice was firm, and I swore he shivered at the command.

"Yes, Coach."

Without breaking eye contact, he unzipped his pants, tugging his cock free. A low groan fell from his lips as he gave it a long, languid pull. Precum glistened at the tip, and I couldn't help but squirm, seeking some sort of relief. My body was crying out for release.

"You're making a mess. Want me to clean it up?" he asked, continuing to pump his hand around his length. Something inside me snapped, and my hands were in his hair, pressing his face between my thighs. His chuckle reached my ears right as he flattened his tongue, running it up the length of my slit like he was licking a damn popsicle.

My eyes began to flutter close, the pleasure too much to keep them open. But they popped back open when he stopped.

"Eyes on me. How else will you know if I'm doing a good job?" He smirked, mouth glistening.

"Show me what you've got then, Thatcher," I challenged, barely holding onto my sanity.

Cocky ass, didn't break eye contact as he swirled his tongue over my clit. "Mmm. Your pussy is the best thing I've ever tasted." The vibration of his moan against me had me tightening my hold on his hair. Stroke after torturous stroke, he held my gaze, until I was grinding against his face.

Thank god athletes had good lung capacity because I didn't give a fuck at that moment if he was breathing.

"Dalton, please..." I didn't know what I was asking for, but he seemed to.

I let out a loud cry that turned into a moan as his palm landed on the side of my bare ass cheek. Somewhere in the back of my mind, I remembered that we were in my office, and someone could walk into the gym at any time, but none of that was enough to keep me quiet.

My eyes flared as he grinned against my pussy, massaging my stinging cheek.

"Get your hand back on your cock, Thatcher. I want to see you come."

Apparently, he liked being bossed around because he latched on to my clit, sucking hard right as he shoved his fingers deep inside me. My heart seized in my chest at the sight of him fucking his hand, matching the pace of his fingers thrusting inside me. "Fuck, you're a good boy." The words fell from my mouth before I could stop them.

Those startling green eyes flared at the compliment, and he literally growled against my core, sending white sparks of pleasure down my spine.

I was seconds away from an orgasm. He knew it, too.

That wicked mouth applied the perfect amount of pressure to my clit, and then he added a third finger.

I broke—rocked by the most intense orgasm of my life, my legs quaking so hard I didn't know if I'd ever be able to get up. I was in such a daze I didn't even realize he was standing until he moaned my name, and ropes of white cum landing on my pelvis. A second wave of pleasure hit me as I watched it drip down between my legs in one of the most erotic sights I'd ever seen. Part of me wanted to ask him to shove it inside, but whatever bit of restraint I still had prevented me from forming the words.

Apparently, that restraint didn't apply to me scooping some up and licking it off my fingers.

His eyes were darker than I'd ever seen, and his face shone with the evidence of my orgasm. "My dirty fucking girl. Next time, I'll come in your mouth so you don't miss a drop," he said, swiping his fingers through our combined release and holding it to my lips.

Who the fuck was I?

When had I decided my favorite new thing to do was suck his fingers clean of cum?

He pressed gentle kisses up across my jaw and down my neck, then back up until he captured my lips, cradling my face and tilting it up.

"Thank you."

"For what?" I asked with a laugh, sliding off the desk. "You're the one who gave both of us orgasms."

"For listening…"

Oh.

He looked away, rubbing a hand across the back of his neck. "For reminding me that there are people in my life who are proud of me…are there for me." The smile he shot me was sheepish, the bold man from a moment ago replaced by one who was more tender—vulnerable.

I wrapped my arms around his waist, holding him close and trying to ignore the fact that we were having a tender moment while I was still naked from the waist down.

"Always, Thatcher. I am always here for you."

For the first time, making that promise wasn't scary at all.

THIRTY-TWO

ARIELLA

IF YOU DON'T LIKE TEXTING CHAPTERS, I FEAR YOU ARE WRONG.

Saturday

THATCHER:

I bought you more sheets for your bed

ME:

What are you talking about? Like for the couch? Thanks, those sheets were super nice.

THATCHER:

No. For your bed here! Also bought a dresser. I think it has like 9 drawers or something…Idk. I picked the one that had the most drawers for your leggings

ME:

What are you talking about? I don't live there, Thatcher.

THATCHER:

…

If you did, we could be making out on my
couch right now

*Our

I could be eating you out right now…

ME:

Who said we're doing that again? That
was a momentary slip in judgment.

THATCHER:

How do I get you to *slip* and land on
my face again?

THIRTY-THREE

DALTON

ANOTHA' ONE *DJ KHALED VOICE*

Sunday

SUNSHINE:

Are you doing your stretches? I know how your hamstrings get tight and we did a lot of explosive movements last practice

ME:

Yes mom.

How about you come stretch me out...

Okay I take back calling you mom now. It's weird when I want you sprawled out in my bed...

SUNSHINE:

Thatcher. Focus. I don't want you to get injured because you didn't do enough recovery work before your preseason game.

You wearing your cowboy hat with your suit?

ME:

No???

SUNSHINE:

Why not?

ME:

My dad wouldn't like it

Wish you were coming

Why aren't you btw?

SUNSHINE:

Well, I like you in your hat Thatcher

Wish you wore it more…

Apparently the paperwork for my travel arrangements was lost.

It's fine though it's just preseason, and I made sure I'm all good from now on. Monroe will be focused on experimenting with line combinations and testing new strategies. I can't help with that anyway.

I already gave him my player evaluations, so really, he doesn't need me there.

ME:

I need you.

SUNSHINE:

You have me, Thatcher.

I'll cheer you on. Always.🤍

THIRTY-FOUR

DALTON

HERE LIES DALTON. KILLED DUE TO HIS
DUMBASS DECISIONS.

WHAT THE FUCK *did it mean if she sent a heart emoji?*

How did I ask her to send me a picture of herself without sounding like a creep?

"Hey, Cap." Jimenez snuck up beside me, jolting me out of the internal question I'd yet to come up with an answer for since the night before. "Woah. When did you become such a fan of sugar-free Red Bull? I don't think I've seen you ever drink an energy drink in our entire ten years of friendship."

I pulled my screen away from the nosy fucker, glaring at him over my shoulder. Instead of getting the silent message and minding his own damn business, his smile spread, eyes twinkling with mischief.

Fuck me. Here we go.

"But I do know of a ball-busting Mexicana who drinks those." He slung an arm over my shoulder. "Cap, are you buying things for Ari?"

"She is my girlfriend," I grumbled, grabbing my bag so we could make our way out to Betty.

He snorted. "I think you can afford something more than a can of Red Bull." If only he'd seen the receipt for the dresser. "God, you've been out of the game that long? You're supposed to get like some lingerie or something for your *girlfriend*."

I glared at him, but his shit-eating grin only grew as we made our way to my car, the others all still licking their wounds from practice in the locker room.

Monroe hadn't let up one bit today. It was like he was on a mission to push us past our limits before preseason started Monday. I could still feel the sting from those relentless puck battles and backchecking drills. My legs were heavier, and my lungs were burning on the ice. Monroe wanted us sharp—hungry.

I glanced over at Jimenez, who was rolling his shoulders and muttering about needing an ice bath. The rookies had looked even worse, seconds away from collapsing. Still, I could feel the fire in the team, that drive simmering just below the surface.

Ari's work with us allowed us to push harder at practice, and I could already see the edge it'd give us.

Jimenez's voice broke me from my musing. "Look, I know you told me this thing with Ari is all fake, but man, you've got it down bad, my man. Anyone with eyes can see how you two...well, let's just say *I'm* not getting whatever personal training she was giving *you* the other day. Plus you're always staring at her amazing ass—"

My chest rumbled. "Talk about her ass again, Jimenez, and you'll be too damaged to play in the game."

The second I looked up at him, I realized I'd played right into his hand.

He just laughed, but his expression and voice turned serious as we walked. "Look, you don't have to say it, but it's pretty clear this isn't pretend anymore...not for you, at least."

A heavy silence settled over us for a moment before I got the balls to say what I'd been thinking for days aloud. "Yeah," I let out a humorless laugh, rubbing at the back of my neck. "I'm so fucking far gone for her, Christian, but I don't know how the hell I go about convincing her to give me a real chance." My chest tightened as the words finally came out. "She's so independent. I don't want to crowd her or make her think I don't respect that..."

He nodded thoughtfully, the playboy persona everyone associated him with gone. The guy was surprisingly insightful with relationship advice. He just didn't take any of his own. "Listen, a lot of women in Mexican culture have to fight extra hard to live life how *they* want. She's likely grown up with the fear that a man might try to take that independent nature of hers away. I'd bet that's why she's so damn strong-willed. She always felt she had to be."

His words made me pause.

"Show her that you love that about her. That you're there to support her in whatever way she needs. That her hopes and dreams are important to you, and she doesn't need to change them because all you want from her is to be in her corner." He shrugged a shoulder as if he didn't spout out some brilliant shit. "She probably thinks that being with you for real will mean she has to give up her ambitions for yours."

I blanched at the insinuation. "I'd never want to

diminish her like that. Why would I ask her to give up what she loves for me when she can have both?" I asked defensively, causing him to smile.

"And *that's* what you need to *show* her," he said. "It shouldn't be too hard for you. You're the opposite of controlling."

I stopped mid-step, my heart stopping. "Shit."

"Shit, what?" My best friend's eyes widened when I didn't move, clearly sensing a confession coming. "Dalton, what did you do?"

I threw my hands up. "She makes me crazy. She's got me doing things—"

"You ain't never done before?"

"Focus."

He smothered his smirk. "What did you do?"

I didn't get a chance to answer before my phone went off. There was no need to look at the screen to know who it was. My stomach did the same stupid swoop it always did when it came to Ari. Even though this time I knew she was calling to chew my ass out.

"Hello?" I answered, trying to sound casual.

"What the hell, Thatcher?" she snapped, tone laced with irritation. "I come home to hear that you had movers come pick up all my stuff? You can't just do shit like that without asking me."

I tossed my gear bag into the back of Betty, grinning despite myself. "You're right, Ari. Normally, I wouldn't have. But...you would've fought me on this, so I did something drastic. Like moving all your stuff into our home." I kept my voice steady as I climbed into the driver's seat. Jimenez practically tried to climb into my lap so he could hear the conversation. His face was right next to the back of my hand, and he pulled the phone away from my ear slightly, trying like hell to catch the ass-chewing I was receiving.

"It's not *our* home, Dalton Thatcher," she snapped. "It's your home, and you stole all my things to move them in without asking me."

Jimenez's eyes widened, and he whispered, "You moved her shit without asking? Do you know how unhinged women can be?"

"*¿Qué dijiste,* Christian?" Ari's voice crackled through the phone, and both of us jumped, stunned she'd heard him.

Jimenez shot me a panicked look, mouthing "see." "Uh, *nada,* Coach. Just telling him how crazy that is. Not you, never you."

Yeah, maybe it was a crazy move.

But I'd spent too many nights lying awake since carrying her out of her cousin's apartment, thinking about how much I hated that she'd gone back to sleeping on a couch. Then she'd let me taste her, and fuck, I was gone. Decided it was better to ask forgiveness than permission.

Of course, that was before Jimenez's advice of respecting her independence, so now I wasn't so sure it was the smartest move.

"Are your hands up in the air, or are you pinching the bridge of your nose?" I asked, curious about what they were doing because I knew they had to be doing something. Ari always spoke with her hands. Her whole body, if I was being honest.

There was a pause on the other end of the line, like

she had just realized that she was, in fact, doing one of those two things.

"Or is it a mix of both?" I teased, pulling onto the road leading toward the airport. Something tightened in my chest at the thought of not seeing Ari over the next few days, but that was exactly why I'd chosen to move her stuff in today.

Was it a little bit sneaky and underhanded? Sure.

Did I feel bad about it? Not one bit.

There was no way I could sleep at night knowing she was lying on someone's couch when I had a perfectly good guest bedroom at my place. At least until I could talk her into my own bed...

"Both," she admitted. "but that's beside the point. I can't just move into your apartment. That's not...it's not..." she growled in frustration, and I took pity on her.

"Look, Ari. If you want, I'll send all of your stuff back to your cousin's. But we both know that my apartment is way bigger than I need. So, why don't you stay there for at least a few days? See how you like it. What's the worst that could happen?"

She could decide not to stay. The thought caused my chest to tighten, but I meant it. If she wanted out, her stuff would be back at her cousin's within the hour.

There was silence, then a sigh. "Fine, Dalton. I'll stay while you're in Nashville," she said, her voice firm. "But I'm not promising anything longer than that. Got it?"

"Got it." There was no hiding the happiness in my voice. "Still going to cheer for me, Sunshine?"

Her voice softened. "Always, Thatcher."

THIRTY-FIVE

ARIELLA

TO BE SEEN IS TO BE LOVED

THERE WAS no way this was a good idea.

Yet here I was anyway, folding my endless collection of leggings and spandex shorts and stuffing them into the drawers of a really freaking nice dresser that hadn't been there last time.

Despite telling Dalton that I wasn't staying past a few days, I couldn't resist setting up all my little things. Each item I unpacked felt like laying another brick on a path I wasn't sure I should be walking down. One that veered away from my originally laid out road. Although, if I were being truthful with myself, it didn't really veer off...it was more like it ran parallel. Because I was still working toward all my goals, there was just an extra person walking alongside me.

Like every time this topic came up in my mind, I shoved it aside, focusing on unpacking instead.

I set up the photo collage of my cousins and me, the neon sign that said *brujita*, and the collection of coconut-

scented candles that filled the room with a sweet, tropical scent that reminded me of my favorite body wash.

"Hello...holy shit," Gracie called out from where she stepped inside the front door. I smirked, knowing full well her jaw was on the floor. Rounding the corner, sure enough, her mouth was in the shape of an O, her eyes as wide as dinner plates.

"If you decide you're not staying here, I'll sure as fuck do it." She walked farther into the open-concept living room, making a beeline for the exact thing I had—the view. "God, this is...I mean...wow. Does he have any single teammates? Hell, I'll put up with that grumpy-ass coach even."

I shook my head. "First of all, I'm not letting you anywhere near my players." She wrinkled her nose at that. "And there's no way in *hell* you and Monroe would work. The most amount of words that man has said was what you heard at the press conference."

She huffed. "After my last date, I think I want a man who doesn't speak." She moved around the space, face still in awe.

"I know, it's the nicest place I've ever seen," I said, reading the unspoken words on her face as I came to stand beside her. Watching all of the cars buzzing around down below was surreal. I'd never imagined seeing Dallas from this vantage point.

"Nice?" She whipped her head toward me, "No, *prima. Es maravillosa.*" She nudged me playfully before moving toward the kitchen, leaving me shaking my head with a smile.

"Go ahead, Gracie. Just make yourself at home." I

teased, trailing behind her, trying to calm the nerves at being in Dalton's space without him. I'd texted him earlier asking if it was okay if she came over, and he'd told me I lived there now and to have anyone I wanted over.

"Damn, girl, how good are they paying you? Maybe I should have been charging you more for rent. You bought *every* type of drink you like?"

"What are you talking about?"

Entering the kitchen, I found her crouched in front of the drink fridge. My heartbeat picked up the closer I got. I peered over her shoulder, shocked at the sight.

The fridge was fully stocked with all my favorite drinks.

"I didn't buy those," I said quietly, staring in disbelief.

She laughed. "What do you mean you didn't buy them? You two just *happen* to like the same drinks?" She looked over her shoulder, smiling until she noted my face, and then her mouth dropped even wider than it had when she saw his apartment. "Wait a minute..."

"Holy shit." She yelled, jumping up and gripping my shoulders. "He stocked the fridge with all of your favorite drinks? How does he even know which ones you like? I mean, he even got the Topo Chico in the—"

"Glass bottles," I finished for her, biting the inside of my cheek, eyes still glued on the drink fridge.

It wasn't that I didn't think he was paying attention to me when he'd asked all of those questions, but I'd never imagined that he was asking them because he would go out and *buy* them for me. My eyes caught on an orange sticky note on the top of the counter.

The exact spot he'd set me on the night I was here.

Before my cousin noticed it, I snatched it up, eager to read the words on there.

The height of luxury is a well-stocked drink fridge. Leave a spicy water for me. P.S. Check the pantry.

My body was on autopilot, moving toward the door tucked away beside the fridge—a lump formed in my throat when I pulled it open. Ten bottles of Tapatío were lined up. I pressed a hand to my mouth to stifle the surge of emotion. "Gracie, when do we start our period?"

"Huh?" She stood behind me, trying to peek at the note, but I held it close.

"I'm hoping that the fact that I feel like crying over this is because I'm PMSing," I answered, dabbing the corner of my eyes. "Because who the hell cries over drinks and hot sauce?"

She moved to stand directly in front of me, her eyes softening. "It's not the drinks, babe. It's the fact that someone took the time to see you."

I groaned as she wrapped me in a hug, squeezing tight. "Don't start," I mumbled into her shoulder, though a part of me clung to the comfort.

"Oh my gosh, a boy likes you, Ari," she sang teasingly, pulling back to beam at me. "And you like a boy."

"Of course, I like him. As a friend."

"Mmmhmmm. I also let my friends eat me out at work." I went to hit her, but she spun away laughing.

"Graciella, I told you that in confidence."

"You know, now that I think about it, I totally would let my friends eat me out at work." She wagged her eyebrows, grabbing a Red Bull. "I'm going to go snoop," she said, skipping off, leaving me to work through the pile of emotions sitting on my chest.

What the hell was I doing here? Ari from three weeks ago would never have agreed to this. But when Gracie had told me that movers showed up at the apartment to get my stuff and take it to Dalton's, my heart had sped up, not in anger, but in excitement. The control I had over the situation between us felt as if it was slipping through my fingers, and now I stood here wondering if I should be worried about the fact that I wasn't worried.

Fuck my head hurts. This is why I avoid relationships and emotions...

Gracie burst back into the kitchen, her face pale and panicked, looking like she'd seen a ghost.

"Code fucking red, Ari," she blurted out, pacing with her arms over her head, breathing like she'd just sprinted a mile. "Or maybe worse. What's worse than red? Whatever it is, that's what we're dealing with."

I moved toward her, gripping her shoulders so I could talk her off the ledge. She had a tendency of being dramatic, so I was sure that whatever she had to say wasn't all that big of a deal.

"Slow down, what's the problem? Did you spill? Break something? I'm sure Dalton wil—"

She cut me off, her eyes wild. "Your brother is coming to town tonight, and I accidentally told him you moved out," she said, biting on her knuckles.

"What?" I nearly yelled. Now I was the one pacing

the oak floors. "Start from the beginning. You just walked out of here, and everything was fine. Now you come in and tell me that Ricky's on his way here? And he knows I'm not at your place?"

"I didn't mean to." Her hands flew up in the air. "I posted a pic to my story when I got here that said, "My *prima's* new spot," forgetting that the dumbass follows my blogger account, too. Then he messaged me asking what the hell you were doing somewhere else besides my place, and I panicked."

I pinched the bridge of my nose, willing my lungs to start working properly because I was currently swallowing mouthfuls of air and on the verge of hyperventilating.

"Don't worry, though. I didn't tell him you were living with a man," she said.

Saliva pooled in my mouth, followed by the urge to throw up because that sentence was the opposite of making me feel like I didn't need to worry.

"I told him the team owned the apartment and put up their new staff here until they find a place."

Some of the nausea subsided because that was actually pretty smart.

When I opened my eyes back up, Gracie was practically gnawing at her manicured nails, brows up in her hairline.

"Okay, now explain to me this whole thing about him coming here *tonight?*" I asked in a measured tone.

The damn wince was back.

"He said he wanted to surprise you, but now that you've moved he needed to know where to go." There was a pause, and I *knew* I would hate whatever came out of her mouth next. "And he's planning on staying at your place, so we need to move all of your shit into Dalton's room and around the apartment so your brother can stay in your room and believe you live here alone," she said quickly, tacking on a smile like it would help keep me from strangling her.

I walked away from her so I wouldn't be tempted, reaching for my phone between measured breaths. There was no time to freak out. I'd have to save that for tonight while I was lying on Dalton's floor and fighting off the panic attack of my brother finding out I'd moved into a man's home.

Fuck me.

"You owe me so big for this, Gracie," I muttered. "Like, clean the tripe for *menudo* every time from now until forever big."

She only nodded, already half to the guest bedroom. "Got it. I'll start moving your things. You...handle Dalton."

I took a deep breath, closing my eyes as I pressed the green call button. The team had left a few hours earlier for Nashville, which was just a short hop on the plane. My lungs burned as I held my breath, waiting for him to pick up the phone. Part of me hoped he wouldn't, and I could leave him the craziest voicemail he'd ever gotten in his life, but at least I wouldn't have to *talk* to him. Gracie said I should text him, but this felt like way too big of an ask for a text.

"Don't pick up, don't pick up, don't—"

"Ari?" Dalton's voice sounded concerned on the other end of the line, and I wrangled in the tornado ricocheting off the walls of my chest. "Everything okay? Something in the apartment giving you trouble? I can call down and have the—"

I cut off his adorable, worried rant. "No, no. Everything with the apartment is great. Perfect, really." There would be a permanent divot in his kitchen floors from my pacing. "Thanks, by the way, for all the drinks in the fridge. You literally got every single one of my favorites. You didn't need to do that."

"Sunshine," there was a smile in his voice, "you're welcome, but I know that's not what you called me for. So spit it out."

I took a deep breath, and the words tumbled out like one long run-on sentence. "Gracie let it slip to my brother that I moved out. He was already on his way to visit, and now he wants to stay with me for the night."

"Okay?" Dalton replied, clearly confused about where I was going with all of this. Which was a shame, because I'd been hoping he'd figure it out and not make me come out and say what I was about to.

"She told him your apartment was my apartment and that the team put me up here until I found a spot, and now I have to stay in your room tonight because he's on his way over," I rushed out before adding on, "but I won't sleep in your bed or go through your stuff."

"Ari."

I ignored him. Now that the words were flowing, I couldn't get them to stop. "I'm just going to sleep on your floor, and he will only be here for the night."

"Ari..."

"I promise I'll keep everything clean, and we wo—"

"Babe," he interrupted, his voice soft but firm.

That got my mouth to snap shut. He'd probably said it for that very reason, but it didn't stop my stomach from swooping and my lady bits from literally tingling.

"I already told you, the place is yours too. If your brother wants to come stay tonight, it's fine with me." The knot in my throat loosened. "But there's one rule." My back straightened at the authority in his voice, and I tried to ignore the way it turned me on. "You're sleeping in my bed, Sunshine."

I could picture him, that steady look in his eyes, the slight quirk of his brow daring me to argue. Which I always would, and now was no different.

"Dalton, I am not sleeping in your bed," I said, making my way toward his bedroom door as if my feet had a mind of their own. My heart beat faster with each step. There was something exciting about the idea of seeing his space. I wondered if it was more personal than the rest of his place.

Would there be any little insights into who he was?

Pushing his door open, I waited for his answer. We both knew I'd sleep in his bed, that I was only pushing back because it was in my nature, and my heart seized at the realization that Dalton didn't mind letting me push back.

He was patient with me. Accepted my independence, except if it meant me sleeping on a couch or the floor, apparently. I peered into the dark room, hit by his overwhelming scent.

"I've had my tongue in your pussy."

I choked on my spit. That was *not* what I'd expected him to say.

He kept on talking, unfazed that I was nearly dying on the other end of the call. "You think I'll have a problem with you in my bed? You're sleeping there, and I want a fucking picture as proof. Clothing is optional. You understand, Ariella?"

I loved how my name rolled off his tongue when he said it. He made the effort to pronounce it the way it was intended.

"And what if I don't?" I teased, finally recovered, and absently biting my lip at the idea of walking into his space. I took a step and froze at Gracie's incoherent yelling from across the apartment.

Shit.

"I've got to go find out what Gracie needs before she causes me to have a panic attack," I said, turning on my heel to track her down.

Dalton let out a low chuckle.

"Fine. But don't test me, Sunshine. I want that photo."

THIRTY-SIX

ARIELLA

PINCHE PENDEJO

THE POOR PALMS of my hands were red and stinging from all the picking I'd done at my callouses, but it barely registered as I leaned against the island. Ricky eyed me suspiciously, his gaze darting around the apartment before landing back on me.

There was no questioning whether we were related. From our skin tone to the deep color of our eyes and hair. Hair my brother currently had buzzed short in a look that usually had women drooling over him and me rolling my eyes. We clearly shared genes, but what sealed the deal was our smiles—nearly identical.

Not that he was smiling right now.

"So, they just put you up in a multi-million dollar apartment?" he asked, arching a skeptical eyebrow. "That's awfully generous of them, Ariella."

"Yup," I squeaked, taking another drink of my water, desperate to keep some moisture in my mouth so that I didn't flounder around when he asked me questions. I could tell by the side-eye he gave me that he was suspi-

cious. I thought Gracie was a shit liar, but I was discovering I wasn't much better.

"How about we cut the shit, and you tell me what the fuck you're doing dating Dalton Langley. Don't try denying it either, Ariella, I watched the interview," he said, crossing his arms over his chest, clearly ready for a fight.

I froze for a second before anger started crawling up my neck.

"*That* was what you latched onto from the interview?" I shot back. "You don't want to congratulate me, or talk about how every reporter there applauded my accomplishments? God, Ricardo, how shitty is it that my brother only cares about who I'm dating?"

I hoped the walls were soundproof because my volume rose with every word.

"Because you never told me," he yelled back, throwing his arms out to the side, hurt in his tone. "This is his apartment, isn't it? You should have stayed at Graciella's."

"Why would I stay at her place when I've got a perfectly good apartment here?"

It was always like this with Ricky. Every conversation was laced with judgment, as if I'd never made a sensible decision.

"Because, Ariella, you are a woman in an unfamiliar city. It's not smart for you to live with a guy you just met. How well do you even know him?" His face was the picture of brotherly disapproval.

I knew he wasn't totally off with his logic, but there was *years* of build-up bubbling over at the moment, and there was no stopping me.

I scoffed.

"Oh yes, because my womanly brain is incapable of figuring out how to navigate life on my own." He tried to interrupt me, but I was on a roll. "Why don't I take my ass back home and live with *mi mamá y mi papá* until someone you all deem worthy to comes to collect me? In fact," I rounded on him, his posture matching mine—tense and ready to fight, "you should make sure the man you choose offers up something in exchange. Money maybe? Some goats? God, but I don't know how much I'm worth because I haven't been cooking and cleaning lately, which is really all I'm good for, right?"

"Oh, and what you're doing here is better, huh? You start dating some wealthy hockey player who probably only wants to get in your pants before he leaves you for someone else. Did you know that was what the articles say about him, Ariella? That he left his ex for a new woman—you."

Red. All I saw was red.

"Don't you dare say anything bad about him," I said, my voice suddenly deadly calm. "He is *nothing* like that. I've never had anyone treat me as well as he does. To care for me and my dreams the way he does. Dalton is the most selfless man I've ever met, and his ex is a fucking reporter who dragged his name through the mud."

He threw his hands in the air. "Well, how was I supposed to know that? I don't know him."

"But you know *me,* Ricky, and that should have been enough for you to trust my choices in who I want to be with."

My chest heaved. The cold from the marble bit into

my palms because I'd slapped them down at some point during my rant. Probably a subconscious reaction to keep from throwing hands with my brother.

We stared at each other in loaded silence for a long moment, and then he sighed, dropping his arms to his side. "You're right." The edge in his voice from earlier had lessened.

I nearly choked on my tongue at the admission. I didn't think he'd ever said those two words to me before.

He waved a hand at my dramatic coughing fit, smiling.

"Okay, okay. Enough. I get it. You didn't expect to hear me say that. I do know you, Ari." He smirked. "And I've never seen a girl cut down a man the way you do. I've always known that whoever could put up with your ass would be a good man—you wouldn't settle for anything less. But you're going to have to cut me some slack, okay?" he said, his eyes coming back up to meet mine. "My whole life, I was told I needed to take care of you and protect you. How can I do that when you live hundreds of miles away? Or when you don't tell me shit?"

I moved closer, relenting and hugging his center like I'd done since we were kids. "*Pendejo*, you can do all those things by being there when I *need* you, not by showing up unannounced and lecturing me." I pushed away. "And if you want me to trust you enough to tell you about what I'm doing, then I need to know you have *my* back and aren't going to run off and tell my Dad."

He looked away sheepishly, and I cut him off when he went to argue.

"I get it. You're close with my Dad, but he treats you differently than he does me, and I am not going to sit around holding my breath for that to change. This is *my* life, Ricky. Mine. I will not sit around and waste it."

He studied me, brows pulled together like he'd never considered this before.

Of course he hadn't. Why would he?

He'd been allowed to make his own decisions since we were teens, while mine had always been questioned and dismissed.

"Alright." He nodded. "I promise that whatever you tell me stays between us," Ricky said sincerely before pulling away and pointing at me. "*Pero quiero conocer a este cabrón, ¿entiendes?*"

I rolled my eyes. "Yes, you can meet my boyfriend. Now enough weird emotional shit. Let's go get some food."

"Does Texas even have good Mexican food?" he asked, grabbing his hat and following me to the elevator.

"Eh. It's not San Jose, but I've found a few places. Come on, I'll pay for your tacos just to prove I can survive in the world," I teased over my shoulder, catching the middle finger he threw my way.

The moment the apartment door closed behind us, it dawned on me that at no point during that argument did I think about my relationship with Dalton as being fake...

HOW THE HELL did I used to start getting *ready* to go out at ten?

I'd probably been hopped up on adrenaline, because

when Gracie and I managed to go out we'd had to lie through our teeth to convince our parents of where we were going, so we made the most of it. But now? Ten rolled around, and my ass was begging for bed.

The low murmurs of a conversation came from the guest room, and the *chismosa* in me desperately wanted to stick my ear to the door to hear who my brother was talking to.

If I were being honest, I was dragging my feet and looking to distract myself, making every possible pit stop on my way to Dalton's bedroom. Who would have guessed the scariest thing I'd done since moving to Dallas was walking into a man's bedroom?

Another buzz went off, practically burning a hole in the back pocket of my shorts. I knew whose name I'd see on the screen. Dalton had been texting me all night. The first few were genuinely wondering how it was going since I'd abruptly cut off our phone call, but after he knew I hadn't been hauled back to San Jose, the texts had become way...dirtier.

> THATCHER:
>
> Don't forget my photo
>
> Also, I decided clothes are *not* optional
>
> Blankets aren't optional either

I didn't answer.

Sexting while your older brother sits across from you putting down some tacos al pastor was not my idea of a good time, but now...

His bedroom door stood before me, tempting me like

the phone in my pocket. I pushed it open, flicking the light switch. A warm glow illuminated the room, and my foot hesitated over the threshold. Being in there felt intimate, like seeing a part of Dalton's life most never would.

"Don't be a little bitch, Ari. It's a *room*," I told myself, finally gaining the courage to enter.

His bedroom had the same moody vibe as the rest of the apartment, but felt more personal—more lived-in. Clothes were draped over a leather chair tucked in the corner, and various knick-knacks lay scattered across his dresser. I ran my fingertips across the wooden top, picking up a cologne that looked barely used. He either liked it a lot and it was an extra, or he hated and kept it for some reason. I uncapped it, catching a whiff of an awful powdery scent.

"Ugh. Definitely hates it," I muttered, picking up something else. I smiled when I realized it was the keys to the Audi, remembering his shy grin the whole ride to the rink after I begged him to drive Betty the morning after I'd spent the night. My gaze snagged back on the cologne. "Why do you do things you don't like, Thatcher?"

The whole time I was walking around the perimeter of his room, I actively avoided looking at his bed. The anticipation was bubbling up inside me, threatening to boil over. But instead of giving in, I walked into the ensuite. Thanks to Dallas's thousand percent humidity levels, I'd been sweating all day, and there was no way I would sleep in someone's bed smelling like swamp-ass. I might as well have been living underwater at this point, or at least that's how it felt coming from a part of California where we panicked if it hit seventy-five.

My mouth dropped when I flicked on the light. His bathroom was massive, easily bigger than Gracie's apartment. His shower alone was big enough to rent out, and there were more shower heads than I knew what to do with. There was no way I was waiting to test it out.

I stripped out of my clothes. Goosebumps pebbled up along my bare skin, a mix of the chilled air-conditioned air and the sheer fact that I was standing naked in the same space that Dalton stood naked.

You're losing it, Ari. Who gets turned on by that?

Me, apparently.

THIRTY-SEVEN

DALTON

DYING OF BLUE BALLS AND BROKEN DREAMS...

I RELEASED A HEAVY, long-held breath, my stomach churning with a mix of frustration and disappointment that Ari hadn't responded yet.

My head hit the starchy pillow as I flopped back onto the hotel bed, shoving another artificially flavored orange and yellow ring into my mouth. Sugar coating my chest.

Jimenez had invited me out with the guys, but I'd told them to head out without me. Now I was starting to regret it because at least it would have distracted me from Ari's radio silence.

Just go. There's no need to stay here and wallow over the fact that she's not answering.

God, I was pathetic. What did I think was going to happen? That she was going to ca—

My phone buzzed, Ari's name flashing across the top. It wasn't just a phone call...she was Facetiming me.

"Ari?"

It took me a second to realize she was calling me from my bathroom. She stood, wrapped in one of my towels, her bare skin peeking out from beneath the white, fluffy fabric in a way that had my blood rushing south.

"Dalton, how the hell do I work this damn thing? Am I supposed to have an engineering degree to turn it on? " she whisper-yelled, blowing a strand of hair out of her face with a huff.

Those pretty brown eyes peered at me from the screen, hair teasing the exposed skin of her collarbone. The dim light softened the edges of her features, making her look ethereal.

It took me a second to process what she was saying, too mesmerized by how fucking sexy she was.

"Quit smiling at me like that." She rolled her eyes. I hadn't even realized I was, and for some reason, that only made the smile grow. "Are you going to tell me or make me stand here all night?"

Right. Shower.

I chuckled when it all clicked into place. "It's going to cost you, Sunshine," I said, tucking an arm behind my head.

"What's that supposed to mean, Thatcher?"

"Drop the towel."

She hesitated, gnawing on that bottom lip that always tasted like strawberries. For a second, I didn't think she was going to do it, but then the white fabric fell away, and the sight of the curve of her breasts had my cock stirring. "There, happy?"

"Not even a little. I can't see anything," I complained, tilting the screen like that would help see more of her body.

She smirked, a glint of mischief in her eyes. "Next

time, be more specific that you're trying to see me naked. Now, cough up the information."

Oh, if she wanted me to spell out specifically what I wanted from her, I would.

"I don't think I will," I said instead, loving the way her mouth fell open. "I mean, *I* am the one who knows how to work the shower, which means I have the bargaining power here."

Her pouty lips fell open, her chest swelling with a deep breath, and I swore her pupils dilated.

"What do you want then, Thatcher?" Her breathy tone has my cock leaking in my underwear.

Fuck.

I motioned for her to lower the camera with my fingers, and she complied, revealing more of her gorgeous tanned skin, stopping right when her nipples started to come into the frame. She *would* cock-tease me like that.

An honest to god growl came out of my mouth. "You know I want to see more of your perfect body."

"I'm just matching what you're showing me."

For the first time since answering, I realized what I was wearing—or, more accurately, *not* wearing. I dragged my eyes up from my bare chest slowly, catching the way she mimicked the movement.

"Are you asking for me to show you more, Sunshine? You want to see if I'm hard?"

Her throat bobbed, her bottom lip firmly between her teeth as she nodded. Who was I to deny the lady? I angled the camera down lower, pulling out my cock. "Because I don't mind showing you exactly what you do to me."

Her glossy lips parted, and I groaned at the sight.

"Fuck, I want those lips wrapped around me." I let my head fall back. When I looked back, she had her camera pointed down more, giving me a clear view of her perfect tits. "They look as good as they felt in my hands," I said, wrapping my fingers around my shaft and pumping up and down.

"Oh god..." Her moaned whisper came out muffled through the speaker. "I'm supposed to be showering, not doing...this."

"We don't have to do this, baby," I said, voice softening as I angled the camera away. "You know I was only teasing—you're one hundred percent in charge here. Say the word, and I'll tell you how to turn the water on and hang up. I don't ever think I'm entitled to your body, Ariella. It doesn't matter how many things we've done or what we never do, every time you will have the final say."

Something flashed in her eyes, too fast for me to catch, but it looked a lot like gratitude. "I'm not ready to hang up yet," she said, her voice going low, and she left me speechless by propping her phone up in one of the wall crevices of my shower, giving me a full frontal view of her gorgeous body. "How are you using that bargaining power now, Thatcher?" Her voice was husky, like a siren's song.

"Slide that finger through the mess I know you've made."

"So confident," she said with a smirk, but did as I said.

"Show me, Sunshine. Show me how fucking wet you are for me." *Who the hell am I?*

I liked sex as much as the next guy, but this? Watching Ari touch herself over facetime as I fucked my hand? This was something completely new.

She held up her fingers, the slick sheen shining under the bathroom lights. And it was like she read my damn mind, raising those glossy fingertips to her lips and closing around them.

A rumbled noise brewed in my chest. "Show me, baby, show me what you'd do if that were my cock."

Goddamn. My hips bucked as I watched her follow instructions, reaching her pointer and middle finger deep into her mouth, bobbing her head up and down.

"What a good fucking girl," I moaned, watching as she fucked her mouth with her fingers, tasting her arousal. Every tiny whimper had me growing harder, and my tongue felt heavy with the need to trace a path down her body.

"Now touch that needy clit, Sunshine."

Her fingers made a wet sound as she dragged them from her mouth. Saliva glistened on her torso as he trailed her hand down her body before dipping them back between her legs. A small moan echoed through the phone the moment she circled her clit, making my cock twitch in my hands. Those noises were better than any crowd cheering.

I matched her pace, eager to watch her fall apart again, even if I couldn't be the one to do it this time. "Just like that, baby," I said, watching her other hand come up to pull on her pebbled nipples.

Ari's eyes popped open, searching for mine.

"Are you doing this too?" The question came out in heady pants, but there was no missing the thread of vulnerability.

"I'm right here with you, darlin'." I angled the phone

so it captured my hand working over my cock before dipping down to tug at my balls, and we both moaned.

My eyes were fixed on her fingers, mesmerized by how they circled and dipped, seeking out her climax.

She was close. We both were.

Lust shot down my spine, remembering how the last time I came, it was on her body.

"Fuck, I love watching you touch yourself." The corner of her mouth pulled up. "If I were there with you, I'd lick and suck that needy pussy of yours. Stretch and fill you with my fingers." My pace picked up, matching her frantic movements. There was no way either of us could last much longer.

"Oh, god," she moaned, eyes closed as her head rocked back and forth.

"Open those pretty eyes, baby." I smiled when she obeyed the command. "I want to watch you come, soak those fingers as you ride them."

Her mouth dropped open, my name tumbling out as she came. Just hearing the pleasure in her voice was enough to send me over the edge. Cum landed on my lower abs, but all I could picture was it dripping down her pussy and how she'd lapped it off her fingers.

Fuck.

If this was what it felt like to mess around with Ari, I needed to know what it was like to be balls deep inside her. To experience her pussy stretched around my cock, all wet and warm. Truthfully, I may not survive it.

Here lies Dalton. Killed by sex that was too hot to handle.

"Earth to, Thatcher. You still with us?"

Ariella's voice pulled me from my post-climax haze. Her lazy smile told me she was in the same state of bliss. I loved that she was still fully on display. Part of me had been worried that she might revert back to covering up. She had a tendency to run from me the moment we got too close, which was fine. I'd chase after her until she was ready to stop.

"No. I'm pretty sure I died and went to heaven." I furrowed my brows. "No, that can't be right. You'd be in bed with me if I were in heaven."

She rolled her eyes, fighting to hide her laugh. "So, have I earned learning how to turn on this shower?"

"Oh, babe, you've earned whatever the fuck you want after that," I said, loving the way her cheeks were tinged with pink. "It's not that complicated. One knob is for the temperature, one is for the body sprays, and the other is for the pressure of the sprays. Let me see you turn them on."

The sound of water, followed by a squeal of delight, filtered through the phone.

She came back into frame, her mouth opening and closing a few times. "I'll be honest, I don't know what the protocol is for ending a phone call like that."

I chuckled. "You're asking the wrong person because I've never done something like that."

"I like knowing I'm the first," she said with a smile, shifting from one foot to another.

"The only. You'll be the only, Ari."

THIRTY-EIGHT

ARIELLA

YOU KNOW THAT THE PAN DULCE SHE GOT
WAS THE CONCHA WITH THE PINK SUGAR
(IF THIS MADE NO SENSE, YOU NEED A
MEXICAN FRIEND IN YOUR LIFE HAHA)

THE PALE PINK box of *pan dulce* balanced precariously on my arm as I dug into my pocket, trying to find the apartment keys. I needed these sweet breads more than air this morning to try and revive me because I certainly hadn't gotten any sleep last night. How could I when fantasies of Dalton bursting through the door, bare-chested with gray sweats hanging low on his toned thighs, kept running through my mind?

Or maybe he'd be wearing nothing but boxer-briefs. Either way, he'd burst through the door, hard on clearly visible, chest heaving as he glared at me with smoldering eyes.

I didn't even know what smoldering eyes were, but he'd have them as he watched me lying there on that cloud of a bed, hand buried down in my underwear, fingers working in and out of my pussy, just like he had on the phone. We'd locked eyes, stuck in that trance we both seemed to get pulled into whenever we were together.

Then he'd walk over, each step sending my adrenaline spiking higher and higher, his large hand reaching out to replace mine...

"Ms. Contreras?"

I let out a yelp, nearly sending the box flying. My heart slammed against my ribs as I spun on my heel to see who the hell was behind me.

"Mr. Langley?" I asked, utterly confused. "What are you doing here?"

He had to know his son wasn't home—he did own the team for god's sake. I looked around the small hallway outside Dalton's apartment like the answer would pop out somewhere.

Am I still dreaming? Because now we're in a nightmare.

His laugh was low and practiced, the kind meant to disarm someone, but instead, it made the hair on the back of my neck stand up. "I could ask you the same question, Ms. Contreras. I don't know that it will bode well for your job if you're breaking into a player's apartment while they are away." He smiled as if it were a joke, but his eyes shone with something darker

Everything this man said to me from the moment I'd met him felt like a thinly-veiled threat, as if my reply was what would determine his response—and my future at the Desperados.

I forced a casual shrug, digging my hand back into my bag, rooting around for the damn key because something told me I'd need the proof that this wasn't a breaking-and-entering situation. "Oh, don't worry, I'm not. I live here now," I said, sighing in relief when I felt cold metal against my fingertips.

His eyes narrowed, his mouth forming more of a grimace as he watched me dangle my key to the apartment. "Live here?" he repeated, tone sharp. "Well, it seems like my son must trust you deeply, to let you move into his space so quickly after meeting." He closed the distance between us, standing close enough to feel like he was looming over me.

Maybe it would have been intimidating if I hadn't yelled at grown men with egos for years now. Still, my back stiffened, and my body sensed something was off. I didn't think he would hurt me, not physically, at least, but the glint in his eye made me wary.

"Yeah, Dalton and I trust each other. I haven't given him any reason not to," I replied, slipping my hand back into my purse and opening up the camera to record our conversation.

Something about this felt...wrong.

His gaze flickered to my hand before settling back on me. "Trust is a delicate thing. Dalton has always been eager to please, to earn approval. He has a habit of attaching himself to people who may not always have his best interests at heart."

My stomach turned. "What are you implying, Mr. Langley?"

His lips curled into a thin smile, powdery cologne suffocating me as he took another step toward me. "Dalton doesn't need someone interfering with his focus, with my plans for him," Vincent continued, his mask of politeness cracking enough to reveal the narcissistic ass beneath.

"You're not going to become a distraction, are you, Ms. Contreras?"

I was point two seconds away from firing back and saying whatever the professional version of, "I'd like to shove my foot up your ass," was, but his next words threw me off balance entirely.

"I'm sure we can make this work, Ariella. Come to an arrangement that works for *all* of us. Emma did." His voice dropped into a smooth, almost flirtatious tone. "She and I had a unique...understanding."

What the fuck?

He'd manipulated Dalton's ex. Used her to control him. And worse, his creepy-ass tone made me think the unspoken insinuation was that his relationship with Emma had crossed a line—a deeply disturbing one.

"I'm afraid you're going to have to spell it out for me, Mr. Langley," I bit out, trying to hide the barely contained rage bubbling inside. "What exactly are you proposing?"

He shrugged a shoulder. "We don't have to have the same arrangement as Emma and me. Though I'm not opposed." He dragged his eyes down my body, making bile rise in my throat. *I should throw up on his expensive shoes to teach him a lesson.* "I know you're ambitious, Ariella. I have connections my son doesn't have. I can make all of your dreams come true. You don't even have to work hard to reach those milestones. I can just place you there, so long as you help keep Dalton where I want."

His father wasn't just an asshole—he was a puppeteer, pulling strings and dangling the illusion of love and approval to keep his son under control. And now he was attempting to do something similar with me, but the asshole should have done his research on who he was propositioning because the last fucking thing I wanted was a handout from a skeezy old white man.

I didn't want to throw up on him any more. Now I wanted to knee him in the balls and watch him writhe in pain at my feet.

"Dalton is a grown man, Mr. Langley. He doesn't need anyone else's approval to make his decisions. Not mine, and definitely not yours. He deserves to have people around him who care about what he wants, who do things with his best interests in mind. Clearly, you're not one of them, but I am."

His face twisted up in a sneer, but before he could respond, the door behind me clicked open, and Ricky's voice broke the tension. "Ari? What's taking you so long?"

Vincent's eyes flicked to Ricky, who stood in the doorway sans shirt, and he pulled his arm out of my path. His smile had returned, but was colder now. "Ah, I see. A man already in the apartment while my son is away. I suppose that's one way to keep yourself entertained, Ms. Contreras," he said, turning and walking toward the door across the hall. "Nice talking to you."

It took a second for his words to register.

"Hey, that's not what's happening," I snapped, but he'd already disappeared inside. The door clicked sounded like a gunshot in the quiet hallway.

I stared after him, my hands trembling with anger and disgust. My brother leaned against the frame, his brows furrowed. "What the hell was that about?"

For a second, I considered not telling him, but after last night, we'd promised to turn a new leaf in our sibling relationship. "I'm pretty sure my boyfriend's dad just tried to bribe me," I said, stepping past him into the apartment.

He trailed behind me into the kitchen. "As in, the man who owns the team you work for?"

"The one and the fucking same."

We locked eyes, concern shining in his. "What are you going to do?"

I toyed with the hem of Dalton's shirt, mind whirling with what'd just happened. "Not a damn clue."

THIRTY-NINE

DALTON

YES, I KNOW IN HOCKEY THEY WOULD HAVE MORE THAN ONE PRESEASON GAME, BUT COME ON, WE BOTH KNOW THIS IS FICTION AND YOU'RE HERE FOR HOT FICTIONAL PEOPLE.

WE'D WON the preseason game 2–1. It wasn't perfect, but I felt good about our performance on the ice. Nashville was a solid mid-tier team, and it'd been a good gauge of where we needed to tighten up before the season opener against San Jose in a week.

The first goal had come off a setup from Jimenez. A crisp tape-to-tape pass from the blue line to Roberts, who read the play perfectly and deflected it past their goalie. Ari would be pumped to know that Monroe took her advice and put him in. Watching the rookie celebrate with the stupid goofy grin that could split his face in two was a highlight of the night.

Second one was a dirty goal from a scramble in front of the net.

I was tied up with their center, but Stephens fought through the traffic, poked the puck loose, and slammed it into the back of the net. The bench erupted in cheers

when he threw his arms in the air and yelled like we'd won the damn Stanley Cup.

But there were cracks we couldn't ignore.

Our transition game was sloppy at times, and we struggled to connect on some breakout plays. Nashville didn't capitalize on it, but a team like San Jose would eat us alive in those situations. If we could work out the kinks in practice, we'd be ready to make waves this season.

The game had gone well, but a rock was still in my stomach.

The walk to my apartment was torturous, and I stretched my arms over my head, trying to release tension in my shoulders and neck.

What if she wasn't there? What if she'd moved out?

I'd been too chicken shit to ask her before boarding my flight.

Those worries disappeared when I pushed the door open, but a whole new set of emotions I hadn't anticipated facing soon took their place.

Now I wished she'd left.

Rejection hit me in the solar plex, all the heat leeching my body, leaving nothing but a cold shell.

It was like the night I'd come home to the note from Emma breaking things off with me, yet somehow so much worse. A million different scenarios had run through my head on the plane of what I'd find when I came home, but none of them were of me stopped dead in my tracks, listening to Ari's grunts and moans coming from my living room.

Sounds that *I* wanted to be the one to pull from her pouty lips.

Not whoever the fuck it was she had in there with her. I was stripped raw at the idea of her with someone else. I'd thought I'd had more time to convince her to give us a real shot. Thought I'd notice a change in our relationship. But apparently I was seeing things that weren't there—hoping for things that weren't real.

The pathetic part? I still wanted to convince her to give me a shot.

Pain radiated from where my nails bit into my palms as I stood there trying to decide if I should barge in and break up whoever she was with or turn back around and go black out at a bar. My jaw ticked when another grunt taunted me.

Fuck that.

There was no way I was letting another man fuck her in my house.

"Ariella!" My voice boomed through the apartment, and I stormed toward the source of the sounds, practically putting my feet through the floor with each step. Asshole better start running because when I got a hold of him, I was going to put my fist into his face. "I know you might not think we are really dating, but you're mine, and I thought I'd made that fucking cle—"

Oh.

There she sat in the living room, legs sprawled out in front of her on the floor, her long hair pulled up in a knot on the top of her head, showing off the long line of her neck, staring up at me with wide eyes, two little lines creased between her brows.

She wasn't with someone.

She was alone, if you didn't count the foam roller, and in *my* shirt.

Instead of the possessive feelings subsiding, it was as if they'd gathered momentum at the sight. I fisted my hands at my side, but not out of anger. Now, it was to try and control the urge to reach for her. To trace my hands along the tan, muscled lines of her legs.

"What the hell are you going on about?" she asked, pulling out one of her earbuds, oblivious to the emotional roller coaster I was currently riding.

I hoped to god she hadn't heard me because I didn't know if there was anything more embarrassing than trying to explain that I thought she was banging someone in my apartment when all she was doing was foam rolling out her muscles.

I rubbed the back of my neck, pulling my eyes away from her bare legs. "Uh, nothing. I was yelling to see if you were home." My smile felt too big for my face. The arch in her brow confirmed it looked as guilty as it felt. But before she could question me, I pointed at the knobbed thing, spouting out, "Those things hurt like a bitch, huh? That's what you were doing in here...alone. Like by yourself...no one else here..."

I'm an idiot.

Ari looked at me like I'd grown a second head as she turned over, propping up on her stomach, her black spandex shorts poking out from under my college tee, the hard foam roller placed under her quad. Of all the positions she could have gotten in, of course she chose the one that looked straight-up pornographic when she moved.

With every roll, she sent her hips and ass back, taunting my self-control. She started moving and let out the same moan that had caused all my problems from a moment ago.

I'd like to identify as that foam roller.

My lids fluttered closed. I had to run a hand over my face to try and hide the reaction the sound caused. The only problem? Hearing it with my eyes closed was ten times worse. My brain provided the image of her bent over the couch as I drove into her wet pussy like I had with my fingers back in her office.

"Thatcher?" Her tone kicked me out of my fantasy. "Did you get a concussion during the game or something? Because you're acting weird."

"Huh? Concussion? No, I didn't get one. I'm just tired."

She was no longer lying on the floor but standing beside me, a yoga mat tucked under her arm. She chuckled, shaking her head.

"So, you're acting weird for no reason, got it." She moved past me, tossing the mat into the second bedroom—her bedroom—before moving toward the kitchen. "You hungry? I made you dinner."

My brows hit my hairline. I hadn't expected her to say that. Other than my mom, I didn't think anyone had ever made me dinner before.

"Why?" I winced when the word left my mouth. It sounded so rude, which wasn't how I'd meant it. But based on the narrowing of her eyes and the slight downward pull of her lips, that was exactly how she'd taken it.

My hands were on her shoulders in two steps, holding her in place before she disappeared into her room.

"I'm sorry. I didn't mean that the way it sounded."

"I'm not sure how many other ways you could have meant *why*." The hurt in her tone made my chest ache and my need to explain myself that much more pressing.

I tilted her face to mine. "I've never had anyone besides my mom cook for me. I wasn't sure why you'd want to do something like that for me."

We locked eyes for a few minutes, neither of us saying anything.

"You're not the only one who can care for someone, Dalton. Let me take care of you, too."

She moved away, oblivious that she'd put my heart in a vice grip with her words.

IF I DIDN'T THINK it would freak her out, I'd ask her to marry me right then and there because my tastebuds had never been as happy as they were shoveling down her food. Leaning back, I patted my stomach—not a brilliant idea given I'd eaten my weight in enchiladas.

"These are the best things I've ever eaten in my life. I didn't realize those were made any other way than a Pyrex dish in the oven."

I laughed at the look she shot me from where she stood on the other side of the island.

"What are you talking about in the oven? Like to keep them warm?" The confusion on her face made me laugh even harder.

"No, some people cook them in there," I explained,

using my hand to hide my smirk when her confusion morphed into what could only be described as disgust.

"Oh, that's just..." she shook her head, bringing another forkful to her mouth. "If you think this is good, wait 'til you have my mom's cooking when we're in San Jose."

I froze. Heart beating faster.

"Is that an invitation?"

She stood there, mouth slightly open like the words had slipped out before she could think it through. Disappointment slammed into my chest because, for a moment, I'd thought maybe she'd been serious.

"Don't worry about it, Sunshine. You can bring me back leftovers." I rubbed the back of my neck, trying to focus on anything but the look on her face.

"Dalton." I lifted my head. She had a soft smile, and her chin rested in the palm of her hand as she leaned on the counter. "No. I don't want to just bring you back leftovers. I want you to come...to meet them."

I stood and walked over to her, loving the way her breath hitched when I caged her in with my arms. The little moles dotting her clavicle killed me. I wanted to run my tongue along them, connecting them. To see how much faster I could get her chest to rise and fall.

Instead, I squatted down and cupped her face with my hands. "Are you sure? Because I don't have to come if that makes you uncomfortable. I'll go out with the guys or relax in the hotel room while you're out."

She peered up at me, vulnerability shining in her eyes as she picked at her callouses. "I panicked because my inside thoughts made it out of my mouth before my head could filter what to say." A stab of sadness hit me, knocking some air from my lungs. But I couldn't say I was surprised. She gripped my hand with hers when I started to pull away, keeping it on her cheek. "Wait, let me finish. I'm glad it slipped out, because that's what I want, Dalton. I want them to meet you."

The weight of her admission settled in the air between us.

I pressed a kiss to her mouth, loving the way she melted under me. "I would love to meet them. I'd love to be a part of anything you'll let me, Ari."

My heart raced as her wide eyes locked on mine, and then, almost instinctively, she glanced toward the hallway.

She was going to run.

I could see it in the way her chest rose and fell, her lips parting as if to speak, but no words came out. My stomach twisted, regret and fear clawing at me for saying too much.

"We should probably get to bed," she said, her voice softer, almost unsure. "You're probably tired from travel and all that..."

"Yeah, right," I managed, leaning down to press a kiss to the top of her head. Her coconut scent taunted me. "Night, Sunshine. I'll clean up from dinner. Sweet dreams."

She hesitated, looking up at me with a faint blush coloring her cheeks. "Night, Thatcher."

And just like that, I stepped back, and she stood and walked down the hallway.

The knife in my chest twisted deeper with every step she took away from me. It took everything in me to let her go, to stay rooted to the spot as she slipped out of sight.

Two steps forward and three steps back.

I ran a hand through my hair, blowing out a breath as I stared at the now-empty kitchen. What the hell was I doing? I'd been hooked on her from the start, yes, but this wasn't some fleeting infatuation. This was more.

This was everything. She was everything.

My world felt brighter when she was around. The weight of expectations, the pressure of my career—it all faded when she was near. She made me feel seen, like I wasn't just Dalton Langley, star hockey player, or the guy trying to prove himself to his father.

With her, I was...me.

I wanted her to let me in.

To let me see all the parts of her she tried so hard to keep guarded. To stop running—not just from me, but from the idea that we could be something real. Something worth fighting for.

I scrubbed a hand over my face, debating if I should go after her. Tell her everything. That I wasn't just playing house, that this wasn't some fake relationship anymore.

That I'd fallen for her. Hard.

But the thought of pushing her, of scaring her off completely, kept me frozen in place. Grabbing the dishes and carrying them to the sink, I sighed, the ache in my chest refusing to fade. I'd give her space, but one thing was for sure—this wasn't over. Not for me.

I just had to hope that when I told her, it wouldn't be over for her either.

FORTY

ARIELLA

WHEN A CHARACTER SAYS THE QUIET PARTS A LITTLE TOO LOUD…

I GROANED, pressing the phone harder against my ear as I flopped onto my bed, clutching the pillow beneath my head, wishing it could somehow smother the chaos swirling inside me.

Pick up already.

"I made him enchiladas and asked him to come home with me in San Jose," I blurted out before Gracie even got a chance to say anything. I dragged my arm across my face as if that would help the pounding of my heart

There was a pause before my cousin's scream shattered the silence, so loud I had to yank the phone away to save whatever was left of my eardrum.

"Shut up, I knew you liked him. Meeting *la familia*, Ariella that's huge. God, you two will—"

"It doesn't matter if I like him," I interrupted, the lie clinging to my tongue, sounding hollow. "I…" The rest trailed off because I didn't know what the hell I was thinking or feeling anymore.

Gracie's tone softened. "Babe, you better not be

moping around telling yourself this isn't worth it. We both know it is." I clenched my jaw, her words cutting close to the truth. "Have you talked to him at all about how you feel?" she pressed.

I didn't answer.

Couldn't answer because I was still shoving the door, holding my thoughts and feelings closed.

"You ran, didn't you?"

"Yup," I said, popping the *p* and causing a long stream of expletives to exit her mouth. "You have no room to talk, Gracie. You're on a different date almost every night of the week, running so far from anything that could even look like a relationship by making sure you only choose shitty dates who won't stick around."

There was a beat of silence before she responded, calm and contained. Not what I'd expected or hoped for. I'd been looking for a fight so I could deflect.

"That's not totally true. I also select ones that would piss off my father," she sassed, but there was an edge to it. "We both know you're being a bitch because you want to get a reaction out of me, so that way, we can move this conversation on from the fact that you like him."

More silence stretched between us.

"I'm scared, Gracie." My voice broke. "Scared of losing myself, of giving up my independence. What if getting involved complicates everything? What if I can't focus on my career?" I sat up, on the verge of hysterics. "Remember I told you his father fucking propositioned me? Like, do I really want to get involved with someone whose father is like that?"

I winced when the words were out because that was a

lame excuse. In fact, part of the reason I'd realized I wanted to be *with* him was because his father was a piece of shit. I wanted to show him how worthy of love and affection he was.

Fuck. Why did I think about the L word?

Gracie took a deep breath, and I could tell she was choosing her words carefully. "I know you've worked hard to get where you are. But pushing people away doesn't protect you, Ariella. It just leaves you... alone." There was a sadness in her voice that made my heart hurt, but I still tried to argue.

"I'd rather be alone than lose myself," I said, but it sounded hollow.

"The right person won't make you lose yourself. They'll help you find parts of yourself you didn't even know existed. By not giving yourself this a chance, you might be missing out on something incredible." I swallowed hard, her words hitting me deeper than I wanted to admit. "From what I can tell, being with Dalton has only made you happy. You have to ask yourself if you're willing to risk missing out on a chance at real happiness."

Images of his smiles, the way he listened, how he remembered the smallest details...they all flashed through my mind.

Dalton made me feel seen in a way I hadn't felt before. "Maybe you're right," I said softly.

"Of course I am. I'm always right. My personal relationships may be shit, but I like to think my daddy issues help me give good advice."

"*Ay Dios mío*, Graciella."

"Seriously though," she said, her tone gentle. "Talk to

him. Don't let fear decide for you. For a woman who *hates* that the *machismo* tells us how to live our life, you've ironically managed to wall yourself in by your own boundaries. Maybe try living, Ari."

Those words were like a sledgehammer, hitting at a reality I'd been blind to.

"What if I'm wrong, and he's just being nice? What if he's just good at playing the part of a fake boyfriend? He just let me go to bed, no kiss or anything..." The confession was barely above a whisper, but Gracie still caught it, making a sympathetic noise.

It was so stupid. It didn't make sense that I had this secret hope Dalton and I were like a romance novel, falling in love even though it was all supposed to be fake.

"You wanted him to run after you," Gracie said, stating aloud what I couldn't. "Fuck that. Go knock on his door. You two literally live together. Throw on some lingerie and strut your ass over."

"Gracie, it's not the same."

"You want him to make the first move to prove it's not fake for him either." She continued to voice everything running through my mind with alarming accuracy, which would be irritating if it wasn't so enlightening to hear aloud. Gracie's tone turned gleeful. "Oh my god, Ari, you're so far gone. You're past 'like' *prima*, I'm pretty sure you're onto another L-word."

I groaned, burying my face in the pillow. "Not helping. How could I love him? We aren't even a real couple."

"Bullshit. What you two have has been real since you met him. You're too stubborn to admit it aloud, but we both know it. The way you care for one another? That's not fake, but you've been using that excuse as a cover every time you get scared. It's time to put your big *chonies* on and fucking admit it." Gracie paused dramatically, then let up on the serious talk like she knew I was at my limit. "You know what you need? Your vibrator and some quality time imagining Dalton clapping them cheeks," she joked, providing sound effects.

"You need to start dating better men. Clapping them cheeks? Really, Gracie, is that what they're saying to you?"

"Pounding your *pompis*?"

That did the trick. A laugh burst from deep in my chest. By the time we stopped laughing, tears were streaming down my face.

"Please put that on a shirt."

"Oh, you know I'm already on that shi—" A loud knock interrupted whatever she would've said next.

I froze, heart leaping into my throat, because there was only one option for who could be at my door in this apartment.

FORTY-ONE

DALTON

YOU KNOW *THE* CHARACTER ART FROM THIS BOOK Y'ALL LOVE…HERE YOU GO!

NEVER IMAGINED walking down my hallway in nothing but my briefs, cowboy boots, and a hat.

I'd finished the dishes and then paced my bedroom for the past twenty minutes, thoughts racing. I knew I'd told myself to give her time, but fuck that. I couldn't keep it to myself any longer.

Tonight was it.

I stood there, flooded with the same nervous energy I got before a puck drop. What if she didn't answer? It was like midnight already. Or worse, what if she answered and then closed the door in my face?

Nervousness shifted into something more akin to unease. Before I could chicken out, I gave a few hard raps on the wooden door.

What the fuck am I doing? Please don't answer, please don't answer, please don't—

My breath caught in my throat at the sight of her.

I didn't care that I was being obvious about checking

her out. She'd answered the door in nothing but a matching silk pajama set. The light pink perfectly complemented her toned, tanned legs. Those fucking shorts showed off the curve of her ass, and there was no air left in the room.

In the background, I heard who I assumed was Gracie yelling something.

All I could focus on was Ari, her dark hair tumbling down around her shoulders, those wide brown eyes looking up at me with a mixture of curiosity and something else, something I hadn't dared to hope for.

"Dalton?" she asked, a crease forming between her brows. "What are you wearing?"

"You said you liked me in my boots and hat," I answered with a shrug, like that explained it.

One corner of her lips curved. I clocked the moment she noticed the pattern on my boxer-briefs. "There are suns on your underwear, Thatcher."

Every time she used my name, it sent a jolt to my heart. But when it rolled off her tongue in that husky tone, it made a detour down to my dick.

"Yes there are, Sunshine."

With two steps, I'd closed the distance between us, wrapping one hand around the back of her head and pushing her against the wall, my hips lined up with hers.

"I can't keep doing this," I rasped out, as all my reservations about showing up at her door like a lovesick puppy went out the goddamn window. Not with the way she was staring at me right now.

Her pink tongue played with my resolve, poking out

and wetting her plump bottom lip. "What...what do you mean?" she whispered.

I wanted to devour her.

To imprint myself so deeply on her, she'd lower all her walls for me. I wanted to leave her struggling to breathe at the thought of us not being together, in the same way she left me.

I took a ragged breath, knowing I needed to answer.

Her heartbeat was wild in the column of her neck, and I couldn't stop myself. Her draw was too enticing. Slowing, I dragged the tip of my nose up her throat, and a trail of goosebumps appeared in its wake. I savored the little gasps that fell from those sinful lips.

Perfect. She was fucking perfect.

My fingers traveled up her thigh until they gripped her hip.

"Dalton." My name was said like a prayer.

"Yeah, baby?"

Anything. Anything she asked for, I would give her. That was how fucking down bad I was. I pulled back enough to take in the unguarded expression on her face. My eyes were glued to her, memorizing everything about her in that moment. The flush on her cheeks, the way emotion swirled in those big chocolate and caramel-colored eyes of hers framed by thick lashes.

I wanted to savor this—her.

She started to say something, and my heart ached in anticipation of what it could be, but it wasn't Ari's voice I heard.

"Please, tell me you're going to fuck. Holy shit, the

heavy breathing? The *need* in y'all's voices." A high-pitched shriek nearly broke the sound barrier. "I fucking told you, Ari. I told you that he was falling fo—"

"Hang up *right* now," Ari shouted, trying to push me away to get to the phone, but I didn't budge.

"Are you still listening, Gracie?" After a few beats of silence, her attention was back on me. "What are you doing here?"

"I'm done pretending, Sunshine. I want you, every part of you that you'll give me. Not as some front or cover but for real." Her plump wet lips parted, her brown eyes blazing with want, but I refused to move, needing to know where she stood. If she wanted me the way I wanted her. "This was never fake, not for me. Every moment with you has meant everything to me."

Her eyes widened, but she had yet to say anything, and my heart felt like it was being squeezed to the point of bursting. I swallowed. If I thought that part was going to be tough, the next part was going to kill me. "If you don't want this, I need you to break my heart, darlin'. Because I don't think I can stop falling for you unless you do." I let out a humorless chuckle. "Hell, I probably still won't, but I'll back off. I won't chase you in private."

She gave a sharp inhale, looking up at me like a deer in headlights as more of my confessions tumbled out.

"I think about you constantly. Wonder what you're doing and if you're thinking about me at all. I want to be there for your wins and your losses. I want to be the one you choose to confide in. The one you run to and not from." I took a deep breath, forcing my hand to still on her head when I desperately wanted to pull her face to mine. I had to get the rest out. "I know that's not what you asked for, Ari. You made it clear this wasn't going anywhere the first night we met, but my head and my heart are confused." I leaned my forehead against hers. It was too difficult to look at her. Scared I'd see her rejection before she actually said the words. I knew she felt things for me, but I didn't know if she'd let herself act on it. So I steeled myself and said the last of it. "But my heart thinks we have a chance to make this real. To be yours."

Something warm and wet dropped onto my skin, and I caught another of her tears with my thumb, looking up at the drop in awe.

Without warning, Ari launched herself at me, wrapping her legs around my waist and burying her face in the crook of my neck.

"I said break my heart, not my back," I laughed out, wrapping my arms around her.

"This is all your fault, Dalton. I was perfectly fine before you came along. And now, going home feels lonely without you. Now, I want to hear your voice. Now, my stomach flips when a text comes in, hoping it will be you." She leaned back, dropping her legs back down to the floor and facing me with her teary eyes. "Now...now I can't remember why I told myself not having you in my life was better, why I had to do this alone, why I didn't deserve to love and live simultaneously."

Love.

She didn't exactly tell me she loved me, but the profession was close enough.

My hands gripped her waist, her skin hot to the touch.

"But what abo—"

She cut me off with her mouth pressed to mine in a hard, fast kiss.

"There's nothing more, Thatcher. I choose you. Everything else, we'll work out. I don't have all the answers in this moment, but I don't need them."

Undone. I was completely undone by her, by her words. My entire existence shifted in that moment, because she was mine.

I moved my hand under her shirt to place it on her bare stomach and held her close. "I've been thinking about doing this with you since our Facetime." I rasped the words against her ear, lost in lust and feelings.

"Yeah?" She ran her fingers over my chest, and a shudder went through my body from her touch. "Me too." Her lips were a hair from mine, her sweet breath hitting my face, and I closed the distance. She parted for me so I could tangle my tongue with hers, whimpering into my mouth, and I swallowed her sweet sounds. I held her tighter against me before picking her up. Her thighs wrapped around me, and I grinned against her, sliding my tongue into her mouth and kissing her deeply. Small hands slid up my bare chest, traveling up over my neck before gripping either side of my face with a tenderness that caused my chest to ache.

I ground against her, and she matched my movements with as much desperation as I had as I carried her to her new dresser, setting her ass on top.

"Dalton," she moaned, keeping her legs around my waist as I used one hand to lift the hem of her sleep shirt.

My movements were frantic and messy as I slid the shirt over her head, revealing her perky tits.

Fuck.

I took one nipple into my mouth, loving how her back arched when I swirled my tongue over it, alternating between sucking hard and soft. I smiled at how her sounds got so desperate, she was barely forming coherent words.

"Tell me what you want, baby," I said, moving to give attention to her other nipple. I was desperate for her, coming apart at the seams. I needed more. The hottest moan I'd ever heard in my life echoed off the walls as I paused my attention to her breasts standing back up to grind myself into her silk-covered pussy.

"Yes," she hissed when I reached for the waistband of her shorts. "Don't stop."

I slid them down her tanned legs, letting my tongue follow their path. A sting radiated from where she tangled her hand in my hair.

"Want me somewhere in particular, Sunshine?" I asked with a chuckle, making no effort to move any faster. I'd fucking waited for this, and I wanted it to last.

Her wet, tight body writhed on the dresser. "Please," she begged, arching her hips toward my mouth.

"That wasn't an answer."

She made an irritated noise, eyes popping open, so much fire in them I swore heat licked up my body. "You want specifics, Thatcher?" Her brow arched in challenge, the sting from my scalp increasing as she tightened her grip, guiding my face so it was an inch from her bare pussy.

I smirked at her ire.

Running my tongue up her wet slit, slow and unhurried, I swirled it around the bundle of nerves, watching the way her eyes fluttered shut. She let out a breathy moan that went straight to my cock. But she wasn't getting off that easily. I pulled away again, loving the way her head hit the wall in frustration.

"You fucking tease."

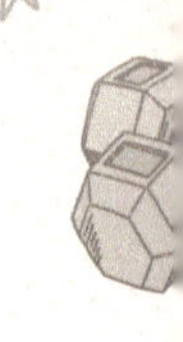

FORTY-TWO

ARIELLA

RAW, NEXT QUESTION…

HE WAS EVERYWHERE and nowhere I needed him all at the same damn time.

"I need you to touch me, Dalton," I pleaded.

He nipped at the sensitive skin on my neck, caressing the sting with his tongue. "I am touching you, Ari. You're going to need to be more specific than that."

Asshole. He knew what I wanted but he was going to make me work for it—beg for it.

My head met the wall again, back arching, and I gave in. "I want you to bury your fucking fingers into my pussy, Thatcher."

He let out a low growl—I hadn't realized men actually made that sound until him—picking me up and practically sprinting to the bed with me in his arms, dropping me on the soft mattress.

"Jesus Christ."

The devilish grin he shot me should have warned me about what he was about to say.

"Think he knew he was dying for the sins we're about

to perform in this bed?" My mouth dropped open as Dalton dropped to his knees, shoving his broad shoulders between my thighs to spread them apart further, just like he had in my office.

I couldn't even tell him how wrong that was to say, too distracted by the rough feel of his palms traveling up my legs.

"Every fucking day I think about these gorgeous legs being wrapped around my head," he growled into my inner thigh. The scruff on his face left a delicious burn on the inside.

"Fuck, you're so warm and wet for me, Sunshine." His fingers traveled to my bare center and we both let out a hiss when he reached his destination.

I was never going to survive this, everything heightened by the emotions we'd just shared.

By the fact that this was real.

"You better fuck me hard, Thatcher," I said back arching off the bed as he pushed into me with his fingers. The delicious fullness had me moaning and wanting more.

"I'll give you anything you want from me, Sunshine," he promised, before latching onto my clit with his mouth, his saliva mixing with my wetness. He hummed, and I nearly leaped off the bed from how fucking good it felt.

His deep grunts had my hands knotting in the sheets. He sounded like he was in as much pleasure as I was. My body was brimming with anticipation with every pump of his fingers and swipe of his hot tongue.

My orgasm was right there, teetering on the edge. I gripped his hair and pulled. It set him off. He swirled his tongue faster, filling me with a third finger. It was like electricity shot down each limb. My body went taut, and every muscle tensed as pleasure rushed through me.

Dalton never stopped touching me, kissing me, until I finally caught my breath.

I gripped his head, dragging his mouth back to mine, needing more of him. He groaned into my mouth, his heartbeat fast, and his touch just as needy.

"God, you're perfect," Dalton muttered in my ear, lazily placing kisses along my body. The frenzy from when he'd show up had slowed, and now it was like we were both seeking something...more. "I need to be inside you," he said, and the emotion in his words had my heart leaping into my throat.

I nodded, but that wasn't enough for him.

"No, I want to hear you say it, Ariella." He stood, pulling off his boxers and pulling out a condom from who knew where.

"I want you to feel you. Nothing between us," I said, the words tumbling out and stunning us both.

His inhale was sharp, and I squirmed under his attention. Maybe that wasn't the right thing to say? Maybe I'd misread the moment...

The bed dipped under his weight, distracting me from my thoughts. He crawled over me, caging me with his body. "Is that what you want, Sunshine?" His voice was so tender it hurt.

How had I ever wondered if he felt something real for me, too?

"I'm on the pill. So if you want to—"

I moaned as he captured my mouth with his lips,

tongue stroking mine. He kept his weight off me, but I could still feel his hard length pressed between my thighs.

My eyes closed, senses heightened. His hands were everywhere, the back of my neck, my breasts, my waist.

"Tell me you're mine, Ari."

"I'm all yours," I breathed. As soon as the words left my lips, he sank the length of his cock inside me.

Dalton's ragged groan drowned out the gasp that ripped from my throat. God, he felt so good. So perfect.

He rocked into me slowly, taking his time.

"So tight," Dalton whispered as I wrapped my legs around his waist. We both groaned, the new angle allowing him to sink in deeper. "You feel so fucking good, Ari." He licked my lips as he continued to pump inside me. "This is everything I want. Your pussy. These lips." He moaned as I swept my tongue against his, lost in his words—in him. "Like goddamn sunshine."

We stayed locked in a passionate kiss as he trailed his hand down, reaching between my legs and smiling against my gasping mouth as he played with my clit, rubbing it at the same hypnotic pace that he fucked me.

"Oh God, Dalton…" I cried out, my pussy contracting around his size as I rotated my hips in search of the friction that'd send me over into bliss.

"Fuck, you're better than I could have ever imagined," he rasped in awe as I grabbed handfuls of the white sheets. "It's never been this good. Tell me it's never been this good for you either," he panted, nipping at my earlobe.

All I could do was nod, too consumed by pleasure to form words.

"I'm going fill you with my cum, Ari, and then I'll

watch it drip from your pussy before I scoop it up and shove it back in where it belongs," he muttered, thrusting deeper, harder with every word.

Holy shit.

"I'm going to come..." I panted as he gripped my hips, fingers dimpling the skin.

"Let go for me. Let me see how beautiful you are when you come."

His dirty talk fucking did it for me, because as if by magic, I fell over the edge at his word. "Dalton," I moaned, pleasure shooting up my spine. The orgasm consumed me. I cried out as he pumped into me, drawing out a release so intense it caused my legs to shake.

Even in my state of delirium, I heard him speak the words I didn't know I'd needed.

"You're mine, Ariella, and I'm never letting you go now," Dalton groaned, spilling inside of me before collapsing on top, careful not to crush me. There were a few beats where neither of us spoke. Our heavy breathing was the only sound, but then he popped up on his elbow, eyes brimming with something I couldn't place. It warmed my heart.

It was as if everything was right where it belonged, where I was supposed to be.

He trailed his fingertip down the side of my face before pulling me in for a kiss, his dick still firmly inside me, our limbs entwined.

Dalton had seeped into my skin, gotten into my head.

Into my heart.

WE LAY there tangled up in one another after another round in the shower.

"When did you even take your boots off?" I asked, thinking back to how tonight had all gone down. I could say I'd never expected this, but that'd be a lie. The even larger lie would be if I said I hadn't hoped for it.

"Fuck, I don't even know how I got out of those so fast. Practically jumped out of them."

He looked over at me, wide smile painted on his face. "I'll keep the hat on next time and you can ride me."

"Shouldn't *I* wear the hat then? Wear the hat, ride the cowboy and all that shit," I responded, waving a hand in the air, laughing at the way his smile morphed into a scowl.

"Where'd you hear that rule from?"

I gnawed on my lip to keep my laughter in check, turning on my side so I could fully face him. "Is that jealousy I'm hearing?"

"Yeah, baby, it is," he said, sealing our lips together and making me melt into him. God, we were insatiable, because I'd have sworn this make out session would lead to his tongue being buried between my thighs for the third time in a handful of hours, but a shrill ring cut through the haze.

"I swear if that's your cousin." He flipped over, fumbling with the light. "Shit. It's my dad."

That short sentence had my heartbeat kicking up. I

almost told him not to answer, but didn't get the words out fast enough.

"Hey, Dad." Dalton's tone was tight, devoid of any of his usual charm. The volume wasn't loud enough for me to hear the other half of the conversation, but I didn't like how he tensed. "What changes are you talking about?" His mouth shut, jaw ticking as he listened to whatever bullshit he was receiving. I threaded my fingers with his, giving a gentle squeeze as a show of support, hating how dejected he looked. "Well, do I get a say in who you're looking at trading? Yeah, I know I'm not an owner, but I am the captain and your son."

Dalton practically spat the last word and it dripped with a condescending tone. Whatever his father's response was, it only caused his frown to deepen, his fingers tightening around mine to the point of discomfort, but I didn't dare pull away.

"Okay. Yeah, that's all I've got to say. I'm not sure what more you want when you call me in the middle of the night and tell me you're shaking up the team, but then refuse to tell me anything more. I don't know what the point of this call was if you didn't want my opinion." He paused, jaw clenching. "Our season opener is this week, at least wait 'til after you watch a game to make decisions." With that, he hung up, eyes finally finding mine. Anger swirled in their green depths. "He's making trades and we haven't even started. He hasn't even seen a fucking game."

The moonlight filtering through the sheer curtains offered enough illumination for me to make out the sharp angles of Dalton's jaw, which was still tightly clenched.

"We'll figure it out, right? I mean, he's probably going

to ask Monroe for his opinion before he makes any decision. And I'm sure he's going to want your opinion—this is your team as much as it is his."

Dalton looked like he was grasping for hope, but I didn't actually know that his dad *would* ask me, or even Monroe. Vincent was a narcissist who loved calling the shots—being in control. This was another power move. But I didn't want to voice those worries aloud.

The interaction with Vincent in the hall was on the tip of my tongue, but I was still wrestling with whether or not to tell Dalton about it.

Something cold settled in my gut, an unease I couldn't quite place.

I heard him move against the sheet, but couldn't make out what he was doing until his little finger gripped mine like a lifeline.

"Promise not tell?" he whispered, the pain in his voice tearing at my heart.

"Pinky."

Dalton let out a deep sigh. "He never wanted to be in my life. My dad knocked up my mom when he was on an away game. She was a bartender at a spot the team partied at. Didn't ask for all the details because thinking about my mom having sex grosses me out." He let out a chuckle, but it was still sad. "Mom said it was a one-time deal. Cell phones weren't a thing back then, and he didn't bother giving her a number, but after she found out she was pregnant, she went full Nancy Drew. That's how she figured out he'd failed to mention he was married—didn't tell her he was a hockey player either."

I gasped at the confession. "What happened?"

"Nothing. He told my mom not to contact him again, that she was lying about being pregnant with his kid or that she'd tampered with the condom, and said if she went to the press he'd bury her."

I pushed up on my elbow, needing to see his face. My heart broke at the sadness written in his expression. His skin was salty when I pressed a kiss to his cheek, peppering his face until I met his lips, then looked at him again.

"Your dad was an asshole."

He rolled his lip between his teeth, staring off. When he spoke, he sounded distant, lost in thought, and I let him release what must have been years of built-up family shit.

"I got a full ride for hockey. I made Rookie of the Year, and put up record-breaking numbers my freshman year. Came back as a sophomore, and when we made playoffs he showed up at practice. Had no clue my biological dad was a hockey player—Mom never told me. We didn't talk about my dad, period. It was the first big fight we had." He ran his hand over the back of his head. "Regret that to this day. But when he took me out to dinner, he painted this picture of my mom keeping him out of my life. And he was so..."

"Convincing?"

He nodded, and even in the dim lighting I knew he wasn't actually *seeing* what he was staring at, too lost in thought.

"Very. It's how I found myself dropping out of college senior year and joining the Desperados. Mom wanted me to finish college and get my degree." He let out a humorless chuff. "But I wanted so badly to please him. To give him a reason to stay." His eyes locked onto mine, bitterness coating his words when he spoke. "He hates it when I call him Dad. We live in the same building, on the same floor, and I've never seen him here. I drive the car he wants me to, wear the name he wants, act the way he wants, and he won't let me call him Dad. Maybe if we win the Stanley this year."

Heartbreak.

My heart was shattered by the way Dalton longed for acceptance. The hope in that last sentence. He believed the lie that he should earn his father's love, that he fell short of deserving it, so he thought he needed to work harder for the affection.

When, in reality, his father was undeserving of him.

I didn't know how to tell him he was better off without the asshole. My gut told me he wasn't ready to hear that yet. So I did the only logical thing.

Used humor to deflect.

"Think it would help your daddy issues if I called you *Papi*?"

He barked out a laugh, giving me the biggest smile, clearly happy for the subject change. The smile didn't dim as he tucked my hair behind my ear, trailing his fingers down the column of my throat, leaving a trail of raised skin in their wake.

"You could probably solve all my issues if you called me *Papi* in bed."

FORTY-THREE

DALTON

WHY AM I SWOONING OVER FICTIONAL CONVERSATIONS?!?

ME:

What's the point of living with my girlfriend if I can never find her?

SUNSHINE:

We were just in bed together.

I'm panic-packing in my room.

ME:

*Guest room

Your room is the same as my room. In fact, while you panic pack, move the rest of your shit over

BTW It's going to be fine

SUNSHINE:

Easy for you to say. You're not the one bringing a white boy to a family party.

Shouldn't you be on the ice?

ME:

Snuck my phone into the rink

Send me a picture of you in our bed…

Without clothes. The way I left you this morning…

SUNSHINE:

Get back to practice!

I swear, if Monroe trades me to another team because you're sexting me…

ME:

I'd follow you.

I told you. I'm keeping you.

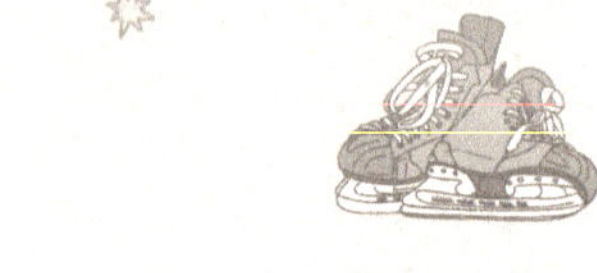

FORTY-FOUR

ARIELLA

"IS THAT A GOAT?"

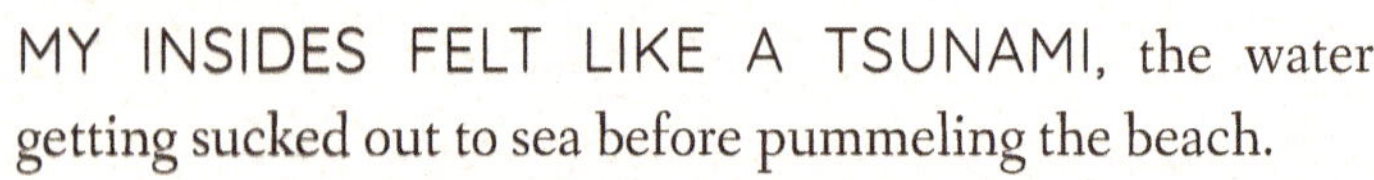

MY INSIDES FELT LIKE A TSUNAMI, the water getting sucked out to sea before pummeling the beach.

"Planning on chewing through your lip there, Contreras?" Monroe asked. The question wasn't quite a green light to sit in the chair in front of his desk and talk about personal issues, but I treated it as such.

"I did something, and I'm not sure how it's going to go over."

He raised a brow, pulling his attention from the computer. "Wow, that wasn't vague as shit. Yes? Like what the fuck are you expecting from me with that information?"

I groaned, head hitting the polyester fabric on the chair's back. "I may or may not have had another jersey made for Dalton and threw out his old one."

Oh look, the urge to throw up was back.

Three full blinks. That was how many it took to get a response. Monroe wasn't pleased. "The fuck do you mean

you threw out his jersey? We get on a plane for our season opener in like an ho—"

"I put Thatcher on the back," I blurted out, copper filling my mouth because I really was chewing a hole in my bottom lip.

Monroe's face blanked before blooming into an honest-to-good smile. It was brief, but I witnessed it.

"Thatcher." He stared at me for a moment, then gave a curt nod. "Listen, whatever the consequences are for that stunt, because you know there will be, you've got my support."

"Yeah. I know."

And I did. His father was not a fan of mine, and I wasn't a fan of his. But unlike him, I cared about his son. Dalton deserved to see what it was like for someone to care about him. To realize he already had all the love and support he needed, and that his sperm donor was nothing but a leech.

"That was the name that should have been on his back the entire time. That kid is like a younger brother to me, and —" he paused, staring at his hands. "Dalton has a heart of gold. Cares for people in a way that is genuine. Sees the best in people. Even those who don't deserve it... so be patient with him if you see him accepting shit behavior he shouldn't. Maybe you can show him how to stick up for himself, too."

The words come tumbling out before I could stop them. "I'm pretty sure his dad propositioned me."

Monroe's eyes flew to mine. I'd been wrong. He didn't walk around with a scowl, *this* was a scowl and it was borderline terrifying. "I want you to be very careful, and very specific, with what you're about to say, Ariella. What makes you think that?"

I bristled at his tone, wishing I could tell him to forget about it and move on, but it was clear that wasn't going to happen. The air was cold in my lungs as I took a deep breath. "I saw him in the hallway outside of Dalton's apartment. He asked me if I was going to be a distraction for Dalton. Make him stray from the plans Vincent has for his son." The lines between Monroe's brows deepened with each word, but he sat there still as a statue. "He told me Emma and he had an *arrangement*, and he could give me all of my dreams if I fell in line."

That made him react. He scoffed, running his hand down his face, muttering what sounded an awful lot like "piece of shit."

"You're sure about his meaning? There's no way you misunderstood him?"

I took out my phone and pressed play. There wasn't anything on the screen, just a shot of the inside of my bag, but Vincent's voice was as clear as day. We sat in silence as the recording played all the way through.

"Send it to me. Then go get ready to head out." His voice was sharp, attention back on his computer, which I took as my sign I was dismissed. "And Contreras," he said, looking up at me as I stood. "I'd take what he said to you as a threat and watch your back. Take it from personal experience...there's a punishment coming because of your response."

I GROANED when we had to drive farther and farther down the street to find parking.

"Wow, you weren't kidding when you said parking was a bitch in San Jose," Dalton said, sliding the little rental into the first open space he saw, which was nearly five houses down from my parents.

"Yeah, parking does suck. But all these cars belong to my family."

Dalton's eyes widened, taking another look at the row of vehicles.

A burst of laughter came from the back seat, and Jimenez's head popped between our shoulders. "This is going to be fun. How many boyfriends have you brought home?"

"Who even invited you?" I asked,

"So none."

My cheeks heated because the asshole was correct, and the grin on his face as he sat back said he knew it too.

We'd landed a little over an hour before and headed right over to my parents' place. I'd specifically told them to keep it small. That we wouldn't have a lot of time to stay before we had to get to the arena, which was conveniently only a few short minutes away.

But it looked like Dalton was about to meet far more people than he bargained for...

Maybe we should just leave.

My heart dropped at that thought. I'd actually been looking forward to seeing everyone...to introducing them to my boyfriend. My mom had been on cloud nine when I told her I was bringing someone. My father was less than thrilled, but Ricky'd piped up and given his approval, which shocked both me and my dad.

Then, to my surprise, the rest of the week I kept getting calls from my dad asking about what Dalton wanted to eat, when we'd be there, he even asked if I knew how to get them into the game.

"*Déjala en paz*, Jimenez," Gracie said , trading places with him and sticking her head up front too. " I don't know why you didn't think my *tía* was going to invite everyone over. By the way, thanks again for the plane tickets, Dalton."

His face had a sheepish grin, but he didn't look at all worried. He'd told me my cousin was coming—he hadn't told me he was the reason she was able to. He rubbed at the back of his neck, glancing over at me. "Ari deserves to have everyone who loves her at her first NHL game. I didn't want it to just be me there." My heart rate kicked up, and I swore I could feel my blood pumping through my veins.

It wasn't exactly an "I love you," but fuck did it feel like that's was what he was trying to say. Between his words and his gesture...

"Well, I'm fucking hungry. So let's go. You two can make out later," Gracie called out, already out of the car and halfway to my parents' backyard.

"I'm with her," Jimenez called out, practically sprinting after her like he was five.

I was still not fully prepared when we walked around the side of the house to the backyard, following the sounds of laughter and conversation. I smiled at the loud sounds of my family we could hear all the way from the street, but as we rounded the corner, something in my chest burst open. Tears welled up in my eyes.

Navy and orange banners hung from the fruit trees, and Desperados-themed party decorations covered almost every surface.

"What is going on?" The words were a broken whisper, and I pushed away the tears spilling over. Ricky jogged over, a wide smile on his face.

"Look at that. Seems we did good, eh? She's even crying, which is a rarity for my sister. She tends to hit or yell instead." He wasn't talking to me. His eyes were behind me—on Dalton. I spun around, completely confused as to what was happening.

"You did this, too?"

"I called your brother after booking Gracie's flight out." He shrugged. "Introduced myself, told him he got a free shot if he wanted it when we met for moving his sister into my house."

"I don't need his permission to mo—"

Dalton's eyes sparkled when he cut in, "Told him that, too." His eyes flicked over to my brother, who stood there with his arms crossed, a smirk on his face.

"Yeah, *este cabrón* told me that you didn't need either of us trying to tell you what to do or where to live. You could handle making those decisions on your own." He paused, nodding his head. "I tend to agree."

This was why Ricky had stepped in for me with my father.

"I still don't understand what's going on here, though?" I looked up into Dalton's warm green eyes.

His hand slipped into mine, giving it a tight squeeze.

"I told you, tonight's special. You deserve to be celebrated."

"I'm not even the one playing. Hell, I'm not even doing any actual coaching tonight. I'm basically another fan."

"You're nothing like a fan. You're so much more, Sunshine." He cupped my face with his hand, and my cheeks heated with the thought of him touching me like this in front of my family. For a brief second, I considered pulling away, but those were remnants of the old me. The one who ran from relationships because I thought they'd cost me my independence, that I'd be forced to support someone at the detriment to my dreams.

Yet here I stood, surrounded by family, never having felt more supported in my life.

And it was all thanks to one man.

Ricky's voice cut through the moment, reminding me of where I was. "You know who *will* be a fan tonight? Me."

I turned. "Wait, you're coming to the game? You don't even like hockey."

Ricky shrugged a shoulder, taking a sip of his beer. "Your boyfriend got us tickets, so we're all going." He paused, looking over the yard where all my aunts and uncles were milling about. "Well, not all of us. My mom just got a little excited and thought everyone needed to come for *birria*."

As if summoned by his words, something dashed between us.

"Is that a goat?"

My face flushed, and my eyes probably looked like

fucking dinner plates. "Oh my god, I forgot that white people don't usually butcher their own animals at family parties." I covered my face with my hands, wishing the ground would swallow me. Meanwhile, Ricky was nearly doubled over in laughter.

We'd just been having this heartfelt moment, and a fucking goat ruined it.

"Ari?" Dalton peeled my hands away.

"I'm sorry, when my parents heard I was bringing someone, they got all excited an—"

"Ari."

I ignored him, the ramble pouring out. "They wanted to do *birria*, but I should have known that would be too weird and told them to do…I don't know, *quesadillas*? Or mayb—"

He pulled me in tight, kissing the top of my head. "I am honored that you brought me, and I want to experience what your family is willing to share with me. I'd never come into their home and ask or expect them to alter their food, culture, way of life, or any of those things." He pulled back, looking down at me. "Same way I'd never ask you to change for me. I want all of it, Ariella."

I wasn't entirely sure he was still talking about the food with that last part.

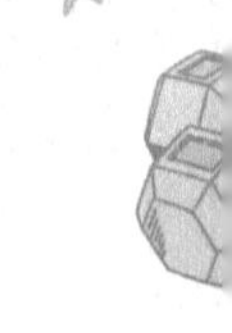

FORTY-FIVE

ARIELLA

I HOPE YOU FIND A PARTNER WHO GIVES
YOU GIFTS THAT PROVE THEY KNOW YOU.

THE CHILL CUT through the fabric of my suit, but I didn't mind. I enjoyed the reprieve from all the anticipation coursing in my body. The atmosphere was electric, and the opener hadn't even started yet.

"So, what do you think?"

Dalton's words rumbled in my ear as I stared out the tunnel we were minutes from walking down.

"I can't believe I'm on the coaching staff for an NHL team."

His warm chuckle traveled down my spine, settling between my thighs.

"I can't believe I'm going to try and play after eating all that food."

"I told you to slow down," I scolded, rounding on him.

"God were they worth it. Your mom told me I can come back after the game for more." He wagged his brows at me, causing the scowl I was trying to give him to fall.

"You should have heard the lecture I got about not letting you eat more." I smiled at the memory. "My mom

said you're a growing boy who needed your food. And I told her I thought the ten tacos you'd already had were probably enough."

Laughter echoed off the tunnel, settling into a comfortable silence between us.

"Thank you."

"For what?"

"For the party, the tickets, flying Gracie out so her annoying ass can sit right behind me at my first NHL game. I'm not even the one playing, and you made sure everyone would be here to support me." God, did that make my heart burst for him.

"You deserve everything and more, Sunshine." He said with a soft smile, stroking my cheek with his thumb. "I've got something else for you," he said, the confidence slipping slightly, his hand coming up to scratch at his neck.

"Wait. Me first." I really shouldn't have eaten so much, because now, all of it was threatening to make a second appearance. I pulled a large folded jersey out of my bag that looked identical to the one he had on—hadn't realized he'd brought spares when I threw out his other one—minus one major change.

His brows pinched together. "I don't—"

"Just look at the back." My tone was almost harsh, but I was seconds away from puking, I was so nervous.

Dalton turned the jersey over, his fingers brushing the fabric. I watched his expression shift, curiosity giving way to disbelief as his eyes landed on the name. THATCHER stretched across the shoulders, bold and unapologetic.

His chest rose and fell, but I could see the crack in his composure, the way his throat bobbed when he swallowed hard. When he finally lifted head, his green eyes were raw and unguarded.

"Ari…" His voice was low, thick with emotion. He looked back down at the name, his thumb tracing the stitched letters "You did this for me?"

I nodded. "You should play under the name *you* want, not the one your dad forced you to."

His lips parted like he wanted to say something, but nothing came out. Instead, he closed the space between us in two steps, pulling me into a tight embrace. His arms wrapped around me, his face buried in my hair. I felt the deep, shuddering breath he took, the tremor in his hold as he tried to keep himself together.

"You have no idea," he murmured, his voice cracking. "No idea what this means to me."

Tears stung the back of my eyes, but I held them back, pressing my palms against his chest.

"Can you take a picture of me in it on the ice? I want to send it to my mom, she's going to love it." He chuckled. "We are probably going to have to have a fan jersey made for her. And darlin', when we get back, will you come to family dinner with me to meet her?" he asked, gripping my chin.

My heart stuttered in my chest. "Of course. I mean, it only seems fair since you just endured meeting five hundred of my family members."

"And I can't wait to be around them again," he said smiling, before it fell slightly, replaced by a nervous expression. "It looks like we had the same idea for a first game present." He pulled a swath of navy fabric from behind his back, handing it to me. Flashes of what looked like orange stitching on the back caught my attention as I unfolded it.

"You know, I'm glad I moved you into my bedroom, because planning surprises is a lot easier when your girlfriend's clothes are hanging in your closet." The nerves were clear in his voice, and it took me a moment to figure out what the hell he was talking about.

But it all clicked when I unfolded a suit jacket. Orange embroidery matching the color and number on his jersey stared back at me.

55.

"I told you I'd find another way to see my number on your back." There was no missing the hint of possessiveness when he spoke. It rolled over me like a caress. "If you don't like it, you don't ha—"

I cut him off, lunging at him and wrapping my arms around his neck. The hard planes of his gear bit into my skin, but I didn't care.

"Woah, there, Ari. In skates here," he laughed, catching me around the waist, his shoulder colliding with the cinderblock wall.

"I love it." *I love you.*

"Really? Because it was a fifty-fifty shot of you reacting like this or telling me off at the idea of being marked by me."

I leaned in, pressing my lips to his. The kiss was slow and deliberate, like we had all the time in the world, like he wanted to savor every second. His hands on my waist tightened, pulling me closer, and I melted against him, my fingers tangling in the hair at the nape of his neck.

The roar of the arena preparing for the game seemed

distant, muffled by the rush of blood in my ears and the way Dalton's lips moved against mine.

When we finally pulled back, his forehead rested against mine, our breath mingling in the quiet space between us. "You have no idea how much you mean to me," he murmured, his voice low and rough.

I smiled, my fingers tracing the edge of his jaw. "I think I have a pretty good idea."

He kissed me again, softer this time

"Alright, Coach, time to put that jacket on and show everyone who you're rooting for."

"SHIT."

Another player, this time from San Jose, slammed into the backboards, rattling the plexiglass, the sound mixing with the shit-talking from players on the bench and chatter of the crowd.

Monroe snorted, suited arms crossed over his chest, clipboard in hand. "Contreras, you've been around hockey how long and you're still reacting to hits?" he taunted.

"Gets me every time," I said, craning my neck to catch Dalton's breakaway.

My comment earned me a snort, his eyes never leaving the gameplay. The guy looked at the rink in the way I analyzed a player's body movements.

Reading. Anticipating.

I could see why the players liked him so well as a coach. Monroe read plays almost as well as Dalton.

My stomach swooped just thinking about him. He was impressive on the ice, skating with an assertiveness that made it hard to pull my eyes away. Every move he made, the numbers on my back warmed. As if the whole arena's eyes were on those two numbers.

We were up by two going into the final period, and the boys were on fire. A loud clang echoed off the ice, the puck nailing the crossbar of our goal. The play caused a scramble for the puck.

San Jose was aggressive in their play. They weren't shy about putting us into the walls.

And I wasn't sure how to feel about it.

As a coach, I winced every time, my mind playing through every injury a hit like that could cause.

Then there was the *other* reaction I had to it. A reaction I was blaming on biology, because I found it incredibly hot every time Dalton slammed a grown man into the plexi.

I thought back to what he'd whispered to me during intermission when he was supposed to be paying attention to Monroe's gameplay prep for the third period.

"Sunshine, there a reason you bit your lip when I plastered Holtz against the glass? Because if I didn't know any better, I'd say it turned you on."

"Good thing you know better then, Thatcher."

Dalton had to have a superpower. It's like he knew when I was thinking about him, because mid-flashback, he shoulder-checked Holtz into the boards next to the penalty back, and he had the audacity to wink at me before skating away.

"Great. How many of my players are using the game to get laid?" Monroe grumbled, throwing a hand in the air.

"Coach, we've *always* used the game to get laid. You should know that." Jimenez laughed, catching his breath on the bench. "Hell, don't tell boss man, but you wouldn't even have to pay me to play this game professionally. Drowning in pussy is payment enough."

"You think anyone is going to want you if you're broke, Jimenez?"

"What do you mean? Of course, Coach. Ari over here is always telling Cap not to pay for shit." He threw an arm out my way, standing and gnawing at his mouthpiece as he waited to go out on the ice for the final minutes of the period.

"That's because Dalton's got a good personality. All you've got going for you is your money, Jimenez," Monroe ribbed, his tone making it obvious he was messing with the defensemen.

"That's cold, Coach. Cold. My good looks are my other selling feature." He flashed a gleaming smile, and I laughed.

Then everything came to a screeching halt.

The energy in the arena shifted instantly, from electric anticipation to something heavy, tense, and wrong.

It started with the collision. Two players slammed into each other at full speed, sticks tangling, skates scraping hard against the ice. Dalton was one of them. The crowd roared, but I barely heard it, my entire focus narrowing on the rink as his body hit the ice at an awkward angle.

He didn't get up.

"Shit," Monroe muttered, his clipboard dropping to

his side as the players on the bench surged forward, craning their necks to see what was happening. Jimenez swore under his breath beside me, his usual grin wiped clean off his face.

Dalton still wasn't moving.

My heart thudded painfully in my chest, each beat echoing in my ears. "Get up, Thatcher," I whispered, my hands gripping the edge of the railing so hard my knuckles turned white.

But he didn't.

The refs blew their whistles, the game grinding to a halt as trainers hurried onto the ice. I couldn't make out what they were saying, but their hurried movements and the way they gestured for the stretcher made my stomach drop.

He's fine. He's fine. He has to be fine.

But my brain didn't believe the lie. The way he was lying there, so still, sent a cold wave of panic crashing over me.

"Shit, this isn't good," Monroe muttered, his usual stoic demeanor cracking as he exchanged a grim look with the assistant coach.

I barely heard him. My thoughts spiraled, every terrifying possibility flashing through my mind. What if it was his spine? His head? What if—

"Ari?" Jimenez's voice snapped me back to reality. He was looking at me, concern etched into his features. "You okay?"

I wasn't, but I nodded anyway, unable to tear my eyes away from the ice as the trainers finally reached Dalton. They were speaking to him now, one of them crouched down by his head. I searched for any sign of movement, anything that would tell me he was okay.

And then, finally, he moved. Just a little—his hand flexed, and his head turned slightly as he spoke to the trainers. Relief should've washed over me, but it didn't. Not fully. Not until I knew exactly what was wrong.

"Come on, Dalton," I whispered again, my voice shaking as they carefully lifted him onto the stretcher. My pulse roared in my ears, and I could feel the sting of unshed tears pricking the backs of my eyes.

I cared for him—more than cared for him. And seeing him like this, vulnerable and hurt, made it impossible not to admit just how much.

As they wheeled him off the ice, the crowd offering a mix of cheers and nervous murmurs, my body moved on autopilot. I turned to Monroe, my voice steadier than I felt. "I'm going with him."

He didn't argue. Didn't even try. He just nodded, giving me a sharp look that said he knew how much this mattered.

"Keep me updated," Monroe said, his tone softer than usual.

FORTY-SIX

ARIELLA

ARE WE STILL BREATHING? NO? OKAY.

THE BUZZ of fluorescent lights seemed louder than normal as I rushed through the hospital doors, the chaos of the emergency room doing nothing to quell the rising panic in my chest, making it hard to breathe. My feet barely paused as I approached the nurse's station, gripping the edge of the counter. I'd narrowly missed catching the ambulance ride, and then gotten stuck in traffic that had left me in a full panic.

"Dalton Thatcher," I blurted, my voice trembling. "Or Langley, maybe. I don't know what last name he'll be under. He was brought in a little while ago. Please, I need to know how he's doing."

The nurse glanced up from her computer, her eyes softening when she took in my frantic expression. "Are you family?" she asked gently.

Fuck.

"Yes. Please, just tell me what's happening."

She scanned the screen in front of her. "He's in

surgery," she said, her tone calm but serious. "A fractured rib punctured his lung, and there was some internal bleeding. The surgical team is working to repair the damage now."

My stomach churned, the weight of her words pressing down on me. "Is he going to be okay?" I managed to ask, my grip tightening on the counter.

"They believe so," she said reassuringly. "The surgery is precautionary to stop the bleeding and stabilize him. He's young, strong, and otherwise healthy. That's in his favor."

The words should have calmed me, but the knot in my chest barely loosened. "When will he wake up?"

She offered a small smile. "It'll be several hours before he's out of surgery, and even then, he'll be under observation for a while. He's going to need time to heal."

I nodded, my throat tight as I swallowed back tears. "Can I wait somewhere? I need to be close."

The nurse gestured down the hall. "He'll be moved to recovery in Room 324 once he's out of surgery. You're welcome to wait there."

"Thank you," I whispered, barely managing to get the words out before turning toward the hallway she'd indicated. Each step felt heavier than the last as I walked, the weight of the situation pressing down on me. I had to see him. Even if he wouldn't wake for hours, even if he was hooked up to every machine imaginable, I had to be there when he opened his eyes.

I'd been too in my head to even see the person who stepped in my way, blocking my path. "Ms. Contreras,"

Vincent Langley said smoothly, as though this were some casual meeting and not a nightmare. His expression was as polished and detached as ever, but his eyes showed an unmistakable gleam of malice.

I squared my shoulders. "I don't have time for this."

"Make time," he snapped. "Dalton's surgery will take hours. You're not doing him any good by pacing the halls like a panicked child."

I flinched but didn't move. "I don't have any interest in speaking with you."

"Oh, I think you'll want to hear this." He reached into his tailored jacket and produced a folded sheet of paper, handing it to me.

"Open it," he barked when I continued to glare at him.

I did, and found a trade agreement from the San Jose Stars.

"What is this?" I demanded, even though the bile in my throat already told me.

"Your new life, Ms. Contreras. The Stars were very happy to hear you were available, turns out they've been trying to get you to work for them for a while." He sounded so fucking smug I wanted to scream, or hit him. "If you truly love Dalton, and I question whether you do, you'll take this opportunity. You'll leave quietly. No good-bye, no lingering mess. Just sign the dotted line, and I'll make sure you're set for life."

Coaching trades were rare, but they did happen—especially if your boyfriend's asshole father wanted to get rid of you.

My chest burned, a mix of anger and anguish. "You

want me to leave him now? While he's in surgery? You think I'd do that to him?"

"If you cared about him, yes," he said, sighing when my only reaction was to glare at him. "This was already in the works, Ms. Contreras. You were never getting on a plane back to Dallas with the team. The accident just underlines that you're not good for him. Dalton has a future ahead of him. A legacy to carry. But he can't focus on that with you around. Your career aspirations and your presence are distractions he can't afford. Tonight was proof of that."

His words sliced deep, but I refused to let him see me falter. "You have no idea what's best for him."

Vincent's lip curled. "I see what you've done to him. This injury? He was reckless, because of you. He wasn't focused, because of you. Don't pretend you don't see it. If you walk away, you'll give him the chance to get back on track. To be the player he's destined to be."

I shook my head, my voice low and trembling. "Dalton is more than a hockey player. And he doesn't need you deciding what's best for him."

His eyes hardened. "I tried to be reasonable. But if you won't take the offer, then I'll fire you. Effective immediately."

I crossed my arms, defiance rising even though my stomach churned. "Fine. Fire me. I know my worth—I can always find a spot on another team. Dalton's worth more than this."

Vincent smirked, like he'd been waiting for that response. "Is he worth his friends' careers too?"

"What?"

"You heard me." His tone was venomous now. "If you don't sign this and leave quietly, I'll go through with the trades I've already arranged for Jimenez and Monroe. They'll be gone by the end of the week. Dalton will lose the teammates who've stood by him for years, and it'll all be because of you."

The air seemed to vanish from my lungs. He was bluffing. He had to be. But the glint in his eye said otherwise. The weight of the paper in my hand felt unbearable.

"You would do that to your own son?"

"I would do what's necessary for my legacy," he said coldly. "Now, Ms. Contreras. What's it going to be?"

My mind raced. My heart screamed to refuse, to stand firm, to protect Dalton in the way he deserved. But the thought of taking away the people he leaned on most, the friendships that kept him grounded?

I couldn't. Not when he was already facing so much.

I swallowed the lump in my throat. "I'll sign it."

His smile was smug, but I barely registered it as I scribbled my name at the bottom of the contract, my hand shaking.

"You made the right decision," he said, taking the paper back and tucking it into his jacket.

I ignored him, spinning on my heel. My legs felt like lead as I walked away, my chest hollow. I'd figure out a way to fix this. To protect Dalton and the people who mattered to him.

I turned a corner to see Gracie and Ricky standing there, the shock and concern on their faces a lifeline. Ricky opened his mouth to speak, but I shook my head sharply.

I didn't want Vincent to hear them.

The moment Dalton woke up, I knew his father would be there to spin his lies. And I needed a plan before that happened.

"Graciella, I need you to do something for me."

FORTY-SEVEN

GRACIELLA

PRIMAS ARE RIDE OR DIE.

WHAT THE HELL *could he possibly be doing that is taking this long to answer?*

I jammed the ivory button three more times, tapping my foot. He would have some old-school doorbell instead of a camera. The guy probably had a flip phone, too.

I shuddered at the thought. My whole life was on my phone. It was what kept me employed.

"I do not have time for this," I muttered, raising my fist to knock against the wooden door. But before it could connect, it opened.

"Monroe, wha—" the rant trailed off.

It wasn't a tall, pissed-off-but-hot man glaring down at me, but instead an adorable girl with a pink princess dress, honeyed curls, and a slightly crooked tiara looking up at me.

"Oh, hello," I said, peering past her, searching for a clue on if I'd gotten the right house.

I was guessing no.

What was the over-under she'd know where to locate a professional hockey coach in the neighborhood?

She pointed at my platform Vans with brightly colored flowers. "I like your shoes."

"I like your crown."

Her little face blossomed into a smile, revealing a missing front tooth.

"Goldie." The stern voice caused us both to nearly jump out of our skin. "What have I told you about answering the door? You need to let Daddy do it. Now, go upstairs and play."

"But Dad—"

"No, buts. Upstairs. Now."

My brain short-circuited a bit when the door was pulled open farther, revealing the very man I was in search of.

Daddy? Holy shit.

I probably should have been more sly, but my impulse control wasn't great, so my eyes shot to his left hand, searching for a ring. Hell, the tan line was the real indicator, but there was none. Which, I guess didn't really mean anything. Relationships took all sorts of different forms. And why did I care if he was in one? I mea—

"What are you doing here?" That gruff tone pulled me back. "How's Ari? What happened? No one will tell me shit. Vincent sent us all on a fucking plane the second the game ended and then said she was no longer on the team and that Dalton was in recovery." He crossed his arms over his chest, his brows pulling so close together they nearly touched.

The mention of my cousin reminded me of why the

hell I was back in Dallas only a handful of hours after that shit-show of a season opener.

"Woah, slow down with the twenty questions, my guy." I pushed past him, stepping into the quaint little entryway dotted with photos of his daughter. "Wow, I didn't know you could smile," I said, picking up a pale green frame and taking in the very grouchy man looking unabashedly happy while throwing his daughter in the air, but it was plucked from my hand before I got to commit the image to memory.

Large hands wrapped around my upper arms, gentle but firm, and the hot man-bear of a coach ducked down to meet my gaze. "What the hell is going on, Graciella?"

Right. Focus.

"You're going to want to sit down for this."

FORTY-EIGHT

DALTON

THIS IS WHY YOU CUT OUT TOXIC PEOPLE.

THE WORLD CAME into focus slowly, like the static clearing on a broken TV screen.

My head pounded, and the soft hum of machines mixed with the muffled sound of someone talking nearby. Blinking against the harsh fluorescent lights, I tried to sit up, but a sharp pain in my side forced me to stay down.

"Dalton," came a familiar voice, smooth but cold. My father.

I turned my head, my eyes meeting his. He sat in a chair beside the hospital bed, his hands clasped in his lap, his suit impeccable, as always.

"You're awake," he said, offering a thin smile. "Good. The doctors have been monitoring you closely. They're pleased with your progress."

"What happened?" My voice was rough, barely above a whisper. I tried to piece together the fragments of memory. The game. The hit. The sharp pain in my chest. Surgery.

"You're back in Dallas," he said, as if that explained

everything. "I had you flown here privately. I thought it best for you to recover somewhere familiar, where you'll have the best care."

Dallas. My mind raced. The last thing I remembered was being in San Jose. And Ari...

Ari.

"Where's Ari?" I croaked, my throat dry. "She was there..."

My father sighed, leaning forward, his expression calculated, sympathetic. "Dalton, about Ariella. She's not here. She left."

His words felt like a punch to the gut.

Something wasn't right.

"What do you mean she left? When will she be back?" *How could she not be here when I woke up?* I reached for my phone. There were a bunch of missed calls and texts from numbers I had saved, some texts from one I didn't, but nothing from her.

"She had plans, Dalton," my father said in a careful tone, as if he were breaking bad news to a child. "Plans to take a position with the San Jose Stars. She accepted the offer before you were even out of surgery. I suspect that was her plan all along."

"No," I said immediately, shaking my head. "She wouldn't do that. She wouldn't just leave."

"I know this is difficult to hear," he continued. "But it's for the best. You need to focus on your recovery, your career. You don't need distractions."

"She wouldn't—"

Doubt crept in despite my protest. Would she? The

way she looked at me, the way she cared. It wasn't fake. It couldn't be.

But then why wasn't she here?

"Son, I know you cared for her, but relationships like that are fleeting." His words hit like a punch in the gut, they were not nearly as hard of a hit as when he handed over a white sheet of paper with Ari's signature. "She's ambitious, and I don't blame her for that. But you can't let someone else's priorities get in the way of your future."

I turned my face away, staring at the sterile ceiling. My chest ached, but not from the injury. It was a deeper, raw pain. Ari wasn't just anyone—she was everything.

"I thought she loved me," I whispered, the admission slipping out before I could stop it.

"You have a bright future ahead of you. The doctors say you'll be back on the ice in time for playoffs. Focus on that. On what's important."

My father spoke like my heart hadn't been ripped out of my chest and stomped on. I glanced over at the door, ready for Ari to burst in and prove that everything he was saying was a lie, but nothing happened.

He caught my stare. "Son, she's not coming. She's not even in the state."

His words dug into me, each one scraping against the hope I'd been clinging to. Maybe I hadn't done enough. Maybe I hadn't earned her love.

My dad stood, smoothing the front of his jacket. "This is for the best, Dalton. You'll see that in time." He placed a hand on my shoulder briefly before turning and leaving the room.

The door clicked shut behind him, and the silence in the room was deafening.

I stared at the ceiling, trying to piece everything together.

She left. She fucking left.

The words echoed in my mind, each repetition heavier than the last.

What had I expected? She'd told me she would from the beginning. She'd put up those barriers the night I met her, and I'd been fighting to get through them ever since. I let out a bitter laugh, angry tears spilling over, and I wiped them away with the back of my hand.

I was an idiot. So fucking in love with her that I was seeing shit that wasn't really there. I'd thought she loved me too, that we meant something to each other—that *I* meant something to her.

The door opened again, pulling me from my thoughts. Monroe stepped inside, his expression a mix of concern and frustration.

"Hey," he said, closing the door behind him. "How you holding up?"

I shrugged, the motion sending a twinge of pain through my ribs. "Been better."

He pulled a chair closer to the bed and sat down, leaning forward with his elbows on his knees. "I ran into your dad on my way in. I take it he's been filling your head with shit."

My jaw tightened. "He said Ari took a job with San Jose. That she left me."

Monroe snorted, his expression darkening. "You really believe that?"

"Well, she's not fucking here, Josh. I wake up days later from surgery, and she's not even in the same damn state anymore." Another bitter laugh fell out. "Only note she left was her signature on a contract. She didn't even text or call."

"Check your, phone you idiot."

"You don't think I did?" I yelled it so loud, I thought nurses would come running. His eyes softened and he nudged the device toward me.

"They wouldn't be coming from her number, Dalton. She's trying to make sure your asshole father thinks she's playing by the rules. Check the unsaved one. Probably the one that's been blowing up your phone."

> UNKNOWN NUMBER:
>
> I know you probably won't see this for a while. I hope you're resting. You need it. Please don't push yourself too hard.
>
> UNKNOWN NUMBER:
>
> Monroe's going to explain everything. I know it's a mess, but...you deserve to know the truth and I can't explain it all through text. Please, just listen to him. Trust him. Trust me.
>
> UNKNOWN NUMBER:
>
> I'm sorry for not being there when you woke up. I wanted to be. More than anything. I don't cry much, Thatcher, but I'm pretty sure I've used up all the tears in my body.
>
> UNKNOWN NUMBER:
>
> You're going to get through this, Thatcher. You're the strongest person I've ever met.

It's okay if you don't believe him. I
promise. I just want to know you're doing
what makes you happy.

UNKNOWN NUMBER:

I miss you. I thought you might have
seen these by now. But maybe not.
Monroe said your dad's not letting
anyone but him see you. So, chances are
you hate me.

Maybe you have seen these...

UNKNOWN NUMBER:

I'll never stop cheering for you, even if I
have to do it from afar.

UNKNOWN NUMBER:

Stupid prepaid phone is out of money or
whatever after this. That's probably my
sign to let you go anyway.

I love you.

I sat there dumbfounded. Nowhere in any of the messages did she say it was her, but I knew it was. "Why... I don't understand."

"She's not here, and she's not texting you from her phone, because your dad cornered her in the hospital when you were in surgery. Traded her and told her to leave—no contact. She told him to shove it up his ass, so he threatened to trade me and Jimenez if she didn't take the trade," Monroe said, sounding more pissed off than I'd ever heard before.

My head snapped toward him, my pulse racing. "What?"

"Gracie told me." Monroe shook his head. "Fucking

flew back here just to get me the truth before your dad talked to me. She heard the whole thing, and that girl's got a fucking impeccable talent for remembering every detail of a conversation." He let out what was as close to a chuckle as he got. "According to her, your dad manipulated Ari. Same fucking way he's done to you since he slithered into your life like the snake he is." He turned away, shaking his head. "I warned her, too, warned her he'd punish her for turning him down back at your apartment. He used her love for you to back her into a corner."

I stared at him, the weight of his words sinking in. "What the hell are you talking about? What happened outside my apartment?" My mind was running a million miles an hour, trying to piece together what he was saying.

He pulled out his phone, slapping it on the hospital tray and pressed play. My father's voice sounded through the speaker.

"We don't have to have the same arrangement as Emma and me. Though I'm not opposed. I know you're ambitious, Ariella. I have connections my son doesn't have. I can make all of your dreams come true. You don't even have to work hard to reach those milestones. I can just place you there, so long as you help keep Dalton where I want."

I was so in shock with what I was hearing, learning how he'd made arrangements with my ex and hearing him proposition Ari, that I almost missed when it changed to her voice.

"Dalton is a grown man, Mr. Langley. He doesn't need anyone else's approval to make his decisions. Not mine and definitely not yours. He deserves to have people around him

who care about what he wants, who do things with his best interests in mind. Clearly, you're not one of them, but I am."

"She chose you. And not just the night of your accident, Dalton. She's been choosing you from the start, giving you the same love and support that, according to her cousin, she never thought she could have. And she offered it to you because you gave it to her first," Monroe said, his tone softening. "You've been so busy trying to keep a toxic man in your life, you can't see the people who actually love you."

I looked away, his words cutting deeper than I wanted to admit. "He's done a lot for me. Brought you both on when I asked."

Monroe shook his head, his voice steady. "You think giving me a job, or Jimenez a chance, makes him a good person? We could've done all of that without him. And so could you."

Swallowing hard, the truth in his words settled like a stone in my chest, along with the rage at fully wrapping my head about what he'd done, and what he'd tried to do, to Ari. I looked up at Josh. "What do I do?"

"You fight for her," he said simply. "You stop living for what your dad wants and start living for what you want."

I closed my eyes, exhaling shakily. He was right. I'd spent the last few years trying to gain my father's approval, but I was never enough. And I never would be, not for him.

I'd let my father manipulate me for too long, and I wasn't going to let him take her away from me too. Ari was worth more than that.

She was worth everything.

"I'm done," I said quietly, but with resolve. "I'm done with him."

Josh clapped a hand on my shoulder, and I winced. "About damn time."

My chest ached, but this time it wasn't from the injury. It was from the hope surging through me. I wasn't letting Ari go—not without a fight.

FORTY-NINE

ARIELLA

SHOUT OUT TO NICK PARKER & ELIZABETH
JAMES FOR THE ENDING INSPIRATION.

WHAT WAS the stage of grieving called where you filled every waking second with work or an activity until you were too tired to think about what was missing from your life?

The stage where you buried yourself under an avalanche of distractions, convincing yourself that productivity was the cure for a shattered heart.

Or when thoughts of the person you lost popped in like an unwanted intruder, feeling like a shot to the heart, and you immediately pushed them away—sometimes with a barbell, sometimes with music so loud it could drown out your own screaming thoughts.

And sometimes, when none of that worked, you found solace at the bottom of a bottle of tequila.

That had been my life for the past week.

Gracie, bless her persistent ass, hadn't let me wallow alone. She'd flown out to Dallas and then turned right back around, called her work, and said she'd be out for a while. Used her vacation time and everything.

Now, for reasons I still didn't understand, she'd dragged me to a sports bar downtown, claiming I needed to get out and stop sulking. I'd gone, because fighting her was pointless. And because, deep down, I didn't want to be alone with my thoughts anymore.

The weights had stopped helping.

Maybe the tequila would.

"You've been staring at that margarita like it's going to tell you the meaning of life," Gracie said, raising an eyebrow as she sipped hers. "Are you going to talk about it, or are we just going to sit here in silence while you mope?"

I sighed. "What the fuck am I supposed to say? I love him. I love him so much, it physically hurts."

She leaned back in her chair, a smug smile playing on her lips. "Well, it's about damn time you admitted it. Took you long enough."

"Don't." I pointed a finger at her, my voice sharper than I intended. "I'm not in the mood. What does it even matter that I realized it? I can't be with him...he doesn't even know I love him." The last part was a whisper because it hurt too much to say it louder.

At least I thought he didn't—he'd never answered any of the texts I'd sent him.

Gracie's face softened, and she leaned forward, resting her elbows on the table. "I know, *mija*. But you need to get this off your chest. Talk to me."

She was right. The weight of my feelings pressed down on me like a barbell I couldn't lift. "I wanted to show him what it's like to be chosen, to show him he deserves someone who puts him first. But..." My voice cracked, and I blinked hard, willing the tears not to fall. "I thought I was protecting him, protecting all of them by walking away, but what if I just broke his heart?"

And mine.

Gracie's covered my hand with hers, squeezing. "Ari, you made a sacrifice. You did what you thought was best for him."

"But what if I was wrong? What if I ruined everything?" A bitter laugh escaped me, the sound sharp and hollow. "It's ironic, isn't it? I spent so much time building a career on my own terms, determined to prove I didn't need anyone and was better alone. And now I have exactly what I thought I wanted but..."

"But?"

"I was fucking wrong," I admitted, my voice cracking under the weight of the words. "I thought a relationship would cage me, hold me down—" I paused, running my finger along the rim of my glass, willing the water collecting along the rim of my eyes not to fall. I shrugged a shoulder, giving her a watery smile. "You were right. When you find someone who truly sees you, someone who believes in you, it doesn't cage you. It frees you. Supports you. It makes you stronger."

She reached out, resting a hand on my arm, unshed tears in her own eyes threatening to spill over. "He gave you that, didn't he?"

The memories of Dalton's unwavering encouragement flooded back. The way he'd listened and pushed me to be better without making me feel less.

"He never made me feel like I wasn't enough, or that I had to choose between him and my dreams. He stood beside me every step of the way." My chest tightened, the ache almost unbearable. "And now he's gone, and I feel like I'm dying. Slowly drowning on dry land."

I paused, trying to settle my labored breathing.

"What if he thinks I didn't care enough to fight for him? What if...what if he never knows I love him."

Gracie's grip tightened, her voice soft but firm. "He knows. And if he doesn't yet, he will. Love like you two have doesn't disappear. It leaves a mark. He'll feel it, even if he doesn't know it yet."

"That's what I'm afraid of." I whispered. "That he's marked me forever and I walked away. He's gone."

Gracie's brow furrowed, her thumb rubbing soothing circles on my arm. "Ari, you don't know that for sure. He's not the kind of man to let something like this go without a fight."

"Yeah, but his dad isn't the kind of man to leave loose ends. He'll be sure Dalton thinks I left because I didn't care. That I chose my career over him. I'll be *persona non grata*. Hell, Emma is probably already moved back into his apartment, nursing him back to health."

"That's why Monroe's there. That man's got the stubbornness of a mule and loyalty to match. He'll tell Dalton the truth."

"Not if Vincent threatened him, too," I countered, the thought like a punch to the gut. "It's been a week, Gracie. A week of nothing. No calls. No texts. Nothing from him. At this point..." My voice cracked. "At this point, I have to accept that I lost him. I lost the love of my life."

Gracie's hand shot out, gripping mine tightly. "No. Don't you dare go down that road. You did what you thought was right. You protected him, even if it meant breaking your own heart. That's not losing him, Ari. That's loving him. And if Dalton has even an ounce of sense, he'll see through his dad's bullshit." She paused, ducking her head down so our eyes were locked. "He just needs time to process everything. He loves you. I know it."

She sounded so sure. But the doubts still clawed at me, sharp and relentless. My heart couldn't take the hope.

Before I could respond, movement on one of the TVs above the bar caught my attention. My heart stumbled as Dalton's name scrolled across the banner at the bottom of the screen, accompanied by his photo.

"Turn it up," I called to the bartender, standing so quickly that my chair scraped against the floor. Even with the volume turned up, the bar's noise made it hard to catch what the announcers said. I stepped closer, trying to read their lips, my heart pounding.

"Is it about his injury?" I asked, panic threading through my voice. My mind raced, thinking of all the worst-case scenarios. Was he okay? Was this about his recovery?

"You're not going to find out from there," came a deep voice from behind me, cutting through the noise.

I froze.

My entire body stiffened, my heart racing like I'd sprinted ten miles. Slowly, I turned around, my breath catching when I saw him.

Dalton stood there, tall and imposing, green eyes locked onto mine with an intensity that rooted me to the spot. My knees threatened to buckle under the weight of the moment.

"Oh my god," the words came out as a choked sob, and

there was no holding back the tears streaming down my cheeks. "Dalton?" I breathed, the name slipping from my lips like a prayer.

He stepped closer, the noise of the bar fading into the background.

"You're here? In San Jose?" My voice cracked as my mind struggled to process what I was seeing.

That he was really here, that I wasn't dreaming.

He nodded, his expression unreadable as he moved closer. "I needed to see you. Needed to hear you say it." His tone was soft but insistent, his green eyes searching mine.

"Say what?" My confusion grew, my heart thundering in my chest as he drew closer, our bodies only inches apart.

This had to be real. I could feel the heat from his body, the scent of his cologne, but I was afraid to touch him.

Because if this wasn't...if this were a cruel trick caused by alcohol and grief, I really would die of a broken heart.

"The last thing you texted me," he said, his voice a whisper now. "Say it, Sunshine."

My emotions crashed over me like a tidal wave, battering my bruised heart.

"I love you, Dalton Thatcher. With every fucking fiber of my being. You don't limit me, and as scary as it was to think of attaching myself to someone, you showed me that all you want to do is see me reach my dreams." Another sob slipped out. "Because doing that doesn't require being alone when it's the right person by your side. And you're the right person, Thatcher."

The second the last words left my mouth, his hands

cupped my face, and his lips crashed onto mine. The kiss was desperate and raw, a collision of love and relief that left me breathless. I twisted my hands into the fabric of his hoodie.

"Your ribs!" I gasped, jumping back in a panic when he winced. "You're supposed to be recovering. Should you even be standing?"

He laughed softly, pulling me back into his body before I could get too far and resting his forehead against mine. "I'm fine, Sunshine. Better than fine now. I needed to see you. I needed to tell you that you're it for me." He cupped my face. "You're everything. I love you, and I'm not losing you. I'm not letting you get away."

Tears streamed down my face as I shook my head. "I'm so sorry. I wanted to be there when you woke up. I wanted—"

"Shh." He pressed a finger to my lips, his eyes soft and full of understanding. "I know. Monroe told me everything."

I swallowed hard, my hands trembling as they rested against his chest. "I didn't want to leave. I swear I didn't. But I couldn't let him trade Monroe and Jimenez. I couldn't take that away from you, or from them."

His jaw tightened, and he wrapped his arms around me, careful of his injuries. "I hate what he did to you. To us. But I'm done letting him control my life, Sunshine. Done."

"What do you mean?" My voice was barely audible.

"It's over. I'm done living for his approval. I'm living for me now. For us."

"But what about your team? What—"

"What I want is you," he interrupted firmly, his voice steady. "It's always been you. Forever and always, that's what I want."

I kissed him again, pouring everything I felt into it.

The bar erupted into cheers, reminding me that our emotional reunion was happening in the middle of a crowd of random people. But I didn't care. This was what mattered.

He was what mattered.

When the noise died down, the TV caught my attention again.

"In an unexpected trade agreement, the San Jose Stars have acquired former Dallas Desperados Coach Josh Monroe, defenseman Christian Jimenez, and star center Dalton Thatcher, despite his recent injury."

My head whipped back to Dalton. "You're playing here?"

He smiled, brushing a tear from my cheek.

"*We're* staying here," Jimenez said, coming out of nowhere and wrapping his arms around us. "Ugh, that was beautiful. Fucking choked me up. Hell, I think Monroe even shed a tear."

I pulled away, looking over Dalton's shoulder toward where Jimenez pointed. Sure enough, my former boss stood stoic, hands shoved into his pockets. But his usual frown was replaced by a slight upturn at the corners of his lips.

"Why...how did you all end up on the Stars?" I asked, mind still reeling.

"Well," Monroe started. "Thatcher's in love, and was coming whether he could play hockey or not. And we didn't want to stay behind and work for that asshole. Not that we had a choice since he signed our trade papers too. And I didn't want to take the blame for the property damage to his car." Monroe's gaze shifted toward Gracie, who was studying her drink like it was the most interesting thing in the world, and took a sip. "The police report I read said Vincent's car appeared to have been hit with a long wooden implement. And wouldn't you know, Gracie, I'm missing a hockey stick from the bed of my truck."

She broke out into a coughing fit. "Damn. That's crazy. You really should put those somewhere more secure," she said, looking him dead in the eye with a blank face.

My face split into a smile. *Pinche, pendeja.* She one hundred percent was guilty. And I was one hundred percent so grateful for her.

"That still doesn't explain how you ended up traded to the Stars," I said, staring into Dalton's eyes, who'd yet to let me go.

"He lied." His face darkened. "When my dad said he'd trade Monroe and Jimenez if you didn't leave. He'd already done the deal. The plan was to remove anyone from my life he thought might pull me away from his goals. So, I got a new agent and secured some things first," he explained, some of the anger slipping away.

"But that's not how trades work. You can't just decide where you want to go..."

Dalton smiled with that boyish grin. "Luckily, even with a bum rib, I've got a good enough record they were interested in me. Plus, I grew up with the captain, Hogan.

He pulled some strings. Finalized the trade papers this morning and had my lawyer send them over to my dad. In fact," he pulled out his phone. "This is the asshole calling about it now, I bet."

He answered the call, and even with it pressed to his ear, there was no mistaking the bark of anger from his father on the other line. "Hello to you too, Vincent." Dalton paused for another string of what I was sure was an ass-chewing. With each word, Dalton's smile grew larger until he finally cut him off.

"Here's the thing, my lawyer did a little digging. Had a nice chat with Emma, too. We pulled together a lot of interesting information about how you run your business. Turns out you can't do a thing about the trade, because if you attempt to mess with me, my team, or my girlfriend in any way, I'll fucking bury you."

Hearing a man threaten his father should not make you wet, yet my body would disagree with that logic.

"I don't give a damn about the Langley empire. It's not my last name attached to it." I swore I heard crashing over the phone, but Dalton just kept talking. "If you have anything else you want to say to me, contact my lawyer."

He ended the call, to a round of applause from our friends.

"Hell, yeah," Jimenez yelled, punching Gracie playfully in the arm. Monroe even flashed a rare smile. I didn't think I'd ever been more proud of someone than I was right then.

"He doesn't deserve you," I whispered, too emotional to get the words out any louder.

Dalton dropped a kiss to the top of my head. "No, he

doesn't, and you showed me that. I love you, Ariella. I was coming even if I couldn't play hockey. I only want to be where you are."

My chest twisted with a rush of emotions that were the polar opposite of the ones I'd had at the beginning of the night.

His lips pressed to mine. Soft and searching at first, before morphing into something more desperate, like our bodies were recognizing how close we'd come to not being together.

How the hell had I ever wondered if this was real?

Or thought I was somehow stronger alone?

"I found the other piece of my heart in you, Sunshine. I want it all, the fairytale happily ever after." Saltiness burst onto my tongue, the tears streaming down my face interfering with our kiss. "You don't have to cry, darlin'," he said softly, pulling away.

"Oh yes I do." My mouth found his again. The tears were from happiness, and I doubted they would be stopping anytime soon. "I love you, Thatcher."

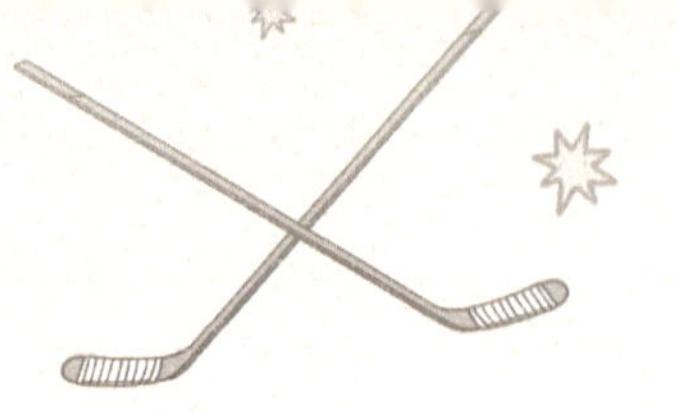

EPILOGUE: DALTON

POP THE CHAMPAGNE AND DON'T THINK ABOUT IF THIS IS STICKY…

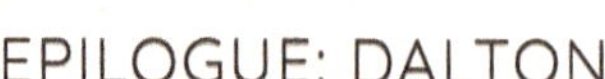

Months Later…clearly.

THE FINAL PERIOD of the Stanley Cup Final was electric.

The air crackled with tension and excitement. Fans of both teams roared, their collective energy vibrating through the boards and up into my chest.

Stars Arena was alive. It felt like all of San Jose was here tonight to witness game seven.

The score was tied, 2-2, with just under a minute left on the clock. Every muscle in my body hummed with adrenaline, trying to fight off the exhaustion, but fuck stopping now. Not when the cup was this close.

I glanced toward the bench, my attention snagging on Ari, her dark eyes focused, shouting directions with Monroe next to her. I chuckled. Her job title might have been strength and conditioning coach, but damn was she a good unofficial assistant coach when it was game time.

She claimed it was because she was forced to live with

"the star center," so she couldn't help herself during a game. Her tailored suit coat moved as she gestured. The number 55 was stitched on the back of this one, too, but I'd made one special addition, and THATCHER ran across the top of her shoulder in a soft blue, matching my jersey.

"Focus," Jimenez growled beside me as we lined up for the faceoff. "We're taking this."

I grinned, my mouthguard flashing. "Damn right, we are."

The puck dropped.

The ice beneath my skates was slick, cold, and unforgiving as I lunged forward, swiping it cleanly and shooting it to Hogan. He darted down the boards, but Nashville's defense closed in like a pack of wolves. I shadowed him, weaving through the chaos, the seconds ticking down.

Twenty seconds.

The puck snapped loose from Hogan's stick, skittering across the blue line. Jimenez charged in, muscling through two Nashville players, and sent it my way. I caught it clean, and for a split second, everything went silent. The noise of the crowd, the players shouting—it all faded as I locked eyes on the net.

Ten seconds.

I wound up and fired, the puck sailing, slipping past the goalie's glove and slamming into the back of the net.

The arena exploded, and it felt like my heart stopped.

The buzzer sounded.

I just stood there, letting the noise wash over me. Then Jimenez barreled into me. "We won the fucking

Stanley Cup," he screamed, knocking me into the boards as our teammates piled on.

As soon as I broke free, my eyes searched for her.

She wasn't shouting anymore, she was beaming, her hands pressed to the sides of her face as tears spilled down her cheeks. Her suit coat gleamed under the arena lights, and I couldn't help it. I skated right to her, tossing my helmet, wrapping my arms around her waist and lifting her off the ground, spinning us in a circle.

"We did it," I whispered against her ear, my breath ragged from the effort and the pure joy coursing through me. "We fucking did it, Sunshine."

She laughed, her hands gripping my shoulders as she looked down at me, her smile radiant. "You did it, Thatcher. You deserve this."

"I deserve you," I countered, my lips brushing her temple before I set her down.

THE LOCKER ROOM WAS CHAOS.

Champagne sprayed everywhere, music blasted, and players shouted, their voices hoarse from celebrating. I'd showered and changed, but my buzz was still running hot, my heart thundering in time with the bass.

Like a damn moth to a flame, I spotted her across the room, surrounded by players and team staff, laughing, her face glowing, and something primal inside me stirred.

This wasn't how I wanted to celebrate.

I grabbed a bottle of champagne and crossed the room

in what felt like two steps, my hand sliding into hers without a word.

"Dalton, what—" she started as I pulled her out of the locker room, silencing her with a smirk. I tugged her into a supply closet and shut the door behind us.

Pine-Sol and bleach permeated the small space, but I didn't fucking care. Nothing mattered except her.

"You're mine, Sunshine," I murmured, my voice low and full of heat, caging her against the wall with my hands. Loving the way her breath hitched, lips parting as I dipped my head to brush my mouth against hers. "Stanley Cup or not, you're my victory."

Her calloused hands fisted in my shirt, slamming my lips down on hers. The kiss was searing. It was like someone pressed a livewire to my skin. Her nails scraped lightly against the back of my neck, sending shivers down my spine. I pressed her tighter against the wall, my body molding to hers as I deepened the kiss, pouring every ounce of gratitude, relief, and love into it.

"Dalton," she whispered against me, her voice breathless, sending a shot of lust to my cock. "I love you."

Fuck. I'd never get tired of that.

The words were everything.

I pulled back just enough to look into her eyes, my chest heaving harder than it had during the game. "And I love you, Sunshine. Always."

Her smile was enough to light up the entire room, and as our mouths found each other again, the sounds of the locker room celebration faded away.

I slid my hands over her strong body and I dropped to

my knees, making quick work of the button on her suit pants.

"What are you doing? Someone could walk in."

"Celebrating," I responded, yanking the fabric down her toned legs to reveal her hot pink silk underwear. I about choked at the sight, my fingers grazing over her ass and her already wet pussy. This pounding in my chest had to be what a heart attack felt like.

Death by pussy sounded like a fucking great way to go to me.

"So wet, darlin'," I growled, pressing her back against the cinderblock and spreading her legs wide. "And I'm about to add to it." I licked over her silk-covered center, relishing in her moan.

Some players dreamt about drinking champagne out of the Stanley Cup, but that wasn't how I wanted my bubbly. Picking up the already opened bottle, I poured it down the front of her white tank top, lapping up the liquid at the apex of her thighs.

"Fuck, Dalton." Her voice shook, and I pressed my mouth against her pussy, teasing her the way I knew she liked. Alternating between hard and soft licks before the fabric got in my way, and I ripped her panties down too.

Those little gasps were like a drug, and I wasted no time pressing the flat of my tongue on her swollen clit until her legs shook around me.

Regular champagne would never be good enough now. Fuck, nothing would be good enough unless I was lapping it up straight from between her thighs.

She begged me for more, hair swishing back and forth as she shook her head. I got her right to the brink before slowing a few times, edging her so I could watch her writhe in pleasure.

"I swear, Dalton."

She shivered as I chuckled against her clit, the vibration causing her to spasm. "You're doing so good," I said, latching back onto her clit and sucking right as I slipped a finger in. Then a second. By the third, she fell apart on my tongue.

"Did I do a good job fucking with my fingers, Coach?" I asked, smiling up at her when she had finally finished shaking. I barely got the words out before she tackled me to the ground.

"Star fucking athlete, but I'd really like you to fuck me with something else." She frantically pulled my shorts down my hips, gripping the length of my cock in her hands.

I was so hard it hurt.

"Fuck," I breathed, my head falling back as she pumped me, dipping down to lick the head of my cock. Those sinfully beautiful eyes locked on me, cataloging every reaction on my face to the witchcraft she was performing with her mouth.

Shouts and laughter started getting louder and we both froze. But then Ari's eyes took on a mischievous glint. "Better hurry, Dalton. See if you can secure one more win tonight before the clock runs out."

I scoffed, reaching over and moving her body so she was straddling my hips. "I'm insulted you think we are only fucking once tonight. You're going to stay naked for *days*."

She giggled, lining up my cock at her entrance before

sinking down, head rolling so far back as sounds of pleasure fell from her lips that the tips of her long hair tickled my thighs.

Later tonight, I'm wrapping my fists around all that hair.

"That's a good girl. Show me how well you take my cock, darlin'.'"

"Where's the damn hat when I need it?" she moaned, bouncing up and down.

We really needed to get back home so I could strip her down completely, but at least the liquid I'd poured down her chest had caused the white fabric to turn see-through, giving me a peek at her pebbled nipples.

"They don't wear those out here," I grunted, my balls tightening every time her ass cheeks brushed them.

"I don't give a shit." Her eyes popped open and she stared me down while she moved on top of me. "You're still going to wear yours, Longest Ride."

I smirked at the nickname she'd used that first night we met, digging my fingers into her hips as she rode me.

"Anything for you," I said, moving my hand so I could circle her clit.

She moaned, arching her back and taking me deeper. God, she was fucking sexy. Feeling her pussy bare was my favorite way to fuck her. Knowing that I could fill her with my cum, and there was something that much hotter about the fact that she'd walk out of this closet dripping our release.

If that was wrong...I didn't give a shit.

"Come on, show me what you've got. Show me how well you take my cock, Coach."

I pistoned into her, unable to hold back any longer. My hands trailed up her body, roaming over every curve and muscle. Breathtaking. So strong, in more ways than just physically.

Suddenly, there was too much space between us.

She cried out as I sat up, staying inside her. The new position made me feel like I was so much deeper, and when she started circling her hips...I forgot how to function.

The sensation nearly sent me to another dimension. A damn factory reset via her pussy, and I knew we were moments away from falling over the edge together.

"Be a good girl and come," I whispered into her ear, pulling the sensitive lobe into my mouth.

Her cries echoed off the walls, her pussy clenching around, sending me into my own release.

I held her in my arms through the aftershocks, burying my face in her hair. "Fuck the afterparty, I'm taking you home to do *that* again...and again."

She laughed, that bright sound filling me with joy and warming me from the inside. She outshone the sun in my life.

"Sunshine, you're the other piece to my soul."

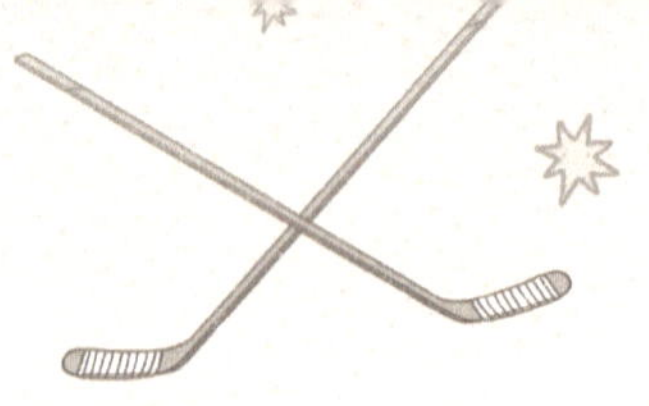

SNEAK PEEK AT BOOK TWO
GRACIELLA

I SHOULD HAVE GOOGLED if breaking into a man's house with a bat was considered attempted assault.

Really, it shouldn't be, especially if you were breaking into said house because he was a lying, cheating bastard who stole your promotion out from under your nose by sleeping with your boss.

I winced at the thump my body made when I half stepped, half fell through his living room window. Some-where in the *deep* recesses of my mind, logic was banging on the door, demanding I think about what I was about to do. Too bad, the tequila I'd downed like water was more convincing.

Besides, there was *some* thought put into this night-time rendevous, and I'd slipped the rideshare driver a twenty to wait out front for me.

Women in STEM: twenty dollars, plus cleavage, times a man who thought he may get laid equals...

A getaway driver.

I paused mid-tip-toe. *Was I making him an accomplice in a crime?*

I shrugged when I couldn't come up with the answer. I just wouldn't get caught. Problem solved. Continuing down the hall, I tried to recall which door led to Caleb's bedroom.

The details from that night a few weeks ago were fuzzy, but I thought it was the last one on the left. Maybe. I should have known from the beginning he was an asshole.

All men named Caleb were assholes.

Thank god he didn't have roommates, so I didn't have to worry about threatening the wrong person—just had to worry about ending up in a hall closet.

A vibration from my back pocket distracted me enough that I managed to miss the grunts emanating beyond the paneled door. Buzzed Graciella had poor situational awareness. Hell, sober Graciella had poor situational awareness but a shocking amount of street smarts. You'd think they'd counteract each other if I were being honest.

ARI:

What are you doing?

Ari's text stared at me, causing guilt to turn in my gut. My prima had a sixth fucking sense when it came to me and trouble. She was a damn bloodhound, sniffing out the shit I was about to be in.

What was more impressive was she was thousands of miles away.

I HAVE A MAFIA SERIES UNDER MARIE
MARAVILLA

Skeletons of Society

Syndicate of Sins

City of Salvation

HEY BOO...

Stabbing is frowned upon in real life...

So I did the next best thing and wrote it in my books (okay, they don't stab in my hockey books, but you bet your ass they are petty).

Writing a book was only supposed to be a bucket list thing to check off; now, here we are. My author brand centers around writing unapologetic feminine rage with FMCs as badass as the boys who fall for them. And now I am trying my hand in the sports romance world!

I currently live in Tennessee and try to survive the cycle of working, writing, mom-ing, and consuming questionable amounts of caffeine.

Keep up with new releases, signed copies & goodies, audiobook deals, and general chaos at:

authormariemaravilla.com

instagram.com/authormariem

tiktok.com/@authormariemaravilla

ACKNOWLEDGMENTS

Oh boy.

This book has been a RIDE to write. January 2024 me had zero clue what was in store. A cross-country move, losing and gaining a job, selling a house, finding a place to live, my kids starting school...seriously, there was SO much that happened that wasn't on my plan. Well, the kids starting school I knew about 😂.

All of that to say, getting this book done alongside all of the other chaos was a feat. One I am very very proud of and one I could not have done without some **amazing people** in my life.

First of all, I have the coolest freakin' readers. Everyone was so supportive when this project got pushed back by months. Not only that, but y'all showed up for me in big ways! Supporting my posts, boosting my ARC sign-ups, and, most importantly, cheering me on. So, thank you so much from the bottom of my heart. 🤍

Then there's my editor, turned friend and cheer-leader, Kearstie. You are a goddess, and I am forever grateful for you. Your support and ability to meet me where I am have made working together such a joy. Truly, I cherish what we have in a professional and personal rela-tionship SO much. We've had plenty of VM back and forth about this so I won't write another novel here, but I couldn't have survived this without you.

Lex, here is where I give you your yearly "I love you." This book wouldn't have existed without you and our nearly daily communication via rambling VM. We have a personal podcast going on with one another at this point. I am so grateful to have made a friend in the business who is so similar to me in so many areas. I don't even have to elaborate on most of my feelings, which is a blessing to an Aquarius. I fear you're stuck with me, boo.

And Lisa, last but not least, thank you for accepting my organized chaos and thought-out impulsiveness. You're the biggest cheerleader, and your heart makes you so special. You were a lifesaver with this project with your organizational skills, taking on the task of dealing with 667 ARC sign-ups 😁.

And my unofficial Prima, Isabella, you are a shining light in this community. Thank you for your friendship, your watchful eyes, and your constant hyping up. Can't wait for us to go to a hockey game for this one.

www.ingramcontent.com/pod-product-compliance
Lightning Source LLC
Chambersburg PA
CBHW030104310726
48970CB00004B/1134